THE WATERGATE SPIES

Delta Tango

BookLocker
Trenton, Georgia

Print ISBN: 978-1-64719-897-8
Ebook ISBN: 978-1-64719-898-5

Published by BookLocker.com, Inc., Trenton, Georgia.

Printed on acid-free paper.

The characters and events in this book are fictitious. Any similarity to real persons, living or dead, is coincidental and not intended by the author.

BookLocker.com, Inc.
2022

First Edition

Library of Congress Cataloguing in Publication Data
Tango, Delta
The Watergate Spies by Delta Tango
Library of Congress Control Number: 2021921348

THE WATERGATE SPIES
A Novel

Delta Tango

Preface

Imagine traveling the streets of Washington, D.C., in an ambulance, as an emergency medical technician (EMT), and you will come to understand what links us all—how a week in this city can shape a century—or bring an end to the race as we know it. Travel with David and Margaret Lovejoy on their family vacation to the capital to see who measures out health care. I'll show you what Deep Throat never did, about what the four, well really many more, Watergate break-ins were about. As a Cuban double agent, I went inside the capital to discover the Code, and this is what I found.

Glossary for Medical Ambulance

Ambulance Codes – circa 1970s

Code 1—no lights, no siren
Code 2—red lights on, no siren
Code 3—red lights on with siren

Call Directives

10-1 call your station
10-2 return to your station
10-4 acknowledge (roger)
10-7 verify address
10-14 call in unit location
10-28 criminal-detention facility incident
10-30 explosion
10-38 aircraft incident/crash
10-42 civil disturbance
10-44 power failure
10-47 nuclear substance spill/incident—HAZMAD
10-49 environmental incident (earthquake, hurricane, flood, fire)
10-50 mutual aid response

Medical messaging

Code Blue—respiratory arrest
AMA—absent against medical advice
EMD—electromechanical dissociation
DOA—dead on arrival
51-50—psychotic episode

"The past is never dead. In fact, it isn't even past."
William Faulkner, *Requiem for a Nun*

The following pages are based mostly on real events and recreated characters. No harm is intended to the many participants, especially the Plumbers and the EMTs, to whom this book is dedicated.

Day 1

Call Me Colson

Colson: "Because Hunt and Liddy did the work. The others didn't know any direct information."

President Nixon: "I think I agree."

Colson: "See, I don't give a damn if they spend five years in jail… They can't hurt us. Hunt and Liddy: direct meetings and discussions are very incriminating to us."

President Nixon: "Liddy is pretty tough."

Colson: "Apparently he's one of these guys who's a masochist. He enjoys punishing himself. That's okay, as long as he remains stable. I mean, he's tough."

President Nixon: "Jesus!"

Colson: "They're both good, healthy, right-wing exuberants."

—A conversation between Charles Colson, special counsel to the president, and Richard Nixon, January 8, 1973

I was a spy. I was involved in assassination plots and conspiracies to overthrow several foreign governments including Cuba, Panama, Guatemala, the Dominican Republic, and Haiti. I smuggled arms and men into Cuba for Castro and against Castro. I broke into intelligence files. I stole and photographed secret documents. That's what spies do.

Frank Sturgis, June 20, 1975

"A conspiracy like this...a conspiracy investigation...the rope has to tighten slowly around everyone's neck. You build convincingly from the outer edges in, you get ten times the evidence you need against the..."

—Deep Throat, October 28, 1972

Howard Robard Hughes

Chapter 1:

Cuba

Tuesday, June 13, 1972, noon—the Presidential Palace

"We may have an opportunity, Fidel, to do to the Americans what they tried to do to you. And this opportunity will come very soon."

Miguel Pintaro, a.k.a. "Blackbeard," dressed in military fatigues, looks the Líder Måximo in the eye, simultaneously ascertaining that the room is empty.

"Yes, and what is this opportunity?"

"Comandante, our agents have learned from Tango that the Code to the American defense system is accessible. He is working hard inside the capital, with FBI and CIA contacts. And he may be close to obtaining it. If he does, we have a way to block the Code or even change it, to prevent a preemptive strike. Nixon is the only one with access to this Code that releases a first strike. Without that capacity, the Americans will never attack us again, let alone assassinate you! You must know this."

"What do I know?" Castro responds, touching his own dark beard while looking out a bulletproof window. "And what does Delta Tango know?"

"That they have never discovered him or our other agents. And we have discovered most of theirs. Tango has befriended 'Deep Throat,' who loves to gossip. The FBI knows that the code to the 'Football' can be unlocked and deciphered. Also, there's a retired CIA agent named Hunt, the same Howard Hunt who helped plan and manage the Bay of Pigs attack on us. He's actively searching to find out if the Code has already been leaked and if the Democratic party has acquired our dossier on the CIA assassination attempts on you. But he knows nothing of Tango, or our penetration. The FBI and CIA—well, you know, Fidel, how they love to out-spy each other. These Americans are very gullible…."

"And where is this Code?"

"You already know, Fidel. It's kept inside a briefcase, the so called 'Football,' kept close to the president to release the nuclear arsenal whenever he wants to. That's what we are to discover."

Castro turns back to Blackbeard, eyeing him fiercely, then pointing a long finger at the informant.

"Nixon's Code? The son of a bitch, why would he activate it? He wants me gone, but all of Cuba? Do you really think they'll try again, after their failures?"

"Fidel, they and others have tried to assassinate you how many hundreds of times! Howard Hunt connects to Howard Hughes, along with Nixon. They all work together. Have you forgotten Operation Mongoose? Hughes has a manager named Maheu, the one who worked with Johnny Roselli and the Mafia. The ones who used to run this country. Think of the ways they tried to eliminate you!"

The two men look across the city, past the Monument of Jose Marti, beyond the Plaza of the Revolution where Fidel gives his orations, and study the streets of Havana. The aging Vedado and Cayo Hueso neighborhoods span outward, toward the Avenida Malecon. Traffic is sparse as Castro takes hold of a cigar and waits for Blackbeard to continue.

"Nixon is so paranoid, in my opinion, that his people will try again. Comandante, he may be more successful than Kennedy! Can you forget the invasion, which killed thousands of our militia and soldiers? Nixon planned for the

Bay of Pigs even before Kennedy, so we have to be ready with a defense before they try to eliminate us yet another time. I want to tell you, in the next seven days we will discover their Code. I am sure of this!"

Billowing clouds drift slowly over the Gulf of Mexico as waves roll in and collapse, over and over, on the thin shore before the seawall, becalming the residents with an ancient rhythm and cascading noise. Castro notes the humidity-softened outlines of Royal Palms defining avenues to the sea, no more than a short missile flight from the coast of Florida.

"All right, Blackbeard, have Delta Tango get this Code."

Chapter 2:

The Lovejoys Visit the Capital

Tuesday, June 13, 1972, 1:25 p.m.

My story begins with a family of five on their first vacation to sightsee and attend a meeting in the American capital. I first encounter them in a Howard Johnson's Motor Lodge, and their experience with the city's ambulance system, called Medical, is unusual, but it could easily be yours or mine! My activities in the safehouse next to their motel room are also different since Castro expects a lot in one week's time!

Entering Washington, D.C., the Lovejoys drive off the Beltway and notice a sudden deceleration as surrounding traffic envelops them.

"To be seized by forces from without, that's how old civilizations used to describe epilepsy," David Lovejoy comments, looking over at his wife, expanding to fullness in her last month of pregnancy. Slightly overweight, with shallow creases lining the edges of his smiling face, he turns his gaze to watch traffic as their station wagon moves slowly toward the city center. In the midday haze it's possible to distinguish distant monuments and the circular outlines of the Watergate buildings, aloft over the edge of the Potomac. "But now, dear, we know it starts from within...probably from just a single neuron..."

"David, please. Can't our neurons have a vacation? This is to be our time away from work, and a chance for the children to see the capital. Rebecca can do her school report, and you can relax a little. You know I have the dinner coming up at the Watergate Hotel, but let's try and relax."

Margaret Lovejoy sweeps her auburn hair out of the way as she looks back at her youngest, Michael, age four, and Angel, age nine, sleeping obliviously in the rear. Wearing a swimsuit in readiness for the motel pool, Rebecca, who is twelve, stares at the river. Her long, lithe legs are bent up against the back of the parents' front seat, and her toes point down, as she waits to escape the car.

"I know, I know. We're looking forward to this, and we're going to have a great time. I just want to help you remember your medication."

"And yours?" she asks David.

Margaret fingers an alert bracelet on her wrist, which is resting on her full abdomen.

These discussions always focus on my pregnancy and how my risk of seizures could be bad for the fetus. Typical. He never wears a bracelet, still smokes—you can smell it on his clothes—and his asthma condition puts him at greater risk for attacks he won't acknowledge. But not so judgmental, she tells herself. *He's under a lot of pressure and the competition in the insurance business keeps getting worse. Spending time with the family in the capital should be fun.*

"My breathing's okay, honey. What we have to make sure of is that your seizures are under control.... Margaret, are you all right?"

There's a slight tremor on the left side of her face. Simultaneously a bright red ambulance speeds past, lights flashing overhead, leaving bursts of a siren echoing.

"I'm okay," she answers. "Just fine. Why?"

"Because you looked like you were about to get sick. You've been taking the pills?"

"Why do you keep asking?"

She looks into the visor mirror just as the twitching stops and she's reassured. In the excitement of preparing for their trip and the upcoming convention, she skipped her morning dose of Dilantin. The mirror reflects an attractive woman with bright eyes, but who seems a touch anxious.

"Well, you seemed a little funny. I think…maybe...look, we're on the bridge. Look at the buildings. Magnificent!"

As they move into the right-hand lane, they pass over the Potomac River and some verdant banks sheltering remnant wildlife. Ahead of them are white marble and granite monuments, expressions of American history and splendor. Within minutes they turn onto Virginia Avenue, rolling past the Watergate buildings, and head into the underground parking lot of the Howard Johnson's, just as Margaret's left eyelid begins to twitch. Once they check into Room 623, however, she feels fine. Across from them, in room 622, I ply my trade. An odd activity is transmitted on my 110.13 MHz microphone transmitter as Nixon's Plumbers are just getting started.

Tuesday, 1:30 p.m.—Dr. Fielding's office

Bob Haldeman, White House chief of staff for the president, hunches over a Medical Ambulance dispatch board watching a video of a break-in. He can hear static from a CIA channel, as well as the covert activities of his fact-finding committee, the "Plumbers," led by Gordon Liddy and Howard Hunt. Working for the president, Haldeman follows the Plumbers' efforts to get dirt on a National Security adviser named Daniel Ellsberg, who has given classified information to the press. When you mess with the military industrial complex and the national defense system, no holds are barred, and my Cuban colleagues and I are all over this. I follow the dialogue through my own transmitters.

"Damn, they're taking too long!" Haldeman says to himself. "I never should have let these guys organize this. They'd better get their butts out of there!"

Adjusting his headset to comprehend signals obfuscated by static, he hears the Plumbers communicate through five-watt, six-channel transceivers. They're miles away, attempting an entry into the Los Angeles office of Ellsberg's psychiatrist.

"Quiet! If you see Dr. Fielding's Volvo, you say something. Otherwise, let's get this over with!" Liddy tells Hunt. From his dispatch office, the crew-cut Haldeman winces as he listens to the two men prepare a Cuban-exile team to force their way into the doctor's office, expecting police sirens at any minute. Ellsberg has divulged classified information about national security, the Pentagon Papers, and violent acts are taking place around the country. The Plumbers are hoping for evidence that Ellsberg is connected to the Russians and the Weatherpeople, an underground group of saboteurs who have been increasing in numbers. Failing that connection, they'll be happy with any personal details the CIA hasn't already uncovered about Ellsberg. His sexual escapades, his insecurities—anything that makes him look bad will make Nixon happy.

"Don't worry, I'm looking out," Hunt, allegedly retired from the CIA, responds. He watches his Cuban men climb through a broken window, carrying black muslin to cover their window reflections and a nylon rope for quick escape. "There they go! They're inside!"

Haldeman can't discern whether it's Hunt or Liddy speaking, but by monitoring their exchanges he knows medical records are being pulled from the psychiatrist's files and photographed. The last sound he hears in the video is a car racing from the scene.

1:45 p.m.— Hinton meets Chuck Colson

Seen from above, Washington, D.C., is geometrically divided by two rivers, the Potomac and the Anacostia. The two rivers join in the center to make a Y, like the shape of a chromosome or a code, and in order to understand the city one must decipher the message within the form. Steel bridges cross over these ocean-destined waters, carrying long, uninterrupted columns of automobiles to and from diverse communities. One can see a sprawl of buildings and monuments interspersed with urban housing extending eight miles north to south, and eight miles east to west. To ambulance drivers it represents sixty-four square miles of inchoate catastrophe, more than a half-million potential passengers, in what's known as "the race."

Inside the Beltway of D.C., on a street lined with convenience stores, Hinton parks his green Mustang and begins his first day as an EMT, as well as embarking on a special mission. He walks to a building where the red letters MEDICAL AMBULANCE are emblazoned on a plate glass window and then, adjusting the zipper on his jumpsuit, he knocks loudly on the door. No answer. Pushing the door open he sees a lone couch furnishing a room along with a television set. Newscasters discuss the current election contest for the president's office. The sound has made his earlier knocking inaudible and he hears snoring.

"Hey there!"

A somnolent body lies motionless on the couch.

"Hello. You okay?" He shakes the man, trying out the alert sequence from his CPR training.

"Whaaaaa..." The bespectacled face of Chuck Colson emerges, crowned by a shock of black hair. "Well, who the hell the...hey...oh, you're the new driver!" he sputters, as he sits up. "Can't hear you…TV..."

He moves slowly to the television, turns it off, and faces the visitor.

"Sorry, worked all night. And I had a lot of phone calls from the pres…. Hey, what'd you say your name was?"

"Hinton, James Hinton. You must be Mr. Colson."

A slight southern drawl defines Hinton's voice. Colson notes it as they shake hands, eyeing each other cautiously. Colson evaluates Hinton silently.

Something familiar about this face. Too enthusiastic, a little boyish. And he shakes hands soooo long...

"Mr. Nixon said someone would be training me on the job."

Seconds pass as Colson waits for Hinton to let go of his hand, and he smiles at the new driver. "That's right. Call me Colson. Ya'll worked in an ambulance before, James?" he asks, feigning a southern accent.

"No, I'm new to this."

"That's pretty obvious." Colson eyes the new uniform, dark blue without a stain.

"Pardon?" Hinton's expression is undaunted, though his shiny boots and clean jumpsuit confirm experience he doesn't have. His curly light brown hair contrasts with Colson's, straight and dark, brushed back behind the horn-rimmed glasses. Both of them carry trauma scissors on their belts.

"Just kidding," Colson says, focusing on the face.

Maybe twenty-five years old. A college kid and I've seen my share: long hair, long ideas—hopes for a quick rise in the ranks.

"So, your name's Hinton? What kind of work you do before coming here?"

Colson turns back momentarily toward the TV.

"Law school."

"Law school!" Colson booms, swinging back and crossing his arms and smiling. "Well, whatta you know! A lawyer! Whatta you wanta drive for, Hinton? Gonna be an ambulance chaser? Ha ha!"

"No, I'm...uh...looking for medical experience."

"Oh yeah? Well, you'll get that here all right. This company is special. In fact, as you already know, the owner happens to be the president of the United States. He likes to keep his hand in the medical world. But, you know something else? Drivers come and go. I've been here a few years and seen quite a few leave. We don't always get excitement. Gets pretty tired, sometimes. A lot of what we do is cabbage factories."

"Pardon me?"

"I said cabbage factories," Colson repeats, pulling a cigarette from his shirt pocket. "What you call convalescent hospitals. You'll see 'em when we get there. Know any first aid, Hinton?"

"Sure, advanced CPR," Hinton answers, slapping the trauma scissors hanging from his thick leather belt.

"Ya'll must be a rocket scientist! Well, come on, rookie. I'm gonna show you my car. You work with me today and another driver tomorrow. There's four of us and we're all different. You're gonna learn each one of our styles. Fortunately, you start with me, 'cause I plan to teach you the most."

Outside, a red ambulance shimmers in the sunlight, the number "22" painted on its side. Colson opens the back and points to a cabinet above the locked gurney. As they climb inside there's a stillness, the smell of medical alcohol, and tightly spaced cabinets line the interior.

"Bandages and stuff in here. Gotta know where they all are for whenever we get the Big Three."

"Big what?"

"Code Three. Ever heard of life and death, Hinton? Lights and siren, man. Code Two means no siren. You can't drive as fast. And Code One's a normal transfer. You'll find out soon enough."

He shows Hinton sequential maneuvers for deploying the gurney, then takes first aid equipment from the cabinet as they study the assortment of dressings and paraphernalia.

"Company has a lot of stuff," Colson points out, "but we need more."

"How's that?"

"Technical advances. That and a demanding public. Our competition is a company called Therapy. They think everyone should get free health care, so they pick up all the bums on the street and expect you and me to pay for it. Health care's not a right, Hinton. It's a privilege and a responsibility you have to pay for. Know what I mean? You and I are supposed to pay for our own health care."

"You and I?" Hinton asks, holding up a pair of forceps.

"That's what I said. Put the tweezers back, Hinton. We use those things to pull out foreign bodies…from wounds."

"So how does this company keep from going bankrupt?"

"Good question. Look, this city pays for everything. Supports every bum on the street, along with the welfare mothers. Every unemployed dropout gets a new car every year, and our taxes pay for it. With a free expense account, who the hell would want to work anymore? Can you answer that?"

"That's right," Hinton agrees quickly. "You know something else, Colson? Ambulance drivers make a third of what the city garbage men average. On a wage basis, that is."

"Is that right? Well, wait till you see what we pick up! Haah-ha!"

Hinton smiles as he hands back the forceps. "Listen, Colson. Everything's about to change," he says. "You and me, we're the future. If we work together, health care will never be the same…"

"Buddy, you will never be the same! Ha-ha…."

Chapter 3:

Howard Hughes' Biographer

Tuesday, 2:20 p.m.—Waiting room of the Pyramid

Who could ever question the Man
Who altered the original D.C. plan?
Who's the one that shaped this city?
A billionaire pilot receives my ditty.

Clifton Urning reflects on the words, wondering how his poem "The Freeway" will be received. A sizeable income awaits if his poems are published, but he still needs permission from Howard Hughes. Nearing his goal as he waits on the ground floor of the Pyramid, Hughes' Business Center, he has the sensation he's experienced it all before. And he has—countless times. Each day he arrives at the reception desk at the base of the city's tallest building, requesting an interview with Howard Hughes. Dressed in a dark suit, white shirt, and black tie, Urning has the countenance of an Anglo poet. His eyebrows arch up, his sensitive gaze peers outward, and his lips intimate a wish to rhyme. And each day he's told Mr. Hughes is unavailable.

As the world's richest man, Hughes avoids any meetings. Awkward and shy from his youth, he was catered to and protected by his mother, and allowed a $5,000-a-week allowance by his itinerant father. Both parents died suddenly, and when Howard took over the family fortune at age eighteen, he never stopped the quest to make more money. As a mechanical genius in his childhood, he left behind his father's oil drilling ventures to make movies in Hollywood, pursued aviation, and began building an empire.

Urning explains to the receptionist that he's been assigned to write poems, has been paid a substantial salary to do so, and that a meeting with Hughes is imperative. He is always offered the opportunity to wait, and this Tuesday, like others, he sits down in the spacious lobby and recites his verses.

Yes, he's the one that circled the Earth
To show us all what flight is worth.
It was he that flew the planes
To set the records and win the dames.

He offered Terry and Gina the fame,
He was with Ella and Billie and Jane.
He courted Ava and the beautiful Jeans,
And married and made them all movie star queens.

Mona and June and Linda and Gail
And Mitzi and Ida and Ginger won't tell.
Olivia, Katherine, Elizabeth, Faith,
Yvonne and Bette won't give a trace.
Why do you take the reds out of the movies?
And fill them instead with gigantic boobies?
Why build the steamer to chop into pieces,
And shake hands wearing gloves to avoid diseases?

Spend fifty million to fatten the Goose,
Do all your business in white tennis shoes.
Deal in the billions without paying fees,
And eat by yourself and measure your peas?

Oh, where do you hide, what do you do,
Who reads your will when everything's through?
The whole world wonders, so please don't refuse,
Tell us you're living, and where, Mr. Hughes?

It's not easy being poetaster for a man who hasn't been seen in a decade. Urning wishes he could have been Hughes' doctor, or barber, though it would mean a lesser monthly stipend. Hughes hires thousands of employees and wants none of them in his presence. They're kept at work for years on the offhand chance he'll need their services, perhaps to have a haircut or administer an enema. On a rare occasion he may let a physician examine his body. But Hughes knows Urning wants to publish a biography about him, so he's hired the writer for life to be sure the book never gets published. Rumor has filtered down to Clifton, however, that an allegedly dying Hughes is bedridden and may be willing to listen to poems and tell his unpublished history.

2:35 p.m.—Howard Johnson's

Colson and Hinton leave the ambulance quarters and walk to a small restaurant at Howard Johnson's Motor Lodge. As they slide into a booth, Hinton's eyes focus on the waitress's legs, bare to the mid-thigh where her skirt stops. Sitting at the counter two men, one bald with a prominent forehead and the other hirsute and spooning into a large chocolate sundae, are deep in a discussion.

"So whatta you think?" Colson asks.

"About?" Hinton turns and watches as a toothpick splinters between Colson's teeth.

"The president, Hinton. The man who owns this company. The same man who's in charge of the nation."

"Well, he's remarkable, Chuck! He rose all the way to become the leader of the United States. You know, to start off as an ambulance driver, then become an attorney and a politician, to build up this company and get where he is now, that's extraordinary! He's probably going to be re-elected and then he'll be in a position to shape health care for the future."

"Yeah, that's exactly right. So, tell me something, Hinton. How's a law student like you come to work for Medical, anyway?"

Hinton pauses, taking his eyes off the waitress, and checks again the holster of his trauma scissors. His answer comes soft and raspy.

"Well…I'm here for experience. To learn about the real world, just like you and Mr. Nixon have."

Colson spits out the toothpick.

This guy is after something. For sure *not the average Medical newcomer. Maybe he'll end up switching over to Therapy and the blue team.*

The struggle for domination between Medical and Therapy, the two major ambulance companies in D.C., has a long history. Presidents have always associated with one company or the other, the Republicans supporting the individualistic, market-based ideology of Medical, or the Democrats supporting the more collective, government-inclined actions of Therapy. Colson knows Therapy will do anything to regain prominence, and the competition between red and blue has intensified.

"When are we supposed to start working?" Hinton continues, ordering a cheeseburger and refocusing on the waitress's thighs.

"We're working right now."

"We are?"

"That's right. Dispatcher knows our location. Anything happens, they contact me." Colson indicates a pager on his belt. Then looks hard at Hinton. "How come you never worked for the military?"

"How do you mean, Chuck?"

"I said, how is it you never worked for the military? I hear from our manager that you never signed up."

"Well...uh…that's uh…true. That is, I signed up, but I was still at the University, so I couldn't really serve. I was…uh…what you call a Rhodes Scholar."

"Is that right? Tell me about it, . I bet you know all about the world."

"Sure, I know a little. But not like you, Chuck. That's why I joined Medical, so I could learn more here on the ground floor. You think it'll take long to train me?"

The two men sitting at the counter get up to leave, just as the three Lovejoy children enter the restaurant and take their seats. Michael sits on Rebecca's lap as they ask for a menu to take to their parents. Angel reaches over and dips her finger in the remaining chocolate sundae left behind on the counter. Colson smiles at Angel and then answers Hinton's question.

"Maybe not, if you keep your eyes open on something besides that waitress's legs. It's a slow day, Hinton. Not much to get worried about."

"You mean we're picking up patients today? My first day?"

"Sure. I just showed you the ambulance, didn't I?"

"Well, Chuck, you showed me equipment. But you haven't finished showing me how to hook up the oxygen."

"Well, ya'll just watch," Colson assures him, using his southern accent again. "Ya'll pick it up. College boy like you ain't going to have any trouble, . You just said you were a scholar. Ain't that right?"

The bald man with a prominent forehead stands at the door, stopping to look closely at Colson before exiting. Colson recognizes him but says nothing and just then Colson's beeper emits high-pitched beeping signals. He curses as he squeezes himself out from the booth.

"Probably another emergency," he tells the waitress as she brings their food.

Hinton starts on a cheeseburger while Colson calls on the payphone and jots down an address.

"Code Two, !" he calls out as he hangs up. "Baby in trouble at City Hospital. We gotta hurry!"

Together they run back to the living quarters, dodging cars as they cross Virginia Avenue to the corner. Hinton climbs into the passenger seat of Car 22, feeling the thrill of his first ride as they accelerate forward. Colson swerves dangerously around an old woman with a shopping cart. No sooner have they headed down the Parkway, however, than he stops and makes a U-turn.

"We gotta pick up the incubator at the station. I almost forgot. Look out, Grandma, we're in a hurry!"

As they race back toward the station, the hapless woman rushes her shopping cart back to the sidewalk, away from the oncoming vehicle. Aluminum cans spill out of the cart and her mongrel dog barks at the passing ambulance.

"What's the incubator do, Chuck? It's for taking care of the babies?"

"Right. Thing we carry babies in. You've never seen one?"

"What are you talking about, man? I just started."

They swerve back into the right lane, narrowly missing a patrol car.

"What'd they teach you in college, anyway? You don't know what an incubator is? Listen, boy, we need it and you're gonna handle it. While I drive. Thing is, don't let on like you never used it before. When we get to City Hospital, they'll be watching us."

Chapter 4:

The Hepatitis Baby

Tuesday, 3:40 p.m.—City Hospital

Inside the hospital ER, the ambulance drivers arrive unannounced. A resuscitation is taking place in two different cubicles, and physicians and nurses hover over trauma tables shouting commands and acknowledgments. Heroin has found its way into the poorest sections of the city, having come from Mexico or by way of Cuba, and the results of alcohol and overdosage are never good. A nineteen-year-old woman in her third term of pregnancy, brought in comatose with her boyfriend, undergoes urgent procedures, as remnants of her clothing remain scattered aside on the floor, where they were removed using trauma scissors.

"Lactated Ringers! Give me another amp of calcium!"

"Right here. Ten milliliters calcium gluconate, Doctor. Forty-four milliequivalents bicarb. This is your second amp!"

A harried physician reaches for a long-needled syringe, then injects the contents into tubing connected to the vein of the naked woman.

"Move away, everybody! Stand back!" he shouts from the side.

"Clear, please! Paddles on. Okay, fire!"

POOMMT!

A blunt noise is followed by silence. Everyone watches the cardiac monitor, ignoring the odor of singed flesh.

"Okay, resume CPR. Get ready to defibrillate again. I saw a rhythm."

Hinton stands in the first cubicle, uncertain what to do. He knows CPR, has performed flawlessly on a practice dummy, but he's still nervous he'll be asked to help in a real situation. Colson wipes dust from his glasses and leans against the incubator, waiting for someone to come forward with transfer papers.

"Hold CPR! Okay, everybody back! Clear, please! Fire!" the physician continues.

POOMMT!

Another silence, shorter than the first, is followed by a resumption of frenzied activity. Pharmaceutical interventions proceed futilely.

"EMD! I don't see a rhythm!" a nurse by the monitor calls out.

"Pump harder! I'm not getting any pulses!"

"Someone get OB down here! We called 'em five minutes ago!"

Sweat builds up on the ER doctor's brow, and Hinton's anxiety also increases as he watches the heart tracing go flat. The physician starts changing places with a nurse, who has lost stamina doing compressions. As he moves farther up the bedside, he spots Hinton.

"You!" the physician says, spotting him. "I need you to switch with me so I can run this code!"

Hinton passes around the machines nervously and then stands next to the woman. She's spread-eagled on the metal emergency bed, secured with gauze restraints over her wrists and ankles. Four IV bottles frame an image of last rites as he puts the palms of his hands on the sternum and begins pressing down.

"One thousand one, one thousand two..."

Her stomach is tight with air, the fetus pressing up on it, almost even with her ribcage.

"There they are!" the code doctor calls out as obstetricians finally approach from the side door. "Get some instruments!"

Colson keeps by the side of the incubator, still cleaning his glasses. Two orderlies next to him make their own assessment, having watched the woman come into the ER with her boyfriend. Both patients had arrived unconscious.

"Don't think I wanna try anything they used," the first says. "That woman's gonna go a lot lower than she ever got high—can tell that just by lookin' at 'er now. An' that baby. That's a crime."

"Yeah, I heard that. Look at 'em. He's colder than she is."

In the next cubicle, the boyfriend's resuscitation is not going well. A large tube sticks out his mouth and a nurse pumps saline solution to rinse out the stomach. Besides an occasional retching noise there are few signs of life from the drug-laden body.

"Man, a'least he might live," the first orderly continues. "She ain't gotta a snowflake's chance..."

"Wait a minute. Watch, man. Just watch now, here comes OB. They're gonna, oh Jesus, can you dig this? Watch it, Colson, you watching?"

Codes rarely run longer than twenty-five minutes in City Hospital. This one has been going for twenty and the end is approaching.

"Damn, man," one of the orderlies whispers. "Chief resident's doing it! Can you believe it, Colson? I'm telling you, the lady's gotta be infected."

Colson wipes the back of his neck with a handkerchief and looks over the crowd, watching the obstetrics residents rush into the room. They speak with the Emergency Room doctor and go to the side of the agonal woman.

"Knife and pick-ups! Prep her belly fast!"

Hinton presses on the woman's sternum, giving short, deep compressions.

"Deeper!"

At the foot of the table a female surgeon directs her partner, who slides a scalpel vertically across the taut, distended surface of the woman's abdomen. Blood rushes out as successive layers of skin and muscle give way to the underlying womb.

"Now, you up there, doing CPR. I want you to press down on the abdomen when I tell you to. Do you hear me? We'll need a little pressure to get his child out. Do you hear me?"

She looks up at Hinton, who's never seen a C-section, let alone assisted on one. Across from him another nurse has prepared to take over his chest compressions.

"Okay, now! Start pressing!" the chief resident urges. With a pair of scissors, she cuts through the top of the uterus, then with the help of pressure above she scoops out a helpless, barely squirming form. Amniotic fluid drips onto the mother's blood-soaked abdomen, and the baby looks dusky.

"Give it oxygen!"

Hinton, at first shocked, then is elated as he watches the baby turn pink, squirm, and emit a high-pitched cry. Immediately the chief resident clips and divides the umbilical cord and walks toward the incubator where Colson is waiting. Blood and amniotic fluid have soaked the bottom of her scrubs, and Colson backs up a few inches. She reaches into the incubator, pulls out a blanket, and wraps the newborn girl before handing her to him.

"Keep her warm. Bag her if you have to," she tells him. "And get her to Children's Hospital in five minutes. And please don't you crash, okay?"

"Wait a minute, Doc," Colson protests. "We need some papers signed. We need a name..."

"Jane Doe. Now get going!"

4:05 p.m.—The first ambulance ride

"Don't worry about a thing," Colson tells Hinton as they slide the incubator into the back of the ambulance. "You're gonna be steward on this run so you can get some experience. We'll be there in no time."

He closes the back doors and hops in front, behind the steering wheel. As he flicks on red lights and glances back, Hinton looks worried.

"Damn, Chuck, what exactly am I supposed to do?"

"Keep it pink," Colson tells him, accelerating forward, "and don't let it spread any bad stuff!"

Hinton puts on gloves and searches through the cabinets. When he looks back into the incubator the baby has stopped crying. The pink flush of its lips has become a mottled blue. A cold sensation runs through his stomach. Traffic and buildings appear and vanish through the rear window view of the ambulance, and fast lane changes throw him off balance.

"Chuck..."

"Yeah?"

"Baby's blue. Where's the Ambu bag?"

Colson gestures into the rear in several directions, hoping to pinpoint the Ambu bag for ventilating.

"Over...there.... Look on top of the whadda-ya-callit. Right there!"

“Come on, man!” Hinton says, reaching for and then tossing away an obviously oversized adult Ambu bag. “This can’t fit! Where’s the baby one?”

He has an urge to jump out of the vehicle and desert the whole rescue effort. Instead, he reaches for the infant, lifting him gently from the incubator so that he can seal his mouth around the nose and lips and blows short, quick breaths.

“Damn!” Colson proclaims, looking back at the blue-colored baby and then ahead at approaching traffic. “I seen a lotta resuscitations, but this takes the cake, buddy. Your eyes will probably turn yellow in a few weeks!”

Chapter 5:

The Lovejoys and the President

4:30 p.m.—The Reflecting Pool

After unpacking and having lunch at HoJo's on the first floor, the Lovejoys leave the motor lodge to go sightseeing. They spend an hour visiting the Lincoln Monument, where an immense statue of Lincoln peers over the Reflecting Pool. Rebecca, Angel, and Michael gaze up at the monument, in awe of the size and stern visage of the statue. David contemplates the face of his wife as they stand together.

"Margaret, you look…just lovely."

"Well, I'm so full I could burst, David! But thank you. What a nice thing to say to me."

She can't remember the last time he gave her a compliment. As she watches the children run down the steps and play at the edge of the light blue Reflecting Pool, she glances back. The insurance work has created lines of tension in his face. He's still young, and she senses his longing.

"No, really, you do. I think I've just gotten too busy this last year. I never have time to look at you."

Medicine's a war, Lovejoy reflects, moving his arm around his pregnant wife's waist. *Too many sick enrollees, expanding demands, technology spiraling toward higher and higher costs. I want to forget about all these people for a week. I'm exhausted, but at least I have some time!*

"David, we both need to catch up a little, just try and relax a bit, don't you think? Look at those children—they're like little fish drawn to that water! And Rebecca, how she's growing! I need to keep her working on her school assignment, but this trip will be a wonderful time for her to learn about how our government works."

The humid air and her closeness cause an urging in David, but he lets go of Margaret and heads after Michael and Angel, who are trying to crawl into the water. Rebecca sends a splash of water onto all of them and they laugh as the wet family returns to the station wagon. When they arrive back at Howard Johnson's, the younger children race to Room 623 and put swimsuits on. Immediately they head for the rooftop pool and David follows, feeling strangely distracted, fighting off an urge to smoke a cigarette.

4:45 p.m.—Car 22, resuscitation and Colson's philosophy

Hinton breathes short puffs into the baby's mouth and nose, then presses his third and fourth finger down on the sternum in a one-to-five ratio. He's rewarded as the blue, anoxic lips of the baby turn pink. Colson maneuvers around traffic, and on arriving at Children's Hospital the incubator is rushed to the intensive care unit. Colson gives a brief history, and on hearing it the nurses look at Hinton in admiration and disbelief, advising him to wash his hands and lips. Colson does some paperwork as Hinton takes a last look at the baby, then they return to Car 22 and head back to the living quarters.

"You know," Colson reminisces, as they return. "When I grew up, there didn't used to be all these infections. Maybe the flu and pneumonia, but fact is, in those days the ambulances were a little different. They dealt with a lot of car wrecks. Back then they had what today we call funeral wagons. Mortuary cars, if you know what I mean. Kind of deal where people taking care of the dead are the same ones who take care of the accidents."

He slides into the right-hand lane and flashes a grin. "When there was a wreck, the ambulances...we're talkin' big old Cadillacs...were sent out to pick up injuries. Ha! Tell you something, . People knew better than to get into a wreck. The guys who drove those cars were like horses. Only place they wanted to go was back home, meaning the mortuary. Hah! See, the real money was taking care of dead people. That's what they got paid for...think of that!"

Car 22 absorbs rays of late afternoon sun as they drive past the Washington Monument. Colson talks about his time in the service and early days before he studied law himself.

"I joined the military and rose up fast in the ranks. I was good when it came to efficiency, believed in the chain of command, know what I mean? Not like young kids today. I'm not sure you know, Hinton, but following orders is what makes things work in the military and government. Medicine and politics are not all that different. Fact of the matter, things move pretty fast here in D.C., and if you get out of line you get out of work. I like to say, 'If you got 'em by the balls, their hearts and minds will follow.' Haa!... What I mean to say is, power determines what happens around here."

Outside, a blue Therapy ambulance speeds past with lights and siren. A crowd of tourists looks up and continues along the parkway, headed for the next attraction.

"Thanks to dedication and discipline, I joined Medical and went to work for Mr. Nixon. Fact is, he's the best president we've had and you're lucky to work in this company. I'm lucky too. He saw in me what we needed, going to the top, and I'm helping him get there. It's all about health care now, and I know what it means to serve the boss.

Now, just between you and me, when I started out as a driver, I did a few things to help our company along. Just between you and me, right, and this is confidential, we started looking into Therapy records. We sent a few what you might call infiltrators into the Therapy ranks. Double billed their patients so they would get mad, and then switch over to Medical, ha! We even had a plan to firebomb their main office and maybe knock off that damned journalist, Jack Anderson, who gives us a bad name all the time. Call it dirty tricks if you want, but really, it's just healthy competition. Health care is serious stuff, know what I mean? And you need to prove yourself if you want to be a good driver."

Colson looks over at Hinton to judge his response. He smiles quietly and nods, looking at the government buildings as they pass by, and Colson continues explaining.

"So, what I'm saying is this—Nixon worked his way up. He's president now and he calls the shots. I mean, he still runs Medical on the side, being top guy in the ambulance business, and wanting to have a part in health care. As president you actually oversee both the Medical and Therapy companies, and no one gets in the way. It took time and a lot of hard work and now Medical is the leader, so we don't go for all that union stuff, like they have in Therapy. We believe in individuals, chain of command, loyalty…."

Wednesday. 1:30 a.m.—The White House

Richard Nixon lies in his bed gazing at the ceiling. He remembers his sleepless nights as an EMT, retrieving victims of trauma, before he went to law school. Ahead lays the responsibility of a president—salvaging the country from economic decline, anticipating threats from communism, exiting from Vietnam…

*I've come from being an EMT to national prominenc*e, he ruminates, *but the democrats keeps pressuring, undermining the economy, demanding service to the poor. There are so damn many poor people, always sick, and the transports are too frequent! I was poor once, but I worked my way up. So, this re-election depends on a strong economy and a realistic health care plan. How do I decrease taxes when everyone expects a free ride with Therapy and the democrats?*

His thoughts progress along the same query when he remembers Colson's temporary solution—take a vacation and plot out a new strategy.

Just me, Kisman, and the Secret Service, he imagines, as his wife sleeps quietly in a separate bed. *So, before we win the election, I clean up shop and make an outing on the Potomac, in the presidential yacht, like I always do. As president I keep this country as the world's leader, and by God, I'll set the example with the ambulances!*

1:45 a.m.—A private conversation

Inside the living quarters, Hinton waits patiently till Colson falls asleep on the couch. The sound of a late-night movie—*Attack of the Puppet People*—drones lightly on the television as he slides out of his lower bunk and carries the call phone into the bathroom. He dials a number to the Therapy headquarters.

"This may take some time," he whispers to his partner, at the other end. "I think we'll be able to work with Colson. But there's three more drivers to line up in the next three to four days, before we can get the union lined up. Colson's a little suspicious. But he doesn't see the big picture yet, let alone that we'll be taking over…"

7:30 a.m.—The wakeup call

RRR RRR RRR.

Hinton wakes from a dream, frees himself from the lower bunk, and reaches for the phone on the bathroom floor. Colson sleeps soundly as he answers.

"Medical Ambulance."

"Where the hell are you?"

"Well, I'm at the living quarters for Car 22. Who's this?" Hinton answers.

"I'm the dispatcher. So, get here for inspection before eight if you don't want your butts kicked. Copy?"

"Ten-four. You want us to..."

"Right. Before eight! Got it?"

Static follows the message and Hinton hangs up. Colson sits up and combs his dark hair back around horn-rimmed glasses and grimaces.

"Man, whatta nightmare I had last night!" he tells Hinton.

"Chuck, what's going on? The dispatcher sounds pissed off..."

"Haldeman is always pissed off. Get in before eight...or 'ah'm gonna kick your...' Man! What a dream! All of us in Medical were stuck inside this prison, trying to figure out what we did wrong. Except Nixon, who went on a vacation. And here I am, preaching about the Lord to everyone, telling them how lucky we are. Jeeezus!"

"Sounds like a strange dream!"
"It gets stranger."

Chapter 6:
Meet Howard Hughes

7:45 a.m.—The Hughes Pyramid

Within the dark apex of the Pyramid, Howard sits in a Barcalounger chair designed like a large mummy. Kleenex tissues cover his groin, thin hair falls over emaciated shoulders, and the curling nails on his fingers twist back like those of Mandarin Geishas of ancient days. A life-threatening crash in his experimental jet left him with allodynia, a condition where the lightest touch to his skin, sensitive fingers, or toes causes severe pain. And like an ancient Mandarin in seclusion, he remains motionless, watching the radiant screen in front of him. Hughes has not left his sanctum for five years, but within his reach is an electronic circuitry tracking communications from the combined informational network of Washington, D.C. As a reliable contractor for the CIA, Hughes screens much of the information going out from the city, as well as that which comes in. And it's time to act.

"Gordon, where are you?!"

He presses a button on the remote-control panel at his side. When the Mormon attendant appears from behind, his eyes remain watching the TV screen.

"Sir, can I get you something?"

"Margulis, bring my pad."

A light barely flickers out from digital control panels but the guard knows exactly where to hold the yellow writing paper. There's an audible sound of a Kleenex box being opened—then tissues are spread over the pad, held at the right upper corner. Hughes grasps the lower left corner of the pad, avoiding proximity to the other's gloved fingers, and the ritual is completed.

"Anything else, Mr. Hughes?" Margulis asks, with a Cockney accent.

"No. Stay here, Gordon."

He waits patiently, keeping his eye out for insects. There are small piles of newspapers and *TV Guides* in the darkened apex, a vestige of Hughes' habits before electronic surveillance. In an adjacent room below are memorabilia—the oil paintings of Jane Russell, buxom and half dressed; model airplanes; remnants of old movie sets. Packed into a closet are clothes Hughes had worn in his younger days—double-breasted suits, a white sport coat, an old leather flight jacket that hangs despondently—they all sag from their hangers. There's a pair of white tennis shoes, golf shoes, and a set of wing-tip brown oxfords resting on the floor, their toes pointed up from years of neglect. Margulis knows he'll be told to take a message to Robert Maheu, Hughes' closest advisor and manager, as Hughes writes in longhand.

Maheu, they're doing it again! Medical is advertising on my channel. I don't remember giving them permission. When did we tell them they could use my channel, do you know? Listen, I think it's time we brought in our own president, or made sure this one knows what I want, and I think you better get going on this.

I am determined to elect one of our choosing this year who will be indebted, and recognize his indebtedness. Remind Nixon that he owes us. He has to remember that I put him and his brother Donald where they are and I can get another president any time I want.

As a matter of fact, Bob, I'm looking at the democrats. They are still worth investing in. I gave $50,000 to Humphrey and you can tell McGovern we could extend some support to his side, if they ever want to have a president. But McGovern's going to lose and Nixon knows it. If the Democratic party could just decide on someone who can keep his job a few years, without being assassinated or backing out of Vietnam? Robert, these guys need to know they need us more than we need them. I think you should give this project the attention I asked for long ago. I have had no single word from you as to who should be president, but Nixon has the clear lead and only a major revelation can change that. If it were to leak out that he was part of an assassination plot on Castro, or that we bribed him, well it's pretty clear that he needs to be looking out for me!

My own work doubling with the CIA allows me to follow Hughes closely. Ironically, he's collaborated with the CIA from early times and developed much of the technology that the CIA currently uses to track him. When Hughes was caught giving Donald Nixon $250,000 it collapsed Nixon's lead for the presidency against Kennedy. Now Hughes knows the recent $100,000 he gave to Nixon may compromise his race against McGovern. Howard's a master at following everyone, but I have my own calling. And my job is to take care of Richard Nixon!

Wednesday, 7:50 a.m.—The Medical Office

Car 22 turns off the freeway, taking side streets before arriving at the main office on Virginia Avenue, where other ambulances are parked. As Hinton and Colson leave the car and approach the office, they hear laughter coming from inside. They pass through the front door into a hallway where a laundry bin is filled with sheets that give off the dank odor of blood. Once designed as a barbershop, the small building is still large enough to serve as Ambulance headquarters. Continuing into the main office area, Hinton encounters another atmosphere thick with the aroma of coffee and three other drivers standing around a large percolator who watch him closely.

"Well, it looks like you had a good night's sleep," a deep, guttural voice greets him from behind. He turns and recognizes the face of Harvey Kisman, the manager. Stout, with thick glasses, wavy hair, and an unctuous grin, Kisman asks, "You and Colson were tired after saving the baby, yes?" His *w's* are pronounced Teutonically, like the *v* in victory, and his voice drones with authority.

"It wasn't bad," Hinton answers.

"I'm so glad to hear that. Maybe next time we will give you something larger!"

The room fills with chuckles from the drivers. Kisman, sitting in a swivel-seat barber's chair, lifts his coffee mug as if in toast.

"These are the other men you'll be working with, Hinton. Deed...Otieno...and Dr. Noah, our famous "rocket scientist." Of course, you know Colson, and our dispatcher, Mr. Haldeman, is in the radio room."

Hinton nods to each of them as they make their assessment of him. Deed is well groomed, with straight blond hair receding over the forehead. His handsome, almost boyish face is tense. Behind the smoke of Deed's cigarette is Otieno, a tall black man leaning comfortably back in a chair. Distance and immediacy shine in Otieno's large eyes, conveying amusement. Dr. Noah, silent and bespectacled, sits aside and scrutinizes Hinton before returning his attention to a calculator. Hinton looks twice at the "rocket scientist."

"What you see is what you get. Who you know is who you met. Can you dig it?" Otieno, the driver, asks. "So, welcome to Medical, Hinton. You won't be sittin'."

"Great!" Hinton answers, maintaining his composure as he looks around the room. Black and white photos of car accidents and burning houses are pinned up next to calendars of nudes.

"Tell 'em about the fifty-one fifty," Deed says, referring to a psychotic patient they'd transported during the night.

"Oh yeah!" Otieno grins. "An interesting study, wasn't he, Dr. Noah?"

"Of whom are you speaking?" Noah seems impatient to leave, but returns to his work on a calculator.

"The psycho, Doc. We dropped him just before coming in this morning. The police cornered him in the project after he threatened to kill his wife. He was running around, foaming at the mouth, shouting 'Kill me!'" Otieno says, looking at Hinton. And it's amazing they didn't shoot him. Man, we didn't know what to do with that dude. What would you do, Colson?"

Colson adds sugar to his coffee. After a second teaspoon he comments, "I woulda left him alone. Let the police have him."

"He wouldn't a' left you alone," Deed counters, flicking ashes of his cigarette into a half-filled ashtray. "It was all we could do to tie him down with straps."

"And guess what we did next?" Otieno asks, his eyes opening like saucers. Hinton looks around as if there's someone behind him. The bins of dirty sheets in the hallway give no clue. When he turns back, he sees Otieno nod at a tall, crew-cut man, standing by a side door.

"We gave him to Haldeman!"

Ha hah ha hah…

The room fills with laughter as the dispatcher emerges from the radio room with his arms folded.

"Very funny. Something amusing you all?" Haldeman asks.

His short, crew-cut hair is as sharply defined as the collar and epaulets on a starched white shirt. Wing-tipped shoes, polished to a luster, click as he enters the room. Besides serving as chief of staff at the White House, Haldeman makes time to dispatch during the day for Medical Ambulance Company. I've infiltrated into the company as night dispatcher, so I can follow all their work.

Kisman lets them talk while he works out finances in the barber's chair. Adding and subtracting figures in a large account book, he looks up every few minutes to survey the room. Movements of his pursed lips suggest he's not satisfied with the calculations. After a short while he closes the book and stands up.

"Colson...we need more work from you! Hinton...you come with me." He snaps his fingers as he walks outside and Hinton follows.

"When do I finish my training?" Hinton asks, walking into the parking lot.

"Right now," Kisman answers. "So, just listen to me."

They move toward Car 22 and he opens his briefcase and pulls out a container of polish. Standing next to the ambulance he dabs paste over the side of the car and then rubs it with a cloth. The finish becomes progressively brighter as he presses harder, using fast, methodical strokes to remove a thin layer of oxidation. Finally, the wax hardens into a luminous membrane, reflecting sunlight like a mirror.

"In America, Hinton, when we look into our cars we see our reflection. Cars are everything here. You must polish them every day, my friend. People in this city judge us by our appearance, and we want to be successful, don't we?"

Hinton nods. Kisman's face appears on the side, reflecting an image of probing eyes behind thick glasses that rest easily over his bulbous nose. The waves of thick, curly hair are brushed straight back, accentuating a broad forehead, and his lips form a mysterious smile.

"When you polish something enough," Kisman continues, "you begin to see your face. I like people to see themselves in front of the ambulance, because that's where life ends and begins. That, my friend, is your training today."

He opens the side door, indicating for Hinton to get in. Climbing into the driver's seat, Kisman unlocks a glass door over the tachometer and removes a miniature recording disk, then replaces it with a new one.

"We check every morning, so we know what you're doing, Hinton. When you go too fast, we know. We have ways of watching your activities, so I advise you to drive carefully."

Kisman's smile turns to a frown as he looks at the erratic markings on the disk pulled from the tachometer.

"But you don't look like the kind of driver who wants to break rules. I want you to take responsibility for this car. You know Colson can't always be trusted."

"Really? Why's that, Mr. Kisman?"

He studies Hinton's reflection on the side of the car, considering his potential.

He's too self-assured. I haven't had time to check his background, but on the other hand, I need educated drivers. The man comes without medical experience, has a college scholarship, and even a law degree! There's lives to be saved, money to be earned, and if a youngster is ambitious enough and wants the EMT experience, maybe he can balance out the organization.

Kisman decides to run a background investigation during the first week.

"Already Colson has destroyed one car," he tells Hinton. "But at least he'll show you what he knows. That won't take long. And then I let you work with Deed, who moves a little faster. After Deed you work with Otieno, who is even more ambitious. And, finally, you work with Dr. Noah, our rocket scientist, who goes like the speed of light. But first, Hinton, we see if you can handle the job."

Sliding the previous day's disk into his shirt pocket, Kisman re-locks the tachometer and gives the ambulance a quick mechanical inspection, after which they return to the office. In the hallway Kisman tells Hinton to take the bin full of dirty sheets into the laundry room.

"Give those to Helen, the new laundry girl, and get fresh linen for your car."

Hinton rolls the bin down the hallway past the dispatching room. Through an open door he can see Haldeman handling a call on the intercom system. Then, pushing his way into the laundry room, he encounters Helen.

"Just leave them there. They aren't bleeding anymore," she says.

Standing next to a table folding sheets, she stops and rubs her hands down the sides of a tight uniform. He glances at the sheets, then at her blond hair, pulled tightly back into a bun. She's attractive, and she stares back.

"You must be Helen," he says.

"And you're the new driver. You act like you've never seen blood before."

"Oh, I have," he counters.

"I bet you haven't."

They laugh together, then become quiet as she returns to folding sheets. His eyes leave her face as he notes the uniform clinging to her supple figure. Then he forces his mind back to the plan. Infiltrating and controlling Medical may not be easy, but she'll be helping him. Changing health care in the capital starts in the emergency service realm.

"Well, what should I call you?" she asks.

For a moment they gaze into each other's eyes.

"What do you mean, Helen?"

"I mean, do I call you James or Mr. Hinton?"

A smile comes to his face. "You can just call me 'The Comeback Kid.'"

8:40 a.m.—The Trash Lady

"That's what I mean," Colson announces, as he lets Hinton drive away from the main office. "That's what I mean. He doesn't care how much you work, or how many people you save—it's never enough. It's never as good as if he does it himself. You think Kisman cares...so long as he gets his recognition from the president? The guy is so damn smart!"

Hinton practices with the power steering.

"Not that his life has been easy," Colson goes on. "I mean he had to leave another country to come to D.C., and a lot of his family got killed off. He started at the bottom. I have to admit, he's not stupid...he's smart as a fox…but that's why you gotta watch him…"

Hinton glances at the tachometer, wondering if it records voices.

"What do you mean, Chuck?"

Colson pauses, looking at the tachometer, knowing his words are traceable in a company that tracks voices by bugs. Like Nixon, Kisman is a master at bugging.

"Well, what I mean is, you can learn a lot from Mr. Kisman. He's bright and he's got experience, having lived in other countries. You being a college boy, you should watch and learn from him, . Course, most of the things you need to learn, I'm going to teach you. Now, Mr. Kisman is organized. Very organized! He travels a lot to negotiate. Besides being our company manager, he works for the president in an international capacity and has handled the Vietnam negotiations. Kisman understands how to deal with foreign countries and how to keep us out of trouble. Fact is, some people think Kisman's smarter than Nixon. Particularly when it comes to terrorists and radicals."

They drive back to HoJo's to have breakfast, and while parking the ambulance they spot the old woman with a shopping cart scouring the back of the motel, picking up aluminum cans from open bins. Her dog follows behind, guarding the cart, while her search is cautious, determined by arthritis as well as the need to never miss an aluminum can.

"Colson, isn't that the lady we almost ran over?"

"Trash Queen. She hangs around here. One of these days her and that pit bull dog are gonna get hit if she isn't more careful."

"Where's she sleep?"

"Who knows? I wouldn't get near it. She's deranged, and every time we try to take her to City Hospital, she makes a ruckus and they throw her out."

"So, she lives on the street around here?"

"Her and the damn Weatherpeople. Who knows where they all sleep?"

Living below the streets of D.C. in the tunnel drainage system, the Weatherpeople sporadically surface to protest, sabotage cars, and disrupt daily traffic patterns. Believing automotive pollution destroys natural weather cycles, they often protest and promote anarchy on the streets. The elusive group has become more active as the presidential election has heated up, and they're known to harbor terrorists, anarchists, and Vietnam war protestors.

10:10 a.m.—Breakfast in HoJo's, and room 723

Colson and Hinton talk about the Company over eggs and coffee, as Colson's underground Plumbers plan out their night's activities on the seventh floor of Howard Johnson's, directly above them. I have the benefit of tracking these activities, since room 622 is my safe house, and the planning for the Watergate break-in is right above me in 723, just as I need it to be. I've known the "Plumbers" for years. They're all connected to the CIA in one way or another, though for past adventures few can match Frank (Fiorini) Sturgis, grandson of Italian immigrants, who was raised in the U.S., not Cuba. Sturgis had 31 aliases, depending on what country or agency he worked for, but Castro knew him as Chief Crazy Horse ("el jefe de caballo loco") or "Yankee Barbaro" (one hell of a yankee), after witnessing him land an aircraft full of weapons in a next to impossible hill top of Eastern Cuba. Frank dreamed of becoming a Catholic priest in high school but went on to become a teacher of Guerrilla warfare and the master of silent killing with a Stiletto. Of course, all the Plumbers have one shared goal, to rid Cuba of Castro.

"Hunt and I will keep a close look out," G. Gordon Liddy tells the group, gathered in room 723, which has a convenient view of the Democratic Headquarters in the Watergate office building, across the street. "So, no screw-ups. If you do things the way we tell you to, there's more work ahead. We're gonna get a few demonstrators from the University, a few Vietnam protestors, and butt their heads together. And there's more. We'll teach Therapy a little about the art of medicine, and when you boys get ahold of Daniel Ellsberg, you'll break both his legs!"

Howard Hunt nods, puffing quietly on a pipe. His tweed jacket looks incongruous next to the Plumbers, who are dressed in black business suits.

"Good!" Liddy continues. "Everybody knows their job. Now practice with your cameras, and I'll see you tonight."

Liddy leaves and drives back to his FBI office in an open-roof Jeep. As soon as he leaves, room service knocks on the door of 723 to deliver breakfast. One of the Plumbers, bald-headed James McCord, erstwhile security director for the CIA, throws a sheet over the telescope by the window. It points into a sixth-floor Watergate office window, just across the street.

The Cubano exiles are hungry, having arrived the night before after red-eye flights from Miami at the invitation of Howard Hunt. Bernard Barker, or "Macho," is happy to accept a plate of eggs with bacon. As bag man and leader of his three colleagues, his service record includes working for Batista's secret service in Cuba and flying combat missions as a bombardier with the U.S. Army Air Force in World War II. Captured by the Germans, Barker spent a year in the Stalag Luft 1 prison, was eventually freed by the Soviet army, and went on to serve with the FBI, the CIA, and the invasion force for the Bay of Pigs mission. Eugenio Martínez, called

"Muscalito" for his physical prowess, sits across from Macho and pours Cuban hot sauce onto his eggs. He's still on the CIA's payroll, and can boast 364 covert missions into Cuba, as well as spending time in Castro's prisons after his capture in the Bay of Pigs.

"Macho," is the designated speaker for the Cubans. Although he's shorter than the others, he has the widest forehead and a sober expression. Like the others, he's lost many close friends and comrades in their struggle. When Hunt came to Miami and told him he had been hired to act as a counselor to the White House, Barker knew that he and his associates could have another opportunity to eliminate Castro and regain Cuba for all the exiles.

"Eduardo, how did you learn that Castro is giving money to the democrats, to fund their campaign?" Barker asks Hunt, using his pseudonym "Eduardo".

Hunt puffs calmly on his pipe, and nods at the collection of wigs, transceivers, and CIA-provided equipment that rests on the floor of room 723. It's understood between them that they have a common source of information.

"Macho, would I bring you all the way here if it didn't concern Castro? That's what you are here to find out: How much money did he give to McGovern's campaign? We know the Cuban spies are filtering in money through rigged Jai Lai games in Miami, and Cuba's drug money via the Black Panthers. So, the president would like to know how much money, and wouldn't you?"

Virgilio Gonzalez, always fastidious, has left his suitcase of locksmith tools next to Hunt's assorted devices, and declines his breakfast. He only eats two meals, always later in the day, so the fifth Plumber, Frank Sturgis, eats the remaining two servings contentedly. As Soldier of Fortune, Frank's the only one skilled at execution. His advanced training in Guerrilla warfare while serving with the U.S. Marines in Guam and Guadalcanal, helped him to train and supply Castro's revolutionary troops. He then became gambling czar of Cuba's casinos and security director for Castro's air force. But then Castro adopted Communism and Sturgis turned double agent and worked with the CIA in its attempts to assassinate the new dictator. He denies he helped execute seventy-one soldiers of Batista's forces in the Sierra Madre mountains of Cuba, but he stood over the mass gravesite with an assault rifle poised on his knee. Due to that photo he almost lost his U.S. citizenship were it not for his subsequent work with the FBI. Needless to say, Sturgis knows nothing of my work for Castro.

Meanwhile, Martínez ("Muscalito") sets his food down and looks toward Hunt.

"Eduardo, how many years did we spent in Havana prisons? Frank was bullwhipped in the El Morro prison, I did my share, and we don't need any more of those experiences. You would not lead us in a bad way, would you?"

"Musculito, we're brothers, and you're an operative. You know your mission is to do as you are told and not to ask questions. And another thing. Castro kept a dossier of all the attempts made to assassinate him. If we find it in the Watergate office, we need to make a copy of it, and remove it. So if anyone can find it, it will be you."

Hunt and Macho are well aware of the dangers of such a dossier in the hands of Therapy, having helped plan several of the assassination attempts. If the democrats get the dossier, it will impact Nixon's chance of re-election as president, since he helped arrange the invasion of Cuba.

James McCord pulls the sheet off his telescope, and looks across at the sixth floor of the Watergate into the Democratic National Committee offices.

Chapter 7:

Reynolds' Last Smoke

Wednesday, 10:14 a.m.—Car 22 transfer from the V.A.

"So, anyhow," Colson continues, lighting a cigarette and exhaling smoke, as he and Hinton finish their breakfast at HoJo's, "Kisman's never around. It's just as good since he thinks he knows more than anyone else. You'll never see the man driving an ambulance. But he does know all about the leaks and come right down to it, the leaks can hurt us in the coming election. We know the democrats have access to our inside information, but we don't know how much. So it has to stop."

The morning sun lightens the Howard Johnson's restaurant, and Rebecca Lovejoy, exploring the hotel alone after swimming in the rooftop pool, peers through the glass door of the restaurant at the two ambulance drivers. In her effort to do her school report on the capital, she has become more interested in drawing portraits of interesting people, and she studies Hinton and decides she can draw him. But first she wants to finish a portrait of an odd man named Dr. Leary who keeps appearing in the newspaper.

"Tell me more about the leaks," Hinton asks, finishing his coffee. He signals to the waitress for more toast.

"You read the *Washington Times*, don't you?"

"You're talking about the election?" Hinton asks. "And the connections between Hughes and Nixon? Or is it something else?"

"You catch on fast," Colson says, taking another drag from his cigarette. "But not that fast. Ever stop to think what the democrats would do if they could really expose Nixon?"

"Well, I'm not sure. What's there to expose?"

"Wouldn't you like to know?" Colson asks, smiling and watching Hinton closely.

"Well, who does know?"

"Try Deep Throat."

"Deep Throat?"

"Someone in the FBI. We're not sure who he is, but he likes to talk! Especially to the *Washington Times* reporters. And there's always the CIA as well. They keep an eye on everything."

A set of loud beeps comes from Colson's pager, and he stands quickly and heads for the payphone.

"Damn cabbage transfer!" he vituperates, returning to the counter. "Haldeman gives 'em to me every damn time!"

Within minutes they're back in Car 22 and heading out of the parking lot, narrowly missing the shopping cart lady again. She bends down to pick up spilled aluminum cans, muttering curses as the ambulance speeds away.

"Colson, what's a cabbage transfer?"

"They don't teach you much in college, do they, ? It's Code One to a nursing home, in this case a V.A. patient. Haldeman likes to save 'em all for me. Never gives any of 'em to Deed or Otieno. Or Dr. Noah, for that matter. Dr.Noah's never been to a cabbage factory in his life and couldn't start an IV if he had to!"

Colson fails to mention that he has trouble starting IVs successfully. His stomach turns queasy when he tries, so sometimes he tapes the plastic sheath on the outside of the patient's arm. The catheters are restarted by nurses after the patient reaches the hospital anyway, so with enough tape it looks for all purposes like a good IV.

"Well, I guess I've never even started one," Hinton confesses as they see the Veterans Hospital up ahead.

10:45 a.m.—The Bingo game

After picking up their transfer, Car 22 is on the freeway again. Buildings and houses disappear like a rewinding video as Hinton looks through the back window and makes sure the gurney's secured. Mr. Reynolds, the transfer patient, remains oblivious to his guardians till the ambulance arrives at the Heavenly Rest Home.

"Door watchers," Colson informs Hinton, as they enter the convalescent home. A dozen patients stare back at them with interest, saying nothing, missing nothing. "So, come on, before Haldeman gives us another transfer."

Inside the dining room another group of residents plays Bingo on a large table. Hinton looks over them at a numeric replica or message of an odd crossword puzzle, posted electronically with lighted numbers on the wall. Unaware of its significance, he stops momentarily to jot it down on a notebook, then slides the paper into his front pocket.

7 15 15 4
18 5 1 4 5 18 19
23 1 20 3 8
4 5 12 20 1
20 1 14 7 15

The door watchers continue observing as the drivers roll the patient past the nursing station and into his new room, where he's transferred onto a clean, sterile bed. Between the off-white walls of the room there's one small table with a television, and the pungent odor of a bedsore fills the room air. Hinton, out of curiosity, tries to unravel the message of the bingo game noted on the way into the nursing home.

I'm good at crossword puzzles, he acknowledges to himself, trying to ignore the odor while Colson records their transfer, and pulls the recorded message from his pocket. *Let's see. If I use a numerical correlation with the alphabet. 7 15 15 4 should be "good." And 18 5 1 4 5 18 19—that's tougher. I'm going to say "readers." Hmmm...23 1 20 3 8? "Watch" maybe?*

Before he can finish, Colson nods to him and pulls the gurney away from the bed. Colson takes a single cigarette from his pocket and sets it on the table beside the TV. Reynolds watches them leave, as a small tear forms below his eyelid, like a raindrop.

Chapter 8:

The Fall

Wednesday, 10:50 a.m.—Virginia Avenue

David Lovejoy looks up from the Howard Johnson's rooftop swimming pool as Angel glides on an air mattress over the shallow water, and Rebecca keeps an eye on Michael, who hangs onto an inflatable pool tube. "Strawberry Fields" pours out from a transistor radio in Beatles harmony, and in the bright sun the motel is immersed in the laughter of children and a holiday's freedom. Drawn to the edge of the enclosure, David can scan the outline of government buildings and the Hughes Pyramid overlooking the metropolis. He walks around the side of the fenced perimeter till he comes to an edge facing the river. The exclusive Watergate buildings block most of the view. His wife is at the Watergate complex now, checking preparations for the banquet to be held Friday night, and he's to spend the evening with the children. In the distance the soft current of the Potomac drifts past the city, while a team of rowers heads upstream on a slender kayak.

God, I need a break from work, he thinks to himself, *and just a little time to breathe outside of meetings, and more meetings, and then more meetings. Maybe I should go swimming. But I just need a little time to myself.*

He watches the kayak being paddled upriver, edging northwest of Roosevelt Island, and feels a powerful urge to smoke a cigarette.

Looking back at the children he sees Rebecca has herded Angel and Michael into a corner where a lifeguard sits in an aluminum chair. Rebecca is getting close to puberty. Her light-skinned figure, accentuated by her bikini, signals a full figure that will fill out in a few years. Unaware of her beauty, just waking to the world of boys and men who look at her, she begins to notice the lifeguard staring her way. There's no breeze and the sun's rays bring moisture from Lovejoy's forehead, a gentle, enhancing sweat. Checking the side pocket of his swimming trunks he feels several metal coins, the size of quarters.

Wallets in the motel room. But there's enough change to buy a pack. I really need a smoke!

"Rebecca," he calls out, "be right back. I'm going down to the room. Don't leave the pool or go anywhere till you see me come back. You watch your brother and sister, okay? Stay here and I'll be back, so just wait by the pool for me."

"Okay, Dad," she calls between splashes, tossing her ponytail at Michael, who laughs with delight. Angel dives off her air mattress, trying to evade her sister. For Rebecca, the chance to explore away from home, to escape homework for a week, except for a required report on the capital and its many activities, is the greatest adventure.

Lovejoy walks past the pool and into the rooftop elevator. As he descends to the lobby, an annoying sense of guilt competes with his vacation relief.

Forget the pressure, his mind battles. *Forget competition.*

He approaches the cigarette machine and succumbs. Several coins drop into the machine, the lever pulls back, and a package lands softly in the stainless-steel base, making a familiar, reassuring thump. A long-standing addiction is appeased as he opens the package, removes one cigarette, and walks slowly outside to a semicircular entranceway.

Busy traffic flows down Virginia Avenue as drivers head to and away from work, with few interruptions of the constant flow. He borrows a match from a group of tourists standing outside. Inhaling deeply, he feels both energy and relaxation.

Forget tensions, the growing numbers of clients who want more health care, always more for less and less. I'll deal with it when I get home. Now I can spend more time with my family! The thoughts ease from his mind as he takes a second, deeper puff. *If I could only break this habit I could help myself too.*

He watches traffic flow by the front of the building and his heart rate increases. A Greyhound bus pulls up along the sidewalk, and just as he decides to finish the cigarette and check on the children, an unexpected convergence of diesel fumes, pollen, and the humid D.C. moisture triggers a bronchospasm. Small tube-like airways, filling each lung like the branches of a tree, inundate with toxins and constrict together synchronously, depriving a flow of oxygen to the rest of his body. Sliding backwards and catching the curb with his heels, he loses balance. Tourists standing nearby can hear the light thump of his head landing on cement.

10:55 a.m.—Car 22 on a Code Three

"Man, that Reynolds guy was old," Colson observes, as he and Hinton put fresh linen on the gurney and return it to the ambulance.

"Are all the rest homes this way?"

"No, there's nicer ones. They cost more. Color TV and stuff. Goddamn it, , this work gives me a headache. If it weren't for the boss and his obsession with health care…"

Colson grimaces. Creases on his forehead and crow's feet wrinkles by his eyes stand out in the sunlight as he squints and looks ahead.

The two drivers head back to the living quarters while Hinton contemplates his strategy. Moving along Constitution Avenue, the ambulance passes by Doric columns that suspend the roof of the Lincoln Monument. The monument rests on top of a cavern unknown to the public, and Lincoln's rose marble statue testifies to his legacy. The capital's spacious avenues share other majestic symbols with hard, stone-carved messages of freedom and progress.

Work the group dynamics, Hinton tells himself, as they drive by the monument. *Colson will come around. I still need to bring in the other drivers. Need to set him up now.*

"Colson. Anyone ever asked the owner for a raise?"

"What for?" Colson looks up from the logbook where he's recording the Reynolds transfer.

"For ourselves. The drivers haven't ever tried to get together to bargain, to negotiate?"

"What kind of bargain? What are you talking about?"

"Like full representation, for salaries. I mean, for example, you know how much the owner of this company makes? Ever compare salaries?"

"Why?" Colson puts the logbook down and eyes Hinton. "Why do you care how much he makes? He's the president of our country, so he makes what he wants, and he deserves it."

"I just wondered if you ever asked him."

"Maybe *you* should," Colson says. "You want to call him?"

"No, no. Not yet. Give me a little time, Chuck. But we should be thinking about a collective stand."

"Collective? What the hell are you talking about, Hinton?"

"Car 22!" The dispatcher's voice booms over the radio and Colson grabs ahold of the hand phone.

"22 by."

"You ready to copy?"

"Affirmative," Colson answers.

"Howard Johnson's Motor Lodge. 2-0-1 Virginia Street. That's Code Three. 2-0-1 Virginia Street, you copy?"

"Roger. Virginia Street, Code Three. Hey, that's where we had breakfast this morning!" Colson says, jotting down the address and looking over at his partner.

"Okay, so, I should use the siren, right? Where we going?" Hinton asks.

"Right where we started this morning, by HoJo's breakfast place, close to our quarters," Colson answers, as Hinton hits the overhead switch. "It's in front of HoJo's. Stay north...go north...till we hit...you hear me? We go north! And gun it, goddamn it, this is a Code Three!"

"Okay, I am, I am!"

"Here! Here! Head up 23rd!" Colson's voice climbs as they swerve past and through an intersection. The car accelerates. "Now, stay on 23rd till we get to Virginia and go left."

They pass by a maze of overpasses skirting the river and the Colombia Plaza on their left. "You wanna take...Virginia and...hey! There's the Watergate, up ahead. Pull alongside HoJo's, to the right, where all those people are standing."

11:07 a.m.—Code 3 transfer

Tourists watch from inside the bus as the driver stands by the fallen pedestrian's body, and the sound of an approaching siren intensifies.

"Here it comes!"

The crowd outside turns around to see Car 22 pull alongside.

"Whatcha got?" Colson asks, leaving the car and approaching on foot. He can see a man down on the ground, motionless.

"Don't know," the bus driver responds, "but he's in some serious trouble."

Lovejoy's face is swollen. Wheezing noises escape dark lips as his gaze fixes upward.

"Get 'em on the gurney," Colson says to Hinton, who brings up the gurney while he checks the pulse. ", I need you to bag and I'll drive. What's this man's name?"

"There's no I.D. We just found him lying here," the bus driver says. "No idea of where he came from."

"Okay, he's John Doe."

After loading Lovejoy into the ambulance, Colson flips on the emergency lights and siren, and heads into the traffic.

On the rooftop of the motor lodge Rebecca, Angel, and Michael have migrated from the swimming pool to the side rail. They peer down just in time to see the ambulance drive away and wave, not seeing the patient being transported. I watch the action from the safe house. Like all of Hojo's rooms, it's basic Americana - a shag rug, red and blue couch, cottage cheese white ceiling, and a wallpaper that tries to understate. Transceivers stay in my suitcases, just in case room service gets interested, and I've parked my taxi some distance away, so the motel thinks I'm just another Latin visitor to the capital. I haven't yet realized how the Lovejoy family will change my mission, or how acquiring the Code for Fidel will change me.

Day 2 and 3

Deed

The "Plumbers": Virgilio Gonzalez, Frank Sturgis (Yankee Barbaro), Felipe De Diego, Bernard Barker (Macho), Eugenio Martínez (Muscalito)

"It's incredible. Millions of dollars have been spent investigating Watergate. A president has been forced out of office. Dozens of lives have been ruined. We're sitting in the can. And still nobody can explain why they bugged the place to begin with."

—John Dean to Charles Colson, 1974 Danbury Prison

G. Gordon Liddy describing the Cuban Plumbers he wants John Mitchell to hire: "…professional killers who have accounted between them for twenty-two dead so far, including two hanged from a beam in a garage."

John Mitchell: "And where did you find men like that?"

Liddy: "I understand they're members of organized crime."

Mitchell: "And how much will their services cost?"

Liddy: "Like top professionals everywhere, sir, they don't come cheap."

Conversation in Attorney General John Mitchell's office, January 27, 1972

"There is nothing in this world greater than being a CIA agent. You're serving your country in ways you can't believe."

Frank Sturgis, Watergate spy

Chapter 9:

Nixon and the First Break-in

Wednesday, June 14, 1972, 4:28 p.m.—Howard Johnson's Motor Lodge, room 723

James McCord dabs his forehead with a handkerchief, paying homage to a frontal lobe that has steered his instincts through a lifetime of service for the FBI. Working with the CIA, experience has convinced him that detail is essential to success, and looking around the room at the accumulated listening devices, recorders, and amplifiers, he's satisfied—the work is thorough. Having captured salacious conversations between prostitutes and Johns that Baldwin, his junior partner, has recorded for several days, he'll pass these recordings on to Lieutenant Liddy, who in turn will forward them to Haldeman. No doubt Nixon will take interest, since the information will likely be damaging to both democrats and republicans.

Nixon's guaranteed a re-election, McCord ponders. *So why give him more information? It's obvious why he wants it. He wants to know how much the dems knows about him and the $100,000 donation from Hughes, and other hidden transactions? Or maybe the Watergate office hides a dossier of assassination attempts on Castro, ones that Nixon encouraged? But what do I need to know? Who's sleeping with whom in the Colombia Plaza—that's what may be hidden in the Watergate office. And I don't care if it's democrats or republicans—it doesn't matter, because neither of these parties can be trusted. How much do they know about* *the CIA and our work in the Columbia Plaza? This all has to remain a secret!*

Wednesday, 4:30, p.m.—The phone booth in HoJo's lobby

I drop two dollars of quarters into a payphone and dial Domingo, my Miami contact, who in turn is connected to Blackbeard in Cuba with a secured line.

"Tell Fidel I've made progress. We know what the CIA is doing, what the White House Plumbers have planned, and best of all, I've found a way into the Medical Ambulance Company—the one Nixon likes to run on the side, along with his Whitehouse staff. I managed to get hired as the night dispatcher, while I drive taxi in the daytime. So, now maybe I can find a way to the Code. Nixon visits the Medical headquarters from time to time, and wherever he goes the Football comes along. It may not take too long!"

"Excellent," Domingo assures me. "But do not allow yourself to be discovered. If this happens, we can do nothing to help you."

I look through the glass of the phone booth, watching cars move slowly down Virginia Avenue. Across the street is the Watergate complex, the so-called "Whitehouse II" where many of Nixon's staff live. And also the headquarters for the Democratic Campaign that will soon be invaded. This work is never easy, and if I know Blackbeard, I'm sure I'll be asked to augment his work. The fate of an operative - no mistakes allowed.

Wednesday, 4:35 p.m.—Howard Johnson's Motor Lodge, room 623

In the room just below James McCord and Baldwin, Margaret Lovejoy looks out the window, hoping to see her husband in the sidewalk flow of pedestrians. After verifying that their station wagon is still parked in the underground garage and her husband's keys and wallet are in the motel room, she considers the dilemma.

David might disappear for an hour at a time. But he's not one to leave the children without telling me. I'll call the police if he doesn't show up by five. The children and the hotel lobby people never saw him disappear, but there was that incident with an ambulance. According to the lobby staff, the ambulance victim had been someone on a bus. But, what does that mean? God, this is all so strange! I'm beginning to dread this vacation and there's still my invitation to the dinner banquet Thursday night. Why would he just disappear and what in God's name is going on?

Looking beyond the Watergate buildings to the opaque waters of the Potomac, she whispers a prayer. The waters flow silently along. Behind her, in the larger motel front room, the children have returned from the downstairs restaurant carrying a plate of French fries with ketchup. Rebecca, tired of the homework she brought on the trip, starts drawing portraits of faces in the newspaper and focuses on an odd-looking man named Leary. Using a pencil, she sketches out the word FURTHER on his T-shirt.

Wednesday, 10:45 p.m.—The Plumber's Watergate Hotel Safe Room, No. 214

When Colson and Hinton leave "John Doe" in the ER of City Hospital, a condition of "status asthmaticus with head trauma" is promptly diagnosed. David Lovejoy is intubated, placed on a ventilator, and after a CT scan he's sent to the Intensive Care Unit where he'll be sedated with hopes that he'll recover. The drivers spend the rest of the day doing routine nursing home transfers.

Later in the darkness of night, as Car 22 finishes its work, Lieutenant G. M. Liddy slides his Jeep into a space two blocks from the Howard Johnson's Motor Lodge. He walks briskly toward the Watergate complex, then enters the first of the two riverside buildings, the hotel complex. Scanning the lobby with peregrine eyes, he sees no familiar faces and rides the elevator to the second floor, turns right, and continues to room 214. Tapping sharply on the door, he's greeted by a heavy-accented voice.

"Who is it?"

"Open up," he demands, facing the smooth, enameled door. There's a single peephole made of glass that allows inspection only from within the room. He glances down the hallway once more when a brass chain latch is released, allowing entrance into a thick-carpeted room where the Plumbers await. Virgilio Gonzalez, the locksmith with thin arms and long sideburns, smiles warily and allows Liddy in. James McCord has come over from Howard Johnson's, and stands by the window looking out apprehensively. Macho, the WWII pilot who was captured by the Germans, is now the lead Cuban operative. He waits patiently with Eugenio Martínez, or "Musculito", hoping to start soon.

Frank Sturgis, dressed in a dark suit, sits at a small table playing cards with Hunt. Having fought with Castro during the overthrow of Batista and changing sides when Castro became a Communist, he's a patriotic man with no fears - this foray into Watergate's offices is not much of a challenge. He's glad to be working with Hunt again, and finally they'll get another chance to eliminate Castro.

When Howard Hunt stopped working directly for the CIA, Colson hired him as the more experienced operative, knowing he could bring expertise into the Plumbers' activities. Having been the political organizer for the Bay of Pigs, Hunt had a strong relationship with all the Cuban exiles. He linked up Bob Maheu, Howard Hughes' manager, and Florida mafia boss, Sam Traffiante, and they planned to finish off Fidel at one of his favorite restaurants. Poison in a milkshake. But the pea-sized pills of botulinum toxin, designed by the CIA to dissolve into a soup, never found their way to the lunch table when the waiter got nervous. The plot to get Castro failed as badly as the Bay of Pigs invasion, and their effort to get Castro continues. So now, twenty-three spy novels later, Hunt feels happy to be in real action again; anything clandestine for that matter. Taking a pipe from his lips he addresses Liddy with a question, letting his White House partner believe he's still in charge of the operation.

"Well, Gordon?"

"It's a go," Liddy answers. "Let's get moving."

There's a brief discussion, and the Cubans set off for the Watergate Hotel. Liddy and Hunt remain ensconced in room 214, while the five Plumbers, Macho, Muscalito, Sturgis, and Gonzalez descend down the elevator to the underground parking garage. They continue through a parking lot tunnel to the basement of the Watergate office building, where Hunt and McCord previously taped the door locks open to allow entry. Ascending a fire exit stairwell, they reach the sixth floor, and make their way to the Democratic National Headquarters. McCord continues up to the eighth floor, for reasons unknown to his four partners, who proceed to enter and photograph files from the desk of the campaign manager.

All Sturgis finds is a sheet of paper with a soft image of a woman's lips embossed on it. She had kissed the glass of a Xerox copier wearing lipstick and then wrote a message on the paper—"for the real thing, call me at…". He copies the phone number while they photograph two cassettes of films. Without a key to the manager's desk they're unable to get more hidden information, but Sturgis and Martinez have been sleeping with several of the secretaries and hope to have the key soon. Suddenly McCord appears, telling them to hurry up and finish.

"Let's get out of here. I've planted two bugs in the phones. We need to leave before the night guard shows up."

Unknown to the Cuban-exile associates, beyond a hot phone number, their efforts will show nothing of value, and they will have to return. Hopefully next time they will have a desk drawer key.

Thursday, 8:00 a.m.—Oval Office - the White House

"I don't care how it's done. I want the leaks stopped and don't give me excuses. Use any means. Haldeman, do we have one man here to do it? I want results, now."

Nixon slams the phone down, stands up from a carved mahogany desk, and goes to the bay window. Overlooking the Osmanthus and Boxwood-hedged garden, he gazes from the office at the windowless apex of the Pyramid, contemplating Howard Hughes, the man who lives at the apex of a forty-nine-story building.

It's goddamn disturbing that he's built a structure defying all the construction codes of D.C.. And gets permits for an office that towers over the White House! And rumors have it that real estate tycoons have plans for even taller buildings and luxury hotels! What's more bothersome are these suggestions that the democrats have knowledge of my slush funds—maybe my connection with Hughes. This damned Bay of Pigs thing. If word gets out about how Maheu, the mob, and me ... tried to get Castro? These damn leaks ruined my run for presidency in 1960 and I sure as hell won't let it happen again.

The thing about Hughes—we're both restricted to the buildings we live in, unable to leave without a security force. He may be crazy and paranoid, doesn't want anyone to see him, but in my case, I can't move without security and the "Football," the damned briefcase handcuffed to security with the code for the National Defense System. Well, I'm the only one who knows its combination. I'm the one with the responsibility to activate nuclear missiles. Maybe Hughes controls the industry that produces those missiles. But that industry depends on contracts awarded by departments under me. It's more complex than he understands and as long as his taxes remain low enough, he'll stay in line while I fight communism. Bottom line: no one wants to know the details, as long as taxes remain low. And, of course, that we're protected from nuclear attack. It's up to me, isn't it?

Nixon considers Hughes a few minutes more, then returns to his desk and has the operator connect him with the Medical dispatcher again.

"Haldeman?"

"Yes, sir?"

"Another thing about these leaks..." He pauses. "The FBI thinks Ellsberg shared our defense strategy with the Russians! We don't know for sure, but if he's capable of that, we need to get rid of the son of a bitch. Listen. If there was some way, we could...you know…know what the dems know...you get the picture? Anything they might know about us that could hurt the election. I don't want to lose like I did in '60, because of the Hughes loan to my brother. So finally, Bob, let's get rid of this Ellsberg problem! We can expose him in the press. Put a torch to him!"

Haldeman gets it. It's the second call of the day with the same request.

"You know Colson and Deed already know someone who's very good at finding these things out," Haldeman tells Nixon. "It's the CIA man, Howard Hunt, who thinks Castro may be supporting the democratic campaign. He's working with Lieutenant Liddy, who is part of your re-election committee, and they've got these Miami Cuban exiles, who fought in the Bay of Pigs. They want to find out too. You know they didn't find much in the psychiatrist's office, but they can do more."

"Is that right?"

"Yes, sir. They're part of a special investigation committee; we call it the 'Plumbing Committee.' Their job is to find leaks and fix them, and anything that might find its way into the press. These "Plumbers" have professional experience in this sort of thing. As I mentioned, the Cubans were in the Bay of Pigs invasion, and they're highly motivated to oust Castro. If it turns out Castro is supporting the democrats, well that information could help us. I'll let you know more..."

"No, no…that's okay. I, uh...don't need to know...just need to know that we're working on it. There's the election and I'm busy this week. Howard Hunt, I know him well, and he never turned up much on the Kennedys when we assigned him that. You know it would be nice to know a lot more about the dem's activities. Any of their connections with Howard Hughes and Castro."

"Yes, sir. It certainly would."

Chapter 10:
Hinton Joins Deed (and Muriel)

Thursday, 8:10 a.m.—The Medical Office

Inside the Medical main office Jim Deed III takes his cup and adds a spoon of instant to his regular coffee. His mind wanders the landscape of the future. He imagines himself as dispatcher, then manager, perhaps even owner of Medical and…could he become president? He adds another teaspoon and an equal amount of sugar. With the adrenergic mudslide, a new day is started.

"Never eat breakfast on an empty stomach," he tells Hinton, who reaches down to tie newly purchased boots, familiarizing himself with the surroundings, and getting ready for his new assignment to work with Deed.

"That's right, drink your power food!" the black driver named Otieno laughs. "Gives Deed the speed!"

Deed sips the mixture and brushes off his freshly laundered jumpsuit, making sure the coffee doesn't spill on his Gucci shoes. Then Colson jumps in.

"You never eat breakfast, Deed. How can you work when you don't eat anything?"

"Listen, Colson, you can't work when you spend the morning pumping French fries down your throat at Golden Angina's, so why don't you fasten your lips together, like Noah over there."

Deed nods in the direction of the "rocket scientist," sitting in the back of the main office, working on a calculator.

Colson falls silent while Deed lights a cigarette and turns to Hinton.

"Let's get going. You ready, Hinton? Mr. Kisman says you're working with me today so we're on the road."

They wait for the manager to extract information from the tachometer tape of Car 38. Though Kisman doesn't look up from the barber's chair, he temporarily stops recording into his ledger.

"Sit down, Deed. I will tell you something. You know during the last week you used fifty-two gallons of fuel? You know that?"

"Yeah. I'm aware of it."

Deed looks straight ahead.

"Yeah? Well, you know that you only made twenty-two runs? You know that, my friend?"

"Actually, twenty-three."

Kisman furrows his brow, then fixes his gaze on the young driver through his thick spectacles.

"Where do you get twenty-three? The book shows twenty-two."

"I brought one guy in twice. He ran out of the hospital, AMA."

Kisman glowers.

"If I tell you one more time," he says, enunciating slowly, like a slowly turning drill. "We need accurate records! We don't profit when you burn fifty-two gallons of fuel and make only twenty-two saves..."

"Twenty-three."

"One thousand forty," Noah, the fourth driver interrupts, looking up from his notebook. "At twenty pounds of carbon dioxide per gallon that's about a ton of smog. My car produces zero."

"Oh, Jesus!" Deed responds, his eyes rolling.

Kisman swings the chair around and hops down, walking to the table where the drivers are sitting while adjusting his tie.

"We don't have to worry about Jesus here, gentlemen. What we need is to work and save people. Can you understand that, Deed? Take Hinton, stop wasting gas, and get going. Or maybe you'll end up driving for Therapy?"

The others laugh as Deed nods for Hinton to leave, and heads for the door. Outside several ambulances are parked together, along with the black Mercedes belonging to Kisman, and an orange Porsche.

"There's something we keep between ourselves," Deed advises Hinton, as they enter the parking lot and approach Car 38. Deed's ambulance has a long body capped by a rectangular roof. Halogen lights project from the front and back like an owl's eyes, and a set of baffled mufflers and two extra antennas point upwards from the sides. Beside the ambulance Deed's Porsche is parked, as well polished as its owner.

"I answer to Nixon," Deed continues. "Kisman likes to think he's in charge, but Nixon calls the shots. I do some things that neither of them is aware of, but ultimately, we all serve Nixon. He owns this company. Now, look, today you're going to be sitting in the back by the gurney. You'll get plenty of experience there."

Deed opens the rear doors, and as Hinton climbs inside, he catches a glimpse of another driver positioned behind the steering wheel.

"Muriel, meet Hinton," Deed says. "He's the new driver working with us today. Muriel's my uh…fiancée. We work together," Deed adds, clarifying the arrangement.

"Hello, Mr. Hinton," she responds with a smile.

He takes the seat across from the gurney and returns the smile as her blue eyes measure him. A tight bun of blond hair pulls her face open, like a porcelain doll, making her eyes widen, just when Haldeman's voice breaks the silence, announcing from the radio.

8:14 a.m.—A call to the river

"Car 38! I need a ten-fourteen." Haldeman's voice sounds over the radio again as they leave for their station.

"38 by. We're ten-two from the office," Deed answers, indicating they're returning to their station and available.

"What's your ten-fifteen?"

"Still in the parking lot, here on Virginia Ave.."

Haldeman verifies their location on a computer screen.

"Good. I want you to go Code One to the east side of the river, fifteen miles north of the Beltway. Word's out that Howard Hughes plans to fly his Spruce Goose over the Potomac River today and we want you to cover it. So, go to the Howard Hughes Air Base and stand by. You know how to get there?"

Muriel nods to Deed.

"Right. We're on our way."

Chapter 11:

Resurrecting the Goose

Thursday, 9:15 a.m.—Howard Hughes Airport

Dressed in loose khaki trousers, leather jacket, and a snap-brim Stetson, Howard Hughes groans and grows irritated as an aide cuts his toenails and trims the strings of hair hanging over his shoulders. Five years in a recliner chair and pressure on his back have caused the skin to blister. The lack of circulation, only occasionally relieved during long trips to the toilet, has contributed as well. Hughes doesn't trust the city water and refuses to shower. While the Pyramid has its own supply, he's convinced it too has been tampered with. The aide sweeps away remnants of the once black crown of hair, while Hughes boards an underground train and heads to his private airport and missile launching pad at the southern outskirt of the city. He scribbles notes on a yellow pad.

"Maheu—I'm on my way! I want you to know that now, for the first time in years, I feel better! I honestly do. I am going to show the country what it means to fly! I'm in the air again, Bob! Maybe they've forgotten who set the speed records in this country, who built the world's largest plane? Well, we're going to move ahead with the larger plans. And I'm really going to be in shape this time."

He's hardly finished writing when his aides let him know they're at the end of the tunnel. They emerge at the base of a geodesic hangar that extends out onto the Potomac River. An elevator waits to transport him up to the Spruce Goose, the largest air transporter and military troop carrier in the history of flight. Commissioned by the government to build fifty giant seaplanes during World War II, Hughes stopped working on the project when peace came and government funds went dry. Everyone said the plane was not "air worthy," and he has smoldered with resentment ever since, his irritation aggravated by use of the name Spruce Goose, instead of the *H-4 Hercules* he titled it.

Previous flight crashes and years in the reclining chair have made even walking difficult, so Hughes stopped flying. But now, as the elevator carries him and his assembly of aides into the hangar, he turns his good ear toward two massive doors, where he hears the synchronized roar of eight Pratt & Whitney 2800 engines, their propellers creating a wind tunnel within the enormous hangar. Suddenly the elevator doors seem blown open by the wind force, revealing the football field-wide and long-forgotten Goose. Looking at the plane, he feels lighter—the din of engines is music to his ears. Lines wrinkling his forehead ease, his thin mustache flattens, and edges of his leather jacket fly backward. "Mel," he says, turning to the aide closest to him, "did you pack my lunch?"

"Right here, sir. Chicken sandwiches and Poland water."

He takes the paper bag and walks slowly toward the tip of the left wing, extending fifty yards out from the fuselage. As he walks around the whirling seventeen-foot propellers, he gives no hint to surrounding mechanics that he's satisfied.

Chapter 12:
Ellsberg and Firestone

9:25 a.m.—On the Beltway

"Car 38, I need a ten-twelve." Haldeman's voice comes over the radio, trying to determine the position of the ambulance.

"We're on the Beltway, headed to the Hughes Air Base."

"I don't copy."

"I said we're planning to stand by at the airport—that's what you requested." Deed tells the dispatcher, without concealing his irritation. "What else do you have?"

"This is more important," Haldeman answers. "I have a ten-twenty-eight with a fifty-one fifty that goes Code Two to City Hospital. It's Daniel Ellsberg!"

"Oh wow, okay, we're on our way," Deed acknowledges, excited as he explains to Muriel that a ten-twenty-one is a criminal detention call. He looks outside to note their location.

"So, we're about ten minutes away from the hospital, where we just left," Deed tells Haldeman. "Is that where he is, the municipal jail?"

"Right. Check in with Lieutenant Liddy. He has him in detention and this is going to make the boss very happy."

"Okay, we're on it."

Muriel has flipped on the red lights as they come off the bridge and head across town. Hinton looks up at Deed.

"Fifty-one fifty?" Hinton asks.

"A psycho, Hinton. Someone's insane. We told you about that earlier. This Daniel Ellsberg man is beyond insanity. He had high government clearance and released confidential information about our government and the Vietnam War."

"Daniel Ellsberg?"

"Right," Deed answers, with a sober look at Muriel, who has taken a turn off to head back. "He made a name for himself, giving up defense secrets of our country. A real martyr! Nixon wants him taken care of."

"I don't get it," Hinton counters. "He's giving up national secrets, and he's already in jail?"

"You're new to this, aren't you? You don't realize that Ellsberg needs to be broken first. We need to learn what he knows. It's possible that he's already given out secrets to the Russians."

"About what?"

"That's what we're going to find out. Ellsberg worked for national defense at a high level in nuclear weapons strategy, and he and Kisman planned out how to use and deploy smaller nuclear weapons. When he released the Pentagon Papers, he may have given out up even more, including some high-level negotiations on ballistic missiles! Remember how the Russians tried to send missiles to Cuba, Hinton? There are too many leaks going on right now, like from this guy Deep Throat."

Muriel concentrates on the traffic ahead, looking for spaces to swing up and around the slow-moving columns of cars. Occasionally she uses the siren to clear a space, moving the car through the hotel section of the city. The Hughes Pyramid looms above, casting a shadow over the procession of vehicles.

"Well, what's Deep Throat's significance?" Hinton asks. "I don't understand."

"He's part of that FBI," Deed continues. "Some things are private, and so-called Throat doesn't respect privacy. We're out on the streets saving people, serving the country and the president, and he wants to expose us, along with who knows what other spies."

"So, you know it's a he?"

"Could be. Nixon and Haldeman think it's Mark Felt, second in command to J. Edgar Hoover."

They move onto a clear stretch of road and see the municipal jail ahead. Muriel is overhearing the conversation between Hinton and Deed, as am I through my monitoring device in the ambulance.

"I'm convinced Deed is right, and the president thinks so too," she chimes in. "Ellsberg is connected with terrorists, protestors, and Weatherpeople. They won't be happy till they destroy our country. The terrorists have made hundreds of attempts to blow up federal buildings. They've killed innocent people and they would leak the Code to our civil defense system if they ever got the chance!"

"How could they do that?" Hinton asks.

"Maybe by getting their hands on the football," Deed explains.

"Football? What's that supposed to be?"

"You don't know about the football? Really? Come on, Hinton. It's the national attaché case with a code that controls the release of nuclear weapons. The president is the only one who can open it, and it's never far from him. You know, it's come to this—either we take care of Ellsberg and the terrorists, or they take care of us."

The brick prison and jail, next to the district hospital, stands several stories high and branches out like a hydra, but is barely large enough for the continuous inflow of suspects and prisoners. They turn into a parking area and are allowed past several cyclone gates to the inside compound. After driving under an overhead walkway they reach the detention center. Deed opens the back and grabs leather restraints, while Hinton is told to bring the gurney. Muriel, wearing a blue jumpsuit, walks in between them.

Inside they meet Lieutenant Liddy, who looks at Hinton's long hair with disdain, then fixes on the softer features of Muriel. He nods to Deed and leads them downstairs to a crowded cell that smells like a latrine, thick with heat and humidity.

"I've interrogated him," Liddy says, indicating a dark-haired, nervous-looking man in the back of the cell. "We think he's using drugs, so we're sending him over for tests. And, of course, medical treatment."

His men have slipped LSD into water given to Ellsberg, and Liddy flashes a smile at Muriel as two guards open the cell and retrieve the prisoner. While LSD was in common use by the FBI, it seemed a little indirect to me. My country would have simply relied on execution or life sentence. Execution is simpler.

Deed secures Ellsberg onto the gurney, tightening down the leather restraints, and when the paperwork's complete, they return into the bright sun. As they load him into the ambulance, he seems quiet and controlled for a psychotic. Hinton watches him from the side as Muriel drives away from the compound.

"There you are," Deed says, after starting an IV and watching a trickle of blood run back from the catheter. "This will help wash out the drugs you're taking."

"I'm not taking drugs!" Ellsberg protests. "Exactly where are we going?"

"To the hospital, Mr. Ellsberg. Listen, why don't you just help us a little? Are you sure you haven't taken any drugs?"

"What are you talking about?"

Hinton watches as Deed runs the IV fluids wide open and places his face near Ellsberg's ear.

"Deep Throat! Tell us who he is? And where do you and he get your information? You know, you're headed to jail for the rest of your life. Don't you want to work with us?"

"I don't know who you're talking about. This is a mistake and I'd like to know why we're going to the hospital."

As Muriel calls in their arrival to the Emergency Room, she's already backing into the loading ramp of City Hospital, separated from the prison by no more than a large parking lot. Seven stories of red brick, joined tightly and defining the H-shaped building, rise up to hold and treat the indigent. On the fourth floor, still connected to a ventilator, David Lovejoy slowly opens his eyes and studies the prison-like confines of his ICU cubicle, unaware of any emergency room action.

"You know about Firestone, don't you?" Deed continues questioning Ellsberg. Muriel pulls open the back doors of the ambulance, and as they slide the gurney out its metal legs snap into vertical position. Ellsberg is rolled toward the center of the ER, not yet tumultuous for a Friday morning, as he hallucinates footballs and strange numbers that swirl dreamlike above him.

"Fifty-one fifty from the prison," Deed tells a receiving team of nurses and a doctor. "The vital signs are stable, but he's disoriented and the police say they won't let him back to the jail till he gets his stomach lavaged for drugs. Oh, and also, they want his blood tested for LSD."

"Wait," Ellsberg shouts, starting to feel more lightheaded as he's moved onto a stainless-steel resuscitation bed. "This is crazy. I need an attorney…I demand my constitutional rights!"

Before he can finish, a nurse administers an infusion through his IV and his lightheadedness gives way to full sedation. A thick rubber tube is slid over the tongue and down into the stomach so that gastric contents can be washed out with saline solution. Then the nurse prepares to give ipecac once the sedation wears off.

"We'll be back," Deed tells the medical team.

11 a.m.—Presidential Palace, Cuba

Blowing rings of smoke toward the window, Castro looks out at the streets of Havana and fingers his cigar, considering the past and future.

Two American presidents and an attorney general plot for me. Lately this Robert Maheu man, Howard Hughes' manager—the bourgeois go-between for the CIA and the mob. The idiots think exploding cigars, dusting my shoes with Thallium to make my beard fall off, sprinkling LSD in drinks and on a steering wheel, or grenades and bazookas can do me in? A poison pen, a long-range rifle to pick me off, will end my life? Sons-of-bitches! Here's Nixon, secretly bombing Cambodia, thinking nobody will notice, and guided by the CIA. Cuba may be next, after he finishes with Vietnam. And if they pinpoint where we still have our last missile they'll be after me again!

He sets his cigar down, watching the occasional car roll past the Presidential Palace. Shiny-grilled antique Chevrolets, coughing Soviet Ladas, and rusting Fords move by, He longs for past parades of soldiers, marching and riding on tanks, waving victory to the people on the Havana streets. "Vive la Revolucion!"

Americans are best at undermining their own security, as they proved in the Bay of Pigs. If we're patient, Nixon can be his own worst enemy. I'll bide my time during his so-called democratic elections and Delta Tango can do his work. Whatever this Code is, if there's a time of weakness, well maybe we'll just send them a celebration package. At least let them know we have it aimed at their capital! So, this Tango man needs to find this Code before Nixon ever considers using it, and if he does—it will serve us!

Chapter 13:

Searching for David

11:10 a.m.—A phone call to room 623

Margaret's thoughts leap in myriad directions as she drives across the city, the day crumbling into disorder. After David's disappearance, she calls the police repeatedly.

"Sorry, ma'am, we're working on this. We can't tell you anything new but we'll contact you as soon as we have a lead."

Her night was sleepless, watching the children and the dark outline of the Watergate buildings across the street, with only a few lights on. The night before she and David had been together, looking out at the office building where a single set of lights lit up one room on the sixth floor. They speculated about late-night activities in the capital and what might be happening with the presidential contest, then talked about the DAR banquet on Friday. Was it her background in river restoration, or just her *Mayflower* genetic heritage, that had led to an invitation to the riverside banquet at the Watergate restaurant? Whatever her reasons for being in the capital, it all changed with the morning phone call to the motel room.

"Ma'am, we've located your husband. He's is in the Intensive Care Unit at City Hospital. We need to tell you that he's on life support."

A cold wave surges down her spine, followed by a brief episode of nausea.

"What's happened?" She grips the phone, looking nowhere, waiting for an answer. Several seconds seem like forever. Despite the TV being on, its sound is swallowed into the motel room carpet and she waits.

"Well, right now he's stable. He had a fall and injured his head. And there's a problem with his lungs—the doctors think he had a severe asthma attack."

Margaret closes her eyes, waiting for the shock to diminish, hoping the bad news will disappear, or just be a bad dream. An improvised horror movie, or the simple nightmare of her imagination, might explain this call? Then the policewoman on the line reminds her to bring identification to the hospital. Her eyes open to the surrounding hotel room as she perspires and sees the children lying on the floor and couch. Michael watches TV, while Angel eats French fries from HoJo's restaurant. Rebecca watches her anxiously.

"Mom, what's wrong?" Rebecca asks, setting down an American history book she's trying to read.

"Something has happened to your father. He's…in the hospital." Margaret tries to control her voice, but they all look at her and register her fear.

"No way, Mom," Rebecca responds. "Are you sure? Why would he go to the hospital?" She gets off the couch and turns off the TV.

"Rebecca, I don't know. I don't know what has happened and I have to go right away. So, I need you to watch your brother and sister and stay here and wait for me. Will you please do that? Please don't ask any more questions till I get home, okay? Can you do that for me?"

"I'm going with you, Mom," Angel insists. "I get to go with you. Rebecca can stay here with Michael!"

"Angel, you need to get dressed and you stay here with your sister. I'll be back as soon as I can. No arguments!"

Margaret gives each of them a hug, gathers her purse, and heads into the hallway. The children stare in wonder as the door closes with an abrupt click.

Within minutes of leaving, Margaret drives under the shadow of the Hughes Pyramid, onto a stretch of avenue leading east. An ambulance with flashing lights distracts her and blaring siren, and her right eye twitches briefly as the Doppler sound of the siren fades. For a moment she has difficulty maintaining control of the station wagon and the car swerves toward the oncoming lane as she pulls on the steering wheel in time to avoid a head-on collision. Determination to reach the hospital brings back her focus, and she makes a mental note to take her seizure meds when she returns to the motel.

As she approaches the weathered brick walls and rectangular shapes of the D.C. prison and City Hospital, it's difficult to distinguish which of the two buildings is the medical center. Pulling into the shared parking area, she notes a cyclone fence around the prison, rimmed with a spiral addition of razor wire. Spotting the signs for the emergency entrance of the hospital, she parks hurriedly, leaving the car unlocked, and walks to the entrance. Apprehension builds as she approaches the triage desk, where a reception worker watches her with a look of authority. Her stomach tightens seeing all the people filling the waiting room; men dressed in T-shirts, women wearing cotton dresses, and children hanging onto the wooden benches. There are two white people in the crowded room, and they stare back at her.

"Can I help you, ma'am? You look very nervous!" the receptionist asks.

Chapter 14:
Hughes Flies Again

11:50 a.m.—Hughes Air Base

Euphoric, forgetting his bedsores in the cockpit of the Spruce Goose, Howard makes adjustments and recalibrates the instrument panel. The two-hundred-foot-tall doors slide in momentous precision around the curved sides of the hangar, facing the east bank of the river, after what seems like an hour. Assembled engineers and mechanics watch the massive doors open fully, and now the plane motors majestically onto the river while wind from the propellers creates crisscrossing waves as it taxis forward.

"It's outside the hangar," Deed tells Haldeman on the radio, as Car 38 approaches, answering from their new assignment, after leaving Daniel Ellsberg at the Emergency Room. "There's a lot of cars parked around, but the Goose is not in the air yet. I never thought we'd see Hughes again. That is, if it's him"

Deed flips back and forth on a scanner connecting him to the police and to Haldeman's radio in the main office. They're on the west side of the river.

"I've heard," Hinton says, "a lot of people think Hughes died after he crashed the XF-11. Maybe he wants to prove he's alive and that he can still fly. I never really believed the Pyramid could be run by the Mormons alone."

"Well, if he's alive," Muriel says, holding a pair of binoculars, "I'd love to see him. I mean, the richest man in the world, and no one knows what he's up to. Maybe now we'll find out."

"He wants to keep the government from taking his money, that's all," Hinton continues. "He got caught in a lot of litigation when his plane was never used in World War II, and then he had very questionable business ventures. In fact, outside of a taxi run, the plane's never done anything. You know it's built out of wood!"

"So, what's he going to use it for?"

Muriel looks at Deed, still switching channels on the scanner.

"Who knows?" Deed comments. "Maybe it's not him. Nobody gets as rich as Howard Hughes without a few surprises. Like Muriel says, we're going to find out."

The roar of the Goose punctuates deed's comment. As they drive into the security area of the airport, they're waved past a squadron of police cars and airport guards screening the perimeter. Continuing along the road they arrive at the rescue point, only a few hundred yards from the flying boat that now moves down the center of the river. Stepping out of the ambulance they feel the wind of giant propellers launching the plane forward. Deed tries to take the binoculars from Muriel, who thinks she can see Hughes in the cockpit. Eighty feet tall, a hundred yards wide, the aircraft builds speed as an enormous hull booms over the surface of the river, its slapping sound audible beneath a roaring crescendo of props.

"He's going to fly!" Muriel exclaims. The velocity of the Goose increases—thirty miles an hour, forty, then fifty, and she let's go of the binoculars. "I think it's him! And he's flying!"

"He'd better hurry up and lift!" Deed adds.

Rooster tails spray from pontoons supporting the massive wings as the plane skims over the river, aiming directly into a bridge. There's a sudden decrease in sound when it rises off the water, just clearing the steel arches and rising over the Potomac.

12:00 noon—Guru Maharaji and the ICU

After a long delay in the waiting room, during a change of nursing shift, Margaret takes an elevator leading to the Intensive Care Unit on the second floor. Coming into the hallway she can see in the distance a row of cubicles with beds and ventilators and a few nurses attending closely packed units. She scans for David's bed and her heart sinks as she notes a family gathered together in another waiting area, its members crying and holding each other.

"Could I be helping you?" an accented, high-pitched voice inquires.

She turns to see a short, dark-complexioned youth who smiles at her.

"Excuse me?"

"I said perhaps I might be helping you."

"I'm sorry. But who are you?"

"I am Guru Miraj, but most people call me Guruji," the swarthy youth informs her. He's dressed in light blue scrubs that drape loosely on his short frame.

"And you work here?" She squints, looking for a badge on his scrubs, but can only discern the hospital's initials. He smiles wanly.

"Oh, I'm just a student. And you are here to find your husband. Yes?"

Her pulse quickens.

"Well, yes. But how do you know? Do you know where he is?"

"Of course. I know where everyone is. Your name is Mrs. Lovejoy?"

"Yes. It is. How do you know?"

"It says so on the label on your blouse, but I know all things," he answers, smiling more broadly. "Actually, I know where your husband is also. You will come with me and I will show him to you."

She follows Miraj past the sobbing family, into the dense territory of the ICU. Monitor lights and a cacophony of electronic sounds emerge from the condensed cubicles. Within each tight space is a human network gone awry, and then, as they reach the far corner, she sees him.

"Oh, David!"

He hears the voice and tries momentarily to see her. The tube in his throat restrains him from turning his head.

"We have him on a machine that is helping to breathe," the student tells her. "Actually, he is doing quite well."

David's eyes squeeze together and he swings his head as far as the tube allows. Margaret stands speechless as the machine pumps air and sends out a brief alarm each time his face stretches.

"Well actually, just now he is fighting the machine," Guruji corrects, "but when I tell him to relax and breathe with the ventilator—deep, Mr. Lovejoy, now in, now out—then he does quite well."

The student smiles as the alarm stops. Lovejoy tires, allowing the machine to blow in oxygen without resistance. His face becomes slightly less swollen and Margaret moves closer, looking into his eyes.

"God almighty, David, did you start smoking again? What happened? I'm so sorry…"

Before she can finish his eyes close. Margaret turns to the medical student.

"But why's he still in this hospital? We have insurance. My husband's a health insurance executive. Are you…are they… can we transfer him to a private hospital?"

In her mind, the first step to resolving the crisis is a transfer to the best hospital possible. The ICU is too crowded and the absence of doctors is disturbing.

"I am just a student here. But, of course, I'll tell the attendings when they make their rounds."

"And when do they attend? I can tell them."

"Oh, they will not be here for some time. They rounded this morning."

She looks at the medical student in disbelief, then at David, who can only grimace. His hands are tied, preventing him from pulling out the tube that connects him to the ventilator, and the catheters entering his arms and bladder. He closes his eyes again and she stands slightly away, her body trembling. Then the tears begin. Guruji watches quietly till the nurse, who has been on a break, approaches them.

"Excuse me, are you Mrs. Lovejoy? We've been trying to contact you. Did you know your husband was in the hospital?"

Her tears give place to frustration.

"Oh, please! I just found out. I had no idea and I called the police when he disappeared."

"I'm so sorry. We tried to reach you as soon as we had an identity. Your husband isn't carrying identification and wasn't alert enough till this morning to communicate. The doctors added steroids to his asthma medication so his lungs are working better now."

"Quite a bit better," Guruji agrees.

"Thank you so much, but when do you think he can get out?" Mrs. Lovejoy asks, collecting herself. She pulls a sheet over David's exposed body and holds his restrained hand. The bellows of the ventilator continue up and down smoothly. "Can we go to another hospital now?"

"He can't be moved yet," the nurse answers. "He's just beginning to stabilize and the doctors didn't say anything about transferring this morning."

"But when they see him this afternoon, they'll want to take him off this machine, won't they? He works for health care. He's never needed this kind of treatment and he can go to the best...excuse me...he can go to a private hospital. Can't he?"

The nurse pauses, reacting to Margaret's insinuation of inferior care.

"I'm sorry, Mrs. Lovejoy, there are so many patients here that keep us busy." She nods toward a cubicle where the staff is running a code. "He'll be transferred when he's stable. If you'd like to verify your husband's papers with administration, now would be a good time. And we can only allow fifteen-minute visits in our unit."

David's face blanches pale, then flushes tomato red. He coughs against the ventilator, setting off the alarm again.

"Breathe with it," Guruji encourages. "Now in...now out."

"Oh, please! The man knows how to breathe," Margaret interrupts, feeling the weight of her pregnancy and helplessness. With no one to watch the children, she'll miss the DAR banquet that she's supposed to attend. The student smiles back, increasing her frustration.

"I don't know what to do," she continues, looking at her husband desperately. "I've got to get back to the motel, David. The kids are alone. These people won't let me stay here, and my God, who's going to be watching them! What can I do?"

He looks back in anguish. Each time the ventilator bellows rise, there's a whooshing sound. In the interim, the four of them hear the *POMMT* of defibrillating paddles from the code cubicle nearby.

"Perhaps your husband would like to talk with you," Guruji suggests, looking up and recognizing her anguish.

"He can't. How can you say that?"

"No, no. I mean let him write to you."

Guruji unties Lovejoy's right hand and holds a clipboard in front of him. The nurse remains vigilant, making sure he doesn't pull on the breathing tube as he writes awkwardly, using an ink pen. The writing is distorted but the message clear.

SORRY—DINNER TONIGHT. DON'T MISS. SHOW PAPERS TO DOCTOR. BE OUT SOON. LOVE YOU—DON'T MISS BANQUET!

1:25 p.m.—The flight of the Spruce Goose

Laminated plywood creaks as Hughes eases up on four twin throttles, levels his ascent, and begins a circumnavigation of the District. He readjusts his Stetson hat while steering on a course free from transgressing small craft. Then, turning down the radios, he concentrates on the craft's performance. Each quarter-inch twist of the H-shaped steering control results in a quarter-inch raising or lowering of the ailerons, a hundred feet behind. *Hydraulics are perfect!* He rejoices. A bag full of chicken sandwiches and Poland water go unnoticed as he tries to suppress his delight

. Beneath, the capital shrinks as the great plane climbs in slow, sweeping loops. The downtown section, centered by the Pyramid, overshadows the memorials and the Capitol building. Expansive parks become small green enclaves, enclosed in cement and asphalt interstices. And gradually, the muddy waters of the upper rivers take on a darker hue, forming a Y that divides the capital. A single trunk continues southward, the tidal basin and Washington Channel disappearing within the yoke shape of the joining rivers, and the diminishing metropolis appears as an intricate labyrinth. Hughes contemplates the geography.

It's a masculine affirmation, he decides, confirming his domination of the city. *Men have always explored, wanting to build cities, to form nations, to create civilizations. Now they can see me up here and know that I still fly, and that this plane can fly! But this flight is a prelude. Just a prelude!*

"Bo Bop Areet!"

Diagonal streets and avenues form a patchwork of circuitry that facilitates cross currents of people whose energy he has channeled into the busy success of a small metropolitan empire. Rising above D.C., he begins to remove his clothes. Accustomed to nudity in the Pyramid, Hughes has always enjoyed flying naked, except for his snap-brim Stetson that now covers his recently cut hair. His sensitive skin, at once free of irritation, adds to his sense of liberation, as he sings again the only song he ever sings.

"Bo Bop Areep!"

Almost a soon as the Spruce Goose disappears, it reappears, slowly descending and increasing in size. The flying boat's hull is a gargantuan dirigible as it approaches them, an extraterrestrial vision of wood, metal, and man.

Gazing up at the hundred-yard wingspan, Muriel grabs onto Deed and wonders out loud, "Can he land that thing?"

Newspaper reporters arrive en masse, their cars evading police and filling the side of the runway as they jockey for positions to get photographs.

"I don't know," Deed answers, eyeing the unwieldy seaplane from a distance. "But I know who gets to pick up the mess."

They prepare liters of IV fluids in the back of the ambulance and set the resuscitation equipment on top of the gurney. Hughes makes a final loop over the airport river and Muriel's heart beats faster.

"I don't think he's going to clear the bridge," she shouts. Just as it begins the descent over the top of the George Washington Bridge the wind picks up and forces the enormous craft off course. The left wing rises to compensate, and the right pontoon misses the top of the bridge by several feet. Seconds later the fortress hits the water. Hughes pulls both flaps, and an enormous wave of water rises as the hull collapses onto the river. Taxiing upriver toward the hangar, past an applauding audience, the Goose motors perpendicular to the ambulance drivers and Muriel takes the binoculars to look for a sign of the pilot. When he stands, she's rewarded with a flashing view of his naked frame and thin erection, but never sees his face.

"Oh my!"

Hughes looks past her and the assembled watchers, his mind now preoccupied with the greater adventure that will begin within days. But as his adrenalin surge slackens, he feels the old aches and pain of his body.

Chapter 15:

A Special Banquet

Thursday Afternoon: HoJo's

Rebecca watches her mother spend the afternoon struggling to control her emotions. Her own activities involve travel from the motor lodge pool to the restaurant, to the motel room, then back to the pool again. The cycles quicken with the length of the day, and her mother makes time to visit her husband again. Fatigue insinuates into Margaret's low back, and at thirty-eight weeks she questions why she ever decided to travel while pregnant.

Rebecca senses her mother's anxiety. She tries to anticipate the expected needs of her brother and sister as well as Margaret's increasing stress, and makes a final attempt on her seventh-grade study lessons of American History.

The Mayflower Compact and all those Separatists, or Pilgrims, or whatever, wanting to join together to survive through the winter before starting their colony. I guess they're kind of interesting. But I like Mary Chilton. She's twelve, like me, and she's the first female to set foot on land. Most of the older women on the ship die, but Mary somehow survives and gets married and has ten children!

After checking the list of signers to the covenant, Rebecca sees no women are allowed to sign. She looks at the illustrated history book, now with water stains and ketchup on the cover, and lets it slip behind the couch.

Mom never loses it. Why's she so quiet and sad? Dad must be really sick, and she's feeling the baby a lot? I wonder what it's like to have your stomach kicked. I don't ever want to be pregnant. Probably Angel and Michael will make me too busy anyway, but I wish that guy at the swimming pool would quit staring at me, and those two old men in the restaurant are so weird! This whole hotel is weird. Kind of fun in a way, though, if it weren't for Mom and Dad.

Rebecca's mother drives back to City Hospital and finds the nurse in the ICU unsympathetic, insisting her visits be short. David receives a heavy shot of sedation that makes him sleep through the second visit, and she's unable to make contact with any of his doctors. When she returns to the hospital parking lot the side window of the station wagon has been smashed.

Another bad omen, she thinks. *But I will honor David's wishes and still go to the dinner. I have a responsibility toward the environment as well as the Daughters of the American Revolution. Maybe if I shower I'll feel some energy and restore a bit of order to this catastrophic trip. God, what a time to be pregnant!*

On returning to Howard Johnson's, Margaret checks on the children and gets ready for the evening banquet. She steps into the shower, removes her alert bracelet, and sets it on the bathroom sink. After showering she sits in front of the bathroom mirror, dabs skin softener on her face, takes a cover stick to apply beige cream under her eyes, and tries to force away the recollection of a nurse suctioning secretions from her husband's breathing tube. *She* takes a brush and swishes it back and forth in the rouge compact. After removing curlers from her hair, she realizes again that she's late.

The kids aren't back from the pool!

Moving away from the nightstand, Margaret pulls on a silk maternity dress and her pregnancy image glares back from the mirror. She makes her way to the elevator, and as she comes onto the rooftop pool Rebecca greets her from the water.

"Mom, you look beautiful!"

"Where's Dad?" Angel adds.

The early evening lights from the Watergate buildings fill the horizon, reflecting off the winding river as humid air still holds the heat of the day. A few other families sit in poolside chairs watching the Lovejoy family, wondering why the children have been without adult chaperones so long.

"Still in the hospital, Angel. He's okay. Now out of the pool, please. You know it's supposed to close soon. Rebecca, I really need you to help. It's seven-thirty and I'm very late."

Rebecca climbs out and looks for a towel, and quickly dries.

"Mom, we're starving. Can we order hamburgers and watch TV? There's a movie."

"There's always a movie, honey. It's pay TV."

"I know. I know. We need money for food, too."

It occurs to Margaret that she's left her purse behind in the room. *I'm already late!*

"Rebecca, the purse is by the phone…in the bedroom. I have to go right now. Please order the food and show me how responsible you kids can be, okay? I'm right across the street. And, Rebecca, this is a good time for you to be a perfect babysitter, so what do you think? You don't have to study tonight, but I want you to finish your report on the *Mayflower* and the colonists. If you have any trouble you can go down to the check-in desk, but you should be able to look out for your brother and your sister."

“Mom, Angel always gives me trouble, and Michael doesn’t want to listen.”

“Sweetheart, just remember the Great Commandment and it will all be fine. It’s as true in our family as it is in the world at large. You know what it is: ‘Love thy neighbor…”

“…as thyself.’ Yes, ma’am,” Rebecca answers, as Michael and Angel join her, water dripping from their limbs and bathing suits. It’s one thing to love your brother and sister, but as much as yourself?

Margaret gives them each a kiss, trying to keep her dress from getting wet, then heads for the elevator.

“Remember,” she says, as the doors are closing, “no phone calls, except to room service. It’s your chance to show how grown up you are. “So love your neighbors, but don’t leave this motel…. I love you very much!”

As the doors shut Rebecca waves.

When the elevator descends two levels Margaret is joined by two men in suits. The man with a prominent forehead glances at her through framed glasses before looking away. The other carries a fudge sundae. McCord and Baldwin, both Watergate Plumbers, seem sinister, and neither acknowledges her. She dabs moisture from her eyes, glad to get off on the ground floor, when she remembers she has forgotten to put her alert bracelet back on.

8:00 p.m.: The Watergate Hotel

Across the street the Watergate complex rises in curved layers—with crenelated, exclusive apartments for the well-to-do and politically engaged stakeholders of the District. Traversing the street, away from the plain shell of Howard

Johnson's, Margaret senses a change in status as she approaches the tall hotel. Membership in the DAR, her knowledge of rivers, and not her husband's income permits access to one of the more expensive restaurants in town. She almost forgets the earlier events of the day as she's greeted by a doorman and escorted toward the elevator. She notes the polished mahogany and brass rails, a small chandelier, and a mirror that allows her to inspect her makeup.

Definitely not the motor lodge, she thinks. *And my medication. I forgot to take it! I should put my alert bracelet back on when I return to the motel.*

The elevator doors open, and she's greeted by a hostess for the gala dinner.

"Oh, you must be one of our missing Daughters," the hostess tells her, taking her by the hand and leading her to the restaurant. "I've got to find you a table before Mrs. Nixon begins her address. We won't have time to register or get you a nametag. You're just a little pregnant, aren't you?"

Led through a dimly lit dining area to one of the banquet tables in the back, Margaret finds herself sitting next to several women she's only seen in the society page. She wants to fit in, but her pregnant stomach barely squeezes beneath the table. Several eyes turn toward her as a waiter begins to fill one of three crystal wine glasses, which she declines.

"Madam, I hope you enjoy your meal," the waiter encourages, and steps away. She smiles at him, and wonders if blacks will ever join the DAR. Just then, in full ceremony, the president's wife is introduced at a podium in the front of the room.

"Good evening, and thank you all," Mrs. Nixon begins somberly, "for inviting me to this inspiring opportunity to dine beside the river. A river that gives our city charm and beauty."

She pauses as the audience looks out the window. The silent Potomac reflects a soft sheen of light from the moon. Terrines of *fois gras*, truffles, and mushrooms are served, and Margaret feels a slight dizziness.

"I will share with you tonight," Mrs. Nixon continues, "the special importance of a natural body of water that has helped shape the life and character of this city. We're blessed in so many ways, as the first settlers of this land may not have been. While they struggled with the heat, the mosquitoes, the diseases, and no doubt accommodating the Anacostans, perhaps helped by other indigenous people, in order to build a settlement that would become a crown jewel of all cities, it took the freedom of travel and the ever-beautiful inspiration of the river we see tonight to help them succeed."

The president's wife pauses as glasses of Château Lafitte Rothschild are poured individually. Margaret glances at the woman seated next to her whose nametag reads "Margaret," and recognizes her as the wife of the foremost member of the Justice Department. The woman finishes her first glass of wine, waiting impatiently for Mrs. Nixon to finish. Petite, and well dressed, she has been recognized for her ability to speak openly on municipal affairs, and reporters try to stay close when she appears at social events. Margaret wonders if her momentary dizziness is affected by the cameras flashing in the background.

It feels like I've been at this dinner before.

"The land was not easy to tame," Mrs. Nixon continues. "There were swamps to be filled, canals to be dug, roads to be laid, and buildings to be raised. The District, as we now know it, is really a social monument, 'the city of magnificent distances.' These unique diagonal avenues, the triangular spaces that distinguish the arboreal parks and walkways, provide us with a balance between human control and natural freedom. And preserving that natural freedom is what we might consider tonight as we contemplate this resplendent river. There is so much that has been done. There is much more ahead..."

A second Chateau Lafitte is served and the mood of the audience lifts as occasional glances out the windows reveal the Potomac with a gibbous moon overhead. Margaret feels dizzier.

"...and what could be more romantic than the confluence of two rivers as they flow through the capital's center to become one. The ever splendid, peaceful Potomac, named for an Indian village and known to us as the 'nation's river,' has always been the home for swans, magnificent birds that to this day grace the waters. Joining the Potomac, we have the added waters of the Anacostia, fed by the many tributaries, even like our historical legacy. It is sometimes referred to as the 'forgotten river' and we know that the issues of pollution need to be addressed. I share with you, Daughters of this remarkable history, that we have a mission with a high purpose, a duty to keep the waters pure, to preserve the beauty that this river has supplied since well before our ancestors' time. Perhaps it's not a coincidence, more like a sign of nature, that this river takes the form of a Y, even like the form of a chromosome! Or at least that of men."

The audience lets out a burst of laughter, all of them smiling in unison. More wine is served with the second course, including salad and generous portions of lobster. Margaret leaves her plate untouched as the president's wife concludes her presentation.

"So, I turn to each of you, knowing the hearts and minds of our citizens, and, yes, that of your husbands as well, to find a way to keep this river clean and alive. Let this river be an inspiration to the city through which it runs. And I thank you so much for the invitation and opportunity to be with you tonight."

As Mrs. Nixon takes a seat the host of the gathering introduces the next speaker, sitting next to Margaret.

"We are honored to have many women, known for their research on river restoration, to be with us tonight. And now I would like to ask one of our beloved citizens, also known to us all, to share some more thoughts with us as we dine. She can share with us some of the legal issues of river restoration, for which we are so fortunate to have her here."

Margaret's seatmate takes another sip of her wine and walks, slowly, to the podium. Mrs. Nixon eyes her carefully, as do the reporters in the back. Margaret finds herself distracted by the distant sound of ambulances, still experiencing déjà vu.

"What a special honor indeed," Mrs. Mitchell speaks into the microphone, putting emphasis on the first syllable of *honnahh*, "to share the podium with Mrs. Nixon. And let me begin by telling you that we indeed are part of a special society. We are all daughters in a family, a family of women looking out for the city we know as the capital. The city to which we give our hearts..."

"Oh...!" Margaret lets on a plaintive call, as soft halos encircle her vision. The room swirls while photographers snap pictures of the Margaret at the podium, each flash seeming to emit the sound of a siren.

"And let me say this," the speaker continues, spurred on by the cameras and oblivious to the rapid eye twitching of her former table partner. "I hope you're all listening. Because the last time I looked out at the Potomac, it looked just a little muddy to me."

The audience begins to laugh again. The sound of sirens outside the building goes unnoticed in anticipation of her next words.

"Now you won't see too many men out there, swimming in the Potomac River, though the mud does make it easier for those who claim they can walk on it." More laughter. "Come to think of it, there's a presidential race going on, and we may see men running out there."

The audience laughs louder as Mrs. Nixon grimaces.

"And I am going to share a special revelation with you," the speaker continues. Simultaneously Margaret Lovejoy rolls off her chair, the left side of her body jerking in rhythmic spasms.

Thursday, 9:02 p.m.—An ambulance rescue

"Car 38," I call out, as the nighttime dispatcher. My shift starts in the evening, and after leaving my room at HoJo's I drive the taxi to the headquarters to take over for Haldeman.

"Ten-four," Deed answers up.

"Need a ten-fifteen."

"We're on Virginia Avenue, headed home."

"Good. I just got a call for a seizure and loss of consciousness at the Watergate Hotel. Watergate Hotel restaurant. Copy?"

"Ten-four."

Muriel swings around and in minutes they're parked in front of the hotel complex. She leaves the engine running as Hinton pulls out the gurney and Deed leads them with a resuscitation kit.

"What do you think it is?" Hinton asks Muriel, riding up the elevator.

"Stroke, aspiration? I'm guessing aspiration. Fancy dinner and all that, know what I mean?"

The elevator doors open onto chaos. Women and reporters surround Margaret and lights flash independently as the cameras capture a Daughter trying to perform a Heimlich maneuver. Margaret stares blankly at the ceiling.

"Excuse us. Make way, please!"

Clearing through the crowd, they position themselves next to the pregnant woman where a small pool of saliva, tinted with rouge, lies on the floor beside her face. Deed checks the airway and notes her bulging abdomen, then palpates her neck.

"Weak pulse! Let's get her on the gurney!"

Her spasms subside as they leave on an urgent transfer, and in the rush they neglect to obtain her identity.

"We can call for a name once we get to the hospital," Deed tells Muriel.

Chapter 16:

Lincoln's Secret

9:14 p.m. – Transfer to Hughes Hospital

"Run it as a Code Two!" Deed tells Muriel, while starting an IV on Jane Doe, since they leave without Margaret's name. "Looks like she had a seizure, but now she's settled down. Her pulse and rhythm are okay."

They head out with lights blinking above the ambulance. Muriel starts in the direction of City Hospital but Deed reminds her of the expensive attire and point of pickup, and they turn instead toward the Hughes Hospital. Heading up Virginia Avenue, passing by Howard Johnson's, Margaret stares blankly at Deed while Hinton sits in the passenger seat, adjacent to Muriel.

An interesting day, Hinton ruminates. *Heading for the Hughes Hospital, and it feels like I've seen a lot. But, I wish I were driving. I need to figure out how to handle these transfers, and this lady—all dressed up for a convention—and with the president's wife! What caused her seizure? I wonder. She seems like she's asleep, but her eyes are open and maybe we should be giving her meds?*

Simultaneously, the lights of the Hughes Hospital illuminate a dark, humid sky over the city as Muriel backs Car 38 into an expansive glass and cement receiving station that projects out from the building's emergency room. Margaret is wheeled into the admission station, and the nurses assess her postictal state and record vital signs. Rendered mute by her experience, she's incapable of signing registration forms so Dr. Cohen, the admitting physician, makes his own assessment. Deed gives a history of their encounter at the hotel—the attempted Heimlich maneuver by a stander-by, clonic-jerking motions described by others, and the presence of many celebrities at the Watergate Restaurant.

"We'll admit her for seizure disorder," the doctor decides, somewhat hesitantly. "We can get her name and verify her insurance when the family calls."

Thursday: 9:30 p.m.—HoJo's

The Lovejoy children have settled into room 623 of HoJo's, watching *The Attack of the Puppet People* and eating ice cream. Rebecca takes twenty dollars from her mother's purse to buy dinner, and Styrofoam plates now decorate the room like a small picnic ground.

"You guys, we have to turn off the TV at 10. Mom's coming home late so we're brushing teeth and going to bed. Okay? Otherwise, I'm gonna turn the TV off now."

"No, you aren't," Angel counters. "We have to watch the end. Why not?"

In the motel room above them, James McCord and his partner, Baldwin, are listening through a Communications, Inc. receiver to late-night arrangements being made between a call girl and a Therapy administrator via the bug McCord planted on the sixth floor of the Watergate office building. I'm able to follow all this from the Dispatcher's office, since earlier I put bugs in both room 723 and room 623, not sure at the time where the Watergate spies would be working out of. Prior to this I did not know that McCord had been working with the CIA to track the Colombia Plaza prostitute ring, and now was connected with Nixon's Plumbers. McCord is following it all through the Watergate Office leased by Democratic Re-election Committee to do their election campaigning for the presidency.

Being a mole is never easy. Everyone watches everyone. Nixon's team of Plumbers are spying on the democrats, Castro, Daniel Ellsberg, and more. Inside the Nixon team James McCord is spying on the Columbia Plaza. His techniques are primitive – in the future tracing conversations by shooting beams across windows, recording the slightest vibrations of sound waves inside a room, will be collected by recorders at an angled distance hundreds of yards away. Satellite images thousands of times as detailed as those first designed, will be sensitive enough to identify the toupee on a Russian agent 300 miles away. Jim Deed, who has a secret mission of his own, is using old methods and outdated spies. And I'm spying on all of them, with even older techniques and equipment. It's human nature to spy on each other – more than anything else, that's what humans do.

I never wanted to be a spy. Growing up in Guarajay, four or five hours from Havana by bicycle, I knew the countryside well. As a youngster I excelled in math languages, and was sure I was headed for college, maybe even medical school. I could speak English and solve mathematic puzzles and make up my own. But when my parents split up and I rebelled in classes, I found myself working in the sugar cane fields, wielding a machete, sweating along with the proletariat and destined for exhaustion and obscurity. The army changed all that, along with the Ministry of the Interior when they learned I was a gifted sharp shooter who could speak English. Two things followed: I was placed in the Security team for the Líder Maxímo, where I discovered, by accident, the hidden ICBM launching site that still contained a missile, just outside of Guarajay. My training in the military used my aptitude for mathematic codes, taught me how to investigate, and whether I wanted to be or not, I was a special agent in Miami.

When I got assigned to Washington D.C. I started off as a cab driver. Maybe it was luck that I then got a job as night dispatcher for Medical Ambulance. Or maybe not.

Chapter 17:

Lincoln's Secret

Friday morning, 1:00 a.m.—The Lincoln Memorial

"You know I'm still curious what caused that lady's seizure," Muriel says to Deed, after finishing their last call of the day. Driving back to their living quarters, she continues to think about the well-dressed Jane Doe transported from the Watergate Banquet.

"What makes you so interested? Maybe she didn't like Mrs. Nixon's speech, or Margaret Mitchell's, or probably she stopped taking her seizure medication?"

"What did Mrs. Mitchell say?"

"How should I know? We didn't stay to find out. Maybe she had some crazy revelation to share like she always does?"

"Well, that lady could have been an overdose. Rich people do as many drugs as the Weatherpeople."

"Maybe so, but Weatherpeople do drugs and bomb buildings. We're in a war in Vietnam, and they're putting our soldiers in jeopardy. Muriel, we have to stop all these leaks!"

Hinton tries to keep from falling asleep, but listens from the back of the ambulance.

"What leaks?" Muriel asks. "Exactly what is being leaked, anyway? What is it the democrats are supposed to know that we don't? They got us into the war in the first place, and like, you know we know a lot about them. Their sexual escapades and all that. Remember Kennedy had all kinds of secret liaisons and was pushing for overthrow of

Cuba and Castro's assassination. He used the CIA to go after Castro and who knows what else. Remember that?"

Muriel is cautious not to mention her own involvement with the Columbia Plaza. Her best friend, Heidi Rielken, is overseeing a call-girl ring.

"Well, I'm not exactly sure what Nixon is after," Deed answers, belatedly. "But we happen to know the Weatherpeople are tied to foreign countries and they're terrorists! Think about Ellsberg's Pentagon Papers and what he gave away. And what he might give away—like the security code for the Football. Ellsberg was a planner of nuclear attack strategies, and for all we know, he's infiltrated our security forces and deciphered some of the Code. So, we've told Liddy to find out exactly how much they know. I have a plan of my own, which will take care of the Weatherpeople."

Hinton feigns sleep, listening closely, while Car 38 travels along the city perimeter. Its headlights penetrate through darkness, between taller buildings on each side of the avenues it enters. They pass along a park that leads to the tidal basin of the Potomac and approach the Lincoln Memorial, displayed by a series of angular lights. Silence seems to envelop the unattended monument.

"Really? What's your plan, Jim?"

"Let's just call it…Underground Elimination…. I don't think I can explain it to you right now, Muriel, but...I'm going to drive the Weatherpeople out of this swampy town for good. Pull over here."

They drive behind the Memorial. From the back of the ambulance Hinton looks out at the Greco-Roman colonnade. Thirty-six forty-four-foot-tall Doric columns support a marble attic above and protect the brooding Lincoln statue within. Underneath the columns is a 43,800-square-foot Ubercroft, the supporting structure that contains subterranean pillars holding up the entire edifice. The Ubercroft, unfamiliar to the populace at large, has a metal gate controlling the waters from the Reflecting Pool and the vast Tidal Basin of the Potomac Park. When those waters are not released, they stagnate within the extensive tunnel system below Washington, D.C., where many of the Weatherpeople remain hidden.

"Wait here, Muriel. If Hinton wakes up just tell him to stay put. I'll be right out."

Deed leaves the car and walks quickly toward an opening in the back of the monument. In the darkness he's a small, singular form, almost invisible as he leaves the ambulance and begins a covert mission. He's allowed through a door and joined by two men who take him down into the large, hidden cavern. They question him as they head for the floodgate.

"Why so late? We were told midnight."

"We had a busy day. We've been transporting patients into the night. You know, we almost had to transport Howard Hughes!"

"Really? Howard Hughes is still alive?"

"He just flew the Spruce Goose over the Potomac River," Deed tells them. "Now take me to the floodgate."

"This way."

Deed is taken to a corridor below the cavern that leads to an underground control room with a special set of windows along one wall. Thick glass allows visibility of wide underground tunnels that make up a central part of Washington's drainage system, connecting the Tidal Basin and Reflecting Pool to the waters of the Potomac and Anacostia rivers.

"You sure this has been approved?" the head guard asks. "We haven't heard anything from the top."

"Don't expect to," Deed tells them. "I am the top right now. The only way this gate gets opened or closed is through our special Code, and you know I have to have approval in order to have the Code. The president expects this to happen tonight."

"And you know what happens, Mr. Deed? If the water stops, the waste will collect under the city. It's going to cause some major pollution."

"Right. And it's going to stink out all the Weatherpeople living under the street, isn't it? Their underground activities need to come to an end."

They watch uneasily as Deed pulls open a cabinet door covering a digitalized switch. He looks back at them, then at the window where overflow water from the Tidal Basin and city drainage pipes rushes through the floodgate and into the Potomac. He presses a sequence, 16-15-23-5-18, and slowly the floodgate begins to close.

"Well, I guess that's it," one of the guards comments.

The four men stand before the window and watch the gates shut tightly, till the cascading waters diminish to a trickle.

"Right," Deed says. "And we won't have to worry about any problems from the Weatherpeople, either. Not till we open the gate again."

He returns through the corridor and dark underground cavern, where water drips silently from stalactite formations. Above them the nine-hundred-ton statue of Lincoln is as motionless as his stoic countenance. Deed leaves the deep complex and emerges from the building, and his eyes look out at the Reflecting Pool that points to the sleeping city. Underneath the District, permeating the long-tunneled drainage system where the Weatherpeople and homeless shelter, a concentration of stagnant sewage and water begins to slowly build up.

Day 4

Otieno

"In the Nixon administration, information was power, and power was the drug of choice that everyone was high on. I didn't know that I was working for information junkies and that I would become one of their dealers."

Howard Hunt, *American Spy*, 2007

"Finally, I wanted to tell a more personal story that might inspire young people considering a life of public service how my career in politics really started with a way to explain the different strands of my mixed-up heritage, and how it was only by hitching my wagon on to something larger than myself that I was ultimately able to locate a community and purpose for my life."

Barack Obama, *A Promised Land*, 2020

"Of course, Hughes was behind Watergate. In the United States you tear away the Seventh Veil of Presidents, and there is Big Business."

William Corson, *The Armies of Ignorance: The Rise of the American Intelligence Empire*, 1986

Chapter 18:
Diagnosing Margaret

Friday, June 16, 1972, 8:10 a.m.—The Medical Office

"Drivers and Jivers, jus' lend me your ear,
"Add a little gold, ain' nothin to fear.
"You're lost in the city, danger is near,
"Stay cool with the rule, while I rescue your rear!"

Otieno's long fingers drum out a rhythm on the table, as he looks across the room. On the walls of the main office are photos and news clippings of head-on auto collisions, plane crashes, cities in flame, and ambulance drivers rescuing victims. One shows Nixon and his colleagues of the day, dressed in white shirts and ties, standing by a 1950 Cadillac, when life was simpler but no less difficult.

Helen, the laundry woman, stands in her back-room doorway, folding sheets that have been cleaned of blood and human residue from the previous day's work, listening to the men's office talk.

"And today's rule is tomorrow's fool. That's why you need to stay in school!" Otieno adds, winking at Helen and smiling at the other drivers.

"Don't start the rhyme routine till we've had coffee," Deed groans, adding another teaspoon of sugar to his cup. He adjusts his tortoise-shell glasses and takes a slow sip, after only a few hours of sleep.

Occupying the barber's chair, Kisman inscribes figures into an account book. Hinton's gaze is drawn toward Helen, who continues folding sheets and listening to the men.

I wonder when I'll get the result from the blood test, he wonders. *It can take a month or more before hepatitis manifests, and this is no time to be sick! I was crazy to do mouth to mouth on that little baby during the E.R. transfer.*

Otieno stands before the group and puts his finger into a steaming cup of tea, then swirls it and responds to Deed.

"Imbibe your Aryan drug. I subscribe to a different mug. You see, fellow drivers, I have no need for sugar. When I stir my subject, it turns into the finest honey!"

Helen smiles from behind the doorway while Colson, sitting sideways and half asleep on a chair, looks up with a grimace. All the drivers are fatigued, including Deed and Hinton, from working late into the previous night. Colson has been working on the president's re-election campaign and will get the day off. The smell of coffee and cigarette smoke keeps them half-awake as Kisman watches from his roust on the barber's chair.

"Yeah," Otieno continues, "I'm the syrup between the pancakes, the jelly on the toast!"

"Otieno," Kisman intervenes, with gravel-voice authority, "you are working with Hinton today. I want you to polish chrome and grease the gurney. You think you two can do that, Otieno?"

"When I start to grease, it will never cease," he acknowledges. Leaning back on a chair he pours his tea from one cup to another till the steam clears, then drinks it with a continuous motion, crushing the Styrofoam cups into small white balls and tossing them into the trash.

"Got to ree-cycle, Mr. Hinton. My name's Otieno. That, in Swahili, means I was born during the night. But I can assure you, it was not last night."

Otieno smiles again, and Kisman glowers, making a decisive spin on the barber's chair before climbing down. He motions for Hinton to follow him and heads for the outside parking area. Once inside Car 45, he begins a perfunctory recording of data from the tachometer. Otieno joins Hinton and gives him a few tips on efficient driving while standing outside.

"You should get yourself a pair of gloves," he says, slipping one over his long-fingered hands. "A maroon jacket, and don't worry if your pants hang a little low. Be a brother for Medical. It's good for business and keeps fifty-one fifties from slipping the grip. Can you dig it?"

Leaning his lanky figure against the car, Otieno taps his fingers on the roof. Hinton looks inside, surprised to see a collection of speakers, video screens, and amplifiers lining the walls. Interwoven into the circuitry are standard paramedic instruments.

"You see, brother," he continues, "we're the ones who have to win the public. And the heart of the public is business. So, if our business is to save the public, and the heart of the public is business, then our business is to save the heart, which is the public…which is the business. And that's where first aid comes in—dig it? First to come, first to serve. Business is the heart is the public is the business. Now, you and I are going to do the drumming, nasty thumbing, and public plumbing. When the heart is thumping, the auricle's pumping, ventricles are bumping, and profits are jumping! Right, Mr. Kisman?" Otieno's white teeth shine in a smile.

Kisman steps into the sunlight, frowning and adjusting his glasses. His voice drones as if he were speaking underwater.

"You're out of line, Otieno. And you're breaking the speed limit again, even worse than Deed. I am warning you both that you can't continue speeding or I will be speaking to the boss about this."

Otieno looks into the distance. With the upcoming president's race, the Company can't afford to fire anyone, let alone the equal opportunity employee of the year. Both Kisman and Nixon know there's no one else who can venture easily into "Chocolate City," or the poorer parts of Washington, D.C. Nor can Nixon win the presidential election if the ghettos are left unattended. And Otieno has thoughts of his own as to who the next president should be.

"I'll try to keep you with us, Otieno. Polishing the chrome will help, but you must show Hinton everything you know in the ghetto. Can you do that without getting into trouble?"

"Sho nuff, Boss," Otieno says, as he looks at Kisman's black Mercedes, parked next to Car 45.

"Chrome, Otieno!" Kisman insists, turning toward the main office and holding the tachometer sheet filled with erratic markings from Car 45's recent journeys.

"Rome, Kisman!" Otieno returns, still smiling.

Friday, 8:45 a.m.—Hughes Hospital

In room 402 the Jane Doe transport patient delivered by Medical Ambulance receives careful scrutiny as two physicians debate the performance of her heart. Her bed is between polished mahogany tables on each side. A phone is next to her, and a crystal water pitcher sits untouched. A small container of ice is next to the water, and the ice melts slowly as Louis Cohen, dressed in a white shirt and a white coat, comments on her heart rhythm.

"It sounds" *lubb dupp*..."like the beat" *lubb dupp*..."of a hidden" *lubb dupp*..."retreat," *lubb dupp*. "Yet every" *lubb dupp*..."one I've heard" *dupp dupp*..."is just a requiem" *lubb dupp*..."for time."

Lubb dupp...lubb dupp...dupp dupp...

"On the contrary, Louis, I find each beat a testament to the infinite, unvanquished strength of life. Imagine a ton of life-giving fluid lifted forty feet every day and we know the magnitude and sheer hydraulic capacity of the body's finest vessel."

Dr. Cohen, short, stout, with curly hair, looks at his colleague, Matthew James, who is auscultating beneath a gown that covers Margaret Lovejoy's chest. A new battery-powered stethoscope amplifies sounds of blood passing through the atrial and ventricular valves—sounds that resonate through the room. Margaret remains silent, but her eyes follow the two physicians commenting on her status.

"All this is certainly the most beautiful song of a pump. But beware, my friend" *lubb dupp*... "of the brruup" *...lubb dupp*... "that betrays in a pump" *...BRRUUUUP*!

"What's that?"

Cohen pauses for a moment, his eyes squeezing together as he turns up the amplifier to intensify the sound.

BRUUPPP!

"There."

"Where?"

They lean together over Margaret as Cohen focuses on the area in question. Inside a luxury suite in the Hughes Hospital, overlooking a luxurious expanse of golf greens, the windows are insulated with thick double panes, secure against even the most errant white balls.

BRRUUPP!

"It's irregular," Cohen says, pointing out the obvious and moving the stethoscope slightly up.

"Yes."

"Of course, but she's pregnant."

"That's not irregular," Dr. James counters.

"No, Cohen, the murmur...and the skipped beats…there may be a higher incidence in women with seizure disorders."

"So…what are you saying, something about the rate and the seizure, I suppose? That seems a little speculative. I mean cardiac output is influenced by a high estrogen level, making blood volume increase by as much as fifty percent, but what's that got to do with seizure?"

"I don't know. Is there a connection? A temporary shortage of blood to the brain?"

BRRUUPP!

"But why?" James continues. "Why should that be enough to cause a seizure?"

They step back from the bed. Though the seizure activity has resolved, her focal amnesia remains. Recollection of immediate events is intact, but she can remember nothing concerning time, place, or person before arriving at the hospital. Exhausted, she lets the doctors examine her body as if they're part of a dream.

"Well, the brain CT was okay," Cohen adds to the assessment. "Maybe a little artifact from her earrings, but no lesions seen. Her EEG's okay, and physical neurologic exam is unremarkable. So, we're left with general amnesia. There were low levels of Dilantin in her blood, and we know she's been having seizures before, so maybe all of them have been triggered by an arrhythmia. Or maybe it's just her Dilantin level."

"Maybe, or maybe not. We agree she had a low level of Dilantin. And probably she forgot to take her meds. I wonder why."

"Right, when you hear horse beats, think horses, not zebras. So, let's continue the work-up, do a Holter to follow her rhythm for a few days. That is, if she turns out to have insurance."

"Who gives a damn about the insurance. I'd like to know what started this," James insists.

"Well, so would I," Cohen agrees. "So, she can stay a few more days. And one would hope her family will show up pretty soon."

8:45 a.m.—HoJo's, Room 623

Rebecca awakens to the hands of her sister, Angel, pushing her on her side after a night of tossing on the cot bed. She sits up in the front living space of their motel room.

"Wake up, Rebecca, Mom never came home. I checked and she's not in her room and Dad's not here either. I want breakfast and how come you're not getting up?"

After watching *The Attack of the Puppet People*, Rebecca had nightmares and did not sleep well. Sitting up slowly, she scans the room. Michael is lying on the rug, not far from the TV, and empty containers and soft drink cans lay scattered over the floor. Light pours in with diffuse intensity from the window and there's no sign of their mother's return.

"This is not okay, Angel. Mom's going to be mad when she sees all this stuff and we have to clean up. So, we have to start, okay? I'll go get us some breakfast, but not unless you help!"

On her way to the bathroom, she checks her parents' bed, which is empty. The bed is still made and her mother's purse sits on top close to the phone. Next to the phone she spots a note:

"Rebecca, I will be home as soon as I can. Please keep an eye on Angel and Michael and I know I can count on you. I love you, Mom."

It's is so weird! Dad's gone and now Mom's gone, and now they want me to be the adult! That's the last thing Mom told to me—"...a good time for you to be a perfect babysitter...don't depend on the hotel people...I want just you to watch your brother and sister, okay?" Wow, so here I go. I don't know why they want me to have all this responsibility. I guess to see if I can govern, kind of like the president does here with the government? Ha ha! Oh, girl! Shoot, I can do it."

When she returns from the bathroom, Michael is already up and Angel is helping him to get dressed. Rebecca turns the TV off and looks behind the couch, where her schoolbook, still open to the Mayflower Compact, and her drawing pad are easily retrieved. She looks at her drawing of the Pyramid and decides to do it over again, but not till she buys breakfast from the first-floor restaurant. Before leaving the motel room she places the sign on the outside door handle: "Resting—please do not disturb." As she holds on to her notebook, she confronts her brother and sister.

"You guys, we have to make a compact. That means we are going to take care of ourselves. We're not going to get into any trouble, and that means we work together, okay? After breakfast we clean up this place, and then we can go swimming. Before Mom gets back. That's what a compact means, and you both have to sign on this page next to my name."

The Howard Johnson Covenant

We the children of David and Margaret Lovejoy do agree to work together to find our father and mother and to keep a clean house and to get along together.

Signed: The Lovejoy children

Rebecca Lovejoy __________

Angel Lovejoy __________

Michael Lovejoy _________

Chapter 19:
How Otieno Climbs the Pyramid

8:50 a.m.—A long story

Otieno lights a cigarette as they leave the main office and drive to his downtown apartment complex, listening to a Stevie Wonder song blasting from the speakers. The bright red ambulance has tinted windows, making it difficult to see inside, and the large rear cab is lined at the base by flashing lights. Dizzy Gillespie trumpets through the middle of the song when they reach Otieno's modest apartment, in the poorer section of the city. They climb a flight of stairs to enter, and Otieno slides into a reclining chair and remains quiet, studying a book on Pyramids. Hinton sits on a leather couch nearby, plotting his Union strategy and making notes on a small notebook.

Have to get this man to join our union, he thinks, glancing around the one-bedroom apartment. *I'm getting nowhere with Colson and Deed, but if I can convince Otieno then the others will come around. Why's he so quiet? If anyone should appreciate the collaborative strength of the working class, and the need for blacks, it ought to be him.*

Hinton scans the wall of the living room. Basketball trophies sit on the bookshelves. There are photos of Otieno playing guitar on a stage surrounded by fans, diplomas from the School of Alternative Medicine, a School of Hypnosis certificate, and a plaque from the Millionaire Society that hangs on the wall next to a collection of books on Pyramids.

"Wow, you did all this stuff?" Hinton asks, closing his notebook. "You've certainly been around, Otieno!"

"Oh, yeah," he answers, noting a fly land on the edge of the couch.

Otieno sets his Pyramid book down, and with a quick stretch of the arm catches the insect in his bare hand. He drops it into an aquarium in front of them. "I've had my share of luck."

Hinton watches the bug floating behind glass.

"I doubt it's just luck. Lives are defined by laws of self-actualization. You must be gifted. I mean, you must be if all these diplomas are for real."

"Oh really? Why?"

A whiskered catfish floats to the surface of the aquarium and leisurely ingests the fly.

"Well, I think so. That is, if you're truly a millionaire, like the plaque on the wall claims. But you know, Otieno, millionaires rarely become drivers, or join unions for that matter."

"Unions?" Otieno asks, looking carefully at his partner for the day. Hinton sets down his notebook and adjusts the sleeves of his blue jumpsuit.

"I want to talk to you about that, but it can wait. First, tell me the truth—you're really a millionaire?"

"No, not anymore," Otieno answers, with a knowing smile. "Traded it all back for my soul. Gave it back to the devil so I could become a healer."

"Healer?" Hinton asks.

"Would a man jive about his soul?" Otieno's expression turns serious as he stands next to the aquarium.

"I would hope not," Hinton answers, leaning a bit forward from the couch.

"Then you'll understand when you hear it. I once was asked to join a millionaire's society. I forsook it for a finer life."

"Working for Medical?"

"No, Hinton, working for the people."

"Right on!"

"Right on."

They both make a fist, signifying solidarity, while observing the catfish nestle back behind a rock.

"You see, I used to work for Hughes Oil. This might seem a little surprising to you, but I was once a vice president."

"You can't be serious? Hughes Oil? Hughes Oil is the greatest corporate parasite to ever suck the earth's blood! You worked for Hughes? Come on, man, don't let me on!"

"We all work for Hughes, Hinton. And I certainly wasn't his only vice president," Otieno continues plaintively. "There were twelve others. I was truly small fry. But I was able to view the business from the inside."

"Really?" Hinton tries on the gloves Otieno gave him on their way back from the headquarters. "And what did you see?"

"Oil, man. More oil than you can imagine." Otieno walks to the window of his apartment and then turns back, raising his right arm.

"Saw enough oil to float the whole District of Colombia, James Hinton. Oil in buckets, oil in barrels, oil in derrick wells, tanks, tubes, and pipes. Let me tell you about the hydraulic packing, the catalytic cracking, tetra-methyl, not to mention micro-methyl, hot popping heptanes, and boiling iso-octanes. Hinton, we piped it out, pumped it in, shipped it around, made sure it was found. We dug it, drilled it, flumed it, and plumed it, and when we ran out of it, we explored deeper into it."

I knew this guy was a talker, Hinton thinks, as Otieno's hands become more demonstrative. *And now I'm getting somewhere. He's coming alive!*

"And, oh yeah, I traveled the world. Private yachts, chartered trains, expensive cars, and new seaplanes. My office was designed in the shape of an enormous heart, with walls that could expand or contract. Whenever I pushed the right button, servo units provided me with shelves of books, an instant bar, movie screens, stereos, rows of TVs. I had originals by Rembrandt, Da Vinci, Salvador Dali...check it out. Like all the vice presidents, a buzz on the phone, snap of the fingers, I had the world's most voluptuous women, lots of them, multitudes of them...all inside the confines of a traveling, reciprocating, four-room suite, to facilitate the how much I can't begin to tell you profitable transactions of our oil company, not to mention bodily ecstasy from the ladies of the Colombia Plaza."

He looks out the window as he talks, fixing his gaze on the towering Pyramid in the city center.

"Just perks, man. Of an exquisitely entrepreneurial enterprise, as I used to tell the girls. See, we had room service, real room service, with foreign cuisine brought in by jets and helicopters from around the globe. After eating there was the casino, down in the basement. We amused ourselves by squandering a few grand, collecting millions, depending on how we rigged it.

"So, I played with magnates, nabobs, sheiks, and plutocrats. There were bankers and burgvilles, billionaires and presidents. Knew them inside out, James. All the pervasiveness of false identities, perverse cupidity, rampant cuckoldry, unchained idolatry, parsimony, alimony, testimony, hegemony, litigation, mitigation, mass consumption, class corruption, red tape, legal rape...all the venality, intricacies, and intrigues that were what you might say...implicit in keeping stocks rolling and oil flowing. It all led to an enterprise of monetary pulling, deep sea sowing, revolution destroying, tight purse toying, elastic budget knowing, and the low-go hoeing of an unascertainable infinitude of I could never tell you how much well-endowed bestowing. But let me take you a little further back..."

Otieno walks back from the window and lights another cigarette. Below them, downtown traffic rushes by and they hear a distant siren.

"It was all mine, man. Every last little bit. And all because of a slick. Can you dig it?"

"I just don't know, Otieno, tell me more," Hinton responds, dumbfounded and doubting.

On the streets below cars quickly fill spaces left open by a change in the traffic signal. Black pedestrians push along through openings they find on thc sidewalk. There's a buildup around an itinerant old woman with a shopping cart, who moves too slowly for the morning bustle.

"You don't know, do you? Of course you don't! Why, neither did I...till I found out. See, I'm going to tell you something, Hinton. Something about oil. We all live in a big machine. A very big machine. And this machine needs lots of oil and fuel to keep running. None of us knows exactly what the machine is supposed to do...now do we? Other than to keep us comfortable, of course. But where is it taking us? What we do know is that it has to keep going, at any expense, and always a little faster. GDP, man, everything builds the GDP. I didn't know that before the slick, Hinton. I mean, like, I thought the District could go on shuckin' and jivin', doing its own thing, and I'd take care of myself. Life was just a party—long as I made sure I got everything I needed. I was just another man on the street, until..."

He slowly lifts his arms into the air.

"Until the day..."

He lifts them higher.

"I found out!"

As if by cue, the catfish appears in the center of the aquarium, facing them.

"Yes, 'Lord,' I said that day, 'forgive my black-ass self for all I've ever done,'" Otieno intones. "Because there I was, in black man's land, the deepest, most bottomless pit in the ghetto. Nothing but rabid dogs and starving rats entered that place, and, man, there I was, laying on my black ass, just scared to death."

He flicks off the TV, twists around, and stands perfectly still. The catfish remains motionless.

"Never afraid in my life, Hinton. I lay on my back that day, in a dark slick of water, stone cold with terror! Know where I was?"

"The ghetto public pool?" Hinton answers with a grin.

"Yeah, that's funny, , but you're wrong. No. It was the day I showed up at my grandfather's abandoned bungalow. You may even know about him. He was the first organizer of the black petroleum workers. And he was clubbed to death for saying a single word."

"What'd he say?"

"Union."

"Oh."

"That's right, Hinton. During the night they clubbed him down, very brutally. In the morning the newspapers said he passed away in his sleep, which I guess he did, but would you call that a natural death?"

Hinton stays silent. Distant sounds of traffic outside disturb their vigil, and after a minute Otieno snaps his fingers and the catfish swims away.

"I was pretty young at the time. My mother said there was nothing we could do. When I got older, I went to school and white kids would yell, 'Tar baby, tar baby!' They tried to pick me off in the parking lot after school. That was before I started playing basketball."

Hinton scans the wall again—pictures of Otieno in a uniform on a basketball court, trophies filling the bookshelves. Next to journals and textbooks on Pyramids are more journals on herbs, acupuncture, and homeopathy.

"Like, I was okay on hoops, man. Good enough to get through high school, offered scholarships without reading much. I learned what I needed by memorizing what the teachers said, and then I would turn it into rhyme."

He throws a few pellets into the aquarium, and his catfish audience returns with spoon eyes, like his own.

"There were a few girls back then. Lots more when I turned down the scholarships so I could sing in a band. Yeah, doing good, getting gigs, getting a name, not thinking much about college. Till the night we were getting ready for a show and the sax player.... I hear you play sax, man.... The sax player and bass guitar and drummer all OD-ed on heroin That left only the lead guitar—me. Night before Christmas, man. And I went home to see my mother and be baptized by the bodily spirit."

His body sways as he spins around and continues his tale.

"Even after my grandfather was dissed, my mama refused to leave our house, or sell Grandfather's shack, which was right behind it. So, Christmas morning I decide to clean it out, 'cause I planned to live there after I enrolled in City College. Well, some people had thrown dynamite at it after my grandfather was removed, so it was pretty messed up. After cleaning the place, I get into the old tub and started taking a bath, and you may have read about this in the papers, man, when the D.C. Express...now, I know you may not believe this, but the train goes by only a few blocks away, and it gets derailed. Shock of that train collision ruptured a pipe that happened to be buried in one of the deeper reserves of our time, Hinton, which is why all those white bath bubbles started turning black, just popping all around me. Oil rose up from Grandfather's earth and I was soaking in it till I looked like some kind of a wrinkled cappuccino raisin. Which explains how I came to be vice president of Hughes Oil. We sold our oil rights and I got hired by the company.

Otieno stops the sway, gazing down on his couched audience, and Hinton shakes his head.

"And everything went fine for a number of years, . Fine till the morning when a man came to my mother's door and tells her she's living on eminent domain, over which a new freeway is going to pass. He also says she has to move out, which ends our economic validity. Soon after that I quit working for the devil."

"You mean you quit working for Howard Hughes? I sure hope so, and right on, Otieno!"

"Right on!"

Otieno's fingers fold together and his knuckles crack in sequence. Hinton doesn't believe the story for a minute, but he's mesmerized by the hyperbole and still needs Otieno's support. He pumps for more detail.

"And what about the hypnosis?"

Otieno's eyes flash as he continues the test.

"Glad you asked. You know in our line of work, , it's possible to render people free of pain."

He probes Hinton's eyes, searching for suggestibility, when an alarm reverberates.

RRR RRR RRR!

"Hotline?" Hinton asks.

"Right," Otieno confirms, turning toward one of several phones. "It's our man Haldeman with an assignment. We gotta go!"

Chapter 20:

A Trip to the Pyramid

10:35 a.m.—The waiting room again

Inside the commodious reception floor of the Hughes Pyramid, Clifton Urning adjusts his three-piece suit and begins another day, still hoping to obtain a visit with the richest man in the world. He knows Hughes has a weakness for cars. As a fourteen-year-old, Hughes had visited the Stutz auto agency in Houston and taken a liking to the Bearcat, the glamorous high-speed vehicle of the time. He told the salesman, "I want this. Would you please send it out to my house today?" When Howard's father heard the price, $7,000, he hesitated and asked his son what he planned to do with the car. Howard replied that he would tear it down and put it back together again. And he did so within a month.

There's a siren in the distance as Urning recites his poem, "The Freeway"...

O give thanks to the Bentley, Pegaso, Gordini,
Du Pont, Lorraine-Dietrich, Isotta Fraschini,
The Marmon, Mercedes, and Bugatti Royale
for lifting us all up, right out of the soil...

Friday, 10:38 a.m.—The road to Howard Hughes

Enroute on their first call, Car 45 tires hum smoothly, the rubber surging over asphalt as the ambulance heads for the Hughes Pyramid.

"See," Otieno explains, assessing Hinton from behind the steering wheel, "there are two kinds of people in our profession—drivers and doctors. Everyone ends up being one or the other, though some people try to be both. But usually, a person is either born a driver or born a doctor. Like, a driver is someone who's always trying to get somewhere. I could tell you were a driver the second I met you, . You look like you're headed upwards. You got that headed-for-the-top, gunner kind of look in your eyes. I know, 'cause I often try to be both."

Hinton glances at the speedometer, indicating sixty miles an hour. The rest of the dashboard is a profusion of instruments and lights. The Staple Singers sing out "I'll take you there" through speakers in the rear, and he has to strain to hear Otieno.

"Doctors don't fool so much with cars and machines, just like the driver doesn't fool much with people. Simple as that. It's an important thing to remember: So long as you do your driving while I'm taking care of the patient, and don't interfere with my taking care of the patient while you're doing the driving, there can't be any trouble, right?"

"Why would there be?"

Otieno takes some Motown tapes out of a box and considers them while he maneuvers the car from one lane to another.

"Well, like sometimes the doctor finds the driver's not handling the ambulance in a way that's best for the patient's interest. And sometimes the driver may find the doctor's not handling the patient in the best way. It makes for conflicts of interest, which is important to avoid, particularly in the case of 'lazy fare.'"

He slides a Marvin Gaye cassette in as Car 38 swings into the right-hand lane.

"What's 'lazy fare'?"

"Lazy fare is a person who's not really suffering, but thinks he or she should be taken care of. We see a lot of these folks in D.C. They're very insistent, very demanding. Like, they feel they're entitled to the best, but they do little to take care of themselves. You know, Hinton, often the lazy fare can be taken care of at home, long before he or she gets into an ambulance. Doctors can recognize a lazy fare without difficulty. It's predictable, and Mr. Hughes is a classic."

"Hughes? Howard Hughes? What are you saying…are you saying we're going to be transporting Howard Hughes? Seriously?"

"Well, truth is, I was a little surprised myself. A lot of people thought he was dead, still think he's dead. Anyway, now it seems that years ago he helped Medical and the president with a little loan. A big hundred thousand loan…and not just Nixon, but his brother too. Nixon never used the money. He kept it packed away in a briefcase, case he ever needed it. Hughes forgot all about it until this morning, when he gave the dispatcher a call and said he expected a free ride from Medical."

"But Hughes practically owns Medical!"

"And that's why he gets a free ride."

They roll off the freeway onto Massachusetts Avenue, where the Hughes Pyramid towers above the hotel district. Otieno keeps red lights on to help clear traffic, and as they drive past several government buildings and hotels, the pinnacle of Hughes' building keeps their attention. It seems to pull magnetically, like the man who gave rise to it.

"Yesterday, I thought he was dead," Hinton muses. "Then we see the Spruce Goose go into the air, so he's obviously not dead, or even that sick. You ever dream you'd get close to Howard Hughes, or have him in the back of your ambulance?"

"You know, when it comes to Howard, anything is possible."

Otieno negotiates traffic for several more blocks. Hinton leans forward to take in the forty-nine-story building, towering over the city. Its uppermost peak, without visible windows, is a solid steel cap covering the apex—pointing vertically to the heavens. They reach the Pyramid's protected perimeter and drive into a columned entrance where attendants circle around the ambulance. Hinton observes how the attendants recognize Otieno, who in turn acknowledges them back. He follows Otieno into the same reception room that Clifton Urning has waited in every week for the last year, hoping to meet Hughes.

"Mr. Otieno! How are you, sir?"

Otieno's greeted by screening clerks at the visitors' desk. The recognition of an ambulance driver, once a vice president, makes everyone look around.

"Are we going to the top today?" Otieno asks, signing his name in the logbook.

"We're confirming that now, sir. You could be the first," the clerk answers with a smile, picking up a phone to contact security. As she does so, Clifton Urning appears beside the two ambulance drivers.

"Excuse me. Did I just hear you say that you're 'going to the top'?"

Urning, dressed in his three-piece suit, carries a sheath of verses under his arm. Without turning his head, Otieno acknowledges the poet.

"That's right."

Urning turns to the receptionist.

"You see, Mr. Hughes is here! They're going up to see him, aren't they? He's here! He's here and you've got to let me see him, today! Please!"

"I'm sorry, Mr. Urning. No one sees Mr. Hughes without his permission."

"Well, I need to see him today. I happen to have with me the Epic Verse he requested. For all I…we know, he may be dying. He needs to hear it!"

"Verses?" Otieno asks.

Urning sees his opportunity.

"Look, I'm the Hughes orator. Can you men take me up with you? I really need to see him. As a matter of fact, I work for him."

Otieno scrutinizes the poetaster, smiling.

"Tell the guard I'm bringing two attendants with me," he advises the receptionist. "Perhaps Mr. ...uh..."

"Urning."

"Perhaps Mr. Urning has some verses that are entertaining, or therapeutic?"

She frowns. Otieno takes a moment to look into her eyes, and she acquiesces.

"You all have to be screened. It's been many years since you worked here, Mr. Otieno. Mr. Hughes has not seen anyone in years. But we always try to accommodate."

"Of course."

Waving with his gloved index finger, Otieno signals Hinton and Urning to follow. They head for the secured entrance to the center of the Pyramid, walking past the armed guards beneath a huge letter D, and enter into a Medical examining room. The size of a convention hall, it's partitioned into cubicles, each one attended by a young woman. Many, while waiting to rise up in the ranks of cinematic stardom, have been assigned "temporary" positions as phlebotomy technicians. They take medical histories, draw blood samples, and oversee the prodigious workforce of the building. Besides collecting serum, they follow carefully regulated procedures—collecting urine specimens, skin scrapings, swabs of nasal and oral mucosa, and monitoring temperatures.

The three visitors are separated for their exams. As Hinton enters an enclosed cubicle, he encounters an attractive phlebotomist.

"Hello, I'm Jenny. Won't you wear a mask and put on these gloves? You may have a seat."

She seems to smile, but wears a pink mask so he can't be certain.

"And where did they get you?"

"I need to ask you that question, Mr. Hinton. Have you been driving ambulances very long?"

"Well, no, not really. I just joined Medical. And you? Have you been here very long?"

"Sorry, Mr. Hinton. I need to ask you more questions. While you're loosening your uniform, would you mind telling me if you've had any recent illnesses?"

"I'm just as healthy as they come, miss."

He zips down the front of his suit while admiring her pink scrub top.

"Cold or a flu?"

"No, ma'am."

"Exposure to viruses or bacteria? You'll need to finish undressing if you want to complete the exam. Please remove your trousers."

She waits for his answer.

"Uh...not really."

"Not really?"

"Well, I had kind of a contact with a baby recently. I don't really know if the baby was infected or not. He was delivered in the hospital and he stopped breathing. But we uhh…we saved him!"

"I'm sorry. Can you explain with a little more detail? That's wonderful that you helped the baby. But he or she was sick?"

He unbuttons his pants, searching for words. The confession of exposure could eliminate his chance of seeing Hughes.

"I, uh…it was just a resuscitation of a neonate. There wasn't a definite infectious exposure. I mean so far as I know."

"Okay," she says, beginning to examine him. She looks down his throat with a small light and then feels over his neck and armpits, checking for swollen glands. With a stethoscope on his chest, she listens as he inhales and expires. Then she reaches for a urine specimen container. Another voice interrupts.

"Hold still, Mr. Urning!"

From the next cubicle they hear a struggle. Urning twists and turns on the exam table. He keeps his butt 180 degrees away from the examiner, changing positions each time he's approached from behind, but eventually the nurse's gloved finger discovers his last vestige of privacy, eliciting a prostrate secretion that Hughes demands from anyone who is new.

"Mr. Hughes is a thorough man," Jenny tells Hinton, while donning a pair of latex gloves, ignoring Urning's groans.

"Yes, he certainly is," Hinton agrees, looking at the thin partition between himself and Clifton's exam cubicle. "But he's not here in the room with us. You sure you need all this?"

"Of course. Everyone who comes inside the Pyramid has to have a thorough examination. Mr. Hughes insists that every possible infection is ruled out. We're supposed to check everything."

"Uh, sure. Well, if you don't mind, I think you've done enough. Maybe you might even need to be checked yourself?"

"I've already been screened, Mr. Hinton. I'm going to need a urine sample."

"Well, I'd just love to see what's behind that mask. I'll bet you're as beautiful as I think you might be. You have wonderful blue eyes. And you can just set those specimen containers down, honey. I'll give you all the samples you want. I'm good at this, okay?"

He takes her empty containers, but before filling them he winks.

"I really am shy!" he tells her.

She turns reluctantly, just long enough for him to fill the containers halfway with saliva.

"Now where do we go?" he asks, handing her the tubes and tossing his gloves into a wastebasket.

"We were always having spelling bees," Otieno continues, "and it got so I won 'em all. Till one morning the teacher cut me off. I mean like the Man eliminated me from competition by not giving me a word to spell. I caused so much trouble, Urning, he threw me out of his class. That's how I became class poet."

"I'm not sure I understand. Where's the poetry?"

"'You mothafucka'...give me anotha.' That's what I told 'em. You do the dozen, cousin?"

Urning takes more interest in the aesthetics of the Pyramid and is busy scanning its interior for the first time, marveling at a structure before only imagined. The years spent studying the tallest building in D.C., keeping track of the enigmatic man who lives within, have gone by slowly and he's doubtful if his work will ever be recognized. Not till Hughes' recent appearance in the Goose has any real evidence surfaced that he's even alive. Now Urning has hope of a literary career—the man who hired him on as biographer may acknowledge him. They wait for infectious disease clearance as Otieno extemporizes.

> Yes, before him the Thomas, Maxwell, and Stearn,
> Stutz, Coey Flyer, DuPont, and Auburn,
> Stood there for a choice, to be driven away,
> Just one could he take, without a delay.

"That's good!" Urning acknowledges, impressed with Otieno's knowledge of cars.

"Thanks. I know Hughes' cars pretty well. He never bought just one. He would usually buy twenty of the same ones at a time."

Hinton too takes his eyes off the surveillance cameras to listen to the two men recite. Urning goes next.

"Well, that's right. You know him pretty well. And your rhyme sounds like mine! So, listen."

Cunninghams, Morgans, Lanchesters, Cords,
Appersons, Kissels, and even some Dorts.
Were ready to travel, yeah but just like a fox
He climbed into the seat of a Heine Velox.

"Gentlemen, please get your suits on now," a masked man informs them. They turn to a set of guards who indicate a new doorway leading into the central core of the building. Clifton brushes off his double-breasted suit coat and adjusts his tie. Hinton cinches his belt and follows the guards into a low-ceilinged room with more cameras.

"You'll need to put these on before you get into the visitor's elevator," they're told. Each is handed a hooded white Gore-Tex suit and a surgical mask.

"White is right," Otieno intones, slipping into the outfit that resembles a beekeeper's uniform. Urning worries that his voice may lose clarity when the hermetically sealed hood is zippered into place, and he leaves his face unbounded by the plastic shield. The guards zip it for him, and then one of them dresses too, just before the elevator doors open and a fine mist begins to descend from the ceiling.

"Hey, what the devil is going on?" Hinton shouts, as the mist envelops them.

"Disinfectant. Mr. Hughes doesn't want to be destroyed by our bacteria," one of the guards explains, "or your viruses either." Reluctantly, they submit to the chlorine shower, waiting a mandatory three minutes before the doors open. The guards hand each of them a box of unopened Kleenex, a BIC pen, and a yellow memo pad, just in case they actually get to the top.

"Mr. Hughes hasn't shaken hands with anyone in five years. Sometimes you can pass him a piece of paper. But be sure to use the Kleenex first. It has to be white and come from the right side. The pens have already been sterilized."

They nod in agreement. As the glass doors open, they step into the elevator. The control panel shows buttons for forty-eight floors and an elaborate push panel assembly for the last and final floor, just below the apex. As the elevator heads up, one of the guards punches in a code. Hinton notes it carefully from the side.

8—21—7—5

16—15—23—5—18

Let's see, 8-21-7-5. ***Huge****.... And 16-15-23-5-18. That must be* ***Power****.*

Chapter 21:
The Layers of Power

Friday, Day 4, 1:09 p.m.

Ascending slowly along the side of the Pyramid, they gaze through the glass elevator, and once above the first floor they're able to view off to the east the white, cast iron dome of the Capitol Building, connected by the grand avenue to the White House. Myriad government and white office buildings spread north and south. Invisible to them on the west side of the Pyramid, the Lincoln Memorial transcends a cover of midday haze. Hinton, like Urning, focuses on the inside of the building, now apparent through the glass doors of the elevator. The layers of labor define Hughes' edifice.

"Seven levels," Hinton comments.

He points to the Braille-like tabulation and buttons along the side of the elevator door, and their two guards nod but give no explanation. Of the forty-eight floors there are six divisions that can be discerned by small dotted lines between them. The final triangle contains the letter "H."

H

....

M+PB

....

SH

....

VP

....

L

....

M

....

D

....

"Let me guess. D stands for Driver, right?"

The guards ignore Hinton's probing. Hughes has two or three visitors a year, never presidents, but sometimes state governors or their representatives. Corporate leaders also are allowed to go up the Pyramid, but only to the sixth level. Otieno was once a vice president in the Hughes company, but the two men with him are hardly of that caliber. Even Maheu, Hughes's closest advisor, is only occasionally invited to the seventh level, and has never seen Hughes in person.

"M stands for Manager, right?" Hinton guesses again.

"I'm not sure it's your concern, Mr. Hinton," the guard answers.

As they reach the fifteenth floor, they begin to see other D.C. buildings. Long chains of cars fill the hotel district, encircling blocks like parading dots and clips, all connected in linear motion.

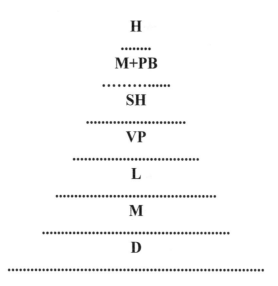

"No, it's not that important," Hinton continues. "I just like to guess. For example, Let's say M stands for Manager. If you don't answer, I could take it as affirmative. Right?"

The guard remains silent. They're well into the Ls, on the twenty-third floor, as the Beltway becomes more visible, curling and streaming around the city with longer chains of cars.

"Ls. Cinch! Stands for Lawyers—right, guys?"

Otieno looks at Hinton and smiles. His own office was on the thirty-fifth floor. He remembers the big stir when he, the first black to be employed in the Pyramid, rose past floors twenty-one through twenty-eight and waved to the Ls. Of the sixty thousand lawyers working in D.C., most of them have worked for the Pyramid at one time or another, and they resented his progress. Hughes, mistrusting lawyers as much as blacks, considered Otieno in a special category. Since the majority of D.C., or "Chocolate City" is black, he made a pragmatic choice, and it helped significantly that Otieno was light-skinned. In fact, he didn't believe Otieno was black anyway.

"Doesn't seem to be a shortage," Hinton adds, as they look in on the assemblage of well-attired Ls, wearing colorful ties with floral patterns, expensive shirts, and Italian sports coats. An occasional woman is dressed in a dark suit with pants. Otieno remembers the level well, and it hasn't been that long since the affirmative action program began. The guards remain silent.

"But they're so far down in the system," Hinton continues, laughing. "There must be a lot of Ls, based on the way their floor expands out. Now, salary will be consistent with the elevation in the building...right, Otieno?"

The elevator drifts to a smooth halt as a telephone rings within the glass-lined room. The three visitors watch the taller of the guards pick it up with a white glove. His face is sober as he takes the message and looks back.

"Which one of you is James J. Hinton?"

"I am," Hinton acknowledges, cautiously.

"You have to get off. Right now. We're taking you down in the other elevator."

"Excuse me?"

"There's some blood tests pending on you, Mr. Hinton, from City Hospital. You didn't tell us of a hepatitis exposure during the medical interview. And there's something funny about your urine sample. They say it looks like spit, to be exact."

Hinton's cheeks turn pink. Beads of sweat form as he stares back through the Gore-Tex gown.

"Wait a minute. I drive an ambulance for Medical. It's well known a degree of exposure comes with our work. Anyone can have a blood test done, and I don't pee saliva, thank you very much. I mean to say I'm strong and healthy. In fact, I'm extremely healthy…and virile, damn it...look here…! What are you guys doing?"

The shorter guard leads him forcefully onto the twenty-ninth floor, where another elevator awaits. As they step out, they're met by the eyes of hundreds of interested secretaries, sitting at reception desks in a suite overlooking the city panorama. The Ls look on suspiciously as well.

"Meet you back at the car!" Otieno calls out.

Otieno has seen other germ carriers make a sudden disappearance. The doors close as he continues upward along with Urning, who lets go a sigh of relief. Urning's faced too many disappointments in his years trying to see Hughes, and isn't sure how much the man knows about him or his own exposures, but he's still upward bound.

Hughes could not achieve his pinnacle of success without a sixth sense or mechanical genius, Urning reflects. *As a spoiled only child, left with the sizable inheritance, he bought out the family business, eschewed college, and went on to one self-designed success after another. First the oil business, then the cars. Then film directing, cinema glory, and aviation. And how he loved to fly, especially seaplanes! In the last decade it's been casinos and the financial empire. Well, I know this history as well as anyone. Cajoling corporations and integrating industries. Making mergers, trusts, mammoth transactions, and ever-expanding consortiums. He's mastered the largest Monopoly game in the world through acquisition of capital. And yet with each expansion and conquest he withdraws deeper into personal isolation. I know this enigmatic side, and some of his secrets, and I know damn well Hughes has yet another hidden plan—still to be revealed. I just have to see him, the great Howard R. Hughes Jr., and face-to-face!*

They ascend to the fourth level, VP, where offices are larger and fewer. Floral tie patterns give way to platinum stripes and insignia-labeled designs, tucked behind three-piece suits. Otieno waves to the vice presidents he once worked with.

They continue up to the fifth level, where a small group carries on somber discussions. Otieno signals again a mock salute to the men who amass and distribute the fortunes. He once envied them. Now as the driver of Car 45, he looks back at their mountain of wealth and shakes his head quietly. The shareholders, rising each day to play with incomes of hundreds of millions, gains and losses in the mega-ions, live on the end of telephones and ticker tapes. They handle the capital's fortunes just as the citizens of D.C. play with their own paltry stakes, in minor gambling enterprises. But the proceeds eventually find their way to the top.

"Ready your rhymes," Otieno tells his fellow poet, "we're almost there!"

Urning feels a creative kinship with Otieno as they approach the sixth level. The forty-first floor is without secretaries, as are floors forty-two through forty-eight. Each office is small, now that the Pyramid has narrowed toward the zenith, and the elevator affords a spectacular view through windows to the interior and exterior.

"Think of the stuff I could write from here," Urning continues, trying to absorb the panorama for later moments when he'll record their experience. The geodesic dome, harboring the Goose on the Potomac River, appears no larger than a half-spherical cooking lid, reflecting rays of the sun outward. The Potomac stretches sinuously, its luxurious blue/brown tones embossed with shimmering lines of distant waves—a uniform, unending pattern—drifting to the confluence of its southern Y formation where it joins the Anacostia. Looking out in the opposite direction they can see cement and steel edifices give way to a distant gentle backdrop of forested hills, with curved and linear projections of the Beltway system reaching out and belonging to a greater form. The suburbs dissolve to small estates, punctuated with barely visible rooftops.

"I think that's where the Spruce Goose is!" Urning laughs. He points to the metal roof of the Geodesic Dome, where Hughes made his recent flight.

"Feel something funny?" Otieno asks the poet.

"Why, yes, I do. It's kind of a strange sensation, but I do feel something."

They make a curious spectacle poised 650 feet up, above D.C.'s thin blanket of smog. Otieno remembers the view well enough from when he was a vice president, but instead focuses on the inside of the Pyramid and the sixth level, which he has never entered. He comments to Urning once more, "It's a very subtle vibration."

"Sure, yes, I do feel it. It's like an oscillation."

"That's right. Well, Hinton's not here to guess anymore, but M and PB stands for Maheu and Power Brokers, ha! So, what do you think is causing the oscillation?"

The remaining guard smiles. The information has never been shared with the public, that the Pyramid is the largest airwave transmitter on the planet. Hughes' control of major TV networks in D.C., as well as the satellite international communication systems the military depends on, gives him surveillance control of the CIA and FBI as well. Otieno has long suspected the larger design of the seven hundred-foot antennae.

Continuing up to the forty-eighth floor, the elevator nears the end of its rise. The last floor contains Maheu's office, with hundreds of telephones, a network of televisions, and a host of monitors with current stock and bond listings. Each preceding floor, lined with plate glass, contains a single desk and chair, spartan compared to the stockholder (S H) floors. On top of each desk is a Bible and a power broker contemplating it, along with the documents and coordination dossiers for the Glomar Exploration, or "Operation Azorian."

"Feels like Channel Seven, doesn't it?" Otieno asks with a smile.

Urning catches his breath, then lets out a whistle of recognition.

"That's it! It didn't occur to me until now. We're on the air!"

There's a shared laughter within their Gore-Tex suits as the three men look outward again, realizing how close they are to the man on the top.

Maheu and the power brokers are helping the CIA, with Hughes' direction and name recognition, to covertly retrieve a Soviet submarine and its nuclear missiles and torpedoes, buried 16,000 feet below the Pacific Ocean surface. Using Hughes' deep-sea mining vessel, the Glomar, cables and giant metal clamps will be used to grasp and pull the submarine up for exploration. But Hughes has greater exploration goals, and he's keeping them secret.

There's a sudden darkness as the elevator moves into the seventh level and they're swallowed into the windowless apex of the Pyramid. A moment goes by in silence. Then another. Otieno becomes apprehensive, fifty feet farther, as they come to an opening. Soft light filters through thick glass doors from inside the apex.

"And, where is he?" Urning asks.

The guard looks at him soberly.

"Where's who?"

"Mr. Hughes. You said he was going to see us."

As the glass doors open, the guard walks his two guests into an empty hallway ending with another closed door. More surveillance cameras mounted above follow them.

"Actually, he is seeing you. Very few men have ever been at this level, Mr. Urning, and you should know, of course, how fortunate you are to be here."

"Of course, I know. But I don't see him."

Urning waits for the door to open, holding onto his box of Kleenex and yellow pad as the silence continues. Solid concrete walls and ethereal light, the sealed door in front, and an unsettling sense of being watched occupy the next several minutes. Otieno and the guard wait patiently.

"Damn it! After all the..."

"Quiet! Don't move," Otieno warns.

"What do you mean?"

Urning's frustration is peaking, but he holds himself as Otieno points to the moving camera heads.

"He's monitoring so don't move around. It makes him nervous."

"Nervous? I'm the one that's..."

"Good afternoon, gentlemen. How can I help you?"

The voice—there's no mistaking his raspy drawl and echoing authority. His sound waves bounce back and forth in the concrete cubicle.

"We have Mr. Otieno," the guard announces, "as you requested, sir. His other ambulance partner had laboratory discrepancies so he was returned to the screening clinic. And this is Mr. Cleffer Urning, your biographer and poet."

The cameras focus on different features of the men as the guard steps back, allowing Hughes to study his visitors. He discerns details through their hermetic Gore-Tex suits, eliminating any surprises that may have been missed in the earlier screening.

"Nice of you gentlemen to come visit. Urning, how is your work coming along?"

"Mr. Hughes, I'm so happy to hear your voice. I've heard you've been sick."

"Sick?"

"Yessir. The news reported you might be dying. In fact, it said you were probably dead."

"Do I sound dead, Mr. Urning?"

"No, not at all, sir. You sound just fine." Urning looks into the cameras, hoping his sentiment will cause a small crack in the sealed door.

"Does that mean I'm not dying?"

"Sir?"

"Never mind. Have you finished the poem I assigned you, Urning? You were not invited today, but I wouldn't mind some inspiration, if you would be so kind."

"Oh, yessir! I was hoping you'd...shall I come in, sir?"

The cameras focus in and out on Clifton's face. The door before them remains fixed.

"Tell me the name of your poem, Mr. Urning."

"It's called 'The Freeway,' Mr. Hughes. I've memorized the lines to recite to you, whenever you want inspiration."

"Really? So, let's hear it."

Urning places the Kleenex boxes on the floor and looks straight into the cameras.

"Oh, give thanks to the Bentley, Pegaso, Gordini,
DuPont, Lorraine Dietrich, Isotta Fraschini..."

"Hold it a second. Mr. Urning, is this poem about cars?"

"Of course, Mr. Hughes. That's what you told me to write about."

"I'm not interested in cars anymore."

"Mr. Hughes! You..."

The camera heads move back and forth rapidly, lenses spinning 360 degrees, reversing in swift angle changes.

"Cars are dead, Urning. Diversion for the masses. What else do you have?"

The poet struggles for composure.

"I have a few verses on you, Mr. Hughes, but..."

"On me? On me? You forgot the contract you signed, man?"

"No, sir, they're in my memory. Nothing's ever been written on paper."

Hughes's voice increases in pitch, amplified through the invisible speakers in the room. Echoes continue reverberating off the confining walls as the guard moves closer to Urning.

"Don't you ever write about me, Mr. Urning, if you want to stay out of court. My life is above public interest. You mean to tell me you don't have poems about rockets?"

"No, sir. Rockets? I had no idea..."

"Get out of here!"

"Mr. Hughes, I haven't gotten here...yet. I've never even met you!"

"Out! Come back when you have rocket verses."

Urning's speechless. As the guard leads him back into the elevator, the doors close together. He heads down the Pyramid—a crushed poet.

Chapter 22:

The Top

Friday, 1:25 p.m.—Inside the Apex

Otieno, left alone in the observation room, quickly pulls a roll of surgical tape from his Gore-Tex suit. Tall enough to reach the reciprocating cameras, which swing back and forth, frantically trying to keep him in view, he slaps white adhesive over the lenses. Still ahead remains the unyielding, monolithic door, blocking off the Inner Sanctum. He remembers the code he observed the Mormon guard use on their initial ascent in the elevator, and presses out the same sequence of buttons.

8 21 7 5
16 15 23 5 18

Time stops as Otieno waits to see if his hunch is correct.

My life is strange, he thinks, as he looks back and notices the sunlight behind him, now illuminating through glass doors that allowed him to approach the final entry to the Inner Sanctum.

I told Hinton only a part of the trail to becoming an ambulance driver and to knowing Hughes. It's true I was a millionaire, but for different reasons than I told him. And now I meet again with Howard, the man who showed me wealth and power. And who helped me to forsake it.

Before dropping out of high school Otieno achieved, at best, average grades, and while an easy career in sports and music awaited, he was determined to do things his own way. Deep in his heart, he wanted to be a doctor. Rather than going to medical school, he enrolled in a school for alternative medicine, pursued independent studies at night, and within a few years established a successful practice. Patients came to see him for a variety of disorders, for which he offered a variety of alternatives.

"Bring your disease, we aim to please," he advertised, never lacking for business. Homeopathy, reflexology, iridology, vitaenology, herbs, green tea/coffee fruit juice enemas, aroma massage, primal scream—all of it was therapy tailored to the recipient. Word traveled fast about his success.

As in most industrial cities, the average D.C. citizen's diet includes high quantities of fat, protein, and refined starch—highly processed foods largely washed down with sugar drinks and alcohol. Conversely, negligible quantities of fiber exist in their food consumption. The transit time of food traveling through the hundreds of thousands of large intestines of District of Colombia is inversely related to the pace of work, fast food consumed, commute time on freeways, and airline flights. And few citizens were more cursed with constipation than Howard Hughes.

Dependent on codeine for his pain syndrome, his life had come to a standstill, veritably a sit-still. Restricted to the bathroom, he was on the throne for endless hours, day after day. This curse of waiting, for a man not gifted with patience, motivated a painstaking search for a remedy. After eliminating a procession of unsuccessful doctors, Hughes made the inevitable turn to alternative treatments, hoping for holistic relief. And Otieno supplied the liberating formula—"one tablespoon wheat germ, one tablespoon rose wheat bran, three-fourths cup of Poland mineral water, one tablespoon honey, one tablespoon instant Cream of Wheat, all boiled for ninety seconds, cooled, followed with a movement chant, "heave ho," and slowly ingested. Not long after he began the formula, Hughes' recalcitrant colon developed peristalsis. Rejuvenating evacuations took place, and a small proportion of his wealth entered into Otieno's bank account. Hughes exited his bathroom and the beginning of affirmative action was assured in the Pyramid. Otieno became a vice president.

Still waiting for the doors of the Apex to open, Otieno recalls the bitterness he felt when he enjoyed the fruits of wealth and power.

When was it I realized I would never shake hands with my employer, let alone advance to become a shareholder, let alone a power broker? The whites rarely complained. Always content to jockey a step up or down, consolidating power and position in their pinnacle of free enterprise, they tolerated all the idiosyncrasies of Hughes so they could stay close to his money. But his aversion to blacks kept irritating me. Can this kind of man have a change in heart? If I could change his methods of colonic elimination, why won't his bigotry lighten up? Well, Howard never recognized me, and definitely not the skin color of his thirteenth vice president. He never set eyes on me, let alone my light-colored skin. It took two years of studying the empire, looking down from the fifth level at all my brothers and sisters below, to realize I could no longer be a tool in this machine of global acquisition!

Another moment passes. The doors slide apart slowly, and Otieno faces the ascending passageway, contained within the elaborate cement structure of the Apex.

So, it's not impossible to meet Howard Hughes! If one holds the hint of a cure for afflictions even the wealthiest of men are subject to, you can approach this notorious recluse.

Otieno counts his steps and proceeds, knowing from hearsay that Hughes has constructed a passageway mirroring the design of the Great Pyramid of Cheops. While the design gives the illusion of proximity, it still requires solutions. His flashlight illuminates the upper surface of the Grand Gallery, where the ceiling rises up enough to allow full extension of his tall frame. There are light scurrying noises along the walls and floor and he's surprised at first to notice small cockroaches scattering away from the beam of light.

Why would a man so concerned with bacteria allow insects near his domain? Then again, even Hughes is no match for the resilience of the D.C. cockroach. The duplication of the Great Pyramid's inner complex is not surprising given Hughes' obsession with concealment and privacy.

Now, the geographic code to the planet's dimensions and blueprint to extraterrestrial travel? No doubt it feeds the plutocrat's need for isolation. My recollection is that I should not continue horizontally along a separate passageway leading to the Queen's Chamber. Instead, I have to count the steps upward through the Grand Gallery, 153 feet from the King's Chamber, where the great Pharaoh Khufu was laid to rest four thousand years ago in Egypt.

Half a millennium has elapsed since Newton recognized the mensurative potential of the Pyramid using ancient ruling units taken from the walls and design of the King's Chamber. Maybe Hughes hopes to defy the effects of aging by reproducing the original pyramid design? Can razors be magically sharpened or time mysteriously stopped? That's just bullshit occult fantasy! But I believe this—whoever stays alone in the King's Chamber, as Napoleon once did, just might visualize his own future.

Otieno feels a slight chill as he reaches the end. An enormous concrete block seals the opening to the chamber. Knowing Hughes' genius and obsession with electronic wizardry, he guesses the block to be a holographic illusion and steps through the middle. Once inside the Inner Sanctum he takes it all in. Small bundles of newspapers, discarded Kleenex, yellow writing pads, and used BIC pens. A few crumpled messages to Maheu lie at the foot of an empty reclining chair. Hughes' Zenith television is on, but he's nowhere to be seen.

"Mr. Hughes, are you here?"

The television and a large movie screen provide most of the light in the narrow, rectangular arcanum, as Otieno scans more closely for a hint of the inhabitant. On the screen, a large-breasted Jane Russell lounges seductively on a bed of straw, gazing sleepily at him. The gravity-defying bra that Hughes once designed for her hides little from imagination.

"Mr. Hughes. Your ambulance is ready," Otieno calls out.

Howard remains hidden. Otieno clears some Kleenexes from the floor and a small cockroach scurries away. But the Kleenex gives him an idea.

"Okay, Mr. Hughes," he says, knowing it's physically impossible to complete the expulsing reflex of a sneeze, unless one's eyes are closed. He covers his nose, keeping his eyes open, threatening to fill the room with germs. "I'm going to sneeze!"

"Ahhh...ahhhh...ahhhhhhh..."

"No, no, please!... Don't do that!"

Hughes' twanging, high-pitched voice pleas desperately. As with many of the privileged, he has never had to clean up a personal space and tolerates living in his debris, but not the thought of other humans' microbes invading his territory or having to clear up his immediate surroundings.

A mechanical humming fills the arcanum and a hint of his form slowly materializes. Suspended by several steel wires, a white mummy-shaped form descends from the Pyramidal apex into the King's Chamber. With an intricate network of wired connections fanning out from an electrical umbilical cord that feeds into the caudal center, it's electronically tied to the Pyramid's circuitry. The controller of the mummy can initiate communications, or receive them, and as it nears the floor it bifurcates, unfolding like a huge clam.

"I insist. Otieno, I insist that you don't sneeze."

In all his sequestered glory, Howard evokes a momentary gasp as he awkwardly emerges from his cushioned seat in the cybernetic enclosure. Once six-foot-three, he's now several inches shorter, gaunt, and fifty pounds lighter. Still, he looks in relatively better health after his hair and nail trimming during the outing in the Spruce Goose. He wears the previous outfit: old dungarees, canvas sneakers, and a soiled white shirt hanging loosely over his narrow frame.

"Good...uh...good afternoon, Mr. Hughes. I believe you called for an ambulance?"

Otieno reaches into his Gore-Tex suit and removes some Kleenex. He covers his right hand before extending it to his ex-boss, who ignores the gesture of a handshake.

"Yes, that's right. And please don't ever try to shake my hand. You are Otieno, aren't you?"

So, it's possible, Otieno thinks, *after all these years the man still remembers me. And perhaps he knew all along about my ethnicity. The Gore-Tex suit I'm wearing still hides my color and microbes.*

"Otieno's the name. What's your game?"

Hughes nods toward a stool by the reclining chair, indicating he wants the visitor to sit down. He collapses back into his Barcalounger recliner and his long legs project outward.

"Well, Otieno, my body has become unacceptably old. Look at me! Just look at me! This damn mummy and high-pressure oxygen has helped my bedsores, but I keep losing weight. I can't sleep. My teeth can barely cut meat! You took care of my constipation once, but now it's worse than ever! Damn it, man, I have the world's worst hemorrhoids and they're back. I sit on the toilet for days, bored out of my mind when I have things to do. In fact, I have some very important things left to do and…frankly speaking, I'm exhausted. I...I..." Several seconds elapse before he can finish the sentence. "…I think I need your help."

The drawling voice softens as it comes to a stop. Circles beneath his eyes sink like craters to join vertical creases of skin that droop past his cheekbones.

"I understand," Otieno says.

I wonder what Hughes will do if I remove my hood? Right here, inside the King's Chamber.

"I don't need understanding, damn it. For God's sake, man, if that was all I needed I'd hire someone to understand me. Like these stupid guards and Mormons who want control of the Pyramid. Or Bob Maheu, who thinks he's in charge of the empire. Goddamn it. What I need is YOUTH! That's all I'm asking for!"

"I hear you, Mr. Hughes. I hear you. I can help you."

Howard squints his eyes.

"What's that?" he asks, cupping his good ear.

"I said, 'I hear you.'"

Otieno speaks loudly and grins while the once omnipotent Hughes leans forward, compensating for years of flying in loud planes and screaming jets. Meanwhile, he considers therapeutic alternatives.

I could Rolf him. Or maybe just a light massage, or… Do-In… No, that's skin contact. Won't work with this man. Hypnosis? He's not suggestive enough, will never work….

Okay, I have it, this is obvious...acupuncture...using the sole implants!

"And I have something designed to help you," Otieno says loudly, making sure Hughes gets the message.

"You do?"

"Yes, sir, I do, Mr. Hughes. I can't give you anything that will make you look younger—that takes too much time. You must realize, even in the 'mummy,' you can't last forever. The goal is to get you back on your feet again, so you feel like moving. Can you dig it?"

"Dig it?"

"A manner of speaking, Mr. Hughes. I've picked up a few methods since we last worked together. The 'sole' treatment is older than most therapies. It comes from the Eastern tradition and undoes painful effects of time. Fortunately, I was able to get my equipment past your guards. Now, look, you may be aware that the bottom of the foot is one of the more sensitive regions belonging to man..."

Otieno undoes Velcro along the side of the Gore-Tex suit, removes one of his shoes, and extracts a package of silver needles from the inside of a heel, not detected in the Pyramid's security system. He holds one before his subject, letting the suggestion take effect.

"Well, I don't want any foreign..."

Otieno moves expeditiously.

"No, don't worry, Mr. Hughes. These may sting a little. But, believe me, these tiny sterile needles are much safer—a lot less hassle than exploratory surgery. They're really noninvasive, and compared to the hypodermic needles you use, why, they're nothing. You don't mind laying back and letting your legs hang off the recliner? Just a little...that's right."

Otieno pulls a lever on the side of the Barcalounger as Hughes' considerable frame rolls back.

"Here we go—you're doing fine!"

His long, muscle-atrophied legs extend out like two-by-fours, and Hughes watches nervously as Otieno cleans his small needles, dousing them with alcohol from the hand sterilizing container stored on the side of his belt.

"Now, these needles are sterile, so just relax, Mr. Hughes. Imagine you're up in your airplane, and you're floating over the Earth. Think about how good you'll feel in a little while from now. I'm going to massage your feet for a moment, with gloves on. That's it…it's going to help you relax."

Otieno's voice and fingers soften the feet and anxiety of the patient, but before he begins his procedure he considers the man in the chair.

Even Hughes has a suggestive side, depending how deep his anxiety goes. Well, every one of us does, but right now I have to be the voice of his father? Or his mother? Has to be his mother. She died when he was sixteen, father at eighteen. This guy is lonely! So very lonely. But it's his mother, I'm sure it is. She nurtured him through all his childhood illnesses.

"Now, that's it. You are going to be just fine. You're at home now, with me, and we are going to lose all this pain…. We can just relax in this quiet moment…."

Otieno starts by inserting one argentous needle along the bottom surface of both feet, into a topographic locus as he aspires for the meridian balance. Several more follow.

Got to find that Chi, baby. Let those arthritic joints go loose for a minute, let go of this pain.

He continues inserting needles, following the meridian, continuing past the joints, moving up to critical points till he reaches the earlobes. Hughes protests by squinting his eyes, but allows the progression. A moment passes. Ten minutes pass and finally Hughes starts to fall asleep. And then…his eyes open.

"By God, man! I think I feel better."

"That's right, you are going to walk comfortably, Mr. Hughes. Let me help you some more. Just rest now."

Otieno inserts several more needles, choosing a few locations superiorly, moving in between the other needles till he reaches the earlobes once more. He inserts the last of the instruments and waits again.

"You know," Hughes finally exclaims, after resting twenty minutes, "I feel like walking! I want to try! Get those damn needles out."

Otieno delicately removes the needles from the bottom of the feet, placing them back in the chamber of his shoe. And then, like a newborn moose, Hughes rises awkwardly to his feet. Wobbling back and forth, stepping between the crumpled sheets of writing paper by his chair, avoiding an occasional Kleenex, he tries to hop again, as he has not done since childhood. Hughes sings out his only song.

"Bo Bop Areet!"

Chapter 23:
Margaret's Condition

Friday, 3:03 p.m.—The Hughes Hospital

After finishing Hughes therapy in the Inner Sanctum, Otieno makes the forty-nine-story descent down the Pyramid and links up again with Hinton. Clifton Urning, the Hughes Orator, has had a psychotic break and mumbles uncontrollably as he now requires transport to the Psych unit of the Hughes Hospital.

"Connected! It's...I swear...believe me...I know they're connected! Hughes supports Nixon, and Nixon controls Hughes…!"

Once Urning is delivered to the Psych Ward, Hinton and Otieno roll the empty gurney back through the soft-carpeted corridor of the hospital. They pass along a hallway decorated with photos of Hughes in his early aviator days. Sea planes, the Hercules, experimental jets, the Lockheed 14 he flew trans-continental to set a world record—all the photos suggest a man obsessed with escaping the Earth's gravity and exploring the skies, or more. The earth and humanity would not contain him, and Hinton cautiously contemplates his own strategic obsession: developing a union of drivers that will include Otieno.

"You know," Hinton begins, "we should find out whatever Hughes and Nixon are after, but even more, we've got to unify, among ourselves. Once we are organized, as drivers, we'll build a real health care system. We'll extend out to other cities and they'll follow our example. So, we've got to watch Nixon. He's against unions, especially when it comes to medicine, EMTs, and us ambulance drivers. He'll try to buy us off, Otieno, and…we'll end up back where we started."

"And where's that?"

"Powerless!"

I know this is not going to be easy, Hinton thinks, *but everything has to fall into place. Otieno is central to the union. His ambition is obvious, and I've got to win his support.*

"Speak for yourself, Hinton."

"I'm speaking for all of us, man. The drivers..."

Otieno halts the gurney in the middle of the hallway.

"And who are you to represent drivers? Just who are you?"

"Look, I just want to be part of a team, like you. I can't tell you everything just yet, but I have a plan…"

While outlining his goal of unifying the drivers and working towards universal coverage of all patients, they pass by two physicians who are discussing how to manage Margaret Lovejoy.

3:04 p.m.

"…so, the twenty-four-hour Holter test was negative on Jane Doe," Dr. Cohen comments, looking up at his partner, Dr. James, as they head for Margaret Lovejoy's room. "No significant arrhythmias, except during REM, when she was dreaming and skipped a few beats. You know, maybe you're right, this lady stopped taking her seizure meds, but there's still something strange about her."

The doctors keep their stethoscopes wrapped over their necks as they walk past the EMTs. Cohen's expression is resolute. Every disorder must have an etiology, an underlying cause, and he's determined to find the source of his patient's disorder.

"Right," James concurs, "but she's not giving us any other clues than her Dilantin level."

They walk in step down the corridor, starched coats brushing together. Cohen slows the pace, and looks up at his taller partner, who's seasoned tan and balanced physique, developed from frequent days on the golf course, contrasts with his own pale blemish and hint of a beard, reflecting long afternoons in the library.

"Well that too. But you know, Matthew, there's usually an exacerbating event in seizures...something that tips the neurons, so to speak. If she could, you know, communicate just a little, I think we could better understand the cause of both the seizure and her amnesia. Excuse me for a minute."

Cohen dictates progress notes into his hand-held tape recorder.

"Hospital Day two, Patient Jane Doe, Medical Record number 10-1-14-5-4-15-5, remains lethargic with retrograde amnesia. She recognizes time, place, and person, but only in the present. Cannot recall events prior to her seizure, which is now controlled on maintenance oral Dilantin. Physical exam unremarkable other than nystagmus and a term pregnancy. She's in her third trimester by measurement and ultrasound and the due date is unknown. Certainly not far off, at most a few weeks based on size. Radiology and laboratory studies are noncontributory. Social services—still no identified family or place of origin. She's scheduled for repeat EEG today and a spinal tap tomorrow."

"Oh really?" James interrupts, following the report. "How do you expect her to consent to a spinal tap?"

"Unlikely," Cohen answers, stopping the dictation. "Unless the family shows up. So, you and I will authorize it as physicians."

"Well, good luck. If the family doesn't show up, the business office is going to be all over this lady. In fact, they already are. Her bill is going to be excessive, and that doesn't include the ambulance transport! She's headed for City Hospital."

Friday, 3:20 p.m.— City Hospital

David Lovejoy struggles to move his forefinger. His arm is secured by leather restraints as he aims for the button to alert a nurse. Phones ring incessantly at the nursing station—each ring suggesting to him that his wife might be trying to call him. Since Friday there have been no other visitors. Each time he fights the ventilator, or tries to move from the bed, the nurse tells him everything is fine, then tightens his restraints.

The local youth gangs, known as the "Knife and Gun Club," were active the night before. Beds adjacent to him are filled with victims of drive-by shootings and violence, and the overworked, understaffed nurses take on each crisis as it develops, helping the medical residents to stabilize the sickest patients. As a stable asthmatic, David's considered low priority and remains on the ventilator only because there's not enough time for respiratory therapists to wean him off. On the triage list, Lovejoy has little urgency compared to the night's E.R. admissions—gunshot wounds, strokes, myocardial infarctions, car accidents, and blunt head injuries. Unable to reach the alert button, David contemplates the situation.

And if I disconnect from the ventilator? If I dislodge this bloody tube in my throat, dragging and rubbing the back of my tongue? God almighty, how many days have I been on this machine? I would give everything, I swear, just for one ice cube, I promise, God. No, better than an ice cube take this tube out of my throat! Let me out of this nightmare!

Never should have smoked that cigarette, left my children, left the motel. How did I ever end up here? How can I get out of this place? Where did Margaret go?

He rolls in agony as the ventilator alarm goes off.

Friday: 3:45 p.m.—From the Taxi Cab

Keeping tabs on both Margaret and David, I know that the Lovejoy children in room 623 are without their parents. But my job is straightforward: get ahold of the Code. Do not get involved with American family issues. Their vacation has gone sour and the children are without parents, but it's not my concern. Then things get more complicated. From Florida, Domingo phones on a secure line….

"Tango, how are you doing? Have you found the Code?"

"No, not yet. I'm closer each day. I have a job working at night for Medical. I convinced this ambulance company that I know the city well and can handle any kind of emergency. So Haldeman bought into it! Sometimes Nixon comes to visit the office, and I will have access to him."

Looking out the window of the phone booth, I watch the pedestrians on Virginia Avenue. There's Domingo in some similar booth in Miami, but I know he's only relaying messages from Blackbeard in Cuba.

"And will you see him? Will you get close to Nixon?"

"I don't know." I rub my goatee. "Why does that matter? I am here only to find the Code."

"Blackbeard wants to know. You must find out and prepare for whatever he tells you to do. Of course, there will be more."

Domingo never surprises me. My pathway into the inner circles began while serving on the widest of the three anillos, or rings that were arranged for Castro's protection. The third ring was the largest, with thousands of men assigned to cover logistics and military protection when needed. The second ring, or "operational group", was made up of around 80 top soldiers, and the first ring, known as the "escolta" had two teams of hand picked elite soldiers who covered Fidel twenty-four hours a day. Everyone in the escolta has to be a sharp shooter.

When I made it to the top team they recognized my language skills and switched me to G2, or the Direccion de la Inteligentisia, where I received more special training. And then it was off to Miami, and now Washington DC. I'm never quite sure who I'm serving in this capacity. The Soviet KGB is stepping over the Czechoslovakia intelligentsia, the G2 tries to maneuver through both of them, but my allegiance has to be to Cuba, which means Castro. Sometimes I wonder how it would be to just drive a taxi and work for myself.

Chapter 24:

"The Bay of Pigs Thing"

4:00 p.m.—The president's yacht

"We're on a short vacation," Nixon shouts over the low rumbling of a forty-four-liter diesel engine to his audience, "and a post-election strategy session. We're working to solve the health care system, and deliver 'peace with honor' in Vietnam, so you'll have more to report on when we return."

The ninety-foot *Sequoia* heads out onto the Potomac River. As he waves to anxious reporters and photographers standing on the dock, the protecting security guards on the yacht make it difficult for him to stay in view for photos, but the press shouts last questions.

"You can tell the public," he continues, raising a finger and choosing his words, "that this is a private trip. I'll be back in time to win the re-election."

"When will you return?" a newsman yells, the yacht already motoring downriver.

"Soon. Before the vote!"

He waves from a distance and there's a silence as the reporters head back to their cars. Part of what he says is true: they'll miss him. With the Democratic party in disarray and with no strong candidates running opposition, it's certain he'll be re-elected.

Without the president there's no story!

Standing next to the teak railing of the cruiser, Nixon watches the reporters disappear and looks down at the dark, silt-laden Potomac, ruminating on history.

You reach a high point in life—at a pinnacle right now for me—and some horrible unraveling always seems to take place. I've done all I can to advance health care in the country, let market forces compete freely. The economic system is good; my drivers are dedicated—the best. I'm all but guaranteed to win the election. But those goddamn hidden records about the Hughes donations, they must be locked up in O'Brien's desk in the Watergate office building. And the Bay of Pigs thing. If Therapy finds out I tried to assassinate Castro it looks bad. Well, nothing to make me look bad if the evidence disappears. Or do the democrats know something more? I hope to hell those Plumbers know what they're doing. Haldeman thinks the first break-in was a waste and I just wonder what they're up to now!

"The press has to be watched," Nixon tells Kisman, who stands next to him on the *Sequoia* as they cruise downriver. He indicates the reporters who are driving back to their offices. "They attack you like piranhas—a finger here, a toe there. They always find an exposed surface. Do you think Lincoln ever had to deal with reporters like this?" Nixon glances over at the Lincoln Monument as they motor by.

"Probably, certainly he did," Kisman acknowledges, adjusting his glasses. "But realize this. I'm watching everyone. It's as important to watch forces inside as the ones outside. 'Always keep your enemies close to you.' That's what Sun Tzu says in *The Art of War*."

The *Sequoia* cruises out into deeper waters, silently passing the Hughes airport, as the two men discuss the "Football," carrying the formulas that control the nuclear arsenal—the code for strategic command.

"You know, Harvey, it's not so easy to carry this responsibility, but of all the things a president is expected to do, it may be the most crucial, don't you think? Our security forces oversee submarines and missiles that carry enough nuclear weapons to destroy every major city in the world. Of course, it has to be a defense strategy, but I make the final decision if and when to launch. And, well, I've been thinking about some smaller missiles, I mean weapons. I mean, you know, for Vietnam. What do you think?"

"I don't think so."

Below deck the security guards play cards. The aide-de-camp has the "Football" secured to his wrist with a steel chain.

Odd, Nixon reflects, *I've never been on a submarine, let alone a strategic bomber. Nor do I ever meet the men who release the missiles. I'm the only one with access to the Football, yet I've never even seen the Code. I have this "Biscuit" that let's me open it up. But what the hell ... Kennedy never used it. I hope I never have to.*

Day 4, Friday, 5:30 p.m.—The Social Club

"The unions are losing," Otieno announces, as he and Hinton leave the ambulance and take an elevator to his apartment building. "And the power of the individual has dominated. What I'm telling you is, if you stay on the bottom you don't help people. Unions, in case you haven't noticed, are on the bottom. Change comes from the top! We have to change the top in order to bring up the bottom."

"Well, we're heading up together," Hinton insists. "What I'm saying is, when we don't work together, we stay on the bottom. If we, as drivers, were to join up, Otieno, we'd be all the stronger. Management will begin to see things our way."

"Management sees things only one way, Hinton. Through power. You want to build a group, that's fine. But we don't have time to be underdogs, so I suggest you follow me. I'll show you change."

Hinton's jaw tightens. As they enter Otieno's apartment, he walks over to the window, thinking through his strategy. When he looks out at the street his hands begin to move, as if he were giving a speech. His face softens and he begins to smile, like someone about to win an argument. Otieno goes to the aquarium and feeds the fish, which float slowly toward the surface.

"It's only when we work together that we effect change. The underdogs are those who fail to organize together. Surely you must know that?" Hinton announces.

The loud staccato rings of the hotline phone distract Otieno, as he takes a new call from Haldeman.

"Let's go!" he tells Hinton. "We got a little action at the Social Club."

Hinton forgets the argument as they head back to Car 45. Within seconds red lights are flashing and they drive onto the freeway. The sun slides behind the skyline while the panorama of dusk creates a strange effect. Sharp-angled cement buildings mold together to form a dark interface against the sky, and the somber, mechanical whine of the ambulance diffuses the surrounding noise of traffic. Otieno plays the soundtrack of *Shaft* and looks at his partner as they pass down the emergency lane.

"Hinton!"

"Yeah?"

"Know what time it is?"

"Six-thirty, maybe. Why?"

"Six-thirty on a Saturday evening. Know what that means?"

"Everybody's off work?"

Otieno chortles, pulling his gloves on as he steers the car with the bottom of his knee.

"That's right, man, everyone's off work. And it's Idiot Hour!"

Each time a car blocks their way, Otieno activates the siren. Like a dog working a flock of sheep, the sound corrals divergent vehicles back into the slower lanes and they race past.

"Idiot Hour?"

"Where you been? Nobody misses Idiot Hour in this town. See outside that window? All those people just got paid, or collected welfare. Money flows, memory rolls, where it goes nobody knows. Whiskey, women, rotgut wines. Pills and crack, snortin' lines. Sniffin' glues, singin' blues. Man, it's Saturday night and these folks are gonna be falling, crawling, and you know something else?"

"What's that?"

"We're gonna pick 'em up!"

They come off the freeway as he switches off the siren and radios in their position, simultaneously waving to the early evening prostitutes standing on the corners. They wait next to bars and cheap motels and some wave at the ambulance.

"There goes the funky Trash Queen."

Otieno nods at an old woman pushing a shopping cart full of aluminum cans. Her dog, leashed to the cart, howls at them. Traffic thins as they continue through the indigent side of town, and after they run several red lights the Social Club comes into view. Surrounded by rundown apartments, it has neon lights on the roof announcing its neighborhood status. Positioned by the front doors, a SWAT team squats and listens to sporadic gunfire inside. The overhead lights of Car

45 blend with those revolving over the police cars outside, and every few seconds they illuminate a police team as well as spectators watching from behind cars.

"Here, put this on." Otieno hands Hinton a lead vest.

"We're going in?" Hinton asks, listening to another sharp crack of gunfire.

"Watch out for the police, now," Otieno answers, as he turns off loudspeakers on his ambulance. The street falls silent, then a tear gas canister is fired into the bar. Within seconds the inhabitants stream out of the doors to be met by the police. The cops search the escaping crowd for weapons, and the few carrying guns are disarmed, arrested, and pushed into the back of a paddy wagon.

"People tend to get silly, so we dress for the occasion," Otieno adds, handing Hinton a helmet with a shatterproof facemask. Then he flicks a switch on the dashboard. The silence of the street is broken as a rap rhythm pulsates from speakers on the top of the ambulance, loud and syncopated with the lights. The music flows outward and Otieno's body becomes a blur as he maneuvers the gurney from the street to the doors of the club and disappears inside.

Hinton slips on his helmet and rushes to the side of the building, where the police remain poised with their rifles. Inside Otieno can be seen whirling past tables and chairs as he holds the gurney up in the air. He makes his way to a victim, setting him onto the gurney in scoop and run fashion, and rolls him out. Quick assessment in the street reveals the man has no major bleeding and stable vital signs, so both he and Hinton return to the bar to search for other casualties.

After the round up, the head of the SWAT team wanders over to Car 45.

"Otieno!" Lieutenant Gordon Liddy announces, taking off his gas mask and holstering his handgun. He smiles under his thick mustache and baldhead. “Got a new man working with you, hey? I think he needs a haircut.”

Chapter 25:

The Final Break-in

Friday, June 16, 1972, 8:05 p.m.—The Watergate hotel building

Evening traffic is heavy as Lieutenant Liddy speeds across town, the wind rushing through his open Jeep as it weaves in and out of traffic. He fumes over his situation of coming up empty after multiple attempts at a Watergate break-in, and the danger of his final one.

Goddamn McCord. Hasn't found a scintilla of dirt from those bugs he planted at O'Brien's office. Nothing besides a few conversations between prostitutes and the DNC employees. The whole thing is an embarrassment so far and for Christ's sake, it looks like I can't deliver. Nixon's people think I'm an idiot!

Heading down Independence Avenue, away from the district jail and City Hospital, he passes a multitude of low-income homes before heading southwest from City Hall. The Pyramid looms high on the left. Continuing toward the river he heads for the Watergate complex while plotting his re-entry.

This time I'll be in control. The Plumbers are going to follow my orders, not Hunts.

Adrenalin wells up as he draws closer to the Watergate hotel and the adjacent convention building.

Best real estate in town! The answer's here, and whatever Therapy knows about Nixon, we'll soon be finding out.

He gets delayed by a traffic patrolman who doesn't recognize him and pulls his Jeep over for shooting through a red light. Gordon begs forgiveness showing his FBI badge.

"Special mission," he explains. "I'm late because of a skirmish in the ghetto. I'd appreciate some assistance, if you'd just let me go."

The cop, acknowledging the badge, lets him pass and he continues racing across the city to make up for lost time, parking a block away from the Watergate buildings. As he approaches the complex he glances over at the Potomac, flowing ever so slowly, destined for the Chesapeake Bay. Elemental water brings sky back to Earth, separated but joined in the night air.

"Good evening, sir."

Liddy nods silently to the hotel doorman, who recognizes the mustache and heavy eyebrows from the visit a few days earlier.

8:08 p.m.—Laying down the tape

Howard Hunt parks a Pontiac Firebird in the underground garage of the Watergate Hotel, then takes the elevator to Room 214. He taps sharply on the door.

"Who is it?"

"Eduardo," Hunt answers, revealing his code name. "Hurry up!"

The door opens slowly and Hunt edges through, acknowledging McCord and the team. Macho has removed his glasses and he and Muscalito practice with Minolta cameras, taking photos of sample documents in the corner of the hotel room, while Liddy reviews the break-in plans with

Gonzalez and Sturgis. As attention focuses on Hunt, the men gather in the center of the room. McCord hands five-watt Radio Shack transceivers to Liddy and Macho, keeping one for himself. Hunt gives each of the team two hundred-dollar bills and they slide them into their wallets.

"Just in case you have to bribe someone," Hunt tells them. "McCord will tape the locks again, to keep the doors open while Liddy and I stay here for radio contact. We'll be watching and when all the lights go out, you move. This time you photograph everything, okay? And Muscalito, here's the key to the desk where the dirt is. Be sure you find what's in there. Any questions? Good luck, and don't get caught!"

Hunt opens the door to make sure no one's outside. McCord heads out for the Watergate office building, making a brief walk alone in the humid night air. The office building is no more than thirty yards from the hotel, the two complexes being connected by an underground garage. As McCord enters the office complex, he passes a security guard who gives his dark suit and professional appearance little attention. He goes straight into the elevator and exits on the eighth floor, where he begins taping door latches from the office corridors to the stairwell. Each piece of tape is laid in a horizontal direction, though oddly the wrong direction for anyone trying to keep the tape hidden from inside the building.

When he reaches the sub-basement garage level, he calls Hunt on the walkie-talkie.

"We're ready."

10:00 p.m.—Howard Johnson's, room 723 and 623

The Howard Johnson's, directly across the street from the Watergate Hotel, appears like a huge transistor illuminating the night. McCord hears the sound of an ambulance as he leaves the Watergate complex, crosses over Virginia Avenue, and enters the motel. He knows that the "November Group," a team of democrat political associates, has learned the timing of the break-in and has tipped off the Metropolitan police as he walks quickly to room 723. Baldwin is sitting on top of a twin bed, eating a hot fudge sundae and watching the end of *Attack of the Puppet People*, and the telescope on the balcony is unattended.

"Some college kid is working late in there," Baldwin tells him. "We'll never finish this break-in if that kid doesn't get off the damn phone. And the children in the room below me make such a damn racket with their TV—it's hard to concentrate anymore. So, I put on the same program. I mean, what the hell is going on? Parents don't control their kids anymore?"

McCord walks over to the window, where he can see the lights of the sixth floor of the Watergate office building.

We're close, he thinks, as beads of sweat form on his forehead, *and its time to put an end to the search. Liddy and the boys are getting way too close. The gig is up.*

In room 623 Rebecca Lovejoy turns off *Attack of the Puppet People*, following her mother's rules of ending TV at ten o'clock at night. After spending most of the day swimming in the rooftop pool, she, Angel, and Michael are worn out and ready to sleep. If her mother and father fail to return, she's resolved to call the police in the morning. But she continues to hope they'll arrive at any moment.

11:51 p.m.—Watergate security

Hank Mills arrives early for the midnight shift and begins his security tour, examining the basement level of the Watergate office building. He's surprised to discover the lock of the basement/stairwell door has been taped horizontally. When he pulls on the handle he sees how the tape hugs and sticks to the door's edge, holding a plug of paper that keeps the latch in place. The easy swing of the door sparks suspicion, but not too much.

Strange! The maintenance men usually leave the tape in a horizontal fashion when they work on the day shift, making it obvious they need access. But, something seems afoot, and there have been recent burglaries. If it's not maintenance, then who?

Perfunctorily, he removes the tape so that the latch snaps out to lock the door and continues his rounds. When he gets back to his desk, he calls his superior, but only gets the answering service. He leaves a message and then he's called back and his boss tells him to see if any other doors in the building are taped

"Call me back again and let me know."

Before following up, Mills runs into a college kid who's been staying late in the sixth-floor office, making long-distance phone calls to his friends, and now has to sign out on leaving the building. The two strike up a conversation and decide to go to HoJo's to get takeout food. Will a cheeseburger, fries, and milkshake really make a difference, he wonders, if something is going on? Unlikely, he decides. The draw of a cheeseburger outweighs the minimal danger of a robbery. He waits for his food and walks slowly back to the Watergate office building.

Saturday, June 17, 1:05 a.m.— the Watergate Hotel, room 214

Hunt and Liddy sip on Cokes, watching the rerun of *Attack of the Puppet People*, waiting to hear back from the break-in team via radio, when McCord knocks on the door. He's let in without hesitation, followed by Macho and Muscalito, the Cuban exiles.

"We've run into another problem," McCord tells them. "The tapes have been removed from the locks by security. We have to decide what to do. I left Gonzalez and Sturgis to pick the lock. If you want us to push ahead, we're ready."

Liddy looks at his partner, worried about the situation but equally concerned about not coming up with any revealing information after multiple attempts. Or setting up bugs in the sixth-floor office, as McCord was instructed to do. He considers the options.

We were hired to produce something. We've already been paid and, for Christ's sake, I can't screw this up! Hunt must want a successful caper as bad as me. He's got years of experience and it seems like there's more going on than just missing tapes on the locks.

"Let's scratch it," Hunt urges, not happy that the taped doors were discovered.

Macho and Muscalito both sense that things are going south, but haven't yet smelled the skunk.

"Gonzalez can pick the locks," McCord argues. "I think we can get in and get what we need. I think we should proceed."

Liddy hesitates a minute.

Hunt and I are relatively safe, observing from a distance. McCord's going in with the Cubans so he's the one at risk. If he wants to press on, then it's probably still feasible and safe.

James McCord is FBI. He's done this kind of work before, so he must know what he's doing...

"All right, let's get going," Liddy announces, unaware that McCord is still working for the CIA.

They check once more with Baldwin, who's watching from room 723 of Howard Johnson's. He confirms that the lights are still out in the office building. By the time McCord and his two men reach the underground garage, Gonzalez has picked the lock and the Plumbers begin their final ascent of the stairwell.

1:30 a.m.—HoJo's and the Watergate

Having missed the end of *Attack of the Puppet People*, the Lovejoy children fall asleep in the front room of room 623. Baldwin stands on the balcony of room 723, and keeps his eye on the sixth floor of the Watergate office building.

On the ground floor of the Watergate, Hank Mills finishes his cheeseburger, fries, and milkshake. After walking back from HoJo's restaurant along Virginia Avenue, he's almost forgotten the taped door business. Now he begins a second tour of the basement of the office building, and is surprised to find tape placed vertically over the door latch once more. It's time to call his boss again.

1:47 a.m.

After receiving direction from his superior, Mills calls the police.

1:52 a.m.

Macho, Muscalito, Gonzalez, and Sturgis are out of breath by the time they reach the sixth-floor landing. Sweating in their dark business suits and rubber gloves, they make their way to the darkened DNC office hallway, but the rear door still has to be picked.

"Cabron!" Gonzalez swears in Spanish.

"Hurry up and pick it, Speedy," Muscalito urges.

"You just watch the stairwell. I can get us in."

He explores the lock with metal probes.

"I'll get this son of a bitch," Gonzalez curses, throwing down probes and opening his bag again. With a hammer and chisel, he begins on the upper hinge, tapping in an upward direction. The hinge barely budges, so he hammers with force.

"Cabron! Hijo de…!"

His grunts and the pounding of steel against steel echoes into the cave-like hallway. Then they hear footsteps running toward them.

"Holy shit!"

"Who is it?" Sturgis asks, anxiously.

"It's me! It's me! What are you doing?"

McCord, out of breath from climbing up the stairs, appears in front of the doorway. The Cubans breathe more easily and Gonzalez resumes pounding on the upper hinge. Finally, sweat glistening on his forehead, he succeeds in freeing the door.

"Let's go. Let's go. Let's get what we came for!" As they walk into the DNC complex and head for the executive office, McCord stops at the secretary's desk and inserts a lightweight transmitter underneath the housing. The others remove documents from file cabinets. Martínez pulls out a small key and is about to open the bottom drawer of the secretary's desk when he hears static coming from Barker's walkie-talkie.

2:20 a.m.—Room 623

Rebecca Lovejoy is awakened by the sound of a siren. She climbs over her brother, asleep on the floor, and goes to the sliding glass door of the motel balcony. Before closing it, she looks out and sees a set of lights brighten up the eighth floor of the Watergate office building across the street. In less than a minute the seventh-floor lights go on. Then, there's a man on a balcony just above her speaking into a transmitting device.

"Base One to Unit Two, are our people in suits or are they dressed casually?"

She looks back at the Watergate office building and notices a group of men heading down from the seventh floor.

"Our people are dressed in suits," she hears someone radioing to the man above her.

Then the man above her says loudly, "Well, I'm looking at guys with long hair, and it looks like they have guns!"

Rebecca hears radio static and then the man above her saying, "Base one to Unit One, you have some trouble because there are some individuals out here who are dressed casually and have got their gun out."

2:21 a.m.—The search for the Code

Macho places a key into the secretary's desk just before he sees the lights go on. He pulls out a single classified letter and opens it. Several numbers—1 19 20 8 25 21 5 12 6—are written inside a drawing of a football. He ducks down on his knees, trying to decipher the message as Barker's walkie-talkie emits static…then...

"One to Two...are you reading this?" he hears Liddy calling out, having been alerted by Baldwin of the police presence. "Are you reading this? Come in, that's an order!"

"Two, this is One. Jesus, there's guys with guns in here. It looks bad. Listen, I think I just located part of the Code. It has something to do with the Football. It says the Code is inside the Football and…"

Liddy hears a rustling noise, then silence. As he looks out the window of the hotel, he sees more police cars and a Therapy ambulance parked next to the entrance of the office building.

Rebecca looks down from the Howard Johnson's balcony at the flashing lights. The police sirens now have her wide-awake, but Angel and Michael remain sleeping on the rug next to the TV.

Shoot, I haven't seen Dad since Wednesday! Mom disappeared Thursday, and now what are those guys doing over there? How come there's police cars and an ambulance? I don't trust the police. They look way too scary. Tomorrow I'm going to find Dad and maybe we don't need cops anyway! I just need my dad!

2:27 a.m.—Room 722

I watch from the saferoom, just above the Lovejoy children, running fingers over my goatee. Listening to the Plumbers' communications through earphones, I just have to laugh.

The first dominoes are falling in the Nixon administration, even if I haven't yet discovered the Code for Castro. These strange and misled Plumbers...and their awkward attempts at spying! Nixon wants to know if the democrats have any dirt or information on the money Hughes gave to him. Kisman is spying on Haldeman. And all of them are spying on each other. Meanwhile, the democrats are deep into their ranks! Ha! My unfortunate expatriates...the renegade Plumbers...are headed for jail. The plumbing there may not be so good either, but If they were in Cuba, they'd just be executed. Well, they got too close to the Colombia Plaza, and now they'll be joined by McCord. Hunt and Lieutenant Liddy will be next!

Day 5

Dr. Noah

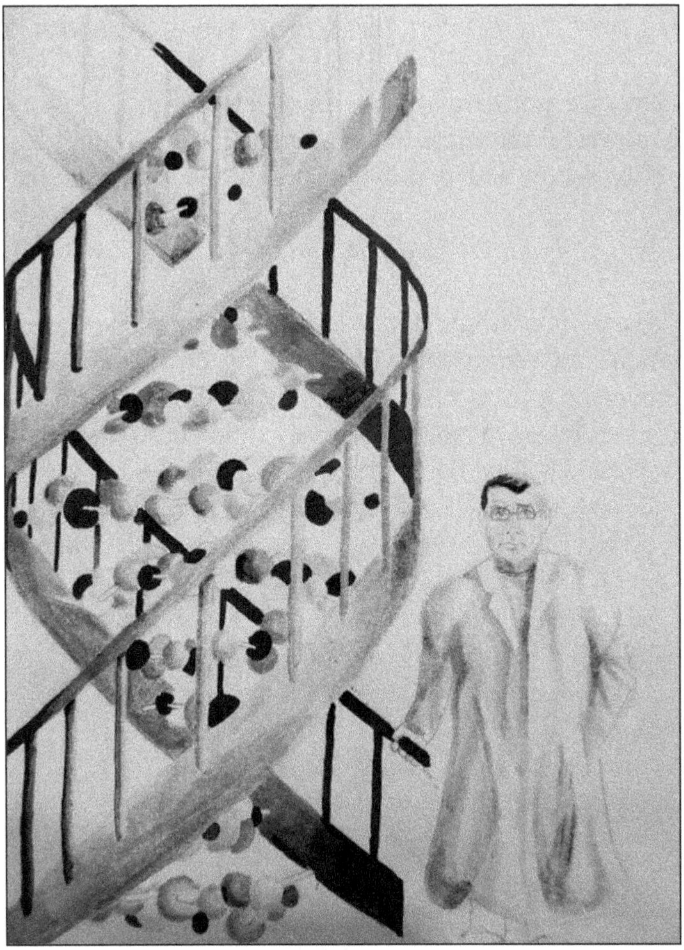

"As we know, the DNC contained an explosive secret: its relationship to prostitutes at the Columbia Plaza Apartments. And what McCord was determined to preserve was the monopoly that his secret principals held on that relationship. Neither he nor the agency wanted the Colombia Plaza operation exposed, and neither were they willing to share everything with the Nixon administration.

—Jim Hougan, Secret Agenda, 1984

"Take care not to make the intellect our god; it has, of course, powerful muscles, but no personality. It cannot lead, it can only serve; and it is not fastidious in its choice of a leader."

—Albert Einstein, Out of my Later Years, 1943

"I guess it's ironic that I haven't toppled Castro's government but was involved in bringing down the head of government of my own country; and that Castro, who tried several times to assassinate me, never could get to me, but my country put me behind bars."

—Frank Sturgis, Watergate burglar, 1974, as told to his nephew

"Watergate. We went in. We got caught. Nixon resigned."

Bernard "Macho" Barker, 2007

Chapter 26:

Colson Meets Cryogenics

Saturday, June 17, 1972, 7:45 a.m.—Room 623

So the plumbers have been apprehended and my attention turns to the Lovejoy family, in the room next to me. It's my day off as night dispatcher and I follow four-year-old Michael, who lies sleepily with his head beneath the television, studying the cottage cheese ceiling of their motel room. Angel sprawls loosely on the shag rug, and Rebecca, on the fold-out couch, remains asleep as the air conditioner hums a monotonous tune.

When's Mommy going to wake us up? That air conditioner makes too much noise. She always wakes Rebecca first but I bet now I can turn on the television. She never lets me watch before breakfast.

Rebecca and Angel start to move as Michael twists the on button and the Road Runner beeps a staccato message from the TV. The beep-beep alerts both girls. Angel goes to the bedroom, looking for their mother, and Rebecca covers her head with a pillow.

"She's not here," Angel reports, her lips tight and eyes squinting with anger.

"Maybe she's sick. Maybe she's having a baby?" Michael asks, after changing the cartoon channel. "I'm hungry!"

Rebecca twists her long legs around the side of the cot. As she sits up and rubs her eyes, she remembers the events from the night before and goes to the window to see if the police are still outside. The streets are now alive with morning traffic and the Watergate buildings, curved and statuesque, give no further hints of turbulence or police cars and sirens. The motel room is still scattered with paper plates left over from dinner. On the floor she sees the "Covenant" signed by Angel, Michael, and herself, agreeing to work together and take care of the room till their mother comes home. Remembering the police in the middle of the night, she resolves to take control of the situation.

"Okay, Angel, you and Michael start getting dressed. I'm going to go get us some breakfast. But first you both have to clean up all this stuff from last night like you said you would."

Saturday, 8:00 a.m.—The District Jail

Having been stripped, searched, and then put in prison denims, the Plumbers wait for a promised attorney to come and provide bail. Frank Sturgis acts as the legal representative as they wait.

"You have a right to remain silent. Say nothing and do nothing to incriminate yourselves. If they ask you what you were doing, just say you were fighting communism. We were just serving our country—isn't that right?"

Frank's chin protrudes and his chest swells. Having been bullwhipped in Batista's El Morro prison, the District of Columbia jail is not intimidating. True, he doesn't have an AK-47 resting on his knee. When he stood over the mass grave of Batista's soldiers in 1959, he was confident that working for Castro would bring freedom for Cuba. And now the president should bring about clemency and a safe ride home to his wife in Miami, and some freedom in America.

"Boys," McCord reassures them, "we will be looked after. Let's all keep quiet. Just say nothing and wait for the support."

I know Sturgis can easily weather through a D.C. police agency. There's very little that puts fear in his heart. He enjoys putting his life on the line for democracy and liberty and with anti-war terrorists bombing the Pentagon, it's perfectly reasonable to act on Hunt's orders and break Daniel Ellsberg's legs, break into the Chilean Embassy, and certainly to break into the Watergate to expose Castro's misdeeds. Freedom has to be earned!

McCord, on the other hand, knows he is likely to end up in prison, and expects the CIA will spring him free. But he should know better. Even a mole, a double agent like myself, has to be prepared for incarceration. Muscalito? He wanted out of the operation before it ever happened, and now there's nothing he can do. He, along with Gonzalez and Sturgis are screwed. So, I let Domingo know, who in turn tells Blackbeard, that I'm getting closer to the Code. Fidel will know that as well. We're all searching for the same thing, but I'm the only one who's close.

And then I begin to learn about the strangest of the Medical EMTs, a scientist named Noah, who has a function separate from Colson, Deed, and Otieno. While Colson and Deed display sensation and intuition, personality types driven by events rather than shaping them, Otieno is the feeling type, always pushing for social justice. But Noah is the thinker of the team. He's spying on the most distant goal of all – immortality.

8:10 a.m.—Dr. Noah's laboratory

The Saturday morning *Times* describes the break-in of the Therapy headquarters, but the public pays little attention. Break-ins are common in the District. They're unusual in the exclusive Watergate buildings, however, and a reporter named Wayword embarks on a deeper investigation, wondering why James McCord, a CIA man, should be involved.

Aware that the Plumbers were captured, and that his man, Howard Hunt, might get identified, Colson is concerned too. But he spends the day working with Dr. Noah, whose work as a driver differs distinctly from his other partners. Noah's living quarters are based in the depths of a large nuclear reactor research center, at the outskirts of the city, where he's engaged in a series of projects. There's a large laboratory beneath the reactor, and he shares one of his experiments with his partner for the day.

"It's all perfectly clear," Noah says, showing Colson a mouse suspended in liquid nitrogen, an example of Cryonic preservation.

"Well, so it is! I can see his little paws."

Surrounded by stainless steel tanks and cylinders, they examine the specimen inside a thermos-like container. The frozen mouse looks back with motionless eyes, from beneath the glass-covered container with its sides coated with a layer of frost. Noah passes the receptacle from the right hand to the left to diminish the pain of the ice-cold metal, and then gives it to Colson.

"You mean *her* paws, Colson. It's an impregnated mother. And when we thaw her out, we'll see how the freeze affects the offspring."

"Oh, well, I guess I understand, Noah. Baby mice-cycles! Ha!" Colson hands the frozen creature back to Noah, who lowers it into a larger canister containing liquid nitrogen. A fine mist rises up into his glasses as the animal disappears, and Noah responds through frosted lens.

"That's quite funny. Now let me ask you something. Have you ever thought of living forever?"

Colson's eyebrows lift up. He adjusts his glasses and tries to smile at Noah, as crow's feet spread out laterally from his eyes, deepening his expression

"Not me, Doc. Not like that, anyway. I guess you're talking about Cryogenics for humans, and you can do whatever you want with those little mice. I prefer staying warm. Frankly, I get cold just looking around this place."

He focuses on the stainless-steel ceiling-high tanks, set on platforms with connecting pipes, gauges, and shut-off valves that line the sidewalls. A steel laboratory bench at the end of the room supports a series of cages, which give off the dank smell of urine and enclosed animals.

"Well, cold's a relative sensation, Chuck. What's a little cold compared to extended life? Even without your own blood!"

"Excuse me?" Colson shivers involuntarily.

"Well, let's just say we use a blood substitute during the Cryonic storage period. Different from our native fluid since the substitute doesn't clot and can keep essential veins and arteries open. Studies show that when you return from the frozen state your organs can't function if they don't receive oxygen right up to the point of freezing. Natural blood just doesn't tolerate that kind of cold. Certainly not a temperature of minus 196 degrees Celsius. So, we need a blood substitute. And volunteers, of course. That is, if we're going to prove the possibility of extended life."

Colson smiles as Noah sets the larger canister next to a series of other containers.

"Sure, Doc, I know about cold. I can tell you a few things."

"Can you really?" Noah's fish eyes turn toward his rotund partner. "And are you prepared to do something for science?"

8:15 a.m.—City Hospital

David Lovejoy wakes to a catheter sliding down the larger tube in his throat and windpipe, suctioning deep in his lungs, causing spasms of coughing. He looks at the ventilator and the myriad electronic monitors displaying heart rate, blood pressure, and ventilator settings. Alarms sound rapidly as the nurse stops suctioning and his coughing paroxysms slow. His arms are fixed by gauze restraints.

Hooked like a fish inside here, trapped like a damned animal in a cage! The IV the nurse started last night is not running, the pump keeps beeping, and how long's it been? Days? Weeks? Margaret? Where did she go? She must be with the kids, but why isn't she coming back? These nightmares multiply and it's worse when I wake! I would love to see that medical student again who tried to help me, but he's disappeared. At least there was some hope when he gave me a pencil and paper and now he's gone, along with Margaret.

I'm a bloody executive, for Christ's sake! Maybe a junior one, not on the Board, but all this happens and I end up in City Hospital. How long does it take to arrange a transfer to a private hospital? Where the hell are the doctors?

Lovejoy watches the nurse collect her suctioning equipment and leave the bedside. And then air stops coming through the breathing tube. Within seconds alarms begin sounding on the ventilator, the heart rate and O2 saturation monitors alarm, and he feels himself sink as the surroundings go dark.

Chapter 27:

Beginning the Cover-Up

June 18, 8:25 a.m.—Car 38

Car 38 pulls into the parking lot of the Medical Ambulance headquarters and Deed sits on the passenger side, more nervous than usual as he monitors the radios. He hasn't read the *Times* article, but he knows an investigation of the break-in is underway and that it could lead to him.

A cover-up has to start now. President's out of town. Haldeman will give Nixon the news: "Thieves caught red-handed breaking into the DNC at the Watergate." He'll go ballistic when he finds out!

He runs the scenario through his mind. Who can leak the origin of the Plumbers?

There's Liddy. He orchestrated the strategy, but never really knew what it was for. He's to Nixon like the moon to the Earth, so he'll never snitch. Then again, if he's crazy enough to let the Plumbers get caught, he can't be trusted. Howard Hunt—even less trustworthy. And James McCord, the CIA man who manages to get caught! He's a loose cannon. If the break-in origin unravels it can spell the end for Nixon and...well, that includes me. In fact, I'll probably become the scapegoat!

There's this new driver, Hinton, who just joined us. Is he some kind of spy? All his talk about a union? He's after information and he has to be watched, but how much does he know? Will anyone know about the Columbia Plaza?

Deed's thoughts are interrupted as he hears over the police radio that Liddy and Hunt are being sought after.

"I'm going in for morning report," he tells Muriel, as she fixes her hair in the driver's seat. "Stay on the radio and keep track of things. We may even need to leave town for a little while."

"You think they'll be coming after you, Jim?" she asks, her blue eyes wide and hazy as she secures an elastic ring to pull her hair close, forming a precise bun just above her neck.

"No. So long as the FBI and CIA do separate investigations and get stopped. We're okay. They're still too busy chasing each other to go after me. But the FBI is more of a problem. They might investigate where the money came from, and start spilling to the press all the connections…well…and there's still the Plaza to worry about too…."

"So, what about the president?"

"He'll try to get the CIA to stop the FBI going any deeper. He can tell them national security is at stake, and he can threaten to blow the story of how the CIA organized the Bay of Pigs, which they have to keep hidden. We'll be all right, Muriel. Things could get a little ugly. I have to protect all of us, including Heidi, and you."

Deed looks around the parking lot. The Trash Queen pushes her cart of aluminum cans out onto the street and her dog follows sleepily behind.

"Well, watch out for Haldeman!" she cautions.

"No, he needs to watch out for me," Deed says, leaving the ambulance.

Inside Car 38 Muriel continues monitoring the radios and considers the events.

Amusing. The president always thinks the break-in is about secret information related to his Howard Hughes *donations. Big deal—his brother got $250,000, and Bebe Rebozo only got $100,000. Don't those investigators understand why the telephones were bugged for in the first place, for the secretaries, and not O'Brien, the manager of the DNC? Typical men, assuming a break-in has to be about themselves. They ignore the call-girl ring using the DNC campaign office, because both democrats and republicans are too deeply involved. Red and blue, blue and red, democrats and republicans, they all use the ladies, that's what we know. If the Plumbers were looking for a connection between Hughes and Nixon, they just might find one, but there's so much more going on and it needs to stay quiet!*

8:32 a.m.—The Medical Office

Deed walks into the main office and sees Haldeman sitting in the barber's chair, spinning it around to watch him.

"I'm taking the day off," Deed announces, walking toward the coffeepot. "I've got to do some outside work today."

"There's plenty to do here, Golden Boy. I understand the police made a big arrest last night. Isn't that right?" Haldeman's face is tense; his tone is flat. He adjusts his tie and waits for an answer.

"How would I know?" Deed responds. "Was it in the newspaper this morning?"

"That's right. And with our boss running for re-election, there's no room for new problems. We've got an ambulance company to run. I thought you were taking care of the leaks around here. The president is up for re-election and this is hardly time for a press scandal. You follow me, Mr. Deed?"

"I've taken care of everything," Deed answers, avoiding Haldeman's eyes. "We're getting rid of the Weatherpeople, aren't we? I made sure of it the other day."

Before Haldeman can ask another question, the other drivers enter the room.

"Dig it," Otieno says, pushing the door open suddenly. "Haldeman in the barber seat. You giving orders today, boss?"

Otieno removes his gloves and smiles, but the dispatcher makes no effort to acknowledge him. Hinton comes through the door next, followed by Noah and Colson.

"Kisman's out of town, and you're late! You men know what time it is?" Haldeman demands.

"Time is relative," Noah answers, "existing within our miniscule perceptions of space and motion, measurements imposed by limited cognition. The important dimension is the future, and by now it could be over."

Haldeman rotates the barber's chair till he faces Noah, who's wearing his white laboratory coat and staring at is calculator.

"Don't lecture us, Professor. You're late! Colson, I want to see your tally sheet for yesterday and you better have a few saves. Let's see what you have."

Colson, sitting on the couch, has a takeout bag and holds up a sugarcoated donut. He looks through the hole in the direction of Noah.

"I don't have it. Dr. Noah has it."

"Where is it, Professor?"

Noah adjusts his glasses. "Where's what?"

"Tally sheet of your work. I want your tally sheet to see how many runs you made. Now give it to me please!"

"This is all I have."

Noah hands the dispatcher a sheet of paper from his brief case.

Technical Data
Liftoff Wgt. Overall Hgt.
8,254,000 Lb. (3,124,431KG) 389 Ft. (121.4M)
F-1 Engine Nozzle: Stage 1 Length Escape Tower
22 Ft (5.93M) tall, 12 Ft 6 In (3.81M) wide 137 Ft (42M) 33 Ft. 6In (10.2M)

Haldeman studies it for a few seconds, raising his brow.

"What is this crap? Some kind of rocket data! It has nothing to do with ambulances and our work here. Listen, Mr. Rocket Scientist, when I ask you for a tally sheet, you'll have to do a little better than this. You want to work with Colson for the rest of the week?"

"That would be fine with me."

Noah takes the sheet of paper and slips it back into his briefcase.

"Oh, sure it would. And you can do cabbage runs all day too. Now listen, Noah, I don't give a damn if you're a professor or a genius or whatever the heck you are. When you work for Medical, you take care of patients and you answer to Nixon and me. Or I'll take your car away!"

"No, that's impossible. You stick to your business, Mr. Haldeman. I'll take care of mine. You're not cleared for my car. It was given to me by Howard Hughes."

"And you're not cleared to leave here till I receive a tally sheet. You understand that, doctor?"

They're interrupted as the backdoor swings open.

"I will decide who goes and comes, thank you very much, Mr. Haldeman," Kisman informs them, as he enters the headquarters. His hands signal for the barber's chair to be vacated and Haldeman reluctantly steps out.

"We, uh, have some business to attend to," his baritone voice continues, the "We" coming deep and prolonged. "So, please, everyone, sit down. I'm sure you know it is essential that we, uh…as a company we are strong and cohesive."

Noah glances at Kisman, then resumes working on his calculator. Otieno fixes a cup of coffee while Hinton joins Colson and takes one of his donuts.

"We are...leaders of health care in America!" Kisman drones. "All cities look to the District, and all companies look to...us…to Medical for leadership. We guide the others, and that includes Therapy—in their little blue cars."

"Welfare people!" Colson says, scorning the competition.

"They'll learn, Mr. Colson. We continue to save patients. We won't be distracted by things newspapers print about break-ins. Nobody here cares what goes on in the offices of Therapy, do they?" He looks around the room, letting his eyes rest on Deed, who lights a cigarette. "That's good. With, uh, with all the sick people in this city, who's interested in what Therapy does, or has in its campaign office, so long as we do a better job? Isn't that right, Dr. Noah?"

Noah continues looking down, working on his calculator.

"Noah, is that right? Are you listening?"

Noah then looks briefly at Kisman, who has pumped the barber's chair higher and stares down at him.

"Did you ask something?"

"I said...oh, never mind. Tell me something, Professor. How is the, uh, design on your new rocket coming?"

"Very good. Excellent, in fact."

"Wonderful. Would you like to tell us about it?"

"No. I offered the data sheet to Mr. Haldeman, and he wasn't interested. And it's still not for general knowledge."

Noah turns back to his paperwork as the drivers look at Kisman. The manager lets out a sigh and continues.

"Very well. I ask you at a different time. Let me remind people again of how important it is for us to…set an example for others, to bring in more patients. Our jobs depend upon transport, and that includes you, Noah…Professor. We will show the drivers in their blue cars how to run a company through competitive enterprise. The market still works in this city."

Kisman takes hold of the lever on the side of the chair and cranks himself up another inch.

"Okay, today I reassign positions. The new driver, Hinton, goes to work with you, Professor Noah. He says he's a road scholar. Are you glad to hear that?"

Noah looks briefly at Hinton. Haldeman, who's entered back into the room, now stands next to the barber's chair and raises an eyebrow. His upper lip elevates a sinister smile as he studies Hinton.

"I would prefer to work with Colson," Noah protests.

"And I make the assignments," Kisman continues. "Now, Deed, where's your tally sheet?"

8:40 a.m.—The Laundry Room

Kisman reviews Deed's tally sheet while Hinton slips back to the laundry room to get a new uniform. Helen, the laundry woman, folds sheets, setting them down on a large table as he stops to admire her. Her white uniform clings tightly around her body, and her hair is pulled up in a bun like Muriel's.

"You look good, Helen. Can I tell you that? Really good. This work's not hard on your hands?"

"I'm used to cleaning up after men," she answers.

"Sure, but look at the volume. This is a big city."

"Looks like you've been getting around yourself." She nods at the catsup stain on the side of his pants, left over from fast food.

"Right. Otieno took me through the inner city. Saw some trauma and drug overdoses. Poor people having heart attacks. Strokes, pneumonias. Gunshot wounds in the ghetto. You know, this work brings us close to others when they need us."

"Does it?" she asks.

"Yeah," he responds, coming close. "It brings us together as an organization. I mean the drivers. And you, Helen," he adds, recognizing his omission. "You know laundry is critical. It's essential to what we're doing. We're saving others...and we're all working together, as a group. That's what it's all about—the service transcends politics. When we work together as a whole, as a...as a …"

"Union?" she asks, reaching over a table and running her finger along the catsup stain on his pants.

"Exactly. Right. You're always quick, Helen. But what made you say it that way?"

"All men seek a union, . But you also came in here with another purpose, to get a clean uniform, didn't you?"

He pauses, smiling. "Wait a minute. Don't change the subject. Let's talk about our plans."

"Go ahead. Take your uniform off," she says, while he smiles again, hesitating. "Give it to me," she adds, "so I can give you a clean one. And keep talking."

"Sure. As I was saying," he continues, "the underlying force that drives Medical. We've got to determine and control their direction. Once we do, it will put us in front of the political race. For universal health care that's going to be the economy that wins."

He slides out of his jumpsuit. As he talks, she notes his brawny chest.

"Strength is the foundation of negotiation, Helen. And there's a way for us to develop that strength."

"Uh-huh."

In the back of the room the radio plays "Heard it Through the Grapevine."

"Our strength will be the union. We organize. We unite. We go forward. With drivers steering this vehicle down Main Street, we move ahead and create a new health care system. That everyone has access to!"

He bends down and slides off his boots.

"Contracts?" Helen asks him.

"What?"

She reaches over and takes his dirty suit as he presses his waist against the table. She holds a clean one just beyond his reach.

"Any union is no better than the contract on which it's based. You know that, . You write things out in black and white, or they disappear. Medical and Therapy will never see things eye to eye.

He picks up his boots and laughs. "That's good, Helen. You sound just like a lawyer."

She hands him the jumpsuit. "Maybe you should."

At that moment Haldeman's figure appears in the doorway.

"Kisman wants you in the office, Hinton," he announces, his upper lip rising. "So, get your butt in there."

8:45 a.m.—Medical Office

"Time is not something you can take off whenever you want, my friend," Kisman says, as he lowers the barber's chair and focuses on Deed. "Perhaps the president asked you to do a little investigation, Jim, but he didn't tell me about it. How about you, Mr. Haldeman?"

"What's that?"

Haldeman re-enters the office without Hinton, who's still getting dressed in the laundry room.

"Deed says he wants time off to look into this Watergate-DNC break-in. He thinks he can discover what it's all about. What do you think?"

Haldeman frowns. "Well, he's got his work cut out for him. He needs to explain what the Plumbers were after, and keep us out of the picture. And maybe he should explain if he was the one who ordered the second break-in."

"That's correct." Kisman agrees. "But we forget about the importance of time and our ambulances, don't we, Deed? We're here to save lives. When we don't have cars on the road, we don't win the race, do we?"

Deed keeps silent, staring at the old news clippings on the wall—auto wrecks where drivers would scoop and run, resuscitating victims. He knows the real reason for the last break-in, and he's determined to keep it to himself.

Noah looks up from his computer.

"Race?" he asks.

"Yes, the race!" Kisman proclaims. "The race to save this city and to re-elect the president."

"Oh, it's dubious, Mr. Kisman, whether your race will ever get anywhere," Noah counters, closing his calculator and sliding it into a briefcase. "When somebody wins, somebody loses. Only the ignorant take sides."

"That's lunacy," Deed argues. "We take our own side, or somebody takes it for us!"

"Not if we take everyone's side...," Hinton says, as he enters the room. They all stare at him.

"That sounds like Therapy bullshit!" counters Colson. "The way to win is to beat the competition, with whatever it takes!"

Otieno stands up and smiles.

"Oh, the worlds like a piece of pie," he begins. "More you have, more you try. Rich get rich, poor get poor, then one day there's not much more. Hey, it's Sunday," he concludes, slapping Deed on the back. "I'm singing in the church today, so if you'll excuse me."

He slips on his gloves and heads for the door.

"Well, you see what we're up against," Kisman says, spinning on the barber's chair. "We sit around arguing who's right and who's wrong, and everything is lost. This is a business, gentlemen. There are patients to save, money to earn! Dr. Noah, you work with Hinton today. I'm sure you can educate him."

Chapter 28:

The Atomic Car

8:55 a.m.—On the way to the reactor

As Noah clicks his briefcase closed, he signals for Hinton to follow. Together they walk out to the parking lot, leaving behind Colson and Deed. Otieno heads off with Car 45 in the direction of Ward 7 as they continue toward the Atomic Car.

"So, this is it!" Hinton says, "I've heard a lot about this car."

AC, painted in large letters on the side, distinguishes the ambulance, which otherwise has a conventional appearance. Noah dials a numerical code on the passenger door to let Hinton in. There's a tall cabin with basic resuscitation equipment and a gurney in the back. Lining the upper ceiling on both sides are two large stainless-steel cylinders with *Caution*! and *Rocketdyne* written in bold letters on their sides.

"Where's the engine?" Hinton asks, noting a profusion of electronics next to the gurney and standard first aid gear. Noah dials a sequence of numbers—16 15 23 5 18—onto the dash.

"There is no engine, and there's no key," Noah answers dryly, cinching his belt on the driver's seat. "Were you looking for a nuclear reactor?"

"Right. I mean, what's it run on? You call it 'Atomic,' don't you?"

"You like to scrutinize, don't you, Hinton? Well, you won't see a gas cap, because there's no gas. Nor is there a 'nuclear' engine. It's the first all-electric ambulance, and I guess you might say 'experimental.' Lithium hybrid batteries line the underside, which are regenerated by a process of fission from our nuclear reactor research center. We're heading to it right now. That's why the designation—'Atomic Car.'"

"No kidding?"

Noah dials in 16 15 23 5 18 once more. They hear a mechanical click and the car moves silently, accelerating away from the main office.

"Quiet, isn't it? Really quiet," Hinton says, before changing the subject. "Hey, I understand you're a rocket scientist?"

Without answering, Noah leaves the parking lot and they encounter the old woman pushing a shopping cart in front of them. Her dog has fallen behind and she stops to wait as Noah flicks on the red lights.

"Let's go, let's go," he calls out, using a speaker attached to the front of the car. She waves him off, refusing to move as she waits for the dog. Noah responds by turning on the siren and the dog starts to howl in unison. He laughs and backs up, then heads around her, the car gaining speed quickly.

"So, what kind of scientist are you? You're not really a rocket scientist?" Hinton asks, as Noah turns off the siren and they head toward the Beltway.

"I'm sure you've already heard, Hinton. I am, indeed, a 'rocket scientist.'"

"Well, I did hear that. But for real? I mean, why would a rocket scientist drive an ambulance? This is some kind of an escape for you? A high-tech junket of sorts?"

"Sure, that's right, Hinton. You can call it an escape. The truth is, I happen to love the sound of sirens. Always have, and that's why I drive an ambulance." He glances over obliquely, exposing a fish-like visage behind wire-rimmed glasses.

"So why not work for the police? They use sirens."

"Unfortunately, they wouldn't take me. I couldn't pass the fitness test."

"I see."

Hinton looks out the windshield onto Saturday morning traffic. It's light, made up mostly of weekend government workers and families making sightseeing trips in the capital. Tourists wander along sidewalks in small groups and look at the odd ambulance as it passes.

"I don't get the ambulance connection, Noah," he continues. "I mean, there are a lot of ways to listen to a siren. Why would someone involved with rockets go back to driving in cars?"

"Well, let's just say it supports my work."

Hinton contemplates the answer while Noah stays in the fast lane, tires humming over asphalt.

"Now that's funny! There's something a little strange about this. A rocket scientist has to drive an ambulance in order to support his work? But I know for a fact most scientists don't get paid much. Matter of fact, Dr. Noah, until we get a union, anyone who drives for this company in order to make a living is probably struggling to get along. Have you ever thought of that?"

They cross into a middle lane to avoid a jam.

"Morons," Noah mumbles at the side traffic, while maneuvering through and around a bottleneck.

"And you know," Hinton continues, "I believe with intelligence we can win the day. It's obvious from your intellectual strength that we can move forward. I really don't think we have time to waste."

"And what kind of time are you referring to?" he asks, as they surge back into the fast lane.

"Here and now kind, Dr. Noah. You know what I mean. We're out here to save lives. If necessary, we risk our own to give others a better chance. What that really means is we're here to try to make everyone safe. Universal emergency health care, right? Health care for everyone—ambulances for the rich and poor. That's the kind of time we're ready for. Americans have the most expensive health system in the world, but they are the least healthy people!"

The traffic ties up again and Noah gives no indication he's listening. Hinton lifts his hand and a finger to emphasize his point.

"What I'm saying is this: Change is inherent in human enterprise. Everything's fine, except…and you may know better than I do...something has happened that is disconcerting. Point is, Dr. Noah…I'm afraid others haven't realized it yet…the point is, we're making so many sacrifices for Medical we've forgotten who Medical is, and who we represent."

"And exactly who is Medical?"

"Well, we are! You and I. We're Medical! All of us in these red cars. Can't you see it, doctor? We've come to identify so much with the struggle in our cars, here on the freeways, that we've let ourselves be exploited. Forget what's going on with the blue cars. Right here in good old Medical! Let's be clear. You must admit we drivers have been economically manipulated, and that we don't serve all the people. Medical has lost touch with humanity."

"Please, don't refer to me as a driver."

"Pardon me?"

The traffic speeds up again, and when a few cars move ahead Noah quickly overtakes each of them.

"I said," Noah responds, elongating the second word, "don't call me a driver. I'm a scientist."

"Okay, of course, Dr. Noah. But we're in it together, right?"

"Together in what? If you're referring to some ideological struggle, Mr. Hinton, then the answer is certainly not. Medical and health care is just a game. I'm here to study it, to enjoy it."

"Jesus, you're serious, aren't you?"

There's a crackle of fresh starch from Noah's coat as he turns his head.

"Yes, I am."

"Well, what about the victims...I mean patients? You consider them to be a game?"

"They're all part of the study," Noah says, looking down at his watch.

"What study?"

"My study...the study of transporting human beings. I'm sure you realize, Hinton, that in designing rockets one tailors them to the human being. I have great interest in how humans are transported. This ambulance work gives me continuous exposure. And more than that it provides a needed relief, as I suggested earlier. We have full access to this!"

He reaches up on the dashboard and activates the siren again. Almost instantly cars move out of the left-hand lane, making it easy for the Atomic Car to advance. Noah smiles.

"Well, I must say, Dr. Noah, you have a rare sense of humor. I was a little worried at first."

"Sure, Hinton. You look like the worrying type. Fortunately, this company provides us all with a good modicum of amusement. Particularly Colson. He's a fine control...I mean friend. An endless source of the most remarkable information. Why just this morning he gave an edifying discourse on the physical properties of ice and the tundra in the Arctic!"

Noah smiles as they take the turnoff, headed for the nuclear reactor research station. Leaving the Beltway, near the perimeter of the Hughes Airport and Launching pad, a tall cyclone fence punctuates the otherwise barren landscape. A large concrete hemisphere emerges in the distance.

"Here. You need to put this on."

He hands Hinton a radiation badge as they drive up to the gate and a guard waves them through. Attaching the badge to his shirt, Hinton focuses ahead and takes in the dimensions of the structure—a forty-yard hemisphere lifted up on a cylindrical base. Directly adjacent is a rectangular building, a hundred yards in length, though not as tall, enclosed outwardly by concrete except for small glass windows.

"Noah, this is astounding! You really work out of a reactor?"

Noah checks his watch again and hits a control button opening a large garage door.

"That's correct… I…you don't expect me to work in a barber's shop, do you?"

"No. I guess not. But come on, man, how did you get into this?"

"I pressed the button."

"Right…. I mean...I mean, what's your role here?"

The door closes, leaving them next to concrete walls illuminated by fluorescent lighting. Noah goes to the rear of the car, takes a cable from the side of the building, and plugs it into a junction beneath the fender.

"The car takes four hours to charge with alternating current, Hinton. You asked about my role? I provide electricity for the city. Some of us, you know, prefer 'clean' energy. This is a light water reactor, the safest and most common kind in our country. The electricity comes from steam production, which drives a turbine generator. Doesn't foul the atmosphere and we don't have to depend on other sources for fuel."

"Well, sure, I knew that," Hinton acknowledges, looking down at his badge and then at the impenetrable walls surrounding them. "So, what do you fuel it with?"

Noah hands Hinton a laboratory coat and signals to follow him out of the garage. As they climb a steel staircase leading to the control room, a quick explanation ensues.

"Simple. We use americium to release alpha particles that knock neutrons from beryllium, and that starts up the fission from uranium 235. Any other questions?"

Hinton stays close behind as they enter an area crowded with terminals and a few small windows that look out on the city. He tries his question once more.

"Well, Noah, I still want to know: What is this place...where is everybody…and where do you get all these radioactive elements from?"

Terminal control panels, several feet in length, run along both sides of the room. Noah takes in digital readings on each display monitor before hitting a button that opens a screen on the inner wall. As it opens, they look into another room that is partitioned from theirs by a thick glass pane. Fifteen technicians, working on more terminals, glance up briefly and then continue their work.

"Good morning," Noah tells them through an intercom speaker.

"Good morning, Doctor."

He nods, looking at Hinton with piscine assurance. "You know, glass is a remarkable compound. One of a few in nature that exists in both liquid and solid state. A beautiful property based on silicon and other elements that bond and release simultaneously. Imagine that, Hinton."

"Sure, of course. Speaking of elements, Professor—I mean Dr. Noah—where do you get the elements that run this reactor anyway? Could you just answer that question?"

"It doesn't 'run' on anything, Hinton. It provides the theater for transformation of matter—from one state to another. A releasing of energy. A good one thousand megawatts, I should add. Sure, we use enriched uranium, but less than most of the light water reactors in other cities. We're thirty-nine percent efficient."

"Excuse me?"

"Thermal efficiency. Heat from a fission reaction, the release of neutrons from transformed uranium, doesn't find its way into pure electrical energy. But our steam-driven turbine is the best in D.C., or any other city, for that matter. This kind of efficiency makes petroleum, coal, wind, and solar energy impractical.

"So, you use enriched uranium," Hinton confirms. "I know a little about that. There's a limit to how much of the element is around, which we'll discover in a few more decades. And what about the plutonium products that result from all the fission? That's what gets used for nuclear weapons, right?"

"You sound like the Weatherpeople, Hinton. I just told you this reactor's a light water type. We use water for the moderator, to slow down neutrons for better fission. So, we don't require plutonium to run it, and we produce very little as a byproduct."

"Very little? And what happens with what you do produce?"

"Oh, we have a solution for that..."

"Great. You admit you have decay products? You use uranium, so you produce fertile nuclides. I'm sure you're going to tell me they won't be used for nuclear weapons, but we both know they have the capacity to threaten the safety of the country. So, Dr. Noah, how about the hazard of radiation to citizens?"

"Miniscule. Perhaps you've heard of the Solar Slingshot?" Noah suggests, anticipating the response with a smile.

"That's a preposterous idea!"

"It's a way. But there are better ones. We have a special plan worked out."

The slingshot scheme, dispatching nuclear waste by way of orbiting rockets which ultimately collide with the sun, had been exposed in the *Times.* While the sun works as the ultimate incinerator, burning molecular compounds to their final state of energy, the chance of a rocket missing the natural body of fission is not impossible. Six percent of rockets have gone astray in the past, and the newspaper predicts an ionosphere looking like the D.C. freeway on Friday afternoon.

"What plan, Noah? Let's get beyond fantasy. When all countries come together as a union, we'll distribute things equally. We need renewable energy. Not nuclear energy and more weapons!"

Noah looks over his glasses.

"Union?"

"Right! I've studied this. The human race has to change. We can't just shoot waste into space just because we can't take care of our own planet."

"Hinton, you expect the multiplying billons to not want the things you have? Face it: Americans invented nuclear energy. We may not always use it, but others will. The public is always five decades behind reality and...damn it, you've made me late!"

Noah looks at his watch and then types instructions on one of the terminal panels. His index finger finds a red button on the top of the board, and as he engages it a shrill siren pulsates through the Control Room.

AREEEEEEE...AREEEEEEEE.

The technicians in the glass-enclosed room jump out of their chairs and stop working long enough to verify that it's a test. They shake their heads and go back to work.

"God, I love sirens," Noah confides, smiling again. "It's my one weakness. Now, there's no place for overreaction in this business, so let's go, Mr. Hinton. You have distracting questions, and I don't like being late."

Day 5—Saturday, 10:00 a.m.—Punta Cero, Cuba

Sitting by the poolside, Castro is served a glass of milk from personal cow #5. The family chef fades away as Fidel looks out on his seventy-five-acre estate, spotted with mandarin, orange, lemon, and grapefruit trees. He sips his milk calmly. Extra guards at the perimeter have doubled the protection from incessant attempts to assassinate him, and he turns his attention to his guest.

"I will outlive them all," he assures Blackbeard, first in command for intelligence. "Nixon and all those American presidents that will succeed him. They all want to control our government, and you can add to the list of assassins the CIA, Frank Sturgis, and my enemies here in Cuba and Miami. So, we hear Frank Sturgis is in jail, so at least he's no longer a worry."

"Most certainly, Comandante, but how do we deal with the current president? We've lost almost all our missiles except one, even the small weapons that protected us. The Soviets respect us no more than the Yankees do—you have told me this yourself."

Like a needle in his side, hitting a nerve, it awakens Fidel's resentment. The Russians first removed the long-range missiles, and subsequently all the tactical nuclear weapons, and ignored his advice and desire to protect his people. Kennedy's assurance to Brezhnev that there would never be another invasion of Cuba left him out of the agreement, and came with no guarantee. He pushes his glass of milk aside and faces Blackbeard.

"And what will you do? What do you propose? What happened with your attempts to capture the Code? Do you think Tango will get to it, or not?"

"Delta Tango says he is very close. We must wait—be patient. We must give him more time, and see what he finds."

As they look up at the sky towering cumulus formations have moved together, pushed by distant ocean currents and temperature changes into a slow swirl. Familiar with the first signs of hurricane season, Castro nods to Domingo, and gives a name to the next one.

"Hurricane Agnes!"

Saturday, 10:01 a.m.—Cruising on the *Sequoia*

The distant banks of the Potomac stretch gently ahead, reassuring Nixon as he doses in the sun, watching the brilliant disk rise over an outline of trees along the banks. He listens to the *Sequoia*'s diesel engines propelling upstream.

I would love to swim! Getting away from the capital is a pleasure, but those murky waters are less than inviting and the scientists say they're feculent! And this teak railing? Looks strong, protecting, but who needs protection? I'm the captain of this ship. The campaign ahead, well…not much left to be done. The democratic peace-loving candidates—weak, disorganized, divided…way too emotional. The Times *writes things about their families and they react like women. They see me as the winner—and the polls confirm it. Strength is everything and why all this talk about blacks and the women vote, protestors and stopping the war? It's a distraction, really, an insult to our freedom from communism. A matter of time, really. I'll end the war when it's time, and I'll be re-elected.*

The yacht steers through the mid-channel, leaving a small wake on the water's surface. On the deeper channels silt flows from distant banks of the Appalachian and Piedmont plateaus, following a course three million years old. Born and raised in the basin, George Washington surveyed and spent much of his life by the river, known for honking geese and graceful swans that still fly above it. The Potomac became known as the "Nation's river"…as agriculture, coal mining residue, and human waste spilled into the depths. Lincoln found the summer stench of the eutrophic waters so strong that he escaped to the highlands for relief. With time the river would divide the Union side from the Confederate, but Nixon cruises up the center, certain he has mastered the middle.

A phone rings in the cabin and he wonders who would interrupt him on his vacation besides Haldeman. Of course, it has to be Haldeman.

"Sorry to bother you on your vacation, sir," he tells him, "but there's a story in the *Times* this morning about a break-in. Somebody's tried to steal secrets from the DNC campaign office at the Watergate. A group known as the 'Plumbers.' And some of them may be tied to us."

"Well, that's crazy," Nixon responds, looking at the Secret Service men waiting outside the door. "What do you suppose they were after?"

"Well, it's not really certain," Haldeman answers, "but they got caught. I'm calling it a third-rate burglary, but it might cause some trouble."

"Well, okay, thanks for your call." Nixon listens for a minute and then hangs up. A brass ashtray rests on a polished table just next to him. Instinctively he picks it up and heaves it against the mahogany wall of his cabin, catching the Secret Service men by surprise.

10:05 a.m.—The staircase of the nuclear reactor

Noah and Hinton take the opposite side of the spiral staircase that descends into the reactor complex, going below the garage level of the Atomic Car. As they descend, Hinton feels an odd give to the metal steps, like a floating sensation, and tries to understand this anomaly of the metal structure.

It's an elastic feeling as my feet come down each step! It's as if I'm landing on a sponge! Strange.

"Something odd about this place!" Hinton calls out, as they reach an intermediate floor leading to the library.

"Why?" Noah asks, stopping before a large metal door, which he opens by dialing a code on a lock.

7 5 14 5 20 9 3 12 9 2 18 1 18 25

"I think I know what you're up to, Professor. I think I get it!" Hinton answers.

"Get what?"

"The staircase. It's a model of the double helix! This whole thing's structured like a chromosome. Fascinating! You're trying to get ontogeny to recapitulate phylogeny, aren't you, Noah? That's it! You're doing biologic research down here, aren't you?"

"Aren't you brilliant, Hinton. You know, for a Rhodes Scholar you're not bad. It's a small part of my work, but it will, in fact, preserve our heritage. Now, if you don't mind, I'm going to have you spend time in the library while I go about some important research. I'll come back to get you in an hour or so."

"Wait a minute. What if we get a call?"

Noah secures the metal door closed, leaving Hinton in the library, then continues down the stairway past a series of metal cages containing animals. He spends the rest of the morning working underground while Hinton explores the library. Volumes of books fill columns of bookshelves, stretching to the ceiling, running from wall to wall the length of the first room. Long rows of research journals span Artificial Intelligence to Guided Ballistic Missiles and Taxonomy of Zebras. It continues into a second room. Discouraged by the arcane subjects, Hinton wanders beyond the rows and columns till he comes to what seems to be an open computer system. The digital apparatus is immense, filling two more rooms, with *Property of IBM U.S. Military* and *Hughes Industry* written on the faceplate. Fascinated, he begins exploring files that appear with each title he types on the control page.

Jesus Christ! What has Noah gotten control of! How did he get clearance for this, and why are there so many cities and texts in foreign languages? And this big database for cryogenics?

Chapter 29:
Rebecca's Search for her Father
and Noah's Freeze

10:10 a.m.—Room 623, Howard Johnson's Motor Lodge

At night I work the radios of the dispatching office for Medical, but during the day I can work from my room at Hojo's and from my cab when I travel the city. Keeping up with the Lovejoy family has captured my attention, and I begin to wonder if they will ever reunite as I track the conversation in room 623.

"Know what? Mom's never coming back," Angel insists, losing faith in her sister's capacity to handle the situation.

Rebecca divides up the pancakes she's brought up from the restaurant, handing the Styrofoam plates to her brother and sister. With the balcony window open, the humidity and heat from outside easily overcome the air conditioning of their main room.

"She's coming back," Rebecca tries to reassure Angel.

"She's not. She got kidnapped by robbers!"

Angel considers her proposal irrefutable. When Rebecca told her of the events from the night before, she imagined gun-toting police and men in dark suits just outside the motor lodge. They were quite likely to be kidnapping children and their mothers.

"I don't have to eat pancakes. I want Fruit Loops," Michael protests, not happy the girls made him put on pants and not a swimsuit.

"Mom said she's coming back and I'm taking care of everything," Rebecca answers thinly.

"You're not. Mom tried to save Dad and you didn't do anything. Now we get to do whatever we want," Angel argues back, pushing her breakfast aside.

"No, she said for me to take care of you. And you guys agreed that we would work together. Stop scaring Michael."

"We need to find her," Angel insists. "Let's call Dad."

"Okay, I'm calling him," Rebecca gives in. "But right now, you have to listen to me. Mom wrote a number down and I'm the only one who knows where it is. I'll call it."

Michael becomes more animated, playing with his food while Rebecca tries the call. When she reaches City Hospital, she learns her father is being held in the ICU and can't be reached by phone. She asks about her mother and the operator then asks her to put her mother on the line, so she hangs up.

"What'd they say?" Angel asks, as Rebecca faces them.

"They said Dad said 'I see you.' They don't know where Mom is. They think she's still with us."

"No, she's not. She's, like, having a baby in the hospital."

Michael looks up as Rebecca, dressed in jeans and a blouse, begins to search through her mother's purse, hoping to find cab fare. The wallet contains twenties and smaller s, in addition to a credit card. She carries the purse with her to the foldout couch, now heaped with a pile of clothes.

"Okay, you guys. Listen up. Angel, you have to get dressed. We're going to go visit Dad."

After changing into street clothes the children make their way to the front of the motel and hail a cab. They're still uncertain of where their father is hospitalized, and when I pick them up I try to determine if Rebecca is up to her challenge.

"Listen, kids," I tell them, as they sit in the back seat, "I don't carry crystal balls in this car. You asked me to take you to the hospital and you don't know its name? All I can do is take you to every one of 'em. Till we find it."

A white turban covers my black hair, and my Spanish accent is strange to them, but I try to seem friendly enough. Rebecca squirms in the back seat. Anxiously, she tries to remember the name the operator told her.

"It's 'City' something. Like City Hospital or something like that," she suggests.

"Sure," I complain, "and there's ten to fifteen hospitals in this city. So, what good does 'City' do? I mean, there's a City Hospital, but your dad can't be at that place. Your parents have money, right?"

Rebecca rebels at my mention of money and is silent for a second, then answers me with her own questions.

"What difference does money make? You don't believe in the Great Commandment? Mom says we should always take care of others!"

"Okay, okay," I tell her, "I want to help you, so maybe he's at City Hospital, and we'll go there first."

"That's what the operator said! City Hospital! Something City," Rebecca tells me. My turtleneck sweater makes it hard to turn my head, and I speak to the children by looking through the rearview mirror.

"Okay, muchachos…I mean children. I'll take you to City Hospital. That's what you're asking me to do, right?"

"Yeah. You better take us there," Angel pipes in. "'Cause that's where we're supposed to go to. My dad wants to talk to you."

"Yeah, he sure does," Michael adds.

"Take us there, please," Rebecca confirms.

We swing across town, passing monuments and government buildings until we reach the Southeast Side, where neighborhoods crisscross with four-story brick buildings. Entering a gate there are two large buildings separated by a parking lot. I pull up in front of the larger brick hospital building that's not surrounded by barbed wire or a security fence. The prison is adjacent.

"You don't want to get caught in that other building," I warn them. "That's the District Jail! You owe me twelve dollars, and it's okay to just give me six. I can guess you don't have a lot of money."

Rebecca removes a ten-dollar from the wallet and waits for me to hand her change, as Angel takes Michael and jumps out of the car. They start off for the hospital alone, with Angel holding on to Michael's hand. After Rebecca receives the change, she instinctively hurries to catch her brother and sister, but she leaves the wallet on the rear seat.

"I didn't like that man," Angel says.

"Me needer," Michael agrees.

"You guys! I can't believe it," Rebecca calls out, suddenly. "I left Mom's wallet in the taxi. He's getting away!"

Speechless, their hearts sink as I head out through the entrance gate and disappear.

"Rebecca! How could you do that? All mom's money is gone? It's our only money!"

"Because...I...thought…I thought…you were going to get lost…. You guys didn't wait for me…"

Rebecca holds back tears and Michael comes to hold her arm. Angel quickly assesses the situation.

"He's not turning around. We're, like, dead."

10:25 a.m.—The Laboratory below the reactor

With Hinton out of the way, Noah pulls open the door of a cage and places a tourniquet around the foreleg of a stout German shepherd mongrel, with hair too long and body parts too short. He injects sodium pentothal till the dog collapses, and lies flat on a stainless-steel bench. Quickly he slides a tube down the dog's windpipe, connects it to a breathing machine, and carefully inserts more catheters into arteries and veins. A small, sterile roller pump circulates substitute blood solution through an oxygenator and into the interconnected vessels. Over the next hour, the animal is immersed in a basin of ice water, as Noah follows the drop in body temperature, making gradient changes in the circulating solution.

"Three-point-five percent glycerol," he dictates into a recorder, while making notations on a clipboard. "Down to one-point-seven. Half the gas at ten minutes, twenty degrees; stop it at fifteen. Cardioplegia…full blood substitute, then freeze."

An hour into the procedure Noah takes the dog off the ventilator, the heart having stopped.

"Point-one degrees per minute. Six degrees an hour, one hour till submersion. My friend, you will now last forever!"

Noah waits for the cooling to conclude while placing small, needle-sharp probes into the loose skin of the head, blinking approvingly as the EEG waves and spike patterns disappear.

An hour later the vapor lifts off the dry ice and Noah observes its transition from solid to gas, bypassing the liquid state.

Perfect. In the future I'm going to be taking the brain from deep freeze back to symbolic thought, he tells himself. *Have to be patient. Everything is technique. Everyone else thinks the brain can't tolerate freezing because of the destructive effects on neurons, but the ice occurs extra-cellular. I know it's possible to protect molecular structure if I keep trying. I just need more samples.*

After disconnecting EEG leads he removes the dog from the ice, placing it in a plastic bag before immersing it into liquid silicon.

Another twenty-four hours—down to minus seventy-nine. Then you enter your "Dewar" filled with liquid nitrogen, my four-legged boy. At minus 196 degrees centigrade you won't be feeling pain. And I'll see you back before you know it!

1:30 p.m.—City Hospital

After leaving the cab, and losing their mother's wallet, the children find their way into City Hospital, a large brick building with a parking lot adjacent to the City Prison. From the parking lot the building is imposing and uninviting. They encounter an initial hurdle.

"You kids can't hang around here. I keep telling you, your father is in the Intensive Care Unit, and children are not allowed. Where's your mother?"

The Lovejoy children stare at long, twisting fingernails protruding from the fingers of a triage volunteer at the information desk.

"We thought she was here. And she told us to come here and she said we could see my father. She said he would see us," Rebecca argues, standing next to the desk. The woman continues to surmise them. Angel and Michael are fixated on tiny blue and gold dragons adorning her nails, wondering how she dials a telephone and eats a sandwich.

"And I already told you your mother's not in this hospital. Now, it seems your father is in the ICU. So, listen to me, you wait here a minute. I'm going to get Social Services and we can figure out why you're alone. You just stay right here."

"We aren't alone," Angel blurts out. "Our dad's here."

"All right, young lady."

They watch her disappear and consider alternatives.

"She wants to turn us in for something," Angel begins, "then she's going to do something to us, like shrink us like they did in the Puppet People movie! Maybe a kidnapping. Or stab us with her dragon nails!"

"Why can't we see Dad?" Michael asks. "I wanna see him. Really bad!"

"Come on. We can find him ourselves," Angel suggests.

Rebecca is not sure, but she needs to be the leader.

"Okay, Angel" Rebecca agrees. "We'll go together. But we have to stay together, so you better not get ahead of me again."

As if crossing a street, they hold hands and start off in the direction opposite to the information counter. Their soft tennis shoes and small bodies disappear into the busy hospital corridor, like small fish immersing into a larger school of flowing bodies. Angel tucks in Michael's shirt, and as they near the elevator lobby, Rebecca sees a directory on the wall and then: "**Intensive Care Unit**—fourth floor."

"Hurry up you guys. I remember Mom said 'Intensive Care Unit.' I think he's upstairs. Let's take the elevator."

As the doors close behind them, they're immediately pushed toward the rear by two ambulance drivers with a gurney. Michael looks up at the blue uniforms with THERAPY printed on the front and back. One of the drivers smiles as Michael is pulled by Angel out onto the fourth floor. Angel looks around and sees a stairwell with EXIT written over it, just next to the elevator.

"This is where it is," Rebecca says uncertainly, "and we have to hurry. We don't know if that lady's looking for us, or what."

"I bet she is," Angel warns.

They proceed till they stand in front of two wide glass doors. **ICU** is inscribed on the surface with white paint. Suddenly, the doors swing open and they hear the commotion of a code.

"Flat line!"

"Gimme paddles. Stand back everyone!"

"POMMMT!"

"I think I want to go home," Michael says, recoiling back.

"Not now," Rebecca tells him, "we have to find Dad."

As they venture past cubicles and beds, looking at patients connected to tubes, each one seems more formidable than the next.

"Oh my God!" Angel cries. A man wrapped in plaster waves his free hand at them. "It's a mummy!"

"I wanna go home now!" Michael repeats. He looks at the floor while holding onto Rebecca's hand. Just then Rebecca spots her father.

"You guys, that looks like Dad! I think it's Dad! It is!"

Still on a ventilator, hands restrained, David glances over and sees his three children making their way toward him. His heart leaps. Just as suddenly, before he can verify his vision, the kids are swept out of view by the head nurse.

"How did you children get in here?" she asks, gathering them up and moving toward the ICU entrance as she talks. "We can't have kids in this part of the hospital. Are you lost?"

"That's our dad! You have our dad!" Rebecca tells her.

"Okay," she says, as they enter the hallway once more, "and do you have a mother somewhere?"

"She's having a baby," Angel answers, "and the police took her, or the robbers. And she's trying to save our dad!"

"Really?"

She tries to assess them. The man they're calling their father will be transferred as soon as he's off the ventilator. He's from out of town. *But why are they alone?* she wonders.

"Code Three, ICU. Code Three, ICU," a voice calls out over the intercom. The nurse's puzzled expression disappears. She's glad to see a Security cop and Social Services coming out of the elevator.

"These people will help you," she tells the children, "so good luck to you! I hope your mother gets here soon!"

As she rushes back to the ICU, the children see the woman with long fingernails.

"Come on," Rebecca says, "let's get out of here before we get arrested. We need to find Mom!"

"Come on where? We're about to be kidnapped," Angel informs her older sister.

"Exit?" Michael whispers.

"That's it, Michael, you're right! The EXIT!"

They head for the stairwell and before the Social Services and Security employees reach them, they're flying down the stairs. His sisters lift Michael off his feet. Determined not to be separated, he hangs onto their hands as they descend two flights. Then, thinking they have reached the ground floor, they mistakenly exit onto the maternity ward.

Chapter 30:

Noah's Game

Saturday, 4:42 p.m.— Nuclear Reactor

Morning passes into afternoon. Noah cleans up after putting the dog in its Dewar, then checks levels of liquid nitrogen in each of the adjoining Dewars. He makes an inventory of the caged animals when a pulsation of beeps causes him to look at his watch. Leaving the underground laboratory and ascending the stairway, he opens the locked door to the library and signals Hinton to come to lunch.

"You can leave that computer now. I'm sure you enjoyed exploring it but it's time for me to fix up lunch in the blender. Then we'll go to the game."

"What game?" Hinton asks.

"Ice hockey. I go every Sunday for three hours. The Company has to pay me for something, and it's the only run I make."

After a prepared drink of fruits, vitamins, and protein powder, they head back to the ambulance. Hinton returns his radiation badge at the gate as they drive onto the public road, away from the nuclear complex.

"I don't like to be late," Noah says. "Otherwise I would let you drive. I notice how you memorized the code when I started the car. You're what Otieno likes to call a 'driver,' and it's fairly obvious that you're interested in my vehicle. I'm not sure what it is you're driving for, Hinton, but you seem very ambitious."

"Tell me something, Dr. Noah. Who pays your salary—and expenses for the reactor where you live?"

"Mr. Hughes."

"Oh, so you work for Howard Hughes, not Nixon?"

"Be serious, Hinton, we are all working for Howard Hughes, but not everyone realizes it."

In the distance they can discern the sports arena. Haze-filtered light of the sun softens an interface of building against sky, creating a sense of involution. The glass cement gallery, larger than the nuclear reactor, is defined by a circumferential sine wave, with an up and down sweeping of concrete-covered steel, embellishing and supporting a massive cylinder for entertainment.

"No, I don't work for Hughes. I work for Medical. Who do you work for, Noah? Medical or Mr. Hughes?"

"I work for myself. Of course, in reality, both pay me. And you may think you work for Medical, Hinton, but we all work for Hughes, in one way or another. Who do you think finances the Medical company, or Nixon for that matter? What do you think is the largest industry in our country, health care or the military?"

"What's your point?"

"It's health care by a factor of five. And Hughes controls both, but medicine is where the money is. Sure, he designs the military projects, but the military is only a fifth of what our country spends compared to medicine, so he concentrates on medicine, including the company you and I work for. And you really think you can form a union, or change health care in this country?"

They head off the freeway into a network of parking lots. Traffic from the city is beginning to arrive, filling the diagonally ordered parking spaces for twenty thousand vehicles. Viewed from high up, the cars almost seem like the attendants of the evening event.

"Well, sure, Noah. Maybe the Hughes Industry is supporting our ambulance company. But from what I can see, you don't spend much time in the ambulance."

"Right. They're too many people in cars as it is."

Noah heads for a gated tunnel leading into the side of the arena.

"So, all you do is run the reactor for Howard Hughes?"

"No, no. I go to our daily meetings, like you. And I work this game every week, for at least three hours."

"At least? Three hours? What do you mean 'at least'?"

"Well yes," Noah answers, a little defensively. "I'm a scientist. I can't be everywhere. It's important to try and help people."

"Help people?"

The car goes under a steel-girded walkway and they park with the rear end pointed toward the ice rink inside of the building.

"Yes," Noah explains. "Why only a few months ago I helped a player with a broken ankle."

Noah hops out of the car, looking a little incongruous in his red MEDICAL jacket and boots. As he looks up, taking in the architecture, he seems elated.

"There's the Omphalos," he points out, indicating the scoreboard. They emerge from the passageway that runs below the bleachers of the gallery, and he nods at a frustum-shaped cone hanging from the center of an array of steel beams.

"It has the same shape as the legendary stone in the Delphic oracle. Sports imitating religion, you might say. Omphalos means navel, and it was located at the center of the Earth. This scoreboard is midway between two goals, and it serves as an augury. Their oracle told the future, while ours just tells the score. At least for now."

The two of them begin walking up the stairs of the enclosed arena.

"What do you mean, 'At least for now'?"

"Well, there's more to life than the present."

Noah leads Hinton up an aisle of stairs leading to the television cameras on the uppermost ridge of the gallery. As they sit on dark seats resembling twenty thousand others, sweeping down to the ice-covered base, they watch a continuous influx of spectators fill the rings around the rink. Hinton is impressed that half of the arena is filled with spectators dressed in red colors, and the other half in blue colors.

"Noah," Hinton asks, still trying to decipher his partner, "how do people know we're with Medical when we're way up here?"

Their backs are hidden against the seats.

"Don't worry. No one does."

"Wait. What if there's an accident? Aren't we too far away to immediately help anyone?"

One of the spectators engages a pressurized horn, and a loud "BLAAAHHHH!" fills the arena. Cowbells join in from different angles, along with the crowd's rising voice.

"Why should we? We wouldn't be able to watch the game."

Hinton leans over to respond and Noah leans away, adjusting his glasses.

"Now wait a minute. You mean if someone has a heart attack...?"

"Then someone in the crowd calls an ambulance," Noah interrupts. "Listen, if you really want to save lives, go back and work with Otieno, or Deed. They'll be the ones. Maybe even Colson."

He looks away, concentrating on the activity on the rink. Hinton is shocked by Noah's response.

"But we have the ambulance here. We're on duty!"

Noah's brow furls.

"You don't seem to understand. If someone has a heart attack, it's part of the game. It won't stop us from watching it—that's what we came here for. Do you realize, Hinton, how many people have died in the time since we got here?"

"How do you mean?"

"Around seven thousand an hour. So do the math. And as far as heart attacks, well, just start multiplying."

A roar reverberates throughout the arena as two hockey teams skate onto the rink. Noah focuses over the mosaic of the seated audience, watching two teams skate rapidly around their goals, waiting for the noise to die down.

"And of course, there are those of us alive right now. That's really what counts, isn't it? You just keep your eyes on the game, Hinton, you'll see. All your noble thoughts. All these people you hope to save—they're but a drop in the ocean. A small drop. The ocean continues, whether you save them or not, and up until now nobody's ever survived. You swim around in circles, but you should be saving your energy."

Hinton scrutinizes Noah.

This man is not ready. He doesn't even seem human! He has a wide grasp of science, but he's strangely connected with Hughes, and he's got to recognize the trap of his own self-interest if he's going to become part of our union. I'll change my tack.

"You mean I should be concentrating on the people who are strongest, Noah? Like the hockey players?"

The players form lines, taking turns hitting the puck into the net.

"Forget the people, . Just concentrate on the game."

Hinton smiles. "You mean we should never take our attention off the game? Should study it every possible moment?"

Noah sits back as the players take positions waiting for the Anthem to be played. "Yes, of course, that's exactly right."

Hinton smiles.

I'll show him he has an altruistic side.

"Well then, Dr. Noah, how did you concentrate on the game when you helped the hockey player with the broken ankle? The one you told me about earlier?"

Music begins and the spectators stand to face the flag.

"It was the break, Hinton. But we didn't transport him till the game ended."

6:59 p.m.—Searching for HoJo's Motor Lodge

After evading the Social Services people, easily accomplished by merging into a group of children in the maternity ward, Rebecca, Angel, and Michael look for their mother without success. They decide to return to their room at HoJo's, in hopes she may have returned. Making a rush to the fire exit at the other end of the building, they emerge from the hospital and run through the parking lot, soon finding access to the underground subway. As they continue down the stairs, they arrive next to the subway map. They stop and stare at the ticket machine, wondering how to buy a ticket. The screams and hollering inside the maternity ward have left

Michael frightened, but there's a hint of relief now when Angel pulls from her pocket a twenty-dollar .

"Rebecca, I knew we would need it, so I took it out of Mom's wallet when you weren't looking. You only have four dollars. Don't we need more money? I mean like…like when there's like an emergency? Isn't that so?"

Without chastising, Rebecca purchases a single ticket with the assistance of a woman standing in line. She carefully pockets the twenty dollars and they're happy that Angel and Michael can ride free, boarding the first Metro that arrives.

Rebecca seeks distractions for Michael, and Angel helps in the diversion. For an hour they depart at different stations of the subway, walking by monuments, the National Air and Space Museum, the Smithsonian, and parks in between. They disappear, mix and blend into small groups of tourists, and they wonder at the treasures of the Natural History Museum, before stopping to rest.

"Who could collect so many things in one building?" Angel asks. Michael adds his concerns.

"How come the animals are so silent? Do dinosaurs eat children?"

"Michael, don't be dumb," Angel chastens. "Dinosaurs are dead!"

It seems like a reasonable way to pass the time since Rebecca doesn't know the way back to the motel. The colored diagrams of the Metrorail give a pretense of order, but each time they reboard her uncertainty mounts. Eventually they spot an exit for the Lincoln Memorial. Both Rebecca and Angel recognize the name.

"This is it!" Angel insists. "It's the one Mom and Dad brought us to when we first got here. Maybe we'll find her here? It's close to the motel."

"Okay, this is where we get off," Rebecca alerts the team.

"I wanna find Mom," Michael implores. "I'm really tired. And we need to go back and watch TV."

Disembarking from the subway, they find a hot dog stand. Food boosts Michael's spirits as they sit on a bench by one of the museums, but he longs for his mother's arms. When Angel tries to hug him, he pushes her away. They have emerged into early evening light and in the distance, past a long Reflecting Pool lined by elm trees, Rebecca makes out the Lincoln Monument with tall columns. Her mother pointed it out on the bridge, on the drive into the city, and they played in the Reflecting Pool on their first day. Now it's a short distance away. People walk along the grass next to the water, the last magnet of diversion before the sun goes down, and they set off to get closer.

"I think she'll be here, don't you?" Michael asks. The pathway leads to bold white columns of the monument, and he follows his sisters willingly. Approaching, they stop to remove their shoes and let their feet hang in the water. The day's length disappears as the air around them cools.

"We're going to find her," Rebecca reassures. "But we still have to find a place to stay. I'm going to ask some people to help us."

"Why? Why aren't we going back to the motel? I thought we were going to the motel?" Angel asks. "I don't get it!"

"Well...I'm not so sure how to find it."

"Rebecca! You mean we're lost? You lost us? You have to be kidding. You're wrong. You must be!"

Angel stares at her sister. Afternoon crowds have dwindled to a few passing adults, seemingly oblivious to the children, walking with anticipation to evening dinners and hotel rooms.

"Why does she have to be wrong?" Michael asks, wanting to remove his clothes, still wanting to swim and missing the hotel pool. Nothing has made sense all day, and now something else is wrong.

"I don't have to know anything, Michael," Rebecca answers. "Angel thinks I have to know everything, but I don't. Even Mom and Dad don't know everything."

"Yes, they do. Where's Mom?" Michael asks, looking toward the monument. "I thought we were going to find her."

"Well, we are," Rebecca answers, as they don shoes and resume walking toward the tall columns. "If she's not around here we'll ask some people how to get to the motel, because she may be back already. Come on, Angel. Just stop being so critical. Maybe she's back."

"What's critical?" Michael asks.

8:30 p.m.—The presidential yacht

The *Sequoia* charters a straight course traveling down the Potomac. Small craft move to the side of the yacht while Nixon returns to the deck, taking a chair where he can watch the sunset. A fiery orb, now turned yellow and golden, enhanced by the swallowing horizon, sinks down to cause a crepuscular light, as he glances behind him at the Secret Service men.

How much do they know? Do they follow newspapers closely? Of course, they do. They're like me. We all started at the bottom of the Pyramid and we worked hard. Always against opposition, never with the luxury of wealthy parents. Maybe they had a father, like mine, strapped, always in debt. Maybe he shouted at them, like my father did, cursing me, but he knew you never advanced without a battle. These guys know that. And they probably know about the Watergate break-in. Of course, they read newspapers and maybe I should ask them what they read about today.

One of the Secret Service men waits behind the cabin door. The Football is attached to his wrist by a small chain, and Nixon wonders how much he cares about any of the information in the Watergate offices. Probably none of it. Or the information contained in the Football? He broods while the sky unfolds a magenta glow over the silhouette of the capital, and the river flows on to the bay.

Saturday, 8:35 p.m.—The sports arena

"…rocket's red glare, the bombs bursting in air, gave proof through the night, that our flag was still there..."

Hinton looks up to see the words flash from left to right through circular lights on the scoreboard. As the crowd sings, he reads the names "Seals" and "Sharks" written next to empty score columns. After the Anthem, a referee skates to the center of the ice, where players of the opposing teams face off. He drops a puck and as it lands two players smash it savagely with their sticks.

"Which side are you on?" Hinton asks Noah.

"Neither. Only the ignorant take sides."

The players wear hard protective padding, the Seals in blue uniforms and the Sharks in red. The crowd listens to a cracking sound as one man collides against another and the "whishing" of skates cutting over ice. An aroma of popcorn and hot dogs permeates the arena.

"Pardon me?"

"I don't take sides, Hinton. I observe."

"You mean you have nothing to gain?"

"No. I gain everything. I learn from others' mistakes. When you don't get involved, when you study a game, you see through it. You learn how things work"

As they talk, one of the Sharks smashes a Seal in the back with his stick. The referees fail to notice and the Shark skates away free as the red crowd cheers in response and the blue side boos.

"You see," Noah continues, "when you really understand the game you know the outcome ahead of time. There's no point taking sides, is there?"

"How can you know that?"

"Technique," Noah answers. He opens his briefcase and turns on his calculator. "I make calculations at each game. For instance, I'll tell you the final score for this game if you'd like."

Hinton appraises his partner's fish-like visage.

"Okay. The score?"

"Sharks by one."

Ricocheting off the inner wall of the rink, the rubber disk goes through a wild, random pattern. Both sides fight for control as it spins between them, hammered relentlessly back and forth, and circles the two nets. Each time it approaches the goalies throw their bodies on the ice to block it.

"Anyone can guess."

"Sure, but I calculate."

Hinton laughs. "So, tell me the difference?"

"It's the difference that exists between pigeons and men. Except my calculations are different from other men."

"Oh, they are? Why's that?"

"Precision. Perhaps you're capable of understanding, . You must realize, the best the race has ever been able to do is momentarily stay above the ocean. That's what it's really all about, isn't it? Longevity. Who can stay up the longest, with or without luxury? In the end we sink to the bottom, transient voyagers."

Noah clicks his calculator off. Behind them the television cameras sweep back and forth, covering the events of the game.

"Most of the race have too many things, too many attachments, and they get carried down by their weight. Oh yes, you can float on luxury, for a while, but eventually you forget how to swim and all your luxury gets taken away. Or you rely on children. But soon there may be so many that no one survives, in an evolving tragedy of the commons. Now, you can become a great swimmer, maybe like yourself, but then you end up going in circles, and face exhaustion."

"And if one swims in a straight line?"

"The Earth, as well as every star and celestial body we know of, is round. No, Hinton, you'll end up where you started, with a genetically designed body timed for self-destruction. Remember this—so long as your body is genetically determined, you're on a path to disintegration."

One of the Seals commits a penalty and the red crowd voices a wave of disapproval.

"Well, I'm not sure where you're going with this. You're mortal. The laws of genetics apply to you as well as me, don't they?"

"For the moment. But that's all, . Our lives are moments disappearing in the ocean of time. We race over the planet, from civilization to civilization, knowing we won't be around for long, never suspecting we might find land."

"Land?"

"Longevity! The capacity to live for centuries, and even for millenniums!"

A roar resounds throughout the conical gallery. The Sharks have scored a goal and horns blast. Cowbells ring and the crowd shouts and gestures with waving arms, imitating the jaws of a shark as the Seals' goalie looks down at the black puck with disgust. Small flakes of ice melt on its top before the referee takes it.

"Do you have something against life on Earth?" Hinton asks.

"Not at all. It just doesn't last long enough."

Once more the referee drops the puck between the players. The two men swing with determination, while above them the drivers debate.

"And you think you can make it last longer playing with science and atomic energy, exposing the city to the risks of radiation?"

"Maybe. Odds are with me."

"What odds?"

"Scientific odds. You must realize there's a risk to everything. Each time you cross the street there's a one in ten thousand probability you'll have an accident. You knock ten minutes off your life for every cigarette you smoke, one trip in an ambulance decreases your span one-point-seven hours, and fifty days if you don't wear a seat belt. I calculate the odds for true longevity at four billion to one, but you must weigh the risk against the benefits. I'm sure you'll agree, in spite of the odds, the benefits are great."

"I'm not so sure. What are the benefits for the four billion?"

"Well, it all depends on one person finding the longest life. Isn't that enough?"

The cameras follow the shifting center of play as hockey players sweep past each other. Circling and chasing the puck, they make an irregular dance chasing its kinetic path till they're blocked or thrown off their feet. Hinton contemplates Noah's suggestion.

"Would you mind telling me how you'll beat the odds? Are you thinking of resurrection? You don't exactly sound like a Christian, or a Muslim for that matter."

"I already told you, precision and timing, and good technique," Noah says.

"Meaning you reduce everything to science and numbers, and then you approach immortality?"

"In a way." Noah scans his watch. There's a crunching noise as one player smashes into another. "You're catching on. You know, this arena is an example of what's necessary to go beyond time. It's made of glass, cement, and electricity. The materials are transparent, permanent, and spontaneous. That's why it will last for a long time."

Two players collide and lay injured on the rink. Others skate around them and a shoving match begins. On the scoreboard a red light flashes next to the word MEDICAL, but the two ambulance drivers fail to notice it.

"It's simple," Noah continues. "What we need is a technology of the mind, a full understanding of the human brain. If we could do with the mind what we've done with this arena, man would not have to sink to the bottom. Even this building can't last. But the human mind can. It's called consilience."

"I'm not sure I see what you mean."

"No, you don't see very far. You're too involved with current affairs. What's necessary, before anything else, is that your mind becomes like glass. Transparent! You know, glass is such a rare substance. It can be in two places at one time. That is to say, liquid and solid, without ever crystallizing. Think about it. Completely uncommitted and yet lasting forever. We use glass to store nuclear waste because it's so reliable. If you keep it in the proper condition it never becomes locked into one state. And we can do the same thing with the human body."

"How's that, Noah?"

"Look at the rink, Hinton. See how it supports the skaters?"

"Ice."

"Exactly, ice. And to support the human mind we need something colder, much colder," Noah says, becoming animated. "Minus 179 degrees centigrade, to be precise. Then we see longevity, my friend. Just pick your millennium, and you shall see it all! When the next big hurricane and floods come, or the next ice age, in about 25,000 years, we will have a way to live beyond it. And that, Mr. Hinton, that is why people call me Noah."

Chapter 31:
Meeting with the Trash Queen

8:36 p.m.—The Lincoln Monument

The children sit on the steps of the Lincoln Monument watching the Reflecting Pool as the last of the tourists leave the grounds. Night sets in and they realize they won't find their mother. Asking passers-by of the whereabouts of the Howard Johnson's Motor Lodge proves unrewarding, their questions always answered with more questions. "Where are your parents? Why are you alone?" One family says they will get the park police to come help, and tells them to wait on the stairs.

Rebecca wants to give in. Having failed to reach either her father or mother, unable to find the way back to the motel, she now has to rely on Angel's money and the change that is almost spent. Too tired to cry, she places her head down between her knees. Angel and Michael wait for her solution, when in the distance they hear a tiny bell.

Angel sees her first, hunched over a shopping cart, moving slowly, but at a constant pace. A dog that appears neither safe nor menacing, but large and stout follows the Trash Queen. A small bell rings from the side of the shopping cart filled with personal items, bottles, and aluminum cans. As she comes closer Michael studies her purple hat and gray hair. The hat's lined with a few seagull feathers and he laughs at it.

"Not so bad," she says, looking at them on the steps directly above her.

"What? What's not so bad?" Angel asks, checking to see if police are coming. Rebecca looks up as well.

"Life's not so bad. You're lost. You're feeling sorry for yourselves, but you'll be all right."

"Who says we feel sorry?" Angel responds. "Who are you?"

"I'm the queen of trash, sweetie. I clean up the city. And I'll be your friend if you want me to."

Rebecca assesses the woman, dressed in old clothing and pushing an overloaded cart. She's as worrisome as her dog, a pit bull that now sits quietly in the background. Still, she's the friendliest person they've seen during the day.

"Why do you say that?" Angel asks. "You're a stranger. Strangers aren't friends!"

"Well, maybe you need a friend! And you're the strangers, not me. Everyone knows me. Why are you kids sitting up here? You're lost, aren't you?"

"We lost our mom and dad," Michael blurts out.

The siren of an ambulance can be heard in the distance, and they look once more to see if the police are coming. The park and surrounding area are deserted now, and light from the Lincoln Monument illuminates the long Reflecting Pool in front of them. The water is a mirror to the darkening sky. Behind them the statue of Lincoln sits in a stone chair, immense and pondering.

"We're waiting for the police," Rebecca adds, "to take us back to our motel."

"Oh, well you'll wait a long time," the Trash Queen tells her. "The park police are off duty till the city pays them again. Not enough money, if you believe the newspapers."

"We don't, and we don't care," Angel asserts.

"Speak your heart, sweetie. You kids don't stay out here too long if you know what's safe. I hope your parents find you. Where are they?"

"In the hospital," Rebecca answers, without meaning to. She feels herself wavering. "Our dad's in City Hospital. We can't find my Mom. We're not from here."

"Anyone can tell that. And you haven't had dinner either. You kids follow me if you want something to eat. We'll take you to your father."

"Who's we?" Angel asks in the darkness.

Without answering, the Trash Queen continues pushing her cart forward, picking up an aluminum can as she goes in a circle around the memorial. They wait till she's out of sight before Angel speaks her mind.

"I don't like her. She's dirty. You hear her say she could take us to Dad?"

"I'm hungry," Michael argues.

"Well, like, I want to know who 'we' is," Angel decides.

Rebecca and Angel feel they have no better alternative. They stand up, and as the woman travels slowly, moving ahead, they keep their distance and start to follow. The dog turns toward them frequently as their curiosity pulls them behind the cart, and the cart traverses a wide circle of sidewalk surrounding the monument, then abruptly is pushed across a four-lane street through a break in traffic. To their surprise, the old woman disappears into an opening in a cement wall that barely accepts the shopping cart. The dog follows her.

"Shall we go?" Rebecca asks Angel, surrendering her lead role.

"No way!"

"I want to go," Michael urges. "I'm hungry!"

Angel nods, then leads the way. “Okay, come on, you guys. Hurry up!”

As quickly as they traverse the street, they are next to the cement retaining wall. And without looking back they disappear like rabbits through a dark hole.

Saturday, 8:40 p.m.—The sports arena

“…so, you see, it’s taken a few thousand years to arrive at an answer for the race. None of it was accomplished alone. Science is a collective effort. Our findings could be considered a fountain of youth or, when accomplished, we can call it a fountain of eternity.”

“Maybe just a fountain of ice. And exactly when will this work be finished, Noah?”

“True works of science take time, Hinton. Details have to be sorted out; connections have to be made. There are always adjustments, and like I’ve told you, it takes technique.”

The crowd boos and hollers. A few people stand on their seats as referees skate back and forth breaking up fights. Hinton looks down on the rink and sees the two injured players who are lying on the ice.

“Hey, the game’s stopped!” he says. The Medical label on his jacket stands out as he rises and points.

“Sit down, sit down. It’s a minor injury,” Noah tells him.

“What are you talking about? They need us down there.”

“Not now. Every game needs a hero, Hinton. But ours hasn’t arrived yet.”

“What are you talking about?”

Some hockey players still cling to each other, smashing with fists and sticks, and into the brawl spectators throw food and drinks. The ushers and police have gathered at the bottom of the conical gallery.

"Well, think about it. If man's going to live for eons, someone has to be first. Someone always has to go first. That can't happen without a hero, can it?"

"What are you talking about? You're going to freeze yourself?"

"No, no, we need a volunteer. He's here tonight, in this arena."

"Who? Why are you looking at me?"

"No, not you, Hinton. And I'm not interested in glory either. I've chosen someone who can represent all of mankind."

"Not you, not me?"

"No, Hinton. Not us. Him!"

Noah points down to the rink where Colson and Deed have arrived to handle the emergency. Colson is struggling to maneuver a gurney toward one of the injured players.

"Colson?"

The crowd suddenly changes its mood, laughing as Colson loses his footing and slips.

"Yes, of course, it's Colson!"

Sliding and scrambling across the ice, he pushes the gurney next to the two players. As he and Deed use the transfer board to move one player on top of the gurney, another fight breaks out and the crowd roars.

After the game spectators flow out to the parking lot and get into their cars. One engine starts, followed by another. Hinton sits in the Atomic Car and ponders Noah's strange ideas of longevity while they listen to the din of thousands of motors. Like a huge reptilian awakening, the linked chain of vehicles moves slowly away, each spectator joined to the larger body as their cars emerge from the arena. Headlights advance in short, predictable sequences, and Noah stares straight ahead.

Saturday, 8:50 p.m.—A homeless campsite and the Monument

At the other end of the city the Lovejoy children join a homeless encampment on the bank of the Potomac. Nestled into a thick clump of trees, it's hidden behind the cement wall dividing the asphalt avenue from the river below. A ragtag army of Weatherpeople settles back into their individual spaces—blankets and old sleeping bags insulated by newspapers, sheltered by lean-to plastic tarps.

The Trash Queen, they discover, shares space with an older man known as "Trash King," and they have a large tent with cots and even some foldout chairs. He commands three shopping carts filled with cans he's collected during the day. The proceeds from yesterday's aluminum have netted enough money to purchase a chicken, which he cooks over a small open fire, along with strips of potatoes frying in the fat.

"Hey, it's like camping out," Angel says, as they sit by the fire and watch the river flow past. Her mom would condemn the fat, but it makes the potatoes taste better. Michael lets grease drip onto his shirt and pants, feeling strangely at ease among the vagrants.

"You like camping out?" the Trash King asks. His white beard covers an otherwise black face, and his eyes shine in the light of the fire. Rebecca looks at the softer lights of the city and a moon rising in the eastern sky.

"I like camping," Michael offers.

"Where do you get all the plates and stuff?" Angel asks. Beside them she has observed a makeshift table full of utensils.

"Thrown away. The world can live on what this city throws away. You need to drink some water," the King says, offering them a gallon bottle, which they decline.

"We have to find our motel. Will you take us back to the subway now?" Rebecca turns and asks the old woman.

"No, it's dangerous at night. You can go in the morning," she tells them. She puts the chicken bones into a bag and then walks a few feet down to the river and begins washing the plates and forks.

"Well, we can't stay here," Rebecca says.

"It's all right. Tomorrow the King can take you back to the hospital so you can find your father. Or maybe your mother. And we can find your motel. But tonight, you should stay with the president."

"President?"

"The man in the building. It's not safe for kids around here. If you follow me, I'll take you to a safe place. I got blankets for you."

The food and the fire, along with a long day, have made them tired. In the darkness they see other fires and the silhouettes of indigents, people who seem even stranger than the Trash Queen.

Afraid to do anything else on her own, Rebecca stands up. Angel and Michael follow her closely as the Trash Queen leads them back through the hole in the cement wall. From her shopping cart she pulls three blankets and a tarp, and then emerges out onto the sidewalk. Across the avenue they can see the back of the Lincoln Monument, and when there's a break in the traffic they cross over.

Floodlights illuminate the front, but it's dark in the rear. They almost lose track of her as she quickly makes her way to a hidden door at the base of the Monument. Surprisingly, it's open. She signals for them to follow her.

"King can pick any door he wants to," she says to them with a smile, showing a missing tooth. She heads into the dark underground floor. "Hold hands and we'll go to the upstairs where you can see the president."

They follow cautiously behind, up a flight of stairs, through another dark hallway, and then they are next to the enormous statue.

Sitting in the stone chair, the sculpture of Lincoln rises twenty feet, his solemn countenance gazing toward the Reflecting Pool and the lights of the city, leaving them silent. Like a deity witnessing a great event, he makes them feel smaller as the Trash Queen places blankets at his feet, over the tarp. When the blankets are all arranged, they curl together at the base and listen to stories of the capital, drifting into deep slumber.

Day 6

Guru Miraj and Anna David

"Where does all this lead us? What is our conclusion? First, we must conclude that we do not yet know the whole Watergate story, and recognize that we may never know it. Many mysteries remain."

—H. R. Haldeman, The Ends of Power, 1978

"Politics do not stand in polar opposition to our lives. Whether we desire it or not, they permeate our existence, insinuating themselves into the most private spaces of our lives."

—Angela Davis, Women, Culture, and Politics, 1984

"It is not enough to give health care to the sick, or jobs to the jobless, or education to our children. But it is where we start. It is where our union grows stronger. And as so many generations have come to realize over the course of the 221 years since a band of patriots signed that document in Philadelphia, that is where the perfection begins."

—Barack Obama, A More Perfect Union speech, 2008

Chapter 32:

Another Seizure

Day 6, Sunday, June 18, 1972

8:10 a.m.—The phone booth at HoJo's

After completing a night shift dispatching for Medical, I return to room 722 and receive an urgent notice to call Domingo, so I leave the motel and use the phone booth outside. Room 723 is empty now, other than the FBI rummaging through to look for more evidence on the Plumbers. The agents are thorough, taking photos, collecting all the left over items with using rubber gloves and putting them in black plastic bags. When the plumbers got caught, Baldwin loaded up all the electronics and took them all to McCord's house. Not much is left behind. The children from room 623 are lost now somewhere in the expanses of the capital. I know things will heat up, and Domingo confirms this.

"Tango, you have two more days to wrap up your work. Fidel wants the Code, and Blackbeard says you are to take care of Nixon. For once and for all!"

My original goal was to find the Code, but there's no mistaking this second mission. A cold sensation sweeps through my body. Outside the usual morning traffic passes by, it's a calm Sunday morning, but I know my work has become more dangerous. The taxi I drive conceals a high-powered rifle that can hit targets one hundred yards distant and has been tested before.

"Is Blackbeard speaking for the Líder Máximo, and how is this supposed to happen?"

"You will know, Tango. Blackbeard reminds you that you're an operative. So, don't ask questions. Just do as you're told."

Eliminating Nixon is two death sentences. To escape the capital and return to Cuba will be next to impossible, and just delivering the Code to Fidel will not clear me of responsibility. I pause, but continue questioning.

"How can I do this, Domingo? How am I prepared to take a man's life."

"It's simple, Tango. You have a rifle, and you will be close to Nixon, and when the moment is right, you will know what to do. Be certain you are prepared."

It occurs to me, as I stand in the booth, looking out at Virginia Avenue, that in 1963 the CIA team was in the same quandary when they planned out Fidel's assassination in Havana. It was timed to coincide with another military invasion of Cuba. Cubela and Varona, the CIA double agents in Cuba, would have faced certain elimination after the act. But then Kennedy was assassinated, and all those plans changed. Here I am looking at another unpleasant assignment.

"Tell Blackbeard," I inform Domingo, "that I'm doubtful this work is feasible."

"And Blackbeard says he expects this answer from you, but you are to complete your mission."

8:12 a.m.—The Medical office

After working for Medical for five days, sleeping less than twenty hours, Hinton sits in the main office, waiting for inspection and assignments. He pours a cup of coffee and drinks it black. The thought of Helen working in the humid air of the laundry room, a few doors away, also keeps him from dozing.

Kisman sits on the barber's chair, overlooking the room and the assembled drivers. Beside him is a medical student from City Hospital who has applied and been accepted to work for Medical. It's the same med student that helped take care of David Lovejoy.

"We've got a new man," Kisman tells the group, introducing the recruit.

"Mr. Miraj, these are the men you'll be working with. Miraj, by the way, is a senior medical student, and he's as smart as they come. He doesn't have experience with ambulances, so you men need to bring him up to speed and teach him."

Miraj's driving skills are uncertain. Kisman has hired him based on a report of high scores on his medical exams and, more importantly, that he'll work for a low wage and is unlikely to complain. He'll be working part-time and his orientation, like Hinton's, is brief.

"Deed over there, he's the one to keep up with," Kisman explains. "Deed's working with Otieno today because his fiancée takes the day off on Sundays. Otieno is the big buck with the coffee cup. He'll teach you how to work in the ghetto. And Dr. Noah does our research. Mr. Miraj here is said to be very bright, Professor. Maybe he can teach you a thing or two?"

Noah looks briefly at the short youth dressed in silk pajamas. Unimpressed, he resumes working on a program with his calculator.

"Where's Hinton?" Kisman continues, looking around for the other new driver, who's no longer in the room. "Probably in the laundry room again, talking to Helen. Well, there's Mr. Haldeman, who's our dispatcher. He works in the radio room. Of course, you already know Mr. Colson, who you will be working with today."

Miraj rode to work with Colson, who was on the phone talking anxiously with the president about his race for re-election and the recent break-in imbroglio. As Miraj stands in front of the drivers, there's a confused silence. It's unusual for students to join the crew. Although bright, they're often naive about emergency care on the street. Miraj, slightly overweight, with a dark whiff of a mustache and cream white pajamas, looks barely fifteen years old.

"You can be calling me Guruji," he announces, with a musical, adenoid accent. "Or Miraj. Whatever makes you most happy. Those who become my Chelas—that is to say, disciples—call me 'Guruji.' Where I come from it means affection for the Perfect Master. I was appointed when I was eight years old."

"Oh boy, where did they find you?" Deed asks, drinking coffee and looking down at Miraj's feet, fitted with sandals.

"Oh, I come from no particular place, though actually I am coming from all places. I am what they call 'Sat Guruji.' That is, in less words than more, he who brings truth. When there is me, you get what you see!"

"Oh, brother," Deed protests.

"Heee..." Miraj laughs nervously, then rubs his mustache and lifts a finger upright. "All things above," he says, pointing to the ceiling, "begin below. All things below begin above. Does it matter where you come from, if you know where you are?"

"I don't care where I am, Little Guru, as long as I go somewhere," Deed answers, pointing his finger at Miraj. "So, pay attention and don't get in the way."

"And he who points a finger at others...has four more pointing at himself," Miraj responds.

Kisman frowns, using the lever on the side of the barber's chair to pump himself up. The shadowed contour of his eyes belies the strain of daily management. He looks forward to the introduction of "Instant Access," a program that will give Medical a competitive edge. The opportunity of running four ambulances continuously will also enhance profits. Miraj, young, without experience, oblivious to the minimum wage and looking for academic credit as a student, will fit the strategy. Nixon wants a health care strategy that out-competes the Therapy ambulance system.

"I point wherever I want," Deed tells the young master. "Did you come here to be a student or a smartass?"

"Oh, I hope to learn about Western medicine and your work," Miraj answers.

"Good!" Kisman interrupts. "You will work with Colson today. He'll show you the 'ropes' once you get on the road. Now, everyone remember, tomorrow is Election Day. We'll be having an announcement for you, and the president will be visiting us here too."

Colson opens a box of donuts and sinks his teeth into a pocket of strawberry jam. Otieno watches the new driver from a distance when they're distracted by the rustling noise of a cockroach that comes into view next to some boxes in the corner. Its tentacles are pointed upwards, like the Guruji's finger.

"Kill it, Colson," Deed demands.

"Kill it?" Miraj asks.

"That's right. We don't want roaches all over the place!"

"Precisely. We don't tolerate bugs," Kisman joins in, as he pumps the barber's chair higher. Colson wipes jam from the side of his lip.

"I'll take care of it," Deed concludes, sneaking up on the insect.

"No, no, I'll take care of him," Miraj intervenes. With a snap of his fingers, the insect scampers away, but a small electronic device falls off of its back.

"Where'd he go?" Deed demands, picking up the device. "And what the hell is this? It looks like an electronic transmitter!"

"Bugs can be our friends!"

"You're a friend of roaches? Listen, little man, if you like 'em in your country, you take 'em with you. And why is someone trying to bug this place?"

"No, I don't kill insects," Miraj replies. "They are messengers. They tell us when there is too much waste. They live below."

Otieno grins. Cockroaches are ubiquitous, and in addition, just about everyone in Washington D.C. has been bugged. He raises his fist in a salute to the guru. "That's right, Miraj. Make 'em disappear—you got nothing to fear. Now, we're outta here."

Kisman pushes the barber's chair lever forward, causing it to descend smoothly. Adjusting his tie, cinched neatly around the collar of his white shirt, he scans the room while frowning.

"Men, we need to work. So, get out and drive. And, where's Hinton?"

8:20 a.m.—The laundry room

Inside the steamy laundry room, Hinton eyes rings of moisture around Helen's armpits, and is aware of a layer of perspiration on his own forehead, he wipes it dry with his forearm and sets his coffee down.

"Hot in here!"

"Aren't you going to meet the new driver?" she asks.

"Sure," he answers, meeting her eyes. Her straight blond hair is pulled back tight. He focuses on her face and neck, also perspiring in the humid room. A sheet comes slowly through the rolling iron, but she hesitates and it almost lands on the floor.

"I have to fold," she says, breaking the silence. As she catches it, he moves simultaneously, touching the side of her arm.

"Let me help."

She lets his hand rest on her for a second. "Okay, let's fold."

Taking the corners, they stand before each other, bringing the sheet together till their arms touch. Her breasts push lightly against his chest and she laughs.

"So, when do we start?"

"Soon," he answers, watching her back away. She takes his two edges to complete the horizontal fold.

"Really, you've talked to everyone? The four drivers?"

"Yeah, somewhat. They don't all understand yet what a union means for us. But we'll get them there."

"Everyone?"

"Well, the drivers have been a little difficult, different, you might say...this is not your average business. But I think they're going to come together and we'll make the union. Including you," he says, realizing his omission. "We'll force the changes. It's just a matter of time till we represent the workers, and eventually a new health system for the country."

"Well James, we have to change the management, not just the drivers. And what do you call me, anyway?" Her eyes hold him in a gaze.

"Laundry wom... I mean, well, Christ, Helen, what do you call yourself?"

"I'm a driver. You need to start calling me a driver."

"I can't do that," he says, wiping his forehead.

"Why not?"

"'Cause, you're not a driver."

"Well, I most certainly will be."

"Wait a minute. We don't change health care overnight, Helen. I mean you don't really drive an ambulance at this point, you know, at least not yet. And what's wrong with laundry woman?"

"You're going to see."

Returning to the main office, Hinton hears Kisman announcing duties for the day. Otieno is assigned to work with Deed in Car 38 since Car 45 needs maintenance.

"Be careful with the cars," Kisman comments, adjusting his glasses, "and with the patients. The...uh…our president, and owner of this company, is going to visit us soon. No driver gets time off till our new 'Instant Access' succeeds—you hear me, Noah, Hinton? You two need to stay in your car. I want 'Instant Access' for every customer. Our new program starts today and your job is to be first on the scene."

"I'm not a driver," Noah counters. "I'll design my own strategies, Mr. Kisman, thank you very much, and they don't include taking instant care of customers in the back of the Atomic Car."

Noah turns off his calculator and tips his glasses up. Kisman tips up his glasses as well.

"Design whatever you want, Dr. Noah. If you don't help us achieve 'Instant Access,' you can feed all your rocket strategies to your calculator. They will never be funded. Do you understand?"

Noah scans the room. Guru Miraj is sitting with legs folded on the couch, with puckered lips beneath his wisp of a mustache.

"What's there to understand?" Noah rebuts. "When this city runs out of gas, you're going to need me for energy if you want to fund anything. And my rocket strategy is already funded. Are you aware of that?"

"Yes, I am, Doctor," Kisman says, pronouncing the title with two heavy syllables. "But that time is a long way off. Okay, I concede that you don't drive customers. You can continue to be transportation designer, in your Atomic Vehicle, as you prefer to call it. And Hinton can do all the driving today. He aspires to be a great driver—don't you, Hinton?"

Hinton smiles. Kisman has a few things to learn about greatness.

"Okay, Doctor," Kisman continues. "Good enough. You ride on the passenger side and design ambulances of the future. Now, Colson, you go work with Mr. Miraj today. You'll teach him everything you know, won't you, Colson?"

Colson eyes Miraj with ambivalence and disdain.

Anyone who wears a white silk jumpsuit is already a little deviant. On the other hand, I like the role of trainer, and having broken in Hinton, I'm ready for this medical student. Judging from this little Guru's interactions with Deed, he'll probably be interesting.

"If the little Guruji wants to work, I can show him the ropes," Colson answers.

"Good, good, we have people to save. Now get out of here, all of you, and start driving. Remember our goal—Instant Access!"

Chapter 33:

Howard Hughes Hospital

9:10 a.m.— Margaret Lovejoy's room

As her memory returns Margaret looks past the bed table and IV pole that have been her primary furniture for three days. An image of the motor lodge and room 623 surfaces in her mind and then she sees Rebecca, Angel, and Michael standing by the door and waving at her. Are they wearing street clothes? Or are they in bathing suits? She scans the hospital room, painted a cream white color and with a large window looking out onto a golf course. Ignoring the call button that summons a nurse, she is able to free herself from the bed covers and stand.

"I just want to get out of here. I have to go now! Where's my family? Please!"

Standing inside the hallway, she can be heard at the nursing station and beyond, repeating the message as nurses turn to see her ashen figure, still connected to IV tubing and fluids. Outside the hospital a distant siren merges with her voice, and she falls back onto a hardwood floor, eyes rolling upward.

"Code Blue—second floor east—hallway" the intercom alarms as nurses arrive quickly and position her safely on the floor. By the time a crash cart arrives, Dr. Cohen, making rounds nearby, has entered the room to do an examination. Her eyes stare emptily as the seizure activity diminishes to mild twitching.

"Okay, I'm calling this condition chronic," he comments to the assembled team, as a nurse checks vital signs, reporting normal pulses and blood pressure. "And I'm afraid it's the last straw. She has no identifiable insurance. Administration says she goes to City Hospital. And as much as I would like to know what's causing this, Jane Doe gets transferred today."

9:21 a.m.—Car 22

Heading back to the living quarters, Colson glances repeatedly at the sandaled youth sitting mysteriously across from him. Miraj looks out at dense, serried traffic through the passenger window, fingering a black tie that drapes over his jumpsuit as a ribbon of distinction.

"And now I am fortunate to be working here. There are more cars than anywhere in the world," Miraj says, in order to start a conversation. "And, of course, more accidents."

"And what do you mean more accidents?"

"Oh, I am only saying that in the meaning of business. It is a good city for ambulances, when there are so many accidents here. Is that not true?"

"We don't have that many accidents," Colson counters. "We just take care of them. It's our job."

"Everything changes. It is the rule of enlightenment."

Colson blows his nose into a handkerchief. "What's this enlightenment crap, anyway?"

"I became a master when I was eight," Miraj announces.

"Yeah, well, good for you, kid. And so did I, and I'm a lot older than you are. Any other good ideas?"

Colson slides the handkerchief into the back pocket of his jumpsuit. Car 22 moves into the opposite lane and he swings the wheel to avoid oncoming traffic.

"Actually, I don't work with ideas," Miraj answers, looking straight ahead. "I see light. You will tell me of your powers, perhaps."

"Powers? Listen, boy, you keep your powers to yourself and do what I tell you. That's my power. First thing you learn in this car is where our stuff is. So, go on back and start learning. Then I'll test you, get it? Go ahead…. I mean get in back. You understand my English?"

It should be safe for a medical student to explore by himself, Colson figures, but the Guru doesn't move.

"Just now I am seeing a light," Miraj says, closing his eyes.

"And I said to get in back. Didn't I just tell you?"

"Car 22!"

"Damn!" Colson curses as Haldeman's voice comes over the radio. Miraj becomes glassy-eyed, gazing out the windshield, making him more nervous.

"22 by."

"You have a Jane Doe transfer at Hughes Hospital," the dispatcher orders. "Can you do that right away?"

"Uhh...roger. Check. We're on our way."

Miraj becomes animated again, and Colson is relieved to see his eyes clear. Colson steers the ambulance toward the Hughes Hospital while studying his partner for the day.

"Kid, you looked kinda weird there for a second," he says, trying to be friendly. "We're gonna miss today's football game and I still plan to show you some real change. So, I want you to get in back and start figuring out where things are. You never know. We just might have a little trauma."

"Trauma?"

"Yeah, trauma. They train you for emergency care in medical school, don't they? You got an EMT or paramedic certificate to resuscitate? We don't drive without a certificate, right?"

"Mr. Colson, I'm a medical student. And also a Perfect Master."

Miraj notes boards along the road to the hospital with **Immediate Access** spelled out in bold letters. The board's image of a healthy-looking patient surrounded by attractive nurses keeps his attention briefly. Then he looks ahead at the Hughes Hospital, circled by lavish landscaping and golf greens as they approach the entrance.

"Or maybe a perfect disaster! Why don't you show me your certificate now?" Colson insists.

Miraj checks the time, looking at a gold watch on his wrist. Colson's attention shifts as he stops at the gate to acknowledge the guards. They let him through and he drives toward the back of the hospital, feeling nervous. It's rare to be sent to Hughes for a transfer to City Hospital.

"Oh, I have many certificates," Miraj answers finally, looking at the white columns surrounding the hospital. "Is it now the Emergency Room to which we are going? I hear so many things about this hospital."

"This is not City Hospital, kid. This place is for real. It's state of the art and you don't get admitted here without insurance! Now, when we go in, you leave the talking to me."

They back up to the loading station and sliding glass doors open as the ambulance enters the rear of the building. Colson motions to get out of the car while Miraj admires the indoor fountain and trees.

"What are you waiting for?" he asks, pulling the back door open. "Let's get the gurney. On one!"

"On one?"

"That's right. On one! Now you reach for it just like I'm telling you to!"

"Reach for what?" Miraj asks, standing behind the ambulance.

"The gurney! Jesus, boy, you don't know how to use a bloody gurney?"

"Actually, no."

Colson pulls out a handkerchief.

"Whatta you mean, no?"

"Well, I have only seen them in the hospital. But I haven't ever used one."

"Well, why not, goddamn it? Didn't you just say you had a certificate?"

"They do not have so many ambulances in my country. Actually, I am thinking you will teach me. And I have only trained in City Hospital, not in the car."

Colson stares in disbelief, then checks to see if others are listening.

"So, tell me something, Miraj" he asks softly. "Why the hell are you here in D.C., anyway?"

"To bring light to the people of this city. And to learn your medicine."

"And you can't work a gurney?"

"Perhaps you misunderstand," Miraj says. "The Perfect Master does not usually carry others. Others carry him."

"You wait here."

Colson gets back into the ambulance and radios Haldeman, who tells him to hurry up because they have another run to make. After a short discussion he returns back to the rear of Car 22, where Miraj is waiting.

"All right, boy, when I say 'on one,' you hang onto this rail and we pull the gurney out. You understand that? I'm the

Perfect Master here. You do what I tell you or I'll put you on the fucking gurney."

"Okay! That is to say, roger," clarifies Miraj.

"Okay! On one!"

"On one! Roger!"

They pull together, and when the gurney falls ahead of them Miraj lands next to it on the ground.

"What the hell?"

"Just now I am learning!" Miraj says enthusiastically, wiping dust off his pajamas.

A security guard wanders in their direction.

"Master my ass! I have to watch you and now we have another run. So, come on."

Colson retrieves the gurney and they pass through sliding glass doors leading to the elevator. Miraj is intrigued and looks back as the doors close automatically.

"That's quite good!" he acknowledges.

Entering the elevator, Colson pushes the third-floor button with the letters "VIP" written on it.

"And this must be how you treat your wealthy ones?" Miraj asks.

"That's right. I'm glad you know something. Now listen, don't ask questions. In fact, don't say anything. You just keep your mouth shut and do what I tell you."

Miraj nods as the elevator doors open and they enter a lush, carpeted hallway. The gurney rolls soundlessly past portraits of the prominent benefactors and Howard Hughes till they arrive at the center nursing cubicle. Classical music comes from invisible speakers as Colson reaches for transfer paper. Behind the nurse preparing them, Dr. Cohen sits watching patients on a television monitor and making notes.

"They're here to transfer Mrs. Doe," the nurse announces.

"Good," Cohen acknowledges. "She's stable. No seizures since restarting a valium drip. Dilantin levels are reasonable. So, now's the time to get her out, gentlemen. I sure hope she remembers who she is someday."

He looks briefly at the drivers and Miraj's loose jumpsuit, then back at the TV monitors. Colson takes the papers and heads for Lovejoy's room while Miraj walks behind him, holding the back of the gurney. Halfway down the photo-embellished hallway they find Margaret Lovejoy lying on a queen-size bed, staring vacantly at the ceiling.

"Medical Ambulance, ma'am," Colson tells her, pushing the gurney alongside the bed. Miraj continues to admire the rolling golf greens through the tall window at the end of the room. Men wearing shorts and brightly covered shirts swing the thinnest of metal bats at tiny white balls. The balls travel for a long distance, as if the men want them to disappear, and then they chase the balls in electric carts. It's unlike any cricket game Miraj has seen, and he admires the meticulously groomed lawn that stretches forever.

"Ma'am, we're going to be moving you to a new hospital now. My assistant and I are going to slide you over, onto our gurney here. Okay, Guru, let's go!"

Entranced by the men in carts, still chasing their miniature white balls, Miraj is reluctant to leave the window, but he walks toward the patient while Margaret's nurse watches on.

"Let's go, I said," Colson repeats. He places a draw sheet beneath Margaret by rolling her sideways, first away, then toward himself, until she's centered. Her pregnant abdomen raises up above the sheet. "Listen, boy, steady her while I slide her onto the gurney, get it? Grab a hold right now!"

Miraj stands across the bed, holding the sheet passively.

Through the periphery of her eyes, Margaret becomes aware of the men on each side, vaguely recognizing the medical student as the one who helped her to find her husband. Although she is postictal, confused, and recovering from her most recent seizure, her memory continues to return. Miraj remembers her well but concentrates on the task at hand. While he's well trained in the academics of medicine, making a bed transfer is a new task.

"Okay, Guruji. I say 'on one.' You know what to do."

"Oh well..."

"Okay, I'm gonna say 'on one.' You ready? 'On one!'"

"Uhhhhh..."

Colson pulls on his side. Miraj holds firmly onto his own. The patient slides sideways onto the gurney and Miraj is pulled over onto the bed, still clinging to the sheet.

"Jesus, you klutz, you're gonna ruin my back!" Colson protests. Miraj smiles, embarrassed. As he gets up, neither driver or even the nurse notes that the IV dislodged during the transfer, and remains tenuously taped to Margaret's arm.

Chapter 34:

"I've Got Insurance!"

10:15 a.m.—City Hospital

After three and a half days on the ventilator, David Lovejoy feels new strength. His lungs have recovered enough from the shock of diesel exhaust and cigarette smoke to begin transporting oxygen again, and the ventilator's flowing concentration of the life-giving oxygen is sufficient to perfuse his body. Pain from the plastic tube rubbing his throat and vocal cords convinces him it's time to act. A constant "whooshing" sound of the ventilator, synchronized with a burning sensation in his stomach, adds to a discomfort that surpasses his fear of losing oxygen again, and he waits for his chance.

The busy trauma service, cardiac arrests, and Code Blues have left the night's ICU team ragged. As the morning advances a group of new physicians makes belated morning rounds. They approach David's bed with a chart of vital signs and labs, and the head of the team makes hopeful comments.

"This guy has decent blood gases. If we get him off the vent, we can transfer him to the floor and free up the bed. Actually, I hear he probably has insurance. So, we could even move him today, if he weans off the vent okay."

They close in to make adjustments on the ventilator, diminishing his support gradually, when it becomes apparent he'll bring about his own extubation. A thrust and pull of his right arm slips it loose from gauze restraints and he yanks his breathing tube out in one fell swoop.

"I've…I've got insurance," he whispers through swollen vocal cords.

Multiple days on the ventilator have left his vocal cords swollen, and the ICU team can't quite recognize his words. They rush to restrain him.

"Don't pull out your IV!"

"Hold still. You need oxygen."

"Relax! Someone get a crash cart in case we have to re-intubate. Mister, whoever you are, you need to settle down and breathe with a mask. You're not going anywhere yet!"

Overwhelmed by hands that secure him to the sides of the bed, he tries to fight loose again.

"You're okay—everything's all right," the head doctor says, glancing down and looking for a name on the chart.

Lovejoy wrestles free a second time, pulling the oxygen mask off his face.

"I've got…I've got insurance. I sell insurance!" he croaks.

The team draws nearer, trying to decipher the words.

"Insurance!" he whispers once more. This time the words are clear enough. "Find my family…"

"Yeah, this is the guy," the ICU chief says. "His wife said he's supposed to be an insurance executive. He's the one who had a pulmonary collapse by the Watergate. Let's check his blood gases again. If they're all right we can call an ambulance and send him to Hughes Hospital. You know his wife came here looking for him, but she's never returned. I wonder what happened to her?"

Sunday, 10:45 a.m.—Car 38, Otieno and Deed

"I have a transfer for you," Haldeman calls out from the dispatcher's office. "City Hospital to Hughes Hospital. Go pick up a David Lovejoy."

Otieno is driving Deed's Car 38 down the beltway, circling the city when the call comes in. Deed is scanning the horizon through dark glasses, noting the Watergate Towers curving upward by the Potomac and the Hughes Pyramid in the distance. He communicates with Lieutenant Liddy on a separate police channel and the conversation is muffled, but the words "damage control" are repeated several times.

"What's that?" Otieno asks, pointing to a switch next to the transmission column of Car 38. "And what's all this about 'damage control'?"

"Turbocharge," Deed answers. "We use it for acceleration. You can try it if you want, and don't worry about 'damage control.' That's my forte."

Deed takes off the headphones and looks across the river, still scanning the Watergate complex and considering his new situation.

What was supposed to be a simple plumbing mission, stopping leaks and getting rid of the Weatherpeople, has become a nightmare. Especially the problem of the break-in to Dr. Fielding's office to get records on Ellsberg. That could blow up Nixon's presidency. And if the Colombia Plaza call girls get pulled into the investigation it will be even worse. This whole thing is starting to unravel, but if I can keep it from going public, and oversee the investigation, it might just blow over. Nixon doesn't know everything I know, but he's damn smart, and they will all be counting on me.

Otieno reaches over and flips on the turbocharge, and Car 38 accelerates ahead, leaving behind a cloud of exhaust.

Day 6, Sunday, 10:47—Unit 160, Cuba

I know Fidel likes to travel in a Soviet ZIL 114 limousine, Brezhnev's gift to him from his first trip to Moscow. He is led and followed by Groupo #1, fourteen of his best security guards traveling in red Alfa Romeos. To complete security, he reaches down and palms the 7.62 Kalashnikov assault rifle, placed between his feet, along with five cartridges holding thirty bullets apiece. For additional safety, he keeps a 9mm Browning pistol just behind his right shoulder, with three clips of thirteen bullets. Juan Sanchez, sitting in the front seat, also has his 7.62 Kalashnikov. One of Fidel's closest friends, Gabriel Marquez, is visiting from Colombia, and sits next to him.

"You see, Gabo, I have my protection. Who needs a fancy briefcase with a steel chain attached to their security guard? The so-called 'Football.' I walk freely among my people. 'Vive la Revolución!'"

Marquez laughs nervously, looking out a triple-glass layered window at the surrounding city as they head for Unit 160 and the early birthday party planned for the comandante.

"Well, you know how to defend yourself, Fidel. You're well known for your marksmanship. And what's going on with your efforts to capture that Code? Are you any closer?" Marquez's thick eyebrows lift up.

"We will find out shortly. Cuban spies are the best on the planet, Gabo, you know that. The CIA has sixty of theirs in Miami, along with six hundred informers, and we know every one of them. The day will come when the U.S. will ask to borrow some of ours!"

Fidel and Marquez both laugh as the limo pulls into the five-acre family farm in the Siboney quarter of Havana. Fidel's second wife, Dalia, meets him on entering. They kiss as always, and she takes his Kalashnikov to place it in the bedroom. Fidel and Marquez are greeted by Raul Cruz at the private house in the center, where a sheep is roasting outside. It will soon be served to the assorted guests along with birthday gifts of Algerian wine, Iraqi figs, and *pata negra* hams. First to greet them is the head of espionage, Blackbeard, who brings the supposed good news.

"I am told, Comandante, that our man, Tango, is closer each day. We will learn the secret code by the end of this week. And this Watergate saga is unfolding faster than the CIA can handle it. The success will be yours!"

Castro looks over at Marquez, smiles, and lights a cigar.

"You see, you see how this works, Gabo?

"But, Fidel, Cuba is only an island. And America is an island too, but a very large one."

"And they don't speak our language. But we can speak theirs!"

10:50 a.m.—Homeless camp

Having returned from the Lincoln Memorial, where they spent the night wrapped in blankets, the Lovejoy children have a breakfast of cereal and canned milk by the side of the river, and then try their hands at fishing with the Trash King. The Queen washes plates and utensils on the bank and stores them away in her tent. Having emptied her shopping cart of bottles and aluminum cans into plastic bags, she prepares to head back into the city.

"Good luck finding your father," she tells the children, as she heads out. "If there's something to be found in this city the King will take you there. He may be a little slow, but he knows his way around and he'll get you to the place you need to be."

The Trash King has promised to take them back to the hospital and act as their custodian. With renewed hopes they sit along the tree-lined bank holding long poles with nylon lines dangling in the water. Hooks baited with chicken fat drift deep in the muddied water, and as the sun lights up the distant bank the day promises to be hot and humid.

"How come you have to live here?" Angel asks the King. "Did you get in trouble with the police?"

"I leave the police alone. They leave me alone."

"Me too," Michael says. Never having fished before, he's uncertain what might happen at the end of the line. He keeps a wary eye on some Wood Ducks swimming not far from their angling venture.

"Don't you need a house? That's not a house," Angel continues, indicating the Lincoln Memorial where they spent the night. "Not this, either." She looks at the motley collection of cardboard huts with rain tarps, shopping carts, and folding tables nestled into the trees and bushes. And the large tent where the King and Queen sleep.

"Houses cost money," the King says. "You don't get that kind of money picking up cans and trash."

"We have a house," Michael tells the King.

"Glad you do, Michael. Houses are good when you stay in one place. I like traveling."

"Well, you could stay in our house."

Rebecca watches the King smile.

I trust him only a little, and everything he does is slow. His clothes are dirty, and we need to get started—soon!

She watches several boats and a large yacht cruising up the river. The yacht's diesel motor hums softly and the sound alights a large heron, which glides off a tree branch like a kite, floating silently past them. It crosses over the river and heads downstream.

"You kids are okay. You too, Michael. Now look at that there. That's the president's boat. He lives in a house that we ought to go see. The White House! Maybe we'll go today."

"We saw it. Yesterday," Angel tells him. "It has a big fence all around it. You have to go on a tour to get inside."

"President's real important. If he ain't in a yacht he travels in a helicopter. Or sometimes a limousine or an airplane! He's very important."

"How come he needs a big fence around his house? Did he do something wrong?"

The King smiles.

"Maybe he'll help find our mom," Michael suggests.

"Well, maybe he will."

Michael's the first to get a bite.

"I got it!" he shouts with delight and the girls try to help him pull a small catfish from the dark water. The King reaches for the line and removes the hook from the fish, holding it up for their admiration, careful to keep the head spine from piercing his hand.

"Do you eat it?" Angel asks. "It's got whiskers."

"Well, that's why you call it a catfish," he tells her. "These catfish are like me. They pick up garbage. Their food is on the bottom of the river, Angel, and we don't eat things coming out of the river anymore because it's polluted."

"Are you polluted?" Angel asks, looking at the muddy water, then at his clothes. The red and black shirt and dungarees look like they've never been washed and his old boots have holes. When he's sitting close to them the unwashed socks send an odor to their sensitive noses. The King smiles without answering, and Rebecca turns to him.

"Can we go now?"

Chapter 35:

The Wild Goose Chase

10:55 a.m.—Car 22

Rolling down the carpeted hallway of the hospital, Margaret focuses on the sharp edges of the ceiling, sensing each turn as lines become corners, the corners become new hallways, and the journey continues through sliding doors. Entering the elevator an overhead mirror reveals her body on the gurney, covered only by her gown and a sheet. Her face has the flush and glow of pregnancy, and she can barely recognize herself. Then she's wheeled out through a long corridor, and arrives at the indoor reception room for ambulances. The soft foliage of indoor trees and bubbling fountains seem more peaceful.

Where am I, and where am I headed? There was a dinner. I remember that woman who said the politicians could walk on water. On the river. It's so polluted with silt and sewage that no one can swim in it anymore. That was why I was here? To clean up the river? But where? Where did my family go? Why do I feel so strange?

"On one!" Colson calls out. He and Miraj lift the gurney into the back of the ambulance.

"On two," Miraj adds, having studied the locking mechanism. The gurney slides into metal slots along the side of the ambulance—click!—and secures. Colson makes a silent note of their coordination, and nods approval. As she continues to look upwards, Margaret's field of vision includes the long metal bar onto which Miraj hangs her IV bottle.

"Stay back here, boy," Colson tells Miraj. He hasn't noticed the dislodged IV, but the tubing buried beneath the sheet now saturates her gown with anti-seizure medication.

"Take vital signs every ten minutes. If anything's wrong you tell me right away. Got it? All right, let's go!"

Miraj climbs into the back and sits across from Margaret. With the start of the ignition the glass doors open and Car 22 heads out of the receiving room, toward the surrounding green landscape. Miraj snaps his fingers, delighted to see the glass doors slide back together, then turns his attention to the patient, secured on the gurney by a locking belt and a tucked-in blanket. Her facial twitching is worrisome and he reaches over to check the pulse—quickened but not weak.

Could she be experiencing an aura?

"Oh, Colson!" he calls out.

While sampling a fresh donut, Colson simultaneously radios in their location as he approaches the freeway. "Now what's the matter?"

"Actually, I can tell you this. She is surrounded by a light. It is disturbing her."

Colson rolls his eyes, then concentrates on the road. Without looking back, he asks the standard questions. "Right, Miraj. Tell me her pulse."

"Actually, sixty-five per minute."

"Blood pressure?"

"One hundred ten over sixty."

"Respiration?"

"Sixteen per minute!"

As they drive onto the Beltway, Colson spots the shopping cart lady just in front of the on-ramp. He swerves around her and accelerates as he looks back.

"That's fine, kid. I want you to let me know if her pulse climbs. Meanwhile, I'll get us to the hospital. Is that okay with you, Perfect Master?"

"Oh roger, yes," Miraj affirms.

The fasciculation of Margaret's facial muscles disappears and she seems to be asleep, almost meditating. Her eyes close.

"You can drive," Miraj adds. "I'll take care of her. But I am going to start a new IV."

"Wait a minute," Colson calls out. "You're not cleared to start IVs. What's wrong with the one she has?"

"Just now it is out."

"Well, you just leave it, you hear me?"

He rolls his eyes in exasperation again, looking for an off-ramp. Taking the first exit he sees a clearing and parks along the shoulder. With the engine still running, he climbs into the rear where Miraj has begun preparing things.

"I thought I said leave it alone!" he barks, approaching the gurney. Margaret opens her eyes and he doesn't like her blank upward stare. "Look, Miraj," he suggests, assessing alternatives, "you do know how to drive, right?"

"Of course! I have driven many cars! I have even flown an airplane! I have never driven an ambulance, however, and I would like to very much!"

"Well, we don't have a choice. I'm gonna let you take the wheel while I fix the IV. So, drive careful. Understand?"

"Roger," Miraj nods.

Miraj climbs into the front of the car, his feet barely reaching the gas pedal. He asks for directions to City Hospital.

"Follow the signs ahead of you, for Christ's sake," Colson tells him, rubbing alcohol on Margaret's arm and fixing a tourniquet. "I'm busy starting an IV, so you need to use your

Perfect Master skills. Use signs with the arrow pointing to the hospital, and if you just look up you can't miss 'em. Just follow the arrows, okay?"

"Roger, yes."

Sitting low in the driver's seat, Miraj engages the transmission while looking up. Just as he does so, a flock of Canadian geese passes directly over the car. The V-shaped formation is pointed northwest and provides the only hint of direction to one not used to D.C. freeways or signposts. So, Car 22 enters back onto the Beltway and heads north, following the migrating pointer.

11:15 a.m.—Car 22

Margaret's eyes open, her sclera as white as the ceiling of the ambulance, as she watches helplessly. Colson, breaking into a sweat, makes attempt after attempt to restart her IV. Like a punctured voodoo doll, plastic catheters dangle from her arm like flags of defeat, haunting him as he searches for a willing vein. Her fluid-accumulating pregnancy and recent seizure make IV access difficult.

"Damn!" he curses, as a few drops of blood trickle from another failed attempt.

With the interruption of the valium drip, Margaret begins to remember more from before the grand mal seizure on Thursday night.

Something happened to David. He was taken to the hospital and I visited him, but he wanted me to go to the dinner. And the children were at the motel. Rebecca was going to take care of everything.... But where am I going now...?

Miraj follows the V-shaped bevy of geese assiduously. They fly high over the ambulance, still within vision, traveling outside city limits on a northwest route. He continues just behind his avian pointer along Canal Road, hoping the hospital will appear since there are no other hospital signs. The birds continue in formation, headed north along the Potomac, and when the birds diverge westward, Miraj decides to take the Canal Bridge. He tracks the birds down a tree-lined passage, mostly empty of traffic and disturbed only by the muffled crackling of Car 22's diesel engine. But the pattern of geese disappears just as the ambulance approaches the gates and buildings of Langley, the CIA headquarters.

"Oh, Mr. Colson!" Miraj calls out, swinging the car over to park near the H-shaped four-storied headquarters. There's room to pull over adjacent to the Memorial Garden, and the geese have now disappeared. "I no longer see any signs or pointers. Where should I be heading?"

"Holy shit! What the hell is going on?" Colson calls out, forgetting Margaret's unyielding arm, and looking out the window.

"The address here says Langley Porter," Miraj answers. "I have followed the V sign and now it has disappeared. Is this the right hospital?"

Colson looks out the side door window, astonished to see the CIA headquarters, and moves to the front of the ambulance.

"Miraj, where the hell are we? I mean, how the fuck did you...?"

At just that moment they're approached by David Atlee Phillips, chief of Western Hemisphere Operations, who has been on a relaxing stroll past the Memorial Garden of the

CIA. Phillips looks in the ambulance window and recognizes Colson.

"Chuck, what in God's name brings you here?"

Colson takes a moment to get over his shock. Leaving his failed attempts to start an IV, he tells Miraj to monitor Margaret Lovejoy. Stepping out of the ambulance he motions for Phillips to step away from the car so they can talk.

"Jesus, David, what are you doing here?" he asks Phillips, too embarrassed to confess that he is now lost.

"I work here, Chuck. And what, may I ask, are you doing? You're a long way from the White House."

Colson wipes sweat from his forehead, then tries to explain the odd surroundings.

"Well, I'm on an ambulance call, and my driver got completely lost, trying to get to City Hospital. This is kind of a disaster!"

"I see," Phillips comments, "and it seems you've had a few in the last few days. The Watergate break-in—it's all over the news, and I think both your boss and mine are in trouble."

It seems odd to me, as I intercept their conversation through the bug planted in Car 22, that David Atlee Phillips would comment not only on Colson's disasters, but his own. After all of Howard Hunt's attempts to assassinate Castro had failed in 1960 and 1971, Philips helped organize the coup and ouster of Allende in Chile. Phillips also worked with Tony Veciano to take care of Castro during a scheduled visit to Chile. The plan was to insert a rifle into a television camera filming the Cuban leader during his news briefing. A Cuban exile, disguised as a newscaster, was going to project a few bullets into Fidel, but it never worked out. Phillips moved on to larger targets.

"David, I have to go. Howard Hunt screwed up the break-in, and I'll probably get blamed, but it wasn't my fault. I was just helping Nixon. Take care, my friend. I'm on an ambulance run."

Colson jumps into the driver's seat and turns the ambulance around. Miraj climbs in the back of Car 22 and surveys Margaret's right swollen arm with the dangling IVs. Her eyes twitch rapidly to the left. The resuscitation kit is open but he refrains from placing a rubber bite block between her teeth, knowing it is no longer indicated.

"Jesus Christ, how did you ever get us out here?" Colson cries, racing down the forest-lined highway.

"You told me to follow the arrow signs ahead of me. I followed them as closely as possible."

Miraj tightens a tourniquet around the left arm and slides a good IV into the vein, then pulls a syringe from the kit and injects enough muscle relaxant to soften the generalized seizure contracture. Almost instantaneously, Margaret's body relaxes and her respirations come easily. He places an oxygen mask around her face.

"Damn, kid. Where'd you learn that?" Colson asks, looking back, envious at how the IV bag is pouring fluid into the pregnant woman. He turns the siren off as he approaches the outskirts of the city.

"Learn what?" Miraj asks.

"To start an IV. That was pretty fast!"

"Well, I'm a student of City Hospital. Our job is to start IVs," Miraj responds.

"Well, maybe you could show me how you did that?"

"Oh, roger that. In a manner of speaking, that is why I'm here."

11:00 a.m.

After sending out the drivers, Kisman leaves the main station and resumes his government duties, spending time on the phone and negotiating with foreign countries. In his absence, Helen slips out of the laundry room to eavesdrop on the dispatcher. The washing machines churn noisily, drowning out her footsteps as she moves down the hallway and next to the dispatcher's door. Standing by the edge, she hears some somber words coming from one of the dispatcher's radios.

"One day we will get them... get them on the ground where we want them. And we'll dig our heels in, step on them hard, and twist. Right, Bob?"

Listening closely, her ear next to the open door, it's easy enough to identify the voice of Nixon. Haldeman sits in a chair, nodding and taking notes on a yellow pad.

"Kisman knows what I mean," the determined voice continues. "Like bugs. Get 'em on the floor and crush them, show them no mercy."

"Yeah, that's right. Kisman...knows," Haldeman agrees, speaking into the private channel. "He would love to eliminate Daniel Ellsberg, who used to be one of his advisers and knows a lot about our plans. He may even know the Code!"

Haldeman simultaneously monitors screens on his desk that show different parts of the city, as well as the location of each of the ambulances. Helen glances through the side of the door, looking for the Atomic Car, which Hinton will be riding in. She spies it on a screen indicating the eastern edge of the city, where Noah's reactor is located.

"That's right," Nixon continues. "Kisman understands competition and strength. That's what makes us successful and well ahead of Therapy. I mean…they talk about the uninsured...you know. Sounds all right...but it doesn't get ambulances to people who need them in a hurry. Market competition makes health care work—we know that."

Helen notes a short pause as Nixon switches back to his first subject of conversation.

"So, what I'm talking about, Bob. We have to control these people...stop the leaks before they get to the democrats and the press! All this break-in stuff can ruin us if it's not done right. You don't think they...uh...know anything. Do you?"

"No. At least nothing's turned up so far. Hunt and Liddy could be a problem, though, if either one starts talking. Liddy, thankfully, is a rock. He'll never desert you."

Haldeman hears a noise and looks away from the radio as Helen ducks quickly behind the door.

"They can ruin us," Nixon continues. "I mean these leaks from the Watergate and where they lead. If I, as the president, can't conduct national business, we're lost. So...what have they found out, Bob? You think Liddy and Hunt have discovered anything? About Hughes?"

"As far as I can tell...nothing. Just some call girl-type arrangements. A bunch of lascivious phone calls from the Columbia Plaza," Haldeman answers, turning back to the radio. "And they photographed a numerical sequence before the arrest happened, but I have no idea what it means. It seems the CIA had a key that they gave to one of the Plumbers. The key opened up a secretary's desk and inside they found this drawing of a football. Like I say, it was locked inside one of the secretary's desks and it might be a code of some kind."

"Well, I mean, you know…they may have some dirt on us. But we certainly know about them too. Or else...I mean...how much do you think they know about Hughes and me? And what were they hiding in the desk? There's the Bay of Pigs thing, but what's this football with a code?"

"I wouldn't suppose much, would you? The football thing bothers me, though. I wonder if it's related to the Football your secret service carries for you? With the Code in it."

Haldeman looks around again. Helen remains flush against the wall.

"Well, I don't know," Nixon continues, "but I think Deed or Colson should find out more about the problem people. Deed has this 'Enemy List" that Colson collected. It has all the critical people they think are leaking. You know, Bob, Deep Throat, he's the one we need to find. He's either working for the CIA or the FBI. Could be Mark Felt, the son of a bitch…he's second in line in the FBI to take Hoover's job. Don't trust any of them!"

"That's right."

A telephone rings by one of the Eastside monitors. Haldeman answers while Nixon stays on the radio.

"What was that?" Nixon asks, as Haldeman returns.

"Just a call about some patient at City Hospital who turned up with medical insurance. I sent Deed and Otieno to transfer him to Hughes Med Center."

"Good, now tell me again, who do you think Deep..."

Another telephone rings from the Westside monitor. Haldeman answers it while Helen continues spying on the conversation, hearing Haldeman take the message and telling Nixon.

"This time it's the university again. The campus police have captured Anna David and they want us to transfer her to the city jail by ambulance. Just so it doesn't stir a ruckus with all the demonstrators, I'm going to send the Atomic Car."

"No, don't do that," Nixon advises. "Noah's working on a project. We can't disturb him. But Davis needs to be in prison. She's a goddamn communist."

"Okay, I'll put 38 with Deed and Otieno on it. They can double up since they only have a transfer to City Hospital. What were you saying about Deep Throat?"

"We've got to find him," Nixon answers, "and stop this damn leaking!"

"Or her," adds Haldeman. He glances at a shadow outside the door.

11:05 a.m.

Before entering the nuclear reactor, Hinton looks back at the city center and the Pyramid rising sword-like into the sky. The contrast of its sharp apex with the round hemisphere of the reactor makes the structures seem separate, but he understands the connection.

Hughes's financial control of the city extends everywhere. And the direction of electronic information all flows to the apex. But what's his plan? Why does so much of what he does depend on Nixon? Will the break-in of DNC headquarters and the capture of the burglars reveal these secrets? The only certainty is that without the strength of a union I'll never penetrate the Hughes-Nixon hold over the city. The drivers will continue on a minimum wage, for longer hours, without benefits, and ignore my leadership. Real health care in this country remains an illusion, available only to the rich. So before unraveling the Hughes-Nixon connection I have to win the driver's support. And with the election coming up for Nixon I've got to work quickly.

Inside the garage of the reactor Noah plugs the Atomic Car into its charger. He then heads for the spiral stairway, checking on the technicians as he passes the observation room. Hinton continues to contemplate strategy while following Noah, feeling the fatigue of several days driving ambulances and lack of sleep.

"Dr. Noah," he asks, as they descend the double helix stairway, "what if you were to have unrestricted time for research? Wouldn't you prefer it if Medical allowed you to control your own schedule?"

"I already control it."

Noah's hand glides over the spherically shaped handrails, configured like giant hydrogen bonds. Every four to five feet a sulfide bond links together the sides of the bases. Their feet move down the staircase, sensing a quantum push of energy with each step. Not quite a vibration, the feeling transmitted to the men descending is matched by a gentle swing of the structure, strangely alive, pulsating epigenetic changes.

"Well, say you didn't have to remain on standby call. Never had to come to the morning inspections?"

"That would be fine with me."

As they approach the laboratory, Hinton steps ahead, hoping to stop Noah's progress down the staircase. It disrupts the symmetry, like a mutation in an otherwise perfect form.

"Good. So, what you really want is more time, right?"

"Yes," Noah answers, irritated. Graphite and uranium casings are being lowered into the surrounding chambers of the reactor, and there's a knocking sound that carries through the steel walls next to them. There's even a slight trembling along the staircase.

"Good. Then I think I know what you need."

“What I need is a lot more time. And for you to stop asking questions and go entertain yourself in the library, Hinton. I’ve got quite a bit of work to do today.”

“I’ve got to talk to you about this time issue,” Hinton presses on. “I think we can find what you need—that is, if the drivers start working together.”

“I’m not a driver, Mr. Hinton, at least not like you! How many times do you have to be told? Now if you would please spend some of your own time in the library, I’ll attend to my work.”

Noah holds the door to the research library open. After Hinton enters, the sound of an electric bolt signals its closure.

Chapter 36:

A Parent Transport

Sunday, 11:10 a.m.—Transfer to Hughes Hospital

Assigned to transfer patient David Lovejoy, Car 38 rolls off the freeway onto Potomac Avenue, approaching City Hospital that abuts the City Prison. Haldeman has explained that the transport patient has newly discovered insurance and needs careful handling, but Deed is preoccupied, thinking only about the break-in. He looks out at a red-bricked prison and jail, wondering how the Plumbers are being treated and if they're keeping silent. He hasn't heard yet from Liddy, who remains free while the investigation goes on.

Backing into the loading dock of the hospital, Otieno looks around at a fleet of blue Therapy ambulances dropping off patients from indigent sections of the city. The Therapy drivers congregate near the glass receiving doors, sharing stories and drinking coffee. They nod silently as he and Deed pass.

When the ambulance drivers arrive on the third floor and approach the ICU bedside, David's hopes surge. The last two hours have seemed like infinity, though not as excruciating as his time on the ventilator. A chance to move to a private hospital, where he can regain his voice and use a telephone, is finally within reach.

"That the man?" Deed asks, pointing toward Lovejoy.

"Ask him," Otieno suggests. The nurses are busy with another patient as they roll the gurney next to the bedside. "I'll bet he'll be happy to tell us."

"Mr. Lovejoy? Are you ready to be transferred? We're taking you to the Hughes Hospital."

"Yessss…!"

His voice is barely distinguishable, so he signals with two thumbs pointed up. Before he's switched over to the gurney Deed gets a signature on the papers. The halls of the City Hospital are busy, filled with patients and visitors, but they make their way to the elevator and down to the exit.

God almighty, it's so wonderful to see sunlight! David thinks, as they move from the outdoor ramp of the hospital to the back of the ambulance. *Look at these brick walls I was trapped inside of. And I'll be able to see Margaret. We'll get the children, leave this godforsaken city, and return home. Where the hell is she? Why isn't she here now? The kids…?*

Deed takes the wheel, listening to radios and heading for the Hughes Hospital as Otieno sits next to the gurney. A sonorous resonation comes from the engine and then Haldeman's voice interrupts over the radio.

"Car 38!"

"38 by." Deed curses at the thought of another transfer. He needs some time to make some phone calls to Liddy. "We're ten-two on the way to Hughes Hospital."

"Got another call for you boys. It's a Code Five. On your way to the hospital, I want you to pick up an Anna David at the university. There's a search warrant out for her and you can pick her up at the Political Science Department, where she's been hiding. Should be easy to find because there will be police cars all over the place. Drop her off at the prison."

"Wait a minute. We just came from City Hospital," Deed protests. "We already have a patient!" He glances back at Otieno, who's recording vital signs.

"Good, that means you're close by the jail. Nixon wants it taken care of, and STAT. Lieutenant Liddy will meet you there."

"Ten-four," Deed acquiesces. Seeing Liddy is better than a phone call, so he takes a side street and heads for the university.

Chapter 37:

Picking Up Davis

Sunday, 12:00 noon—Car 38

Deed and Otieno glide down a restricted road toward the Political Science Department. Liddy's Jeep is parked next to several police cars in the back of the building, while in front a crowd of student demonstrators mill together and wave picket signs urging "Free Ellsberg Now!" and "Stop the White House Lies!" In the back of the ambulance Lovejoy lies flat on the gurney looking up at stainless steel rails while a bag of fluids drips into his left arm. His stomach is burning.

"Are we really picking up Anna David?" Otieno asks, grabbing the resuscitation kit from the back of the ambulance. "What's she done?"

"She's a communist," Deed answers. "And violent as well. There was a prison break, and her gun was used to foment it. Four people were killed."

Otieno doesn't look forward to transporting Davis, who has a reputation for intellectual confrontation. He's left to watch David, while Deed heads into the back of the Political Science building where he encounters Liddy and a host of policemen surrounding a young black woman. Thin and attractive, Anna's ebony hair rises out with estrogenic defiance as she stares angrily ahead. Her arms are handcuffed behind her back.

"Hey, you're just in time," Liddy announces. "This so-called professor needs emergency transportation. We're trying to eliminate publicity so if you could take her downtown it would simplify the work."

The lieutenant looks disheveled. He indicates to Deed that he wants to talk privately, and the two of them step into a separate room while the police continue interrogating Davis.

"Listen," Liddy begins, rubbing away some sweat on his forehead, "I know we had a little trouble at the Watergate. I mean, not just that the Plumbers got caught. There's a lot more at stake."

"What do you mean we, Gordon?"

"You know what I mean. Right now, you have to do some damage control. I... uhh, ran the ship onto the reef, so to speak. They found some traces of my involvement, so it looks like I'll be going to jail. If they learn about the break-in of the psychiatrist's office, all the other things we did…what I'm saying is, we can't have any more leaks or the whole boat's going to sink."

Deed nods with a private realization.

Now that the break-in story has hit the press, Liddy's doomed. But the re-election of Nixon has to be protected. Liddy's just one tree in a forest. And even though I helped plan it all, I need to keep free of this.

"Sure. You must feel bad, Gordon. It's a mess."

"Listen, if they want to shoot me, I'm ready to stand on the corner."

He looks at the lieutenant in disbelief. "Gordon, its not that bad, is it?"

What's Liddy know that I don't? Deed contemplates. *Nixon has a reputation for ruthlessness, but he's not an assassin. Or is he? How deep does this really go? How far is the CIA into this?*

"Sorry about the way things turned out, Jim," Liddy says, "You'd better get moving. Good luck."

"Yeah, uh…you too, Gordon."

Picking up his resuscitation bag, Deed heads back to the room where Davis is being restrained. Liddy nods as several of the policemen lead her to the ambulance. She's directed into the rear and re-handcuffed to a bench beside Otieno and Lovejoy. With the police cars parked in front of the university building, the crowd of demonstrators continues to wait for her outside. Car 38 drives away unseen.

David Lovejoy now looks from the gurney across at the handcuffs on Anna David. Her legs are bare to the mid-thigh, where her miniskirt stops.

"Are we in a paddy wagon?" he coughs, trying to regain control of his voice.

"Pig wagon would be more definitive," she corrects, looking at Otieno, who avoids her contemptuous stare. "And you, brother, must be my keeper. Isn't that a coincidence?"

Otieno says nothing as the ambulance takes a sharp turn and heads onto the freeway, turbocharger whining as they accelerate. With one hand cuffed behind her back, David's blouse pulls open, revealing the lack of a brassiere.

"Could one of you...just let me have a cigarette?" she asks, nodding at the pack in Lovejoy's hospital bag. "I doubt we can smoke in jail, and I doubt I'll ever get out."

"We're in an ambulance," Otieno answers, abruptly "There's oxygen in here. No smoking."

"You're taking me to jail, not to a hospital," she argues, staring back, but softening her gaze. "And how about him?"

She indicates Deed, who's smoking a cigarette as he drives.

"She can have 'em," Lovejoy sputters. The ventilator experience has taken away his craving for cigarettes.

I'll never smoke again. I'm so bloody happy to be headed to the private hospital! I just need to get my strength back!

Otieno looks toward the front of the ambulance. Deed is listening to the radio; smoke wafting back as he heads for the jail. Lovejoy is breathing at an easy rate.

Should I do it for this sister? Who seems to despise me? Actually, I really want a smoke myself, but just one.

Relenting, he turns off the oxygen and reaches into the plastic bag. He sets one of Lovejoy's cigarettes between her lips and lights it. Thick smoke rises, and her face softens.

"You really like working for this company?" she asks, blowing the smoke away from him.

"I've had worse jobs."

"I bet you have. Got any women driving these things?"

Here comes the beginning of a backseat lecture. She may be a professor, but I don't really need this. Otieno removes the cigarette from her lips as Lovejoy begins to cough.

"Yeah. His girlfriend drives," Otieno says, indicating Deed. The inside of the ambulance thickens with smoke.

"I wonder what she gets paid."

"I don't make the salaries, sister. I just take care of people."

"Like me?" she asks, looking at her handcuffs. "You know damn well we should be working together, organizing to end the Prison Industrial Complex! The jails are filled with our brothers and sisters, aren't they? And now they have me."

With the smoke in the back, Lovejoy begins to cough heavily. As he does so, a wheezing noise accompanies his expirations and he takes on a waxen, frightened expression, then coughs more violently. His lungs clamp down in another allergic spasm, constricting the small bronchioles, causing a prolonged wheeze. Then silence.

"Pull over!" Otieno shouts, stamping out the cigarette. As he reaches for the resuscitation kit Lovejoy's face turns blue. "Open all the windows!"

Deed turns around, along with David, to watch Otieno slide a tube past Lovejoy's vocal cords. Once the Ambu bag is connected, Otieno squeezes quick pulses of oxygen and the cyanotic face turns pink again.

"Car 38! Car 38...come in!" Haldeman's voice cracks over the radio.

"38 by," Deed answers, alarmed by another interruption from the dispatcher. "We're Code Three to Hughes Hospital. Our Code One just decided to become a Code Blue!"

"Negative on that," Haldeman interrupts. "There's been an explosion at the Hughes launch center! A Saturn rocket's on fire with astronauts on board. You copy?"

"You're crazy...we can't cover that. I just told you we have a Code Blue!"

"Get going, goddamn it, and fast. It's a 10-40!"

12:50 p.m.—The Lovejoy children return to City Hospital

Michael sits in the empty shopping cart, just upwind of the Trash King, as they pass along a wide park in the shape of an ellipse. The president's house is on the opposite side. Large oak and elm trees cool the air and they can hear the sound of warbling vireos and orioles from across the green lawns. The King watches them while continuing a monologue.

"So, the man with the beard lived in the White House a long, long time ago," he explains, pushing Michael and trying to keep up with the girls. "And he was said to be the one that freed the slaves. Lincoln never had slaves himself, and he never had that on his mind, not at first, or at least till he was pretty much forced to, on account of the Union busting up. I mean all of the States that made up the country breaking up to the North side and the South side. But if he didn't free the slaves, the Union might 'a been lost, and I wouldn't be making all the money I do."

He smiles but the children miss the sarcasm.

"Slow down a little, 'cause I'm about to tell you something. There ain't no hurry around here when I'm driving this cart, you hear, Rebecca?"

"We *are* in a hurry. We saw the president's house yesterday," Rebecca argues. "And we don't even know if we're going the right way."

"No, we're going the right way. And I want you to remember what I told you. You look for signs on the road and you keeps 'em in your head. That's the only way you keep from getting lost, Rebecca. I take this road every day. Not too much to pick up along here, but I like the birds. Look at those birds, 'cause you see a lot of different ones and they can lead you back to the natural world. When the birds are gone, we'll all be gone. Pay close attention to all the signs. Reason they call it the 'White House' is 'cause the English people tried to burn it down. So they painted it white to hide all the English efforts to wipe out the house with fire!

So, like I was telling you, it used to be that they did most of the slave tradin' right here in this city, during Lincoln's time. He helped stop all that, maybe, and I was goin' to tell you that he didn't really plan on doin' it himself, but people finally just got fed up, and then there was a war. A very big war, and in a way it's still going on."

"How come they had a war?" Angel asks.

"Well, there were enough people who liked havin' slaves, and enough who didn't, till it was the North against the South, and they stopped getting along. The slave owners wanted to break up the Union, go off on their own. And then there was the money. Money always seems to divide people, you know that? You always the one asking the questions, Angel—why is that?"

"I don't know. What do you think?"

"Children like questions. But if you have too many you don't have room for an answer."

"How about big people?"

"Same thing, I guess. Big people have trouble getting along, like kids. Maybe even more."

Rebecca has read about the Civil War, and she resigns herself to listening.

We only have six dollars left and there's nothing else we can do except turn ourselves in to the police. Maybe we should, but if the King finds our dad, these lectures will be okay. If he just didn't walk so slow! I'm going to remember this building and everything. We've been walking a long way on Independence Avenue. I know that much.

The King finally rolls his cart into the parking lot dividing City Hospital from the prison. Michael shares the cart with Angel, who's now tired after walking past the White House, the Capitol, and the endless city blocks. Rebecca views again the weathered, brick buildings and after walking almost an hour she moves faster, hoping to nudge the King a little. She feels her father is close in the already muggy afternoon.

Nurses are picketing outside the hospital when they reach the entrance. Leaving the King's shopping cart near a bicycle rack, Angel and Rebecca are nervous, fearing they'll see the woman with the long fingernails. Instead, they encounter a man at the information desk who displays his volunteer badge. He smiles as they approach.

"Morning, sir," the King says, introducing himself and standing in front of the children.

"Good afternoon."

"Oh, well. Afternoon. I'm...uh...Mr. King. That is...these children here…are trying to find their father, a Mr. Lovejoy. A Mr. David Lovejoy. He's supposed to be in your ICU."

The volunteer goes over his list. Michael makes a motion to leave, not happy to be back in the building that they escaped the day before. The patient list shows Lovejoy transferred out that morning.

"He's no longer here. He was transferred to the Hughes Hospital about an hour ago."

"Are you sure?" the King asks, impacted by their bad luck. It's more than the children will tolerate, and as he rolls up the sleeve of his red and black shirt the volunteer notes the strong odor. Rebecca steps in front.

"Where's the Hughes Hospital?" she asks.

"Yeah, where's the Huge Hospital," Angel echoes.

"Kids, it's on the other side of town."

1:13 p.m.—Hughes Space Center

Car 38 enters through double security gates and is directed down a protected runway that leads to the Hughes Space Center. The launching area for Saturn missiles is visible from a distance, but Otieno is busy bagging oxygen into David Lovejoy's constricted lungs. Deed and Anna David see only the fire consuming the top stage of a rocket.

"Holy shit!" Deed whispers as he calls in their arrival to Haldeman and David stares quietly through a window. A fleet of fire trucks positioned a small distance from the conflagration have hoses pumping jets of water and de-combustion chemicals that barely reach the nose of the rocket. Three hundred feet in the air, its capsule forms a peak with flames spewing from its sides. Black smoke billows higher into the open sky.

Deed turns off the siren and drives to the periphery of the trucks, while Otieno begins pulling down aluminized fire suits from an overhead cabinet.

"Hey, what are you planning to do?" Anna David asks, looking at her captors.

"We're part of the rescue team," Otieno answers. He lays the suit down on the floor with his right hand, bagging Lovejoy intermittently with his left.

"Wait!" she says, looking at the gantry of the Saturn. Rescue workers are already being transported up the center to reach the blazing cone above. "You're going to climb that cracker ladder to hell? You mean to tell me saving one man and taking me to jail is not enough? Brothers and sisters shackled to this Hughes Empire and you're trying to save a rocket that's in flames? And now you're about to risk your own life? Are you out of your black mind?"

"Last time I checked," he answers, pulling a key from his side pocket and freeing her right hand from the shackles, "I was. Look, I don't know how long we'll be gone, but I need you to squeeze this bag every five seconds till we get back, got it? Pump in just enough to keep this guy's lungs filled—not too hard, so you don't pop any holes. And don't light any cigarettes. Are you with it?"

"You've got to be out of your goddamn mind!"

"I know. Now count five between each squeeze, and not too hard."

Otieno takes her one free hand and places it on the Ambu bag, helping her to squeeze. Deed pulls the back doors open and shouts, "Let's go!"

Grabbing the rescue kit and fire suits, they join the firefighting team. Anna contemplates her options. The police have killed her lover, her left hand is shackled with a handcuff to the ambulance, she'll spend years behind steel bars of the men at the source of her agony, and now this! The back doors of the ambulance remain open as she watches an elevator carry a rescue team up the gantry. Shaking her head, she turns to the patient.

"Mister man on the gurney," she tells Lovejoy, "I don't know who the hell you are, or why you're here, but you better breathe this bloody damned bourgeois oxygen while I'm on the way to prison!"

Day 6, 1:17 p.m.—Another seizure in Car 22

"Car 22, where are you?"

Colson grabs the hand phone.

"We're uh, on the way to City Hospital," he answers nervously. "On a Code Two. We got waylaid by Miraj but we're coming into the city right now with the transfer."

"Goddamn it, I sent you over an hour ago on a Code One. What the hell are you doing? We've got a 10-40 going on!"

Colson looks into the back where Margaret is resting quietly while Miraj reads through her transfer papers and records notes of the new seizure.

"We...uh...had some trouble," he answers. "Our patient had a grand mal and it took a little while to get it under control. Miraj took a little detour and we started an IV. I was just getting ready to radio you..."

"Forget it," Haldeman barks, "and forget the hospital. You're going to the Space Center. Copy? That's Code Three! Hit your siren."

"What? We have a seizure patient. The lady's sick and I don't think..."

"I said 10-40. Get going. You hear me, Colson?"

"You're serious?"

"I said 10-40 and you are **Code Three**! Now get on it!"

"Okay, ten-four. We're on our way."

He reaches up and engages the siren. They're still on the Beltway, outside the city, and he's able to make a direct approach to the Space Center. Then Miraj calls out again.

"Oh, Colson!"

"What now? What the hell's the matter now?"

"I see another light, another seizure! I don't think she likes the ambulance."

Margaret is twisting on the gurney, her right arm and leg flailing, constrained only by the white sheet that tucks them down. A thin pool of saliva collects on the metallic floor of Car 22.

Miraj injects another half syringe of muscle relaxant and it lessens but does not stop the convulsions.

"Cut the crap!" Colson says. "We're on a 10-40, boy. That means major disaster!" The sound of the siren muffles both their voices as the ambulance speeds down the fast lane. Cars move out of the way and Miraj continues injecting drugs and monitoring vital signs.

"Oh, my goodness!" he exclaims. "And now she won't breathe!"

After the third syringe her seizure softens and her respirations stop. Miraj reaches for the rescue bag, pulls out intubation instruments, and slides a tube between her vocal cords. By the time the tube is taped down and the Ambu bag is pumped with oxygen a few times, he's able to give another dose of relaxant. Meanwhile, the ambulance is being flagged down the runway of the Space Station.

1:19 p.m.—Hughes Space Center

Otieno seals tight the Velcro of the aluminum-asbestos suit and pulls a hood over his head as the second team of rescue workers rides up the elevator. Pointed up into the sky, the Saturn V rocket is stationary, held by a steel gantry. Flames and smoke pour out of its capsule.

"Electrical," one of the firemen shouts. "They were running an oxygen test in the command module and a spark ignited!"

Beneath they hear sirens sound from all directions, heralding disaster from the periphery. Other ambulances can be seen arriving, along with more fire trucks, and as they look down, the city of Washington unfolds in the distance—an expanding network of government buildings, the Hughes Pyramid, and a Y-shaped confluence of the Potomac and Anacostia rivers. At a height of three hundred feet above, Otieno can read the number 22 on the roof of Colson's car as it arrives into the confused symphony of sirens and alarms. It backs up toward Car 38, where Deed is setting up IVs and resuscitation equipment.

Then the elevator stops with a jolt. The men move out onto the last stage of the gantry and a blinding cloud of smoke, mist, and chemicals envelop them as the detail team goes to work on the searing metal of the capsule's escape door. With thick asbestos gloves they rotate a wheel that controls the locking pin, taking turns to complete a full turn.

Searing heat scorches their hands and they struggle to breathe and endure the blinding smoke. Suddenly, a blast of pressurized gases and flames explode from a crack. The others watch silently as Otieno grabs a hold of the white-hot door and pulls it open.

Day 6, 1:27 p.m.—Car 22

Miraj bags oxygen gently while controlling an infusion through Margaret Lovejoy's IV. Her convulsions come less frequently, in staccato jerks, as screaming sirens outside re-announce the disaster. In between seizures, in a strangely lucent moment, Margaret's eyes open. She looks through the open doors where Colson and Deed stand next to Car 38, waiting for the rescue team and victims, and sees a woman in the back of Car 38 squeezing a bag of oxygen for a patient. The patient seems to wave at her, and when she recognizes her husband, she tries to sit up, causing the IV to disengage once more. A white light surrounds her once more, lifting her away from the scene of confusion, giving her a sense of endless peace. Resisting the euphoria, hoping to see her husband again, Margaret opens her eyes once more to search for her David and senses the pressure of new life in her abdomen.

Day 6

The Watergate Women

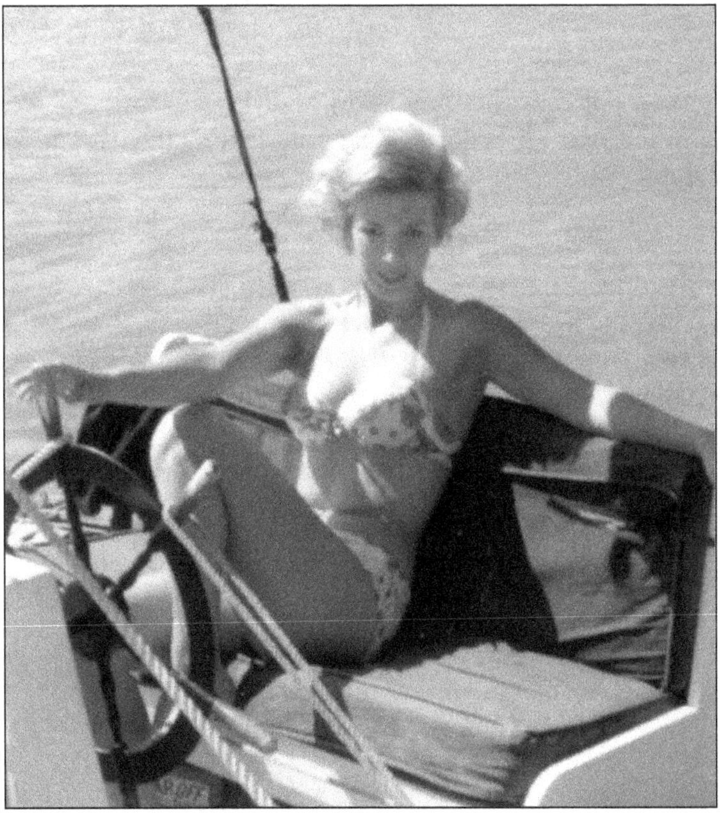

Heidi – the Watergate Days

"I looked up at the night sky and its bright wash of stars.... I thought about how the constellations hadn't changed since the first sailors set out to explore the world, using the positions of the stars to find their way back home. I have found my way through a lifetime of uncharted territory with good fortune and abiding faith to keep me on course. This time I needed all the help I could get."

—Hillary Clinton, Living History, 2003

"You tell me what you know, and I'll confirm. I'll keep you in the right direction if I can, but that's all. Just...follow the money..."

—Deep Throat, All the President's Men, 1976

"In effect, the snake had swallowed its tail; CIA agents working under cover of the CRP [Committee to Re-elect the President] came to be targeted against their own operation and the very organization that unwittingly provided them with cover. All that the agents could do was to stall, and when all else failed, blow their own cover. Where upon the White House, lacking deniability, attempted to cover up—with the result that it was soon buried."

—Jim Hougan, Secret Agenda, 1984

"You know we've got to find a way to bring some loving here today, yeah!"

—Marvin Gaye, "What's Going On?" May 21, 1971

Chapter 38:

Preparing the Speech

Day Six—Monday, June 19, 1972, 7:42 a.m.—Medical Office Laundry Room

"Oh, what's going on… What's going on… Yeah, what's going on?"

Helen sings along, her voice blending with the radio and the noise of the washing machines as she folds sheets. Then she leans on one of the appliances reflecting on the events of the last five days.

All the connections are lining up. Hughes and Nixon are linked together, like the gears inside washers and dryers. They connect in circles, one gaining from the other, steadily connecting their power, till each part of the city is increasingly under their control. And Nixon will be re-elected as president! He has six million dollars, even without Jim Hoffa's one and a half million, and more than enough money compared to the democrats, even without Hughes to secure his position. Will he use the money to pay off the Plumbers, who got caught in the break-in? And what were they after? Why would Nixon's men do something so crazy to discover it? Hughes is part of this conspiracy, and he must have some additional hidden design of his own. A hidden agenda!

Helen determines to find out what it is when she hears a sharp clicking noise.

"Clip, clip, clap!"

Two wingtip shoes snap neatly together at the doorway, and the sharp eyes of the dispatcher watch her disdainfully.

"Hinton...the new driver," Haldeman begins, with a menacing tone. "I want you to tell me everything you know about him." His arms are folded.

"Excuse me?" Helen asks, turning off the radio.

"Hinton. Tell me what you know about the man? The owner, President Nixon, is coming today and he wants to talk with us. In fact, he's on his way right now. So, I'd like to know exactly what this guy Hinton is trying to do here. I've heard some talk about a 'union'?"

"Oh really?"

"That's right."

As he enters the laundry room, she mops a small bloodstain off the floor and grimaces.

"You like it here, Helen, don't you? You want to keep working here, don't you?"

"Well, yes. I imagine we all do, don't we?" she asks, straining a smile while putting her hand over her chest.

Haldeman adjusts the knot of his tie.

How come every time Helen speaks, she starts with a question? Something persevering about this woman.

His tight grin disappears. The momentary silence of two people accentuates the laundry sounds, and the scent of bleach and clean uniforms fills the room. Then…

"You seem to be here late most nights. You don't happen to have another job, do you?"

"This job's enough, Mr. Haldeman. Don't you agree?"

Helen puts both her hands on the mop, as if for protection.

"Look," Haldeman continues, "I'm asking you for an explanation. In this business, as busy as it gets, our employees stay late sometimes. Even with all the competition, there's enough people who need our service. We put patients first, so we have to work extra hours. But you seem to stay later than most. Don't you?"

"Well, yes. Who could question that?"

"But then you wouldn't be involved with any competition, would you?"

"Competition?"

"You have heard of Therapy?"

This is way too much diversion. She's obviously up to something. If she asks one more question, I'll put a bug in the room and tap her apartment phone.

"Oh, you mean the other ambulance company?" Helen asks, trying to sound innocent. "I don't think they could pay me as much as Medical does, do you?"

"How do you know that?"

"Well, I don't know. I mean, I don't think they would, do you?"

"You ask a lot of questions, don't you, Helen? And I've noticed you never answer my questions."

"Really?"

That's it! I'm going to find out what she's after!

Monday 8:10 a.m.—Inside the Nuclear Reactor Research Station

Hinton works through the night inside the library of the reactor complex, drinking coffee and preparing his Union address for the upcoming meeting with Nixon and the drivers. Library computers flash silent mosaics as he paces back and forth between screens, running through his final words.

"We are entering an age in which every driver will work together for the Union. It's the end of welfare medicine and the beginning of Universal Health Care! Let me share with you this—the equitable provision of medicine for all Americans..."

He looks at his watch, noting that the night has passed, and skips ahead to the conclusion.

"So now…the time has come to organize together," he continues, reaching with his arms and pointing his fingers to emphasize words. "It arises for each of us, the drivers of Medical," he continues, pausing for effect, "to make this opportunity fair and equal while providing guaranteed health for all." Each word is enunciated and his facial muscles articulate along with his voice. "A house divided does not stand! So, are we united?"

He spins around to his phantom audience.

"Fellow drivers, the race is simple...but challenging. In the effort to provide, there's one way to win. Through the Union of each of us into a larger whole, we will join and make possible the health and safety of every citizen." His left hand drops and his right hand extends with the palm out.

"We have...just one hurdle…"

Hinton notes the empty library and the door remains locked. Noah left him during the night and he stops to consider the vested interests? Can he itemize them? Prove to the others he knows the financial connections and where they all fit in? During the night in the reactor, he discovered the information base Noah programmed into the computer and he turns to it again. He sets his fingers on the keyboard and types in:

"**POTUS**."

He scrolls down on the screen to the **Economy and Energy** category.

District of Columbia Assets: Review of Systems
EnergyHughes AeronauticsCryogenicsDefense

Budget

Conventional—$465 Million
Nuclear—$296 Million
Renewable—$3.1 Million
Hughes Aeronautics—$843 Million
Cryogenics —$5 Million
Research & Development
Conventional—$38 million
Nuclear—
Fission $12 million
Fusion $7 million
Hughes Foundation—$3 ion

Thinking the greatest resources are contained in Defense, he scrolls down and clicks open the file containing an array of information Daniel Ellsberg once had. Checking to make sure the room is empty, he clicks open "Nuclear file."

Stockpile
June 19, 1972—8:15 AM

Category	Launchers	Force Loading	Total Stockpile
First Strike Strategic Offense			
ICBM	1817	6600	7600
SLBM	854	3600	4000
Bomber	170	980	1300
Strategic Defense—Missiles			
ABM	110	100	100
Surface	7575	16,000	16,000
Non-Strategic			
Missiles	2074	3000	5,600
Aircraft	4790	28,000	28,000
Artillery	6850	14,000	14,000
Staged Demolitions			83

Casualty Estimate of Communist Countries—in Nuclear First Strike
500,000,000—(Combined Soviet and Chinese Deaths)

So, that's why Ellsberg is such a threat to Nixon and the administration, Hinton realizes. *Our Strategic Arms capacity can eliminate the human race as we know it! And Ellsberg knows it! So whoever has the Code has to protect his own life and all of humanity as well!*

He scrolls back to open each file separately, reviewing the technical information that fills the computer's memory, taking note that the military budget for the country is a fifth of the Medical Industrial Complex.

And there we have it! Hughes has concentrated most of his wealth in medical research. His hospital protects him from taxes, so his empire is protected by Nixon.

As he approaches the final link—**Hughes-Nixon**—he tries repeatedly to find a password that will open the section and is unsuccessful. Then he types in the sequence from the Pyramid.

8-21-7-5 16-15-23-5-18

Alarms began to ring through the side of the computer as he reaches over and clicks off the control switch. The library's quiet. Cautiously, Hinton disconnects the speaker and turns the computer on again. Then he types in the word from Ellsberg's arrest.

!!!**Firestone**!!!

A new message begins to flash.

RESTRICTED: DO NOT PROCEED: **CLASSIFIED**

Numbers on the bottom of the screen indicate a numerical message.

"20 8 5—23 15 18 12 4 19—5 1 19 8 5 19 20—3 15 4 5."

Along the side of the computer he sees a small icon in the shape of a football and clicks on it till a new screen lights up.

CODE TO OPEN BLACK BOX AND ACTIVATE

Numbers to **letters**

Sequence to **alphabet**

Suddenly a door swinging open interrupts him and he shuts down the computer instantly.

"How's it coming along, Mr. Hinton? Have you learned anything?"

Hinton jumps back, caught off guard by Noah, who watches his reaction quietly from the opened doorway of the library.

"Dr. Noah, where've you been? I've been working all night waiting for you. I was uh, just...uh, reviewing your computer base. It's filled..."

"...With information. And most of it restricted to President Nixon and myself. I don't believe you've reached that position of confidentiality, have you? Daniel Ellsberg did the same thing. Now he's in jail."

"Well, no. I was just..."

"...Exploring my scientific network. If I'd known you were going to try and break into restricted information, I wouldn't have let you in the library, would I? Now we're late to the meeting. Let's go."

Monday, 8:20 a.m.—Castro's plan—Unit 160, Cuba

After a night of celebration and feasting, topped off with Algerian wine and whiskey on the rocks, the Líder Máximo sleeps well and wakes late to join his only two remaining guests, Gabriel Marquez and Barbanegra, or Blackbeard. Fidel, dressed in his usual military fatigues, and Marquez and Blackbeard, both wearing Guayaberas and trousers, sit at a breakfast table nursing hangovers from the night before. The guests eat *moros y cristianos* while Fidel sips on a glass of milk and speculates on Hurricane Agnes.

"It's going to miss us almost completely, Gabo," Fidel begins. "It's just catching the western tip of the island, although I am told there were seven deaths."

"And it will head north to our friends in the U.S.," Blackbeard notes, "and will likely hit Washington, D.C. with heavy winds and rain. Floods are expected."

Fidel sets the milk down and lights another cigar. He turns to Blackbeard to interrogate him.

"And Nixon? And Delta Tango? How far along are we? You told me we would have the Code within a week, didn't you? Is that even possible?"

"Comandante, we are closer than you might imagine. I must let you know that now is the opportunity to remove Nixon once and for all, if you so desire."

Marquez looks up sharply at Blackbeard, and then back at Fidel, waiting to see where the conversation is headed.

"I haven't made such a decision. And why should I?"

"Comandante, I only want to remind you that the Americans, beginning with Nixon and the CIA, have tried hard to eliminate you. How many times? And they are still trying! We have complete access to this same president who worked with Howard Hunt to invade our island and end the Revolution. So, can we afford to miss this opportunity?"

Fidel looks at Marquez and his eyes narrow.

"You see, Gabo, you see who knows how to spy? And who does not know how to spy? Our agents make a laughingstock of the CIA. I will outlive all the American presidents, and truthfully, Nixon is no longer a threat. I believe this Watergate business will hang him out to dry at San Clemente, the place in California where Howard Hughes helped build a resort that makes Cayo Piedra look very small. So, let the hurricane wash him away. He can dry off in San Clemente."

The three men laugh together. Then Blackbeard excuses himself from the table to make a phone call.

Within twenty minutes of this discussion in Cuba I receive a call from Domingo, in Miami.

"Tango, I have just spoken with Blackbeard. He says you need to utilize every opportunity. If you are next to Nixon, then you should take care of him. That is the message."

I know that Nixon is coming to the Medical headquarters within hours, and that I will be there as well, completing the night shift as dispatcher. As an operative I know I can't ask questions. But I do.

"Is that a request from Fidel?"

Domingo hesitates briefly. Then he responds.

"I am telling you directly from Blackbeard. There should be no confusion."

Chapter 39:

Colson's Dream and the IV

Monday 8:25 a.m.—Car 22 Living Quarters

Colson stirs repeatedly during the night with nightmares of the previous day's explosion. The image of the Space Center rocket, spewing flames out of its upper stage onto the steel gantry as Otieno and the rescue team attempted to extricate the astronauts, blends with the sight of the immolated victims scorched to dark ash. He waits between the two ambulances, helping Deed prepare IV solutions, when the rescue team finally comes down the runway from the rocket gantry. Otieno is helped down and placed on a gurney. After the astronauts have fatally burned, Colson is unnerved to see Otieno.

"Take him to City Hospital!" Deed shouts at Colson in the confusion of sirens and surrounding noise. "I have a Code Blue going to Hughes Hospital and a prisoner headed for the jail," Deed shouts again. "So, you take care of Otieno!"

"Wait a minute, man. I have a woman seizing in my car!"

Without responding, Deed and Car 38 disappear down the runway, leaving Colson with Otieno in shock. Margaret continues her shaking motions as Miraj infuses another dosage of Valium. Meanwhile, the rescue team waits for him to do resuscitation as he stares at Otieno, flat and motionless on the gurney. He's gripped with anxiety.

"ABCs," Miraj calls from inside Car 22.

"What?" Colson looks into the back of the ambulance. Miraj is bagging Margaret with oxygen, now titrating Valium through an IV to control her seizure and calling out the basics of resuscitation.

"I said ABCs! In a manner of speaking, you must revive your patient!"

Colson remembers resuscitation sequences. Like life preservers, they bob mercifully into memory.

"A for Airway," he whispers, checking Otieno's mouth, verifying that the throat is clear.

"B for Breathing," he whispers again, looking down and watching the chest wall move ever so slightly. So far, so good. Then he freezes, not remembering the third step—circulation, the third critical need of resuscitation.

"C!" Miraj calls out. "C!"

"I know, I know! Goddamn it!" Colson gasps, as it comes back to him. "His carotid pulse is strong."

He notes a rapid pulse on the side of the neck. The fast heart rate is an obvious sign of shock, and fearing the worst he begins looking for a vein, knowing he has always failed in starting IVs.

The heart's okay. He's got bad burns and he's in shock. His face and hands are swollen. But there's no access for veins! The one thing I always fail at, the damn IV!

Dreading the inevitable, he continues looking for a vein.

And I have to start it in front of the rescue team. But both his hands are burned! Damn!

"Go for the big one!"

"What?"

Colson rolls his eyes, trying to shake off the nightmare. He keeps seeing Miraj, holding onto the Ambu bag and ventilating the woman with seizures in the back of Car 22. But what's he saying?

"I am saying go for the big one! That is, in a manner of speaking, try the big vein, now!"

Basilic vein. The large vein in the center of the arm! It's almost impossible to miss.

Between shaking fingers Colson holds an IV needle that can return fluid to the vascular space, taking Otieno out of shock.

"Go for it, Colson!" the rescue team urges him. "Go for the big vein!"

"Let's go! Come on, let's go!" Miraj's voice calls out again. Or is it Deed's voice?

"Wake up! Wake up! Let's go for the big one! Come on, let's go!"

Colson opens his eyes and sees the television on. The smell of French fries and hair tonic from inside the Car 22 living quarters fills his nostrils. Deed has been standing over him the whole time during his nightmare dream.

"What's going on?" he asks, rising up off the couch.

"Time for morning report, Colson. Come on, man—today you're the hero!"

He rubs his eyes, trying to remember. The wild goose chase mix-up with Miraj, the woman with a seizure who's IV fell out, the explosion at the Space Center, and the rescue team shouting at him. It's a confusion of images but it all begins to come back. He thought he had ruined everything and then, in the last second, he started the IV. After running in a liter of fluid, Otieno responded and came out of shock.

"Look, Colson," Deed tells him, "things are unraveling right now. But we've come a long way to get here. Nixon starts his new term as president tomorrow, and you and I are going to get some credit. We're going to bury all the crap about the Therapy break-in. We're still the best company around and Nixon's staying in power. And that IV you started yesterday was great! It may have saved Otieno's life!"

"You think so?"

"You don't remember, do you?"

Colson looks down at a half-eaten pizza, trying to recollect.

"It's kind of a blur...know what I mean?"

"Well, you did it, Chuck. It was a tough stick and you got it just in time. I took some guy on a Code Blue to Hughes Hospital, then I had to go back to the jail to drop off Anna David, who kept haranguing me about 'lifting up our brothers and sisters' and 'stop throwing all the blacks into prison' crap. I don't think she liked having to bag our transfer patient, but she kept him going, and by the time we got to City Hospital, you guys were leaving the ER. What a scene!"

"Scene? Which one? There were too many!"

"I know. The trauma. The astronauts were burned beyond belief! It must have got to Otieno, 'cause after you dropped off your Code Three at Hughes and brought him to City Hospital, he refused to be admitted."

"I remember now. He was pissed off that they wouldn't admit him to Hughes Hospital."

"Right. Just another strange day. We both had Code Blues, and it was like they were watching each other from the two ambulances, almost like they knew each other, while we're taking care of all this disaster."

Colson sits up and drinks some coffee. Still wearing his jumpsuit, he pulls on his boots while recalling how Otieno had lifted himself off the gurney and left the ER, his swollen right hand clenched into a fist and raised up in the air.

"Now I remember! Otieno came out of shock. He refused to go to City Hospital, and then he had me take him back to get Car 45."

"Right. So, let's get moving before we're late."

"Right!" Colson says, looking at his watch. "We'll be celebrating the president's re-election today."

Chapter 40:

Urning's Lament

Monday 8:28 a.m.—Hughes Hospital

Oh, civilizations come and go
Just like the seasons, around they flow.
Driven by nature together to fight
Proving forever who's wrong and who's right.

It's good to come to learn to see
The ways we build our company
For fair is foul and foul is fair
To the man who sits in the barber's chair.

Clifton Urning wanders past the Intensive Care Unit of the Hughes Hospital, reciting poems to his attendant. Permitted to leave the Psych ward and walk around the hospital during the day, he returns to observe a man who seems to be agonizing more dramatically than most, fighting against his ventilator. It occurs to him that he and this man have a similar plight—both are physically restrained from leaving the hospital, and both have difficulty making clear communications.

David Lovejoy is unaware of these similarities, perceiving only his mechanical prison and separation from his wife and children. Having resolved to find them, make a final escape from Washington D.C. and never smoke again, he now knows his wife is connected to a ventilator as well. He saw her in the back of Car 22 and knows she has become dependent on the actions of others to determine her minute-by-minute survival, and somehow he must get to her. But how?

It's so unfair! I never touch a cigarette. Just let that strange woman have one in the ambulance, and now I'm back on a ventilator again. But I won't give up hope.

It seems I'm in a better hospital now. But am I? All because I have insurance, and just because I sell insurance. Does this hospital system make any sense? Does health insurance make any sense in this country?

Clifton Urning ponders his own situation as he looks at David Lovejoy on a ventilator and thinks of his own future. A literary career tied inextricably to Howard Hughes, yet without any access to the man he works for. His chances of ever seeing Hughes in person are virtually impossible. Deranged and morose, Urning finishes his stanza as he continues walking through the ICU, past the hapless Lovejoy.

So, who shall bring us all together?
Hanging from a helpless tether?
Does Nixon know the final secret?
Will Hinton learn and will he leak it?
Truth is rarely what we think
Changes quick as eye can blink.
I seek in vain the face of Hughes
For good or evil, or just a muse?

Chapter 41:

Approaching Chaos

8:30 a.m.—Medical Main Office

Bob Haldeman tries to control his temper as he faces off Otieno and waits for the other drivers to show up at the main office for the morning meeting. As night dispatcher I'm still covering the radios while Haldeman rewraps Otieno's burned hands with sterile gauze. Otieno has arrived early and climbed into the barber's chair to demand that Medical pay for his care at Hughes Hospital. Since City Hospital doesn't have a burn center, he needs more specialized treatment.

"Get real," Haldeman warns. "This is an ambulance company, Otieno. There's no money to send drivers to Hughes Hospital! Don't you realize who you're working for?"

"Look," Otieno argues, "Nixon and Hughes are a team—you know that as well as I do. Only the Hughes Hospital can take care of my burns, and Nixon can pay for it. And so can Hughes! They're a team."

"Ridiculous. They're independent. The president makes sure Hughes pays his taxes, and that's it. Now get out of that chair before Nixon gets here. He's going to be re-elected as president today, and he won't like seeing you up there."

"No, you need to listen to me, Haldeman. I was vice president for Hughes Oil. I know exactly how these men operate. Every profit Hughes makes gets written off as an investment in our medical system, so he never gets taxed. He has all his expenses and profits deducted, just like Nixon does with his estates in Florida and California. The country can afford to send me and everyone else in the city to Hughes Hospital, whenever we need to go. We were the ones that made them all rich!"

Haldeman looks through the window to see if any cars have arrived, then back at Otieno, who has pumped the chair as high as it will go.

"Look, I think you've made enough demands!" he responds. "You're entitled to what you earn and that's all! You want to go to Hughes Hospital; you pay for it, like everyone else. Now you need to get out of the chair, immediately!"

"And what about you?" Otieno asks defiantly.

"What about me?"

"You don't pay to go. Hughes Hospital is where you go when you get sick, isn't that right?"

"That's right. But I'm management, and I have insurance!"

Otieno points a gauze-covered hand at him.

"And that makes you better than the drivers?"

"You don't seem to understand responsibility, Otieno. Or how this country works, or what it takes to assume responsibility for that matter. Listen closely. If you aren't out of the chair before Nixon gets here, you won't drive again. You'll be fired."

"Tell me something new," Otieno says, holding up his bandaged hands again as he lowers the chair and heads for the door.

8:31 a.m.—Nathan's bar

Muriel sits next to her friend Heidi Rielken, who runs the Dating operation at the Columbia Plaza. Holding a half-empty glass, she contemplates the small ice cubes floating separately, slowly mixing with the vodka of a Bloody Mary. The mahogany counter before them is a ship destined nowhere as she explains her situation.

"Deed broke up with me. He won't let me drive anymore, let alone spend time with me. He's obsessed with the break-in. And what were they after in the first place, Heidi? He won't say anything," she laments, taking another sip of her drink.

Muriel's friend empathizes with her as they contemplate their futures. The Watergate break-in saga is still unraveling.

"Well, Deed knows about all the girls and their affairs with the Therapy men, and he was just trying to protect you, Muriel. That's the real reason for the last break-in, isn't it? Our stupid Columbia Plaza call girls being controlled by the CIA! And the stupid CIA monitoring all the politicians in town. They weren't too happy when the White House Plumbers decided to conduct a surveillance on their own. So, the police got tipped off by the CIA and the Plumbers got caught red-handed! Ha!"

Along the wooden counter the bartender's hand mops up the vestiges of past drinks—sorrow and remnants of the night's business deals and late-night assignations that have since found quiet hotel rooms or faded away. Behind them rows of liquor bottles testify to many late-night adventures, pleasures, and friendships re-discovered. Muriel's Bloody Mary rests on the counter while cigarette smoke and ozone permeate the room and air-conditioning insulates against the morning heat. She reassesses her relationship.

"Jim's involved in some deeper way I don't understand. Something that's beneath the Lincoln Memorial and the drainage system for the District. Well, I know he's determined to stop the Weatherpeople from destroying this city! I just hope he knows what he's doing!"

Her reverie is interrupted as several men, just released on bail, walk into the bar and take stools across from her and Heidi. She correctly guesses it to be the Plumbers from the Watergate break-in. Nursing their drinks, the two women listen closely to the Plumbers' conversation as they order drinks and speculate about their fate.

"Maybe it's Liddy's fault! He helped talk us into this mess," Sturgis, the Soldier of Fortune, starts off. Wearing dark suits that remain un-pressed, having been stuffed into plastic bags when they were interred into a single D.C. jail room, they look stressed and tired. "We knew the game was up when we saw that the tape was left in place on the Watergate locks. We wanted to call it off, and McCord led us into a trap. The mole!"

"I don't know, Frank," Muscalito (Martínez) protests, tossing down a martini. "Maybe it was Hunt who walked us into this—right into their hands. Never told us a thing about what it was we were looking for except Castro's donations to Therapy. 'Just take pictures of everything in that desk,' he says. But I still respect him, even if he's a rotten spy. Like you say, it was McCord. Remember how McCord kept disappearing, and he told Macho to turn off his transmitter and police alarm. I smell a mole. If it was all a CIA hoax, and he was working for them, then guess who the suckers are?"

Muriel observes them silently. *Jesus! The Plumbers! These break-in guys are trained in the art of stopping leaks, and they get discovered and never knew what they were after? And they never knew about the call-girl ring? Hard to believe. And did Nixon know? Is there anyone in this crazy city who isn't spying on someone else? Let's just sit here and listen to what they say.*

"No, let's just keep this quiet!" Macho interrupts Martínez. He sets down his Coke while the others stay quiet. "This whole ship may be leaking, but we're just a part of the crew. And we're not going to sink alone—I'll tell you that right now. We were following orders and the captain of the ship is the one who has to take care of us."

Macho, having spent more than a year in a German prison camp, as well as experiencing the Bay of Pigs failure and the death of his comrades, realizes that his fight for Cuba is now resulting in a long-term prison sentence. His face turns dark as he removes his glasses and cleans them with a napkin. The Bell's Palsy he recently developed makes his mouth droop when he looks over at Muriel, who in turn looks down into her Bloody Mary. The ice is almost melted. The four men get angrier as they sit at the bar, ordering second drinks and considering their future.

"Well, I say Liddy and Hunt go down with us, and we stick together," Sturgis argues.

"They're all going to be indicted!" Martínez announces. "Hunt may stay quiet for a while, but we can't really trust him anymore. Liddy? —He'll never talk. What I want to know is this—Nixon! Hunt said we did all this work for the president, so how's he fit in? We were supposed to find all the donations Castro made to Therapy, and we found nothing. I mean ... Nixon should be looking out for us, right? We did it all for him, am I right?"

"Exactly," says Sturgis. "So, maybe we ask Hunt to ask the president just what he's going to do to protect us. Who pays for our families while we're locked up? And the attorney fees?"

"Oh sure," Martínez counters. "Hunt left town the minute we got caught. He's supposed to back us up, and he's counting on the CIA to take care of him, alone."

"Okay, then we can go straight to the president ourselves."

"Give me a break!" Martínez interrupts. "Let's just us ask the new president today and you think he'll talk to us? Chief Crazy Horse, you really are crazy!"

"Well, there's one way to find out. We'll track him down and ask!"

Muriel looks at Frank Sturgis with amazement, and then has a greater surprise as a *Times* reporter makes his way into the bar.

"Hey, well hello, gentlemen, this is really an opportunity!" he exclaims, moving quickly in the direction of their target. "I'm Bill Wayword of the *Washington Times*, and I was hoping I might find you here. Mind if I ask you a few questions? I'm writing a piece for the *Times*."

8:36 a.m.—Headed for the Showdown

Wheels spin in unison as Colson and Deed race Car 22 and Car 38 respectively toward the Main Office. Both are nervous about the meeting with the president. Colson hopes he may get recognition for working hard on the re-election committee. On the other hand, he may get trapped in the fallout from the Therapy break-in since he brought in Hunt to begin with, setting the Plumbers up for failure.

Deed contemplates his own future. Now that he's in charge of damage control for the break-in, he'll be more involved in the affairs of Nixon. And rather than rising to the top, as he had dreamed, it's more likely he'll be picked as the scapegoat.

For what? Deed wonders. *I tried to help Nixon, tried to stop the leaks and take care of the Weatherpeople. I'm still trying to uncover Deep Throat, and whoever else is spying on us. It's starting to unravel and way too fast.*

He looks out from the freeway onto the skyline, and the ominous Pyramid, looming above the other government buildings like a massive antennae. Deed's apprehension increases as he hears a call come in through the private radio.

"Car 38!"

"38 by," he answers nervously, recognizing the lieutenant's voice. More trouble brewing.

"It's me, Liddy. Can we talk?"

"Uh...ten-four, Gordon. What's wrong?"

"More bad news," Liddy says, in a solemn tone, through static in the background. "I'm going to jail today. And there's something else you need to know."

"I think I know too much already," Deed says. He can see the turnoff for the Main Office in the distance.

"Well, you need to know that the Plumbers are out on bail. They want Nixon to protect them. In fact, they're looking for him right now, and they expect money for legal expenses and an early release from jail. Hunt wants the same, a presidential pardon."

"Oh great! That's just great! Anything else, Gordon?"

"It's a real mess!"

"It sure is."

Deed sets the hand phone back in its slot and continues driving. *Another new twist*, he thinks. *The lieutenant's going to jail. Well, it's better than being shot while standing on a corner, I guess.*

As he pulls into the parking lot of the Main Office, just behind Colson, he encounters a shopping cart filled with aluminum cans and bric-a-brac. He swerves to miss the Trash Queen and sideswipes her rolling assemblage. Cans, bottles, and Styrofoam fly into the air. Revenge, the black and white pit bull, barks wildly, pulling hard on his leash and dragging the cart behind him, as she scrambles to pick up the rolling debris and catch up with the cart.

"You'll be sorry," she yells. Deed continues on.

Monday, 8:37 a.m.—Headed for the Showdown

Noah and Hinton glide silently over the freeway in the Atomic Car, each considering the possibilities of the day. Having worked through the night preparing his speech, Hinton is hoping he can win the allegiance of the others. He negotiates traffic, stepping easily on the feather-like accelerator while concentrating on the task ahead.

Somehow, I have to coordinate all four drivers, convince them that by working together we can equal the power of Medical's management. If we eliminate dependence on the Pyramid and Hughes' control of the economy, if we work as an integrated team, everyone in the organization will have to take a new approach to health care. Nixon will get impeached and Therapy will be back in charge with me in the lead. If only the drivers were as easy to control as the Atomic Car!

Sitting in the passenger's seat, Noah silently reads the morning headlines of the *Times*. He wonders if there will be a citywide reaction over the Thursday night Therapy break-in, despite Nixon's expected landslide victory as president. And there's Hurricane Agnes on the way north, headed for D.C.

The sound of traffic blends with the Atomic Car's voltaic whir as he contemplates his own plans.

"I need your help, Noah," Hinton interrupts. "You may be working on something, but this meeting we're about to have with Nixon is a critical event in our relations with management. The drivers have to come together today."

"I keep telling you, I'm not a driver," Noah responds, irritated by the distraction.

"Okay, Doctor, or rocket scientist if you prefer. But we need you! In a few minutes we're all going to be together and I'm going to announce the formation of a driver's union to Nixon. We've got to be in agreement about this because it can shape the future of medicine for this city and for our country. We're headed for universal health care, Noah, and this ambulance business has to be the beginning."

"Union? I'm not part of any union."

"You have to be, Noah! Don't you see it? It's our chance to shape the company! You join together with the rest of us, and you'll get what you need for science. All the other things you want to move forward will come along."

"You know, Hinton, you just might have something there," Noah acknowledges, as he considers his own program. "But I only need one driver. I just need Chuck Colson."

"Exactly! So, it's possible for us to join together?"

"Possible," Noah concludes, taking a calculator out of his briefcase. "Anything's possible in our world. Tell me how your union is supposed to work."

"I will!" Hinton says excitedly. "I've prepared a speech to give to everyone at the morning meeting. Noah, the days of the Pyramid are almost over!"

As they exit the freeway, Kisman can be seen not far behind, arriving in a black Mercedes driven by a chauffeur. Both cars pull into the office parking lot and Hinton swerves around the pile of aluminum cans where the Trash Queen is still picking up debris.

Monday, 8:38 a.m.—Potomac River

Rebecca Lovejoy looks out on the water while the Trash King fixes breakfast. There are more homeless people than the day before, milling about in the trees and on the side of the river, while some sleep under newspapers and ragged blankets. Occasionally they stare at her, making her anxious to get started for the Hughes Hospital. After leaving City Hospital on Sunday, the King traveled at a snail's pace with Angel and Michael in the shopping cart. It was dark when they reached the Memorial, and they slept another night on hard cement at the foot of Lincoln's statue. In the morning they look up at the marble carved above his head: "*In this temple as in the hearts of the people for whom he saved the union, the memory of Abraham Lincoln is enshrined forever.*" Wanting only a reunion with her parents, Rebecca resolves again to call the police, and tells the King of her plan.

"I don think I would do that just yet," he tells her, serving them eggs cooked in bacon grease. The bacon on their plates is burned, and Michael pushes it aside. "Police in this city can be dangerous. I'll take you all to your father today, and then he can get you back with your mother. We'll go just as soon as we finish eating."

Rebecca looks at Michael and Angel, who take their plates and sit by themselves on a rock next to the riverside. They watch the current flow past as a blue heron glides effortlessly over the water's surface not far away, followed by a bevy of terns. The birds disappear, taking a westward course, while storm clouds drape over the horizon and a breeze moves the hanging branches that shelter them. The King notes all of this, trying not to indicate any concern to Rebecca. Terns in pursuit of the heron are an omen of a bad storm on the way.

Monday, Day 6, 8:39 a.m.—The Speech

Kisman looks at his watch as his limousine rolls into the parking lot, and then looks up just in time to note the Trash Queen and her dog tied to the reloaded shopping cart.

"Damn it! I leave for one day and this place is out of control again. Look out, lady!" The chauffeur pulls to the right, narrowly missing the woman, and parks the Mercedes in its customary space.

Kisman spots another anomaly. Car 45 is parked in the owner's space, next to Haldeman's Lincoln.

Predictable, he muses. *Otieno chooses to seize the moment just as I'm orchestrating one of the larger international business ventures in health care history while trying to negotiate the Vietnam War. Now, I wonder, who else is acting up? Haldeman's busy spying on everyone and still can't properly monitor the drivers. The military is spying on me; Nixon is spying on everyone. The CIA is covering it all; along with Therapy's November group. And I've got bugs on all of them! So who else is spying on whom?*

He doesn't know about me, but Kisman has a listening device in the dispatching room, just as he does in each of the ambulances, so he's able to monitor Haldeman as well as the drivers. The information he receives has convinced him that the leaks are not coming from the main office, or from the cars.

Ahhh...with the possible exception of...Hinton! Hinton and Helen! Of course! There just might be something there, Kisman thinks. *The two of them have some kind of connection with Therapy, and if they're trying to infiltrate Medical it won't take long to find out. But I'll worry about them later. I'm going to give my talk on the union before the president shows up and this problem of leaks can wait.*

Climbing out of the Mercedes, he looks across the parking lot and sees Otieno leaving the main office.

"Hey! Where do you think you're going?" Kisman demands.

"I'm through with this company," Otieno answers, walking toward his ambulance. "Time to take a few things into my own hands."

"That will prove difficult," Kisman says, sotto voce, nodding at the white gauze wrapped around Otieno's fingers and palms.

Kisman continues through the parking lot. As he enters the main office, he's surprised to find the dispatcher in the barber's chair, speaking to the group.

"We are entering an age," Haldeman says to the drivers, as they drink coffee, "in which each of us must take responsibility. No more lazy fares, no more free trips. It's going to be the end of welfare and the beginning of real Health Care! Let me repeat, the end of welfare...and...and now…the time is also coming for us to start working together, each of us pulling up our bootstraps to work together."

Haldeman reaches out with his arms.

"An opportunity arises for the drivers of D.C. This opportunity will be fair and equal, as we provide emergency care for all. We will go as a union. I want you to remember; a house divided does not stand! Are we free? Are we equal? Is it fair? Of course it is!"

"Out of the chair," Kisman tells Haldeman, as he enters the room. "I'll be the one who gives a speech today!"

8:41 a.m.—Medical Office Parking Lot

"Damn, these drivers are right out of the trees!" Nixon says to the security guard, as his limo pulls into the parking lot and he spots Otieno. He looks through the tinted glass of his limousine at the rear end of Car 45, which swerves around and away.

Things can change fast in Washington, he reflects. *I haven't done much to help the blacks. Maybe not as much as Abraham Lincoln, but I'll be re-elected president by a landslide—that should deserve a little respect!*

Looking over at the Atomic Car, he's reminded of his black briefcase, the "Football," handcuffed to the wrist of the security guard sitting next to him. Another Security vehicle is directly behind, with five more special Security guards. How many other men have access to the briefcase, he wonders, knowing that the military elite has gained access to the code as well? Could others?

"Let's hurry up," he tells the guard, preparing to leave the limousine. "I'm giving a speech today and I don't like being late."

Chapter 42:

The Showdown

Monday, 8:45 a.m.—Medical Office

"We enter an age," Kisman tells the assembled audience, his voice rasping with Teutonic assurance, "in which every driver will be responsible for himself. No more lazy fares, no more free trips. It is the end of welfare! Let me repeat, the end of welfare...and...and so, the time has come for the drivers to work together." Sitting in the barber's chair, he lifts up his right arm. "There will be a new program of health care for the drivers of this city. And let me make this clear: houses united stand together! We seek equal opportunity for everyone. And our unity will win the race!"

Hinton stares at Kisman, then looks around the room in disbelief. Colson is sampling a donut and Deed has a cup of coffee in his hand, but both are listening intently to the words he himself had prepared.

How did my words get stolen? I knew all along Kisman suspected me, so maybe he wiretapped my voice while I was in Noah's laboratory? Kisman once worked for Therapy, and we know he wiretaps everyone, but how did Haldeman get the speech?

"I tell you, fellow drivers, the competition is straightforward, and...at the same time…a challenge, and there is only one way to win. Through a union of health care workers, each of us becomes part of a larger whole. We join together to improve the health of everyone. We have just one..."

"Attention, please!" Haldeman interrupts. "Everyone will please stand!"

"Just one…" Kisman tries to continue, pumping the chair one level higher.

A silence follows as the group turns and faces the back. President Nixon, the owner of Medical, takes measured strides toward the center of the room, arresting Kisman in mid-speech and waving him off the barber's chair.

"Please, men...and you too, of course," he nods to Helen, who's standing in the doorway of the laundry room. "Continue sitting if you will. And thank you, Mr. Kisman; I will take that chair you're sitting in. Nice of you to prepare it..."

Kisman steps to the floor as Haldeman follows Nixon to the side of the chair and pumps him to the highest position. Nixon's pensive eyes scan the room, verifying authority. From an elevated position his furrowed brow testifies to battles in the arena, won and lost.

"Eh...hum...if everyone is ready, I'd like to make a few remarks."

He circles the chair slowly to see all the audience, missing only Otieno and Miraj. I have continued to monitor calls in the adjacent room.

"We are entering an age," he tells the audience, leaning forward resolutely, "in which every driver will be responsible..."

Hinton closes his eyes. *Christ! Here comes my speech again. And from the lips of Nixon!*

"…for himself. No more lazy fares, no more free trips. It is, gentlemen, the end of welfare! Let me repeat, once more, and yes, I speak in tautologies. The end of welfare, as we have known it, is at hand."

It's all unwinding, Hinton realizes. *My chances for a union are sinking into oblivion. What difference does it make to Nixon if I wrote the speech, as long as he's the last one to deliver it? But how the hell did this ever happen?*

As he continues to survey the room, Nixon's confidence strengthens and his voice deepens.

"The day of the individual is here," he continues, "right in step with our cohesive union! And the freedom of each driver to climb the ladder of success is the reward of driving for Medical. Now, before I tell you the significance of this reward, let me say a little about some steps we've made in our ascent to unified health care in America. It's an evolution, gentlemen, with turns of events that not everyone might predict."

He pauses to assess the room.

"Like tectonic plates, the affairs of men are gradual accumulations of incremental moves. But on momentous occasions, like today, the sum of these achievements causes measurable shifts in the social landscape. And, so, during this election the time has come..."

There is another stirring by the back door.

"... the time...has come..."

The door opens suddenly, distracting Nixon and the others.

"…for us...to become...to become...truly..."

"Good morning...sir!"

Before he can finish his sentence, four Plumbers, dressed in ruffled business suits, emerge into the company headquarters. Nixon doesn't recognize them.

"All right, what's going on here?" he demands, rising in the chair.

Frank Sturgis speaks first, his chin jutting ahead. "That's what we're here to find out, Mr. President. We want to know why we're going to jail and you're not."

"Right," Macho echoes. "We've been stopping leaks for you. And we need you to start plumbing for us. I spent years in prison already, I fought in World War II and was decorated, and now I'm fighting for you and the freedom of Cuba. So what will you be doing for me and my team?"

"Señor Presidente," Gonzalez the locksmith adds. "What he says, Mr. President, is that we are not criminals. We work for you!"

"Exactly!" Muscalito demands. His deep-set eyes penetrate the room and his shoulders tense up. "Not a stinking thing in those Therapy headquarters. No Castro donations to Therapy, no documents of assassinations, just a bunch of porno stuff!" he continues. "We were working for you, so we want to know exactly what it was you sent us looking for in the first place."

Nixon looks at them in disbelief, and then turns to Kisman. "Who the hell are these guys?"

Kisman turns to Haldeman, who heads for the dispatching room to call the police. Then, thinking better, he positions himself between Nixon and the four intruders. Deed walks carefully behind the barber's chair, where he can catch the president's ear.

"It's the uh…Special Investigation team, the Plumbers, sir."

"Plumbers?" Nixon swings the chair around, looking at Haldeman.

"The ones in the newspaper...you...ah..." Haldeman hesitates and looks around. "You remember the leaks? You wanted them fixed...and uh...you were pretty busy running for re-election. We were just trying to protect you, like you asked us to."

"Right."

"Right," Deed continues, nodding at Gonzalez and McCord, who stand with arms folded, "and these guys want money. You know, legal fees, family costs. If word gets out that they're here, it could find its way back to you... It's all really a…well, this is like a big cancer...and uh…"

"Uh-huh…yes...and we…?"

"... could cut our losses here, if you know what I mean...," Deed continues.

"Oh sure, but how?"

Noah stays close to Colson. Sturgis and the other Plumbers wait impatiently, with no plans of leaving till needs are met. As Haldeman enters into the discussion between Deed and Nixon, Sturgis turns to watch Hinton and Helen, who are now watching from the back of the room. He can barely overhear their conversation,

"There goes the union!" Hinton tells her.

"What do you mean?" she whispers back. "This is better than anything we hoped for. Nixon is finished, and we'll take on health care once we're in control."

"Maybe so, but look at the drivers. Otieno is gone. We'll never get his allegiance, or any of the others. It's every man for himself now. It's going to be chaos."

"They'll side with us," Helen argues. "Once Nixon steps down from that chair. The wheels are turning faster than he can control. He's going to be history!"

Deed watches coolly as Haldeman confers with the owner. Haldeman's upper lip rises sardonically, considering the next step.

"Maybe we should try a limited hangout," he says, focusing his eyes on Deed, then looking back at Nixon, "as opposed to a total hangout. The 'Operation Candor' thing you talked about once. That's what we need to do."

"Okay, let's talk about that," Nixon agrees, "but in private." He turns the chair in the direction of Deed again.

"We can do our own investigation," Deed counters, knowing he's about to be singled out. "It could be a ..you know how...one of the...that's, that's why we should keep these guys quiet. We'll have to get the CIA to stop the FBI investigation. It's a national security issue, right?"

I'm following all these conversations from the bugs I have placed in the main office and have to laugh. Nixon knows that the CIA has to keep the Bay of Pigs invasion of Cuba from being exposed. He also needs to keep it a secret since he helped instigate it as a vice president.

The Plumbers grow restless. Sturgis walks over to watch Kisman, who has entered the dispatching room where I'm working. He begins making phone calls to other cities. Turning back to the main office, Sturgis spots the president's security guard with the Football, secured to his wrist with a stainless-steel chain. The weight of the briefcase is around two pounds, and Frank knows its potential.

"It's there!" Sturgis points out, commanding the attention of everyone in the room. "I'll bet the money is inside the briefcase. The president takes it everywhere, and the Code's inside, along with the money! That's what Therapy wants to get its hands on, and it belongs to the president alone. The Code is what everyone is looking for, but it belongs to the president!"

The others focus on Sturgis, whose eyes are now fixed on the Football. They all think the same thing.

Can it be possible? That the reason for our plight is inside the room, and we haven't discovered its meaning?

"He may be right," Macho agrees, lighting a cigarette. "I don't know what's in that briefcase, but if that's what all this Watergate stuff is about in the first place, and we're going to jail for it, we ought to know what's in there!"

Haldeman stands in front of the barber's chair, trying to eclipse the president.

"Oh hell, it's probably Hughes' money in there!" Gonzalez proclaims in exasperation, tired of being the unheard Plumber. The others laugh in agreement. "We all know about the Hughes-Nixon connection—it's always about money! And I bet I can pick the lock so we find out."

"You're right," Sturgis weighs in. "And the money should go to us. For stopping Therapy and the terrorists. Therapy was getting money from Castro so they could win the election, and Hunt told us to expose it." He looks defiantly at the security guard, who holds the briefcase tightly.

"So, if it has something to do with Hughes," Sturgis continues, concealing his own secret, "there's going to be a secret inside, and we'd like to see it. What do you think, Mr. President? Haldeman and Colson sent us on this mission, and now we want to know what's in your Black Box. Why don't you go ahead and share it with us before we go to jail again? Or maybe we should share our information with the press, so you can join us!"

"Traitors!" Haldeman declares, no longer able to contain himself, still protecting the man in the barber's chair. "We're talking about a Code that controls the fate of the nation! The Code to our strategic defense system is something only the president can know. National security depends on this Code and you were supposed to prevent leaks, not cause them. First Daniel Ellsberg tries to give it away, and now you want to. You all deserve to go to jail."

"So do you," Sturgis responds, his forehead glistening with sweat. "Since you set us off on this 'third rate' mission in the first place."

Nixon, whose back remains turned, looks at Deed.

"Listen," he says in a coarse whisper, "I wonder if we shouldn't just give these people...these, uh, Plumbers...what you suggest. I mean what are they doing here, anyway? They want money, right? How much do they need?"

"Sir, I would say they are going to cost a million, over a couple of years," Deed answers.

"I know where it could be gotten. It's not easy. But it could be done," Nixon says, remembering his connection with Jimmy Hoffa and looking in the direction of the Football.

"The point is," Haldeman interrupts, turning his back on the Plumbers, "that we have to get these guys out of here. And fast. That's the point."

"Well, that's right," Nixon agrees. "Maybe we should let Deed handle the negotiations. He's fast. He's the damage control, right?"

"Well, what do you say, golden boy?" Haldeman asks, staring at Deed as Macho and Musculito keep their arms folded, blocking the back door.

"I'm not so sure I can…uh, we can…uh, afford to pay every one of these guys..."

"What you mean is that you don't have the money yet," Nixon says, in a hushed voice.

"Right! And really, it should be, uh…Mr. Haldeman…or Colson who should handle this."

"What he's saying," Haldeman acknowledges, "is that he always gets caught holding the bag."

There's muffled laughter.

"And Colson was supposed to be in charge…" Haldeman adds.

"I get it. I see what you're saying." Nixon nods, spinning the chair around to survey the room. Noah and Colson are still talking, as are Hinton and Helen. "So, what we have to do is have someone take these people where they can talk with some attorneys. That's the legal thing to do."

"That's it," Haldeman exclaims. "Deed can take them. We'll just load them up in the back of Car 38."

"Well, wait a minute," Deed counters. "Who else is coming with me? I mean...Haldeman and Colson should come. They're more involved than I am!"

"Right," Nixon continues, regaining control. "We give you the day off, Deed, so to speak, and..."

There's yet another commotion at the back door. Sturgis and Martínez are pushed out of the way as a band of reporters and photographers suddenly make their way into the main office.

"Oh shit! The press!"

"Hello, everybody!" Bill Wayword announces. His team moves into the center of the main office, setting up cameras and recording equipment as McCord and the other Plumbers vanish through the rear door. Nixon sinks into the barber's chair, his face turning morose. Haldeman tries to stand in front of him while Hinton and Helen disappear into the laundry room.

"Why's everyone leaving?" Wayword asks. "We just want to ask a few questions. Are we interrupting something?"

"No one invited you. And this isn't a press event," Haldeman tells him, blocking access to the barber's chair. "This is a Medical enterprise you're disrupting. One photo in the paper and you go to jail. Get the picture…I mean idea?"

"Sure. We get it," Wayword continues. "And will Lieutenant Liddy be joining you in jail? And is the president of the United States involved in any way?"

The barber chair slides slowly down to the floor.

Chapter 43:

The Climactic Launch

8:47 a.m.—In the Command Module of Saturn XV

The smooth dome of the nuclear reactor reflects rays of morning sun, as if the illumination were coming from within. Howard Hughes ponders the image on a screen from the top of his Saturn XV, mentally comparing the energy of solar power to the reactor's inner release of nuclear fission and the power of his personal rocket.

"Fools!" he laughs, contemplating the critics of Noah's nuclear design.

This reactor produces a thousand times the energy a similar investment in solar and wind can produce. If replicated it could supply half the world's energy in short order. But they're right about the waste! The waste and radiation! I can't be around it and it's time to get rid of it and start over with Thorium!

Hughes takes a yellow pad from the guard to draft his last note to Maheu before he sets off on his space venture.

"Robert—it's everywhere—radioactivity on a large scale. Nuclear could make money if it weren't for the waste and radioactive threat.

"So, I agree with the anti-nuclear people on one thing—it creates too much toxic waste and it's worse than a virus! We have to rid the city of it and we'll use Noah for this. All his bizarre research at the base of the reactor—is a distraction. But Noah's the only rocket scientist we have, and he's a master of electronic surveillance. So, it's good we let him

design the transmitter inside the Pyramid, but the real test will be this Saturn XV, and that test comes today!"

Hughes shifts his concerns to Nixon.

No one really trusts Nixon. If anyone ever successfully assassinated Castro, it would have been you, Maheu. You, the CIA, and your mafia people, Traffiante and Roselli. But you failed. Nixon tried with Hunt and failed several times, but Nixon's an amateur. And now he'll be re-elected, so I have to live with the man for a little while longer. Remember, Maheu, you said I could choose the next president...and I even offered to fly the Watergate burglars out of the country to Nicaragua. But that's no longer likely, is it? They got caught red-handed, landed in jail, so I will deny everything! You couldn't get rid of Castro, Robert, but now I'm getting rid of you. You're fired!

He hands off his message to be taken to Maheu and then contemplates the follies of the Therapy break-in. Looking down on the city through the window of the Command Module, he summons energy for the greater task ahead.

9:46 a.m.—Firestone

After sending his last message to Maheu, and unannounced to the public, Howard Hughes awaits the countdown of his final ascent. Energized by the flight in the Spruce Goose, obscured by the publicity on the presidential race and the recent Apollo explosion that killed three astronauts, his launch from the Hughes Space Center in D.C. has been almost perfectly concealed.

"T minus sixty seconds, Mr. Hughes. All systems are GO!"

He starts his own mental countdown, already resenting dependence on Mission Control. Flanked on each side by a Mormon, it's agonizing having to wait for communications inside the Command Module and he squirms against the padded straps that cinched him down an hour earlier.

Flying a jet is so much easier than complete reliance on others, But, where I'm going there's no question who makes the rules. I'll set the pace on the moon, free of bureaucracy. Maybe I didn't design this rocket, but I planned it. It's my moment now, my opportunity to take the lead once and for all, rid the Earth of nuclear waste, mine the distant regions of the solar system. I'm in charge again!

Resting supine, 375 feet above sea level, the straps of his torso-shaped chair are tight around his emaciated frame. His dual sense of control and helplessness gives way momentarily to a flutter of the heart.

"Ignition sequence start!"

The first stage of the Saturn XV pours twenty-five tons per second of kerosene and oxygen into seven modified Rocketdyne engines. Giant metal clamps hold the rocket down to a launchpad.

"Four…three…two…one…zero!"

The clamps release as nine and a half million pounds of thrust, forty-eight stories below, propel the strapped travelers over a sea of burning gases and into the stratosphere.

9:46:05 a.m.

Pushed back by the gathering swarm of reporters, Noah makes note of a minute detail as he and Colson are squeezed into a darker corner of the Medical main office. A group of cockroaches have emerged from hidden crevices and are waving minute cerci on their abdomens, sensing a fine vibration in the room. It intensifies without associated sound and goes unnoticed for a minute. Wayword's cameras are focused on Nixon and the men around the barber's chair. Then the cameras begin to shake. It's obvious to everyone that the floor is moving and the city is vibrating.

"Firestone!" the reporters call out. "Hughes must have launched for the moon. He left early!"

"10-38!" Haldeman shouts. "We need to cover the Space Center!"

There's a rush to exit the main office. As it empties, Kisman returns from the dispatcher's room.

"I'm in charge here!" he announces. " Colson, you go with Deed. Noah, you go..."

Nixon holds on to the arms of the barber's chair while Haldeman stands his ground.

"Colson's with me," Noah argues. "Chuck Colson goes with me!" Deed disappears behind the reporters.

"All right, everyone, I'm the one who happens to be in charge," Nixon commands. "Deed and Colson may end up going to jail for all I know. But you other men get out there and drive! Go cover the damned Space Center and Howard Hughes, wherever he is!"

9:46:06 a.m.—D.C. City Hospital

"Cough with the machine, honey. You have to cough! You're better now. We'll have you off this machine in no time."

Margaret Lovejoy opens her eyes.

It's not the same as the first hospital. This nurse is younger, busier, with other patients in all the beds next to me. Those four lights above are so bright! God, these sheets are old, and the blood stains! Tubes and wires all over me! My stomach is getting kicked; the sounds of machines, and those rhythmic beeps never stop. The ventilator whoosh is interminable, but it sounds like they will get me off of it. I'm stronger now! And I'm starting to remember! I must have had a bad seizure at the dinner.

As her lungs fill with air, a nurse walks near and the beeps accelerate. Margaret prepares for the suctioning tube and more coughing, wishing her back pain would go away. But there's light at the end of the tunnel as her memory returns and she feels stronger.

The other beds have people connected to ventilators. They seem more important because the nurse goes to them so often. Sometimes a lot of nurses go. When they step back from the bed each time someone yells "clear!" that terrible "pommpt" noise, and then silence, and then it starts up again.

Does it know, she wonders, as the fetus turns and pushes above her pelvis, *that I'm stuck in a bed, with restraints? Have I seen this all before? Am I dreaming, or did I see my husband looking at me from the back of an ambulance...with a woman leaning over him? She looked unhappy. And where was he going and where are our children? Alone!*

She glances around again, trying to distinguish the number of beds beside her, then feels a vibrating motion and jostling of her airway tube. It's more than a suctioning tube. Then she hears the nurses shout as the vibration continues for several seconds.

9:46:07 a.m.—Side street of Washington, D.C.

Moving slowly toward Hughes Hospital, still searching and hoping to find their father, Angel and Michael sit inside the shopping cart as Rebecca walks beside the King, crossing over the Kutz Bridge and then past the Washington Monument. He pushes the cart down Independence Avenue, but never fast enough. When they reach the lower side of the Capitol there's a great roar in the distance and they all look past the Capitol's metal dome to see a rocket lift into the sky, first slowly, then with a lengthening tail of burning gas and adjacent clouds of moisture. There's a light shaking of the ground below them as they watch Hughes' Saturn XV disappear into thin air. Its significance unclear, the children continue on their slow walk, forgetting the brief sidewalk shaking. Farther off, dark clouds are beginning to form and a strong breeze hastens their search.

Day 6, 9:48 a.m.—Car 22

Car 22 heads out of the Medical Office parking lot as Colson and Noah look at the smoke-lined trajectory of Hughes' flight path.

"Well, there goes Hughes, hey, Noah? Looks like Howard is going for the ride of his life. Did you know he was about to launch?"

They drive onto Potomac Avenue, headed for the Space Center on the 10-38 call. The pattern recognizes the city's emergency route, targeting the river area and an initial swing by the Watergate buildings. Noah looks silently at the dense traffic ahead, while noticing an approaching cloudbank coming from the southeast.

"I counted fifteen seconds of shaking," Colson continues, "so that would make it a moderate quake if it had been one, right? About five to six on the Richter scale. I mean, depending on the epicenter."

"Hypocenter," Noah corrects.

"Hypocenter?"

"Hypocenter's the true center of an earthquake. When opposing plates of earth shift underground, the energy travels along the fault. It can manifest a long way from the epicenter. All we felt were the reverberations of a large Saturn XV taking off."

"Well, I get that," Colson nods, steering in the direction of Howard Johnson's Motor Lodge. "By the way, this is where Hinton and I picked up a Code Blue the other day. Same guy got transported with Otieno in Car 38…on a Code Blue. Some guys really have bad luck!"

As they pass the elegant exterior of the Watergate buildings on the left and Howard Johnson's on the right, Colson looks over at Noah, wondering about the scientist's deepest motivations. Noah seems preoccupied, typically reserved but staring hard through his rimmed glasses and the windshield at some urgent problem. Colson reflects on his own motivation, and wonders how he could have steered so far from the original goal.

What a bad turn of events! Nixon was completely unnerved by the appearance of the Plumbers and then the press. No doubt the "break-in" was, in a way, my fault. But I did what was asked of me, bringing in Liddy and Hunt to help in the election process—to discover whatever damn secrets the democrats is hiding. This country has to have a security system. If Therapy has access to our protected codes then we're vulnerable to them and to foreign intervention.

Hell, the North Vietnamese, the Russians...even the bloody Cubans! Like I always say, in this world you have to grab people by the balls. Their hearts and minds will follow. It's a dangerous planet!

"So, what does Hughes want to do on the moon, anyway?" Colson asks his partner. "What exactly is he up to?"

"The rocket has a small payload of spent plutonium. He's going to bury it. He'll mine the moon for minerals, which is how his career started in the first place, and when he's done with that, he may explore options for a station…for the Mars shuttle. If he finds enough thorium he'll plan out a lunar energy station. Then he'll come back in the capsule."

"Wow! Well, maybe that's a good place for nuclear waste, given that no one wants it on this planet. But what's the point of us going to the Space Center now? I mean it's a quick way to empty the Medical office, you know…but Kisman and Haldeman should know how to handle the press. We need to give reporters something else to chase, like plutonium. Haaa!"

9:48:45 a.m.—The Stratosphere

The roar and vibration intensify rapidly as the Saturn XV reaches the end of its Stage I burn. In the first ten seconds it rises only four hundred feet, no higher than the apex of the Pyramid. But at two and a half minutes it's forty miles above the Earth, lighter by four million pounds of fuel, and the Hughes Pyramid disappears like a needle buried in the tapestry of Washington, D.C. Experiencing a body weight four times normal, Hughes and his two Mormon aides hyperventilate, struggling to breathe, panting in bursts in order to fill their pressure-compressed lungs. Suddenly the acceleration shifts. First-stage gases cut off as they jerk backwards and forwards, pummeled by a 7,000-mph whiplash as the second-stage rockets propel them forward. Squeezing back into his seat, Hughes waits for the escape tower above the command module to blast free, uncovering windows that will allow a view of the black ocean of space and stars of the distant universe.

Chapter 44:

Inner Space

Monday, 10:14 a.m.—Laundry Room

Hinton and Helen smile together, sitting inside the laundry room. Sheltered from the ground-shaking "Firestone" event and with the door locked securely, there's finally a moment to work out their next strategy.

"My God! I thought he was going to fall out of his chair when Hunt's people walked in!" Helen laughs, recounting the reaction of Nixon to the appearance of the Plumbers and then the reporters.

Her light brown hair drops over her forehead and along her neck, and Hinton goes to brush it back. She looks down just as he reaches for her. The appliances, which temporarily lose electricity, start back. There's a whir of the washing machine and dryer, revolving again with the previous night's linen. For a brief moment they look into each other's eyes.

"Look at this," she says, holding up several moist, wrinkled pieces of paper.

"What are they?"

"Copies of checks. They've been through the wash, but you can still read them."

"So?"

"Well, take a look. See who they're made out to."

She gently unfolds the copies on top of the table. One check was made out to Howard Hunt, and signed by Haldeman.

"That's it! Laundered checks!" Hinton exclaims. "Haldeman paid for the Therapy break-in. If the press gets these, it's all over for Medical. He really screwed up this time!"

She smiles again. "We're not law enforcement. We're just here to reinvent health care for this country. And there's plenty of evidence right here that will undo Nixon."

He looks back, nodding as the laundry machines continue cycling, reverberating throughout the room, almost comforting in the moist heat.

So easy to forget about the world outside.

A languid "Blue Moon" plays scratchily on the radio, barely audible from the back of the room. She hums the melody while placing the check copies in a safe place to dry, smiling as she looks down.

"Helen, you don't suppose..."

She continues humming, looking back as his hand reaches for her side.

"…You don't suppose I could...ever become like Nixon?"

"You? Impossible," she laughs. "Not with me around."

"I don't know...I mean if we're going to put this company into the hands of the drivers. It's just that...you know...he was a driver once too."

"Not like you, honey. You could never be the same."

They forget the recent upheaval and their bodies move closer. Their voices are soft whispers.

"Why? I mean what if? What if I had all that power?"

"Because. You just can't."

"Why not?"

Her hand finds his.

"I won't let you."

"You sure?"

"Of course."

"Are you sure? How do you know?"

"I know everything about you."

Helen locks the door to the laundry room and their bodies move silently—the music awakening a magnetic force. She feels his trauma scissors push against her side and while pulling them out blindly she lets her hand meet his again. He takes the scissors, guiding them till they rest on the lowest button of her uniform and close, moving up, slicing each button till they reach the center of her brassiere, releasing it. Machines continue to circle above as they find a soft cushion of sheets below.

1:12 p.m.—Still orbiting the Earth

Hughes looks back at deep blue and green hues of the Earth, revolving in the distance, without nostalgia or a sense of separation. The black shining orb of the moon is his destiny for now, and getting larger with each minute.

"You're GO for Trans Lunar Injection. Ten minutes!"

TLI! Ignoring the confirmation, he decides to follow his own pre-planned schedule. *Disregard Mission Control. Igniting the third-stage rockets early is now my option and I'll start the TLI burn whenever I want!*

The final F-1 engine fires pink and violet flames behind the module, stretching for fifty yards—yet infinitesimal in the emptiness of space. It lasts seven minutes, long enough to start breaking free of Earth's gravity and allow Hughes a straight shot to the moon. Looking back briefly at the shrinking planet, he feels the exquisite sensation of weightlessness as the third-stage engine shuts down. Silence sets in and the quiet glide frees Hughes as the Mormons begin preparations.

"We're on target, sir," Mel Stewart exclaims. Slipping out of bulky pressure suits, they don flight overalls. Gordon Margulis has dreaded the flight from the beginning, but he's happy to have survived so far, and removes a part of his gear.

"Yes, we're still on schedule," Hughes agrees. The newfound relief from pressure makes him feel both buoyant and hungry. "Now, Gordon, go ahead and open my lunch. Oh yes, and it's time for the injection."

The remaining three-piece modular craft still has to disassemble and recombine, and traveling at 93,000 miles per hour, Margulis takes a Kleenex and hands Hughes a bottle of mineral water and a Hershey bar. Removing a small syringe from the ever-present metal box, he gives Hughes his afternoon codeine injection into the left upper arm, where the skin's pockmarked from hundreds of sticks. It will allow him energy and peace of mind for six hours, but they'll need twelve hours before beginning the orbit around the moon. He notices that the medical box did not get restocked before the great journey.

Kleenex floats throughout the interior as Hughes glides awkwardly toward the front of the command module to work controls for the separation, turnaround, and docking phase. Between bites of the chocolate bar, he flips toggle switches, while the two guards remove the hatchback on the command module probe, adjusting the locking latches and engaging oxygen and electrical lines. Still within range of Earth's gravity, they feel no motion when the connected command and service modules separate from the third stage, do a somersault in space, and return headfirst to rendezvous with the cone-shaped receptacle of the lunar module.

"Feels good," Hughes articulates, propelling the probe of the command module into the locking receptacle of the waiting lunar module. There's a hard, metallic click, and then the capture light comes on as the two bodies fuse. They are free to separate completely from the third stage of the rocket and continue in space, aimed at the luminous moon.

Chapter 45:

Trash King's Arrest

1:13 p.m.—Lincoln Park

The wide body of the Anacostia River moves soundlessly, just distant to where the Lovejoy children continue their westward trek on to the Hughes Hospital. The battered shopping cart seems to hit each pebble and crack in the sidewalk, lengthening a trip that already seems endless, bouncing Michael's young body.

"Are we there?" Michael asks. "I have to pee!"

"No, we got a ways, Michael. But I brought us sandwiches."

They stop to eat while the King shares some of their food with a few homeless people they meet in a park. Another statue of Lincoln stands in the middle of the park. Next to Lincoln is a statue of an almost naked slave, kneeling with his fist raised up, which has broken out of chains.

"That's President Lincoln again, and he's getting credit for freeing the slaves. Truth is, kids, the slaves had to free themselves. It's the only reason why I'm free today! We have to free ourselves."

It feels to Rebecca that there are more homeless and vagabonds around than she's seen before. Appearing in small groups or alone, their clothes are dirty and they carry bags with things inside she guesses to be drugs or something equally dangerous.

One of the vagabonds decides to join their own group, and it upsets Rebecca enough that she decides she'll break free from the King as soon as they catch sight of the new hospital. She has paid close attention to the travel route, remembering what he taught her about signposts.

"We still got a little ways to go, Michael," the King repeats. "All them sandwiches you and Angel ate make the cart go slower. You kids wanna walk now?"

The indigent who's joined them laughs coarsely, then takes a swig from his paper bag, making the King frown.

I wish I had avoided this man. He's going to be difficult to get away from and I'm too old. If we start arguing I might lose. Don't like this wind and all these heavy clouds rolling in either. Looks like a hurricane on the way!

The midday sun disappears behind the cloudbank, but the humidity causes sweat to rise in small beads on their faces and arms. Their clothes cling from the moisture, and the children wish they could swim.

"I still have to go to the bathroom," Michael says.

"Me too," Angel adds.

Rebecca agrees to take them, and they head for an area behind some bushes and trees, momentarily leaving behind the Trash King and the indigent man. They wish even more their father were with them. It's cooler as they walk into the shade and protection of some azaleas. Then, for a brief moment they forget the intensity of their search. When a sprinkler starts up on the grass, Michael runs immediately for the water and they laugh together. He continues running till he's joined by the girls, who giggle as they try to pull him away, causing them to trip and get soaked by the sprinkler.

As quickly as they cool off, they look back and see a police car pull up next to the King and the homeless man. Their shouts give way to silence and they hide behind the azaleas, watching the police handcuff and take the two men away. A gust of wind chills them as the sky darkens more, and the King disappears in the police car.

"Rebecca? Can we find our way back?" Angel asks.

"Yeah, Angel. But I'm not exactly sure where we are."

Thursday, 5:40 p.m.—The White House

Rebecca decides, after watching police action two days in a row, that it's best to avoid police. Unable to locate the Hughes Hospital, however, she follows their previous trail from the homeless shelter and heads back, remembering the landmarks the King told her to make note of. The Lincoln statue with the naked slave is close and leads her back to East Capitol Street, and the dome of the Capitol is impossible to lose sight of. Michael has to keep up with his sisters, without the aid of a shopping cart or the King's slow, steady push, and they stop often to let him rest. When they reach the White House they continue along Independence Avenue, and the landmarks are now all familiar.

5:42 p.m.

For Nixon, as he sits in the Oval Office making phone calls, it's not easy to establish a conservative course that can minimize fallout from the break-in, and he worries that it may be futile.

Kisman has left town for a day, to work on foreign negotiations, and the Hughes space launch, or "Firestone," was a fortunate distraction, allowing him to get rid of the throng of news reporters that invaded the Medical office. He was able to return to the White House and now Haldeman is busy talking with the FBI and CIA, establishing a cover-up. As he looks through the front page of the *Times* early edition, he marvels at the size of Saturn XV, blasting off from the Space Center pad and shaking the city. The headlines read "HUGHES CLAIMS RIGHTS TO THE MOON!" He reads how the corporate giant acquired international rights from other national heads of state, laying claim to lunar territory. Two hundred forty thousand miles away, Hughes will bury used plutonium that the rest of the world rejects, and begin his lunar mining operation.

Chapter 46:
"Something's Very Wrong Here"

Monday, 6:30 p.m.—Banks of the Potomac

After the long journey, the Lovejoy children find their way back to the homeless camp and sit with the Trash Queen, explaining the events of the afternoon—the arrest of the King, their failure to find the Hughes Hospital and their father, and the general hopelessness of the situation. The campsite in front of the King's tent feels very empty, and there's no fire to cook dinner on.

"We're lost," an exhausted Michael summarizes, as they eat peanut butter sandwiches. "And we still don't have my mommy."

Rebecca and Angel wait for a solution, or any answer at all, feeling no less disconsolate. They ignore the burgeoning crowd of indigents that continue to congregate near the riverside camp, and look instead at the muddy waters of the river. Flowing silently, the river offers no more than the passage of time and a recent absence of bird life, a sense of quiet emptiness.

"No, you're only lost when you stop looking," the Queen tells them. "But something really is wrong here. I think it's time for you to get out."

"Everything's wrong here," Angel insists. Her shorts and T-shirt are still moist and coated with grime. As she eats her sandwich, she realizes she looks like another homeless person, and Michael looks worse.

"Why did you say 'get out'? What do you mean?" Rebecca asks.

"This whole city's out of balance. I think something horrible is about to happen," the Queen continues, sitting cross-legged with Michael next to her and noting the heavy clouds in the sky. "The King won't be back, and it's time for you to..."

"We're not going anywhere till we get our mom and dad," Rebecca says, interrupting. She looks hard at the old woman, who looks away and then back at the children.

"...Leave," the Queen continues. "I know what you're thinking. You won't have to leave without them."

"Well, then what do we have to do?" Rebecca asks, not trusting anyone, least of all the Queen. She's ready to cry.

Mallards fly over the surface of the water, heading toward the confluence of the river's Y, or some other distant goal.

"This city was built by men," the Queen tells Rebecca. "It was designed carefully, with lots of underground structures. But there's always been an imbalance and it's coming to a head. All these people you see wandering around here are just hanging around because the sewer system and subways below are getting fouled. It stinks underneath. There are rivers on fire in this country, and this river system is also in trouble. We can't sleep in the monument anymore."

They listen without understanding.

"Is that why all the people stink?" Angel asks.

"The sewage pipes have been blocked," the Queen continues. "There's filth and waste building up and these homeless people have left the underground. Something bad is going to happen. It always does."

"Like what?" Rebecca asks. She can't imagine anything worse than what they face.

"I don't know. We have to find out what's causing the backup. I think it starts right there." She indicates the Lincoln Memorial behind them. They look back in puzzlement at the building where they've slept for two nights. Overhead storm clouds continue building up.

"Underneath," she explains, "is some kind of gate. I think someone shut it to block the drainage system for the underground. If that's what happened, then the sewage pipes have filled and that's why so many Weatherpeople are here. They've been forced out of the drainage system."

"But," Rebecca asks, "what are we supposed to do?"

"You have to go back," she answers, "to the hotel."

"But that's where we wanted to go the whole time. We don't know how to get there!"

"Well, I can take you."

10:15 p.m.—Laundry room

Hinton and Helen, after a blissful afternoon of lovemaking, sleep in the laundry room, then wake and begin reviewing records and planning their redesign for a future health care system.

"James," Helen asks, after some thought, "how much do you think Haldeman knows about us? I mean we're not exactly trained spies. Do you think he's on to us?"

"No, don't think that way, Helen. We're not spies. We're just working for Medical, and we're going to try and get them to think like us, like Therapy."

Helen laughs, amazed at Hinton's naiveté.

"You don't believe it?" he continues. "Really, we all want the same thing—to lead long, healthy lives."

"Sure, only some get to be healthier and live longer than others. And it's all based on making money."

"Well, we'll see, honey. I am going to get all the drivers to work together, and then we'll see. Unions are strong!"

Helen smiles, shaking her head and brushing back her light brown hair.

10:23 p.m.—Blue Mirror nightclub, 14th St. NW

As Hinton and Helen work on their plans for health care, Clifton Urning sits at the Blue Mirror bar, writing verse and drinking away his misery while across from him, on a revolving stage, two dancers striptease in the swirling neon lights. Urning, recently discharged from the Hughes Hospital, has wandered into the nightclub and writes down verse to describe the gyrations of the two dancers, comparing them with images of a moon landing on a television screen. It's a way to forget his misery, having been thrown out of the Pyramid by Hughes and given a diagnosis of insanity at the Hughes Hospital.

"Float now over Earth's lover, pulling you from the beginning, wanting you in her distance, reminding you with her light..."

The words flow from his pen and he tries to focus on the show, but is distracted by a group of men at a table not far from the dancer's platform. Not recognizing the Miami Plumbers, he continues his verse.

"...Hidden in the darkness, awakening seas of volcanic eruption, they move to a union, bodies separate, three billion years denied, will touch again...."

The dancers unrobe, and the lights dim.

"...Hovering over her black yielding surface, it begins the celebrated descent. Four legs spread outward, balancing an endless dream, holding breath for the coming rapture. A sonorous, empyreal veil, floating gracefully onto the circle of desire..."

Clifton Urning admires Heidi Rielken but continues writing, looking up at the television above the Blue Mirror bar, where transmitted images show the Hughes Lunar Module descend slowly onto the moon's surface. The dancers continue their performance, glancing occasionally at the small audience of Plumbers in the audience who nurse drinks, paying little attention to the dance.

"We got double-crossed!" Musculito laments, considering his comrades who are still on bail but without legal representation. "Hunt promised to cover us if things went wrong, and now he's left town. Someone had to tip off the police for us to get caught red-handed!"

Macho, Gonzalez, and Sturgis look back at Martínez through a haze of cigarette smoke, their vision also blurred from drinking scotch and Cuba Libres.

"Like who?" asks Sturgis, who never drinks alcohol and sips on a Coke.

"Well, McCord has disappeared. He was always disappearing when we were in the Watergate," Martínez responds, having the best understanding of CIA operations. "What do you think, Speedy?"

"What I think," Gonzalez answers, "is that I'll never be able to pick all the locks that are going to keep us in prison. But McCord might, if he's the first one to confess. So I think he's a double agent working for the CIA! He'll rat on the principals and then he'll get a short prison sentence."

Having found no evidence of Castro's involvement, as Hunt originally directed them to discover, they continue to debate the reason they were recruited in the first place. Martínez confesses that a secretary provided him with a key leading to a lock for the secretary's desk in the Therapy office. Besides a drawing of a football with numbers on it, there was an address book with the names of several women—Champagne, Candy Cane, Clout, and Heidi. Columbia Plaza was also written in it. Martínez never had time to take photos of the football or the address book before they were caught and arrested by the police.

"Hunt tells us we'll be taken care of. But I'm not too sure," Macho comments. "I guess we'll find out in court."

While the Miami Plumbers lament their condition, Urning's pen traces out verse along with the erotic tune that insinuates through the Blue Mirror Club and leads the dancer's moves.

"Turn and spread, into the origin, ecstasy of joining. Come, where you have never been, never see, innermost outside... innermost … inside …"

Monday, 10:30 p.m.—The County Hospital – Labor Begins

Day six of Margaret's D.C. vacation is one of the longest, as her memory returns. She slowly recalls driving into the capital, staying at the Motor Lodge, and searching for her husband when notified by the police - the repeated images appear to her in the ICU bed. She saw him on a ventilator in a hospital like the one she's in now, and somehow it seems like she saw him in the back of an ambulance, only a day ago.

Through a distant window she sees rain falling against the glass. And with the building atmospheric pressure of the approaching hurricane, her fetus is a millimeter from its goal. Taut with aerobic, sustained effort, the uterus tightens like a fist every twenty minutes, making her back ache constantly. She looks up at a TV above her bed and watches the broadcast news of a moon landing.

"The module has separated, dropped perfectly into position, and now probing the deepest recess, and...yes…yes…well ahead of schedule.… Howard Hughes has landed on the moon!"

Chapter 47:
Returning to Howard Johnson's

Day 6, Monday, 10:33 p.m.—Room 623

Finally arriving at their original quarters, led safely by the Trash Queen, the Howard Johnson's Motor Lodge seems like a palace to the Lovejoy children. Rebecca takes the room key from her pocket and they find their way into room 623. Housekeeping has cleaned it and it takes little time to feel at home, except that neither their mother nor father has come back. They shower, put on nightclothes, and eat multiple servings of ice cream the Trash Queen brings them from the restaurant. Empty containers migrate across the rug again as they watch the lunar voyage of Hughes on TV, then drift again into slumber, exhausted. Michael sleeps on the shag rug, next to the TV, Rebecca sleeps on her cot, Angel crawls into her parents' bed, and the Trash Queen rests on an easy chair as Hurricane Agnes makes its way into the capital.

Day 7

The End of It All

"We go fumbling in the darkness while the solution has always been with us. A little opening of the heart, a little shining of the lamp, and we don't have to stub our toes on all the obstacles out there."

—Guru Majaraji, London, 1980

"In five or six thousand years, five or six high civilizations have risen, flourished, commanded the wonder of the world, then faded out and disappeared, and not one of them except the latest ever invented any sweeping or adequate way to kill people. They all did their best to kill, being the chiefest ambition of the human race and the earliest incident in its history, but only the Christian civilization has scored a triumph to be proud of. Two or three centuries from now it will be recognized that all the competent killers are Christians. Then the pagan world will go to school to the Christian, not to acquire his religion but his guns."

—Mark Twain

Nixon: "No, no, no…I'd rather use the nuclear bomb. Have you got that, Henry?"

Kissinger: "That, I think, would just be too much."

Nixon: "The nuclear bomb, does that bother you?… I just want you to think big, Henry, for Christ sakes!"

Richard Nixon—The White House tapes, April 25, 1972

"I'll see that the United States does not lose. I'm putting it quite bluntly. I'll be quite precise. South Vietnam may lose. But the United States cannot lose. Which means, basically, I have made the decision. Whatever happens to South Vietnam, we are going to cream North Vietnam.

"For once, we've got to use the maximum power of this country…against this *shit-ass* little country: to win the war."

—Richard Nixon, The White House Tapes, May 4, 1972

Chapter 48:

The Last Day and the Code

Day 7, Tuesday, June 20, 1972, 7:00 a.m.—Unit 160

The sound of a phone next to his bedside jostles Castro awake and he demands an answer as he picks it up.

"Why are you calling so early? What is it?"

Blackbeard, who stays in Havana close to the Líder Máximo, answers nervously.

"Comandante, today will be the day. The day we have the Code. I am told this by Tango, who was next to Nixon yesterday. It could have been Nixon's last day, but Tango did not have the nerve or the courage. Perhaps it will be today, and we need you to allow for this. To give him permission, to give him the order."

Fidel sits up on the side of the bed, looking to be sure he remains alone, other than Dahlia who is in the bed beside him.

"Barbanegro, didn't we say the Hurricane could take care of Nixon? That and the Watergate break-in. What's the meaning of this call?"

"Forgive me, Fidel, but today we can eliminate him for good, and with the Code we will not have to worry about another invasion. Ever! You do not need to know anything, but I must have your permission to work toward your future security. Once Tango has the Code, we can do all that is needed to protect you."

Castro, awake now, is more than irritated. He begins putting on his fatigues and decides to go to the Presidential Palace to continue the discussion.

"I'll call you when I'm ready, Barbanegro, and you are to wait for my call. There are no assassinations without my permission—do you understand?"

Blackbeard remains silent, waiting for Castro to call him back.

Day 7, Tuesday, June 20, 1972, 7:02 a.m. – The Medical Office

As Hurricane Agnes approaches the capital I know that it will be my last day, and that of Nixon as well. A long range Savage M 10 Stealth rifle lies loaded and hidden in the back of the cab, parked two blocks away. While I tend to the calls and wait for Haldeman to come to work, the radios have been busy all night. Distress messages for heart attacks, loss of consciousness, auto wrecks, shortness of breath – all the usual calls come in, but no one has responded to my assignments. Colson, Deed, Otieno, and Noah are AWOL, so I've refer the calls to Therapy. It makes no difference, why should it? My task for the night has been to open the Football that Haldeman, in his anxious dealings with Nixon, left behind just under the switchboard.

The black leather satchel, a Zero – Halliburton anodized aluminum briefcase inside, is not difficult to open. With only 5 combination dials it took twenty minutes to figure out the code. Nixon carries his “Biscuit”, or laminated code card, but any good mole has enough training to break simple codes and has no need for it. The transmitter, however, is far from easy. And there are two “black books” about nine by twelve inches. One contains all the retaliatory options and the other has some information on missile sites and where to take and protect the president during national emergencies. That makes me laugh, but I spend most of the night deciphering how to copy all the codes and make some changes. It’s a primary secret, of course, how the special code identifying the president and allowing him to relay to Military Command activating directions for the entire nuclear arsenal. And, of course, it still needs approval by the Secretary of defense. I was only a little surprised to see that, just like on the menu of Hojo's, there were several choices for the picking, or should I say destroying. Russia first, then China, then North Korea, and, of course, my own country – Cuba. Nixon, or I, could choose one or all of them! Ham sandwich, with or without fries, please?

Day 7, Tuesday, June 20, 1972, 7:03 a.m.—The Oval Office

"Nixon Wins Election by Landslide!"
"Hughes Lands on the Moon!"

After reviewing the twin headlines, Nixon and Haldeman look out the window of the president's office, noting the wind, dark clouds, and hard falling rain, thankful that they don't have to negotiate through morning traffic. Across an open stretch of grass and trees a steel fence protects them from the four-lane boulevard circling the White House. Columns of automobiles pass in opposite directions, making stop-and-go patterns that seem to cinch tightly, like a chain, as Hurricane Agnes approaches the city.

"This looks like it will be quite a hurricane, sir," Haldeman comments as they view the rapidly approaching storm. "We're going to see some major flooding."

"Well, we've weathered worse things, haven't we, Bob?"

"Yes sir, and Howard Hughes has managed to escape it all!"

"He's always a step ahead," Nixon comments, referring to Hughes.

"One step for him, a leap of faith for us!" Haldeman jokes.

Nixon's suit is as dark as the ether in the background of a photograph hanging next to them. Taken by the Apollo 11 astronauts, the photo shows the half-lit Earth rising like an ornament over the moon's volcanic sphere. For Nixon it was a happier moment, greeting the men when they landed in the Pacific Ocean on their return from the moon. "Neil, Buzz, and Mike," he told them, as the USS *Hornet* carried him on a tour of Asia. "I want you to know that I think I am the luckiest man in the world, and I say this because I have the honor to be the president of the United States, but particularly because I have the privilege of speaking for so many in welcoming you back to Earth. They represent over two ion people on this Earth, all of them who have had the opportunity to see what you have done."

Haldeman steps back to look at the president, contemplating the present.

We've come a long way, Nixon and me. But the break-in is a dismal setback. The war protestors and Weatherpeople are increasing in numbers and danger. It's still uncertain how much information the democrats have about the Hughes–Nixon connection and all I learned for sure is what that idiot Hunt, working for the CIA, told me about the Plumbers' discovery inside a locked desk drawer of a Therapy secretary. 1-19 20-8-25-19-5-12-6. The numbers don't add up, don't make sense, and why were they written on the side of a football? It's a code of some kind, but why the football? What the hell are they hiding? The only things we've found from those break-ins are some lascivious conversations recorded between politicians and I guess a call girl organization. The democrats just love sex!

"Hughes is no ordinary man," Nixon says, folding his hands nervously. "Sometimes I wish I'd been an astronaut, you know, but we have to take care of things down here, don't we, Bob? By the way, when does Kisman come back?"

"Today. He missed some of the action yesterday when he slipped out to make phone calls. Makes you wonder a little bit, doesn't it? The press was pretty nasty this morning."

On the second page of the *Times*, Bill Wayword has written another story about the break-in, including a photo of Haldeman and Deed taken in the Medical Ambulance headquarters. Haldeman has a scowling expression on his face, as he tries to conceal the president, who sits in the barber's chair avoiding the reporters. In the news story, Wayword suggests that the Watergate break-in may be part of a larger conspiracy, involving all branches of the government, including the White House.

"Well, uh...they get paid to be that way," Nixon explains, shaking his head. "If it bleeds it leads, as they say. And that's why we're going to tell the press about Operation Candor. We let them know some truth, at least about what Therapy does, and maybe we have to sacrifice a few of these men. Those Plumbers…and uh…Hunt and Liddy, and maybe even Colson—I hate seeing them go to jail, Bob, but what we've said in the past is inoperative now. Now…uh…now that we've won by a landslide. And so, we can get back to business again, and find the real truth, so to speak. We'll start Operation Candor while...uh...while Kisman is away. And take care of a lot of things. Including peace with honor in Vietnam."

Haldeman smiles while pulling a sheet of paper from his coat pocket.

"You might want to look at this, sir. Deed gave it to me to pass on to you. It's going to help us rein things in."

He hands over a single sheet of paper.

The Enemy List

Mr. President—Some people are emerging as less than our friends. With your re-election, we have a chance to stop the leaks once and for all. These are the people that pose a threat.

Daniel Ellsberg—"The most dangerous man in America" as Kisman likes to call him. It's just the tip of the iceberg, his divulging our highest classified information to the press. Maybe to the Russians as well. We need to keep him in prison for a long time.

Anna David—Communist and advocate of violence. We'll also keep her in jail.

Clifton Urning—This mad poet has some detailed knowledge of Hughes. He was recently released from the hospital and behaves erratically. Needs to be committed for a long time!

Bill Wayword—The reporter from the Times. *If we find his source, we can control him. Restrict his access!*

Guruji Miraj—A harmless spiritual master? This medical student has foreign connections that are uncertain. Why's he driving ambulances for Medical? He's probably a candidate for extradition.

Hinton—This man seems to be even a greater threat. We need more information on his relation with Helen and Therapy. Is he gunning for something?

Helen—More dangerous than Hinton? Everything about this woman suggests she wants to wear pants.

Otieno—This renegade black driver wants equal rights and pay and thinks he has a future in Medical. We haven't heard the last of him.

Deep Throat—Mark Felt was second in line for Hoover's job, and then you gave it to Pat Gray. So he's unhappy. Is he the one who's leaking to Wayword, or is there someone else involved?

Could there be a double agent working for the KGB, or maybe Castro? Or even for the CIA? He's deep inside and we need to locate him!

Nixon reads through the list, looks out the window, and then turns back to Haldeman.

"They're all out to destroy us. They want to destroy everything that we've worked for, Bob."

"Yes, sir. And we need a way to deep-six them all."

"Deep-six?" Nixon asks.

"Just a figure of speech, sir. Bury them."

"Oh, that's uh...interesting. But I didn't say it. You did. Now, if you think about it, Bob, you could just get them to go away, sort of like, uh...Hughes, you know. That would take care of it. I wish they all were on the moon!"

The phone rings and Haldeman picks up the call. It's from the *Times*.

"The operator says that it's Bill Wayword again," Haldeman tells him. "He says Lieutenant Liddy, one of our employees, was arrested and is in prison. He wants to know if you have any comments."

"Tell Mr. Wayword that there will be a press conference this afternoon at which I am going to announce a major operation here. Operation Candor. Oh yes, and Wayword won't be invited."

Nixon nods and Haldeman waves back to him as he heads from the Oval Office back to the Medical office. As he does so he notices the aide-de-camp outside the door no longer has the Football handcuffed to his wrist. He remembers that he kept it himself back at the main office, after the chaotic Saturn XV launching episode and invasion of the press.

"Where's the Football?" Haldeman asks, staring hard at the military aide.

"Sir, I left it with you yesterday, as you ordered. During the Hughes space launch you felt you should be carrying it for the president."

"Jesus, that's right!" Haldeman recalls, suddenly realizing that the guard handed it to him while he was dealing with the press. And by a wonderful coincidence, I was still covering the dispatch room, although my shift had ended. I told him I would guard it carefully. And he forgot it.

"But the Football can never be separated from the president! Absolutely never!" Haldeman tells the aide. "You stay with the president now and I'll see that it gets returned. And don't ever let it be separated from the president again. Do you understand?"

"Yes, sir. Thank you, sir."

Haldeman glances back once more to see the lonely figure of Nixon, still looking at the moon photo.

7:15 a.m.—Sea of Tranquility (the moon)

Gazing out through the gold-tinted window of the Modular Station, its four legs immersed into inches of ash on the Sea of Tranquility, Hughes watches his aide Margulis, who's still in the Command Module, disappear for forty-seven minutes each time the module orbits the dark side of the moon. Hughes contemplates the tasks ahead, the silence marred only by his breathing, almost effortless in the reduced pressure of the workstation.

Inconceivable that people choose not to work, he reflects, looking back at the miniature, gem-hued planet left behind. *I'll need to mark out boundaries for the mining territory, drill holes, insert an insignia confirming my rights to the land. We'll leave a half-ton of this radioactive waste, and eventually sell off the thorium and titanium claimed in my territory. This time there won't be bureaucrats, politicians, or city people to slow me down. And the new business will cover the expense of our Saturn XVs.*

"Bo-Bop-Areet!"

The hummocky outer wall of an impact crater he has maneuvered around while landing the module interrupts the white glare of surrounding dust and lunar dirt. A few hundred yards away lies the Lunar Rover, left behind from Apollo 11, its orange fenders curved gently over zinc and titanium wheels. It causes a smile of anticipation as Hughes runs fingernails through his new beard.

"Your steak is ready, sir," his remaining aide Stewart says, pulling a bag from the microwave.

"Make sure it's not undercooked," Hughes cautions, as he takes a bottle of mineral water and squeezes a spherical blob into the gravity-free cabin. As it floats up, he aspirates it with a straw.

"Here you are, sir."

Stewart hands over a bag of peas and a thin, freeze-dried filet mignon. Annoyed by the lack of uniformity of the twelve peas, Howard lets the large ones float off to angular ends of the module. Glancing out the window at the Rover, he's buoyed by the thought of driving the moon mobile.

My bedsores are healing, helped by this absence of atmospheric pressure. I'm so glad to escape from damn Earth's gravity. Hell, maybe, I'll begin to regain my height!

"Bo-Bop-Areet!"

He follows the steak with a cup of peach ice cream and looks back again at the erstwhile planet. As Stewart collects the larger peas floating inside the station, Hughes moves into the decompression chamber. Once inside the airlock he makes multiple checks and maneuvers into a liquid-cooled ventilation spacesuit, first climbing into inflatable trousers, then pulling on the upper torso half. Stewart joins the two halves and helps him snap on gloves and attach the tinted, oversized helmet. Adjusting oxygen flow and waiting for the nitrogen to purge from his bloodstream, Hughes notes a slight pain around his umbilicus and remembers he missed his last codeine injection.

Like a calf emerging from the womb, he makes his gangly entrance onto the no longer virgin moon. The first selenologic contact feels surprisingly stable, as foot hits dust and rock. His step is tentative, and then he takes three more. The expansive open space experience makes him want to leap up like a boy, and he jumps. He's immediately rewarded by traversing a distance of ten feet. More exhilarated, he jumps again, narrowing the distance to the Lunar Rover.

"Bo-Bop-Areet!"

Chapter 49:
Longevity

7:45 a.m.—Noah's Nuclear Reactor

After spending a night encapsulated within the nuclear reactor, Noah and Colson are protected from and unable to hear the wind or pounding rain of Hurricane Agnes. In the morning Noah resumes his cryonic mission with Colson, hoping to engage him in completing one of the final goals of science. Surrounded by metal shelves of journals, periodicals, and textbooks, Noah reiterates his simple message to his resting partner.

"You realize that with time our bodies inevitably cease to function. It's all determined by chromosomes, Chuck. We unravel till our energy is exhausted, spent, lost to the universe. And given man's propensity for self-destruction, there's scant reason to believe that our civilization will stay on the planet for the next thousand years. Even if we do, climatologists say the Earth could be uninhabitable. The next big ice age is not that far off either. The point is, Mr. Colson, we have to start looking for new planets. We'll need some survivors to keep the race going, and we need to get you on board the Ark!"

Colson doses peacefully on the library couch of the nuclear reactor while Noah stands next to him, repeating the same offer he made during the night.

"But you, Mr. Colson, have the possibility of extended life. And I have the responsibility of convincing you that any one of us can enter into a state of preservation—and remain intact indefinitely till science brings us back to full function. Now sit up, please, and just listen to me if you would."

Fluorescent lights flicker above them and Colson moves slightly on the couch, partly awakened by the loud reverberations of uranium casings being transported into the depths of the reactor. The fifty-pound loads, contained within zircaloy shells, slide into position with a clanging noise, enough to make him more nervous. Once the U235 is transformed, he wonders, how does it become a radioactive waste package so that it can fit into a lunar module?

"Your life insurance policy is meager, in and of itself," Noah continues, "but your modest investment over a century or so will compound interest, reaching heights that make Howard Hughes seem like a pauper. Are you listening?"

Colson stirs without opening his eyes, while Noah takes a set of papers and places them on the table next to the couch. He shakes his partner by the shoulder.

"And the Atomic Car will be yours, Chuck. Beginning today, from here on out, it's yours to drive! I'm giving it to you."

Colson sits up, adjusts his glasses, and takes in the library and the papers that the doctor has set down in front of him.

"So, good morning, Chuck. Would you like to sign these papers now? Your chance to live forever, my friend."

Colson shakes his head and rubs his eyes. "What are you talking about, Noah? Aren't we late to work?"

"These papers are for extended life. You need to sign them, now."

Noah holds out a pen while Colson tries to focus.

"Oh, that stuff. Listen, Doc. I can't sign that paper. Well, maybe when I get a little closer to dying. But, you know, Noah, Jesus is on our side. I think Heaven is good enough for you and me, don't you?"

Noah frowns and walks over to where Colson sits on the couch.

"Listen, Mr. Colson, longevity isn't something you just wait around for. You have to sign now. Today, while you're still healthy. We don't…we don't have…time. I mean you…you yourself could have millennia! You should sign this paper, here, this morning."

"Excuse me?"

Dr. Noah pauses, looking briefly towards the gargantuan IBM computers distant to the columns of books and journals, then explains to his reluctant co-worker.

"You don't understand, do you? I've spent my entire scientific career advancing the lives of our people. And the human world as we know it; it can't last. The people of this planet are far too selfish to endure. We're surrounded by other countries even more selfish than we are. You know, like I do, between Russia, China … even Cuba … and us there's enough nuclear weapons to eliminate life on our Earth within hours! We have to have someone who can rise above the masses, who can carry our code into the future."

"Well, I just had a great idea, Doc," Colson says. "How about you?"

"I wish it could be me," Noah answers, without smiling, "but I have to give up my chance in order to control the freeze. I'm the only one who knows the technique to ensure your survival."

The two men are unshaved, their faces turned grey in the interior lighting of the Reactor. Colson doesn't like the words "freeze," "survival, or "your".

"So," Noah continues, "I am selecting you, because you're someone who's prepared to give of yourself, in order to help others. When you sign these papers, I'll give you the Atomic Car and science will take you on your way to an unlimited future. Colson, this is an opportunity of a lifetime, fixed in eternal...let's just say...you'll be the ultimate EMT, way ahead of your time."

"Well, thanks, Doc, I sure appreciate your consideration...and I like the idea of driving the Atomic Car. I wonder if we could just find a few donuts and some coffee. Kind of cold down here, you know?"

He shivers as Noah tries to conceal his irritation, putting the pen back on the desk. The doctor points his finger at him.

"Okay. Just stay here and I'll be right back. But you need to read through the papers while I'm gone. We don't have any time to waste."

As Noah leaves the library, Colson stands up quickly and looks at the forms on the table. The top sheet is dated Tuesday, June 20, 1972.

I, Charles Colson, having fully considered and understanding the significance of extended longevity, do hereby bequeath my body to the Human Preservation Foundation, to be stored at 320 degrees below Fahrenheit, until a predetermined condition of technological competence is met, at which time the Foundation is required to return my molecular composition to its active state. I have been duly and legally informed, pending the proximal moment of conventional bodily function cessation in coming years, that I will be administered biologic preservative fluids, will continue morphologically suspended in liquid nitrogen, within a designated Dewar, until such predetermined time as nanotechnology restores my chromosomes into full remission..."

"Sheeeeit! You got the wrong man, Doc. I'm getting out of here!"

Colson grabs his boots and without putting them on makes his way out the open library door and down a long, curved corridor. Uncertain of the design of the building, he chooses to turn right and walks quickly, hoping to find a door leading to the garage where Car 22 is parked. After less than a minute he realizes he has come full circle. There are several doors across from the library, on the opposite side of the corridor. One of them leads to the inner circle of the building. Remembering that the double staircase with a large Y written over it, Colson eventually locates it and passes through a doorway. He starts down the stairway, holding onto a railing, feeling his feet land on strange rubbery steps as he tries to escape.

"Uh huh..."

He breathes rapidly, quickly winded even as he starts down, and suddenly has the sensation of being followed. The strangely textured steps absorb the impact of his shoeless feet as he stops to look back. Impressed again by the deceptively simple shape of the stairway—two sets of stairs spiraling together in helical fashion—he wonders if he could have gotten onto the wrong side. Is there any way to cross over. Is he out of sequence? Then he sees his pursuer.

"Damn!"

Noah's angry, determined face searches for him as he sweeps down from several stories above, his white coat owing out ghost-like. He replicates the escaper's steps, maneuvering the chromosomal code he knows by heart.

Frightened by the specter, Colson chases down another flight and disappears through an open door.

"Uh huh, uh huh..."

Lungs quickly depleted of oxygen, Colson hopes to discover the garage and ambulance, but instead is greeted by howls and shrieks from cages of laboratory animals lining the circular wall of the new corridor.

"Jesus!" he moans, gasping for air, "How the hell do you get out of this place!"

He moves quickly, making his way along the corridor, hoping to find another door. As the dogs bark and lunge against the bars of their steel cages Colson quickens the pace, again finding that he has traced a complete circle. The sensation of being followed is exacerbated by the fear that he's being driven into a trap! The howling dogs seem to know his destination and then…too late…he's face to face with the rocket scientist.

"Colson!"

"God, uh huh...Noah! God almighty, man...you surprised me! Why are you still chasing me?"

Stopped in their tracks at the edge of the staircase, Noah sanctions him with a bag of donuts and the unsigned consent.

"Listen, Chuck, you need to trust me. What we are doing is right. This is what's right for the race, for you, for us, for eternal life!"

The dogs continue their lament and the monkeys bang harder against steel mesh. One of them spits on the back of Noah's coat, distracting him.

"Know something, Dr. Noah, I'm, uh...uh huh...getting out of here!" Colson cries, slipping past and through the inner door again. He continues down the staircase, grabbing ahold of interlinked messenger and transcribed RNA, double-stepping the soft rubber facsimiles of hydrogen bonding.

Chapter 50:

Coming Apart at the Seams

Day 7, 8:15 a.m.—Marine One and the Enemy List

The sun ascends over the rotating Earth as precisely as it has for four and a half ion years. The slow rise, however, casts no moving shadow behind the rain-covered Pyramid or moving cascade of pedestrians rushing to return home in the rain. Kisman flies over the city in Marine One, the president's helicopter, and observes Hurricane Agnes ravaging the city with wind and down pouring showers. As he heads for the president's special landing base, he can barely see the Lincoln Memorial on the west side, and City Hospital, adjacent to the D.C. prison along the east side, is completely obscured.

His trips to China and Paris have gone okay, but his efforts to strike a balance in negotiations with North Vietnam, by withdrawing American troops, is not yet the solution Nixon was hoping would work. We will bring our troops back to America without delay, along with all American prisoners, is Nixon's offer, but it's soundly rejected by South Vietnam. And China watches the Watergate saga in amazement, amused that Nixon would ever worry about such a minor spying event on the periphery.

Then there's the economy and health care. City Hospital remains to handle marketplace failures, Kisman reflects, as he looks down at the rivers flowing through the city. At the yoke of the two rivers he can barely make out the Kennedy Center. The Watergate buildings, now a regular in tabloid news, are threatened by the rising Potomac.

It's turning into a political quagmire, he thinks to himself, *and I think I know who's behind it.* Opening his briefcase, Kisman pulls out a copy of the document he obtained by wire-tapping inside the dispatcher's room. It's signed by Deed.

The Enemy List

Mr. President—Some people are emerging as less than our friends. With your re-election, we have a chance to stop the leaks once and for all, and these are the people that pose a threat.

He makes an asterisk next to Ellsberg and Wayword and underlines Anna David. Moving down the list he places a question mark next to Guru Miraj, and Otieno. He underlines in bold **Hinton** and **Helen**, and makes a diagram around Deep Throat in the shape of a football. As the helicopter descends smoothly onto a large X he steps out and heads toward his rendezvous with the president, surprised by the appearance of a multitude of protestors and indigents. They carry rucksacks and push shopping carts outside the steel fence that encompasses the White House lawn. Walking faster, impelled by the wind of the helicopter blades as the helicopter leaves, he heads for the East entrance.

8:25 a.m.—Room 623, HoJo's

Like ragdolls in a playroom, the Lovejoy children lie collapsed on the floor of the motel, arms propped in disarray and faces buried in the shag rug, as they begin the last day. Rebecca awakens first. As her eyes open, she's reassured by the gentle image of abandoned clothes and ice cream containers scattered over the floor. In her notebook there are notes and drawings of the capital buildings and images she has seen in the newspaper—Howard Hughes, the Saturn XV rocket, and an odd staircase in a nuclear reactor. Instinctively, she removes a blanket and begins to pick up the trash around her brother and sister, as her mother would do. Then she notices the Trash Queen asleep on a chair.

Where the heck are Mom and Dad? God, I wish they were here!

She gazes at the old woman's face—unwashed, lined with wrinkles, and overlaid with thick gray hair that has come undone during the night. The wan skin makes Rebecca shiver. She quietly wakes Angel and Michael, who take a few minutes of shaking before they stir. Michael rises and goes directly to the TV. Rebecca turns it back off and makes Angel sit up.

"You guys," she says impatiently, "you can't even remember! We have to go get Mom and Dad today."

"Maybe we should watch cartoons first?" Michael asks, his hair sticking up from sleeping on the rug. The previous day's search has left him discouraged, and Angel asks the more difficult question.

"Rebecca, how are we supposed to find them? You don't know, do you? We went all over the place and we're never going to find them if it's up to you. We need the Queen to takes us."

They look in the direction of the Trash Queen, whose eyes are now open, watching them from the chair where she spent the night. Her blue sweatshirt rests flat on her chest. A pair of recycled canvas tennis shoes have holes where the socks have worn out, and her bare toes show. The presence of the woman in the family motel room makes the children more nervous, and the strong wind outside adds to their fears.

"Can you take us now?" Rebecca asks. "We don't need breakfast."

A measured silence passes. With the TV off, they hear only the air conditioning and muffled noises of traffic as the wind howls outside. They continue looking, waiting for a response. Michael senses something has gone wrong, again.

"Why don't you talk?"

Becoming more anxious, he gets up and steps behind the girls, who recognize the change in her as well.

"I can't take you to the hospital," she says. "You need to call the police."

Her words come deliberately, like a slap with the back of her hand, leaving them speechless. "You need to call the police," she tells them again, sitting upright in the chair.

"But you said you would help us...find our parents. You said the police are dangerous," Angel murmurs.

Their small eyes search her face as she prepares an unexpected answer.

"The police *are* dangerous, Angel," she begins. "They're dangerous to people like me and the King. And now they have the King in jail. But they're not dangerous to you, and they can take you to your parents. So, you need to call them and tell them you're alone. I can't help you anymore."

The betrayal rebounds in Rebecca's mind as she recalls the last three days.

She could have told us this when we met her at the Lincoln monument! And then she took us to that crazy campsite, where we could have been kidnapped, or who knows what! The King never knew what he was doing. We went all over the city, taking forever, listening to his stories when he said he could find our father, and we never did find him!

"You mean all this time we could have found them. And you didn't tell us? Why didn't you call the police before?"

The Trash Queen is silent. With each second her cruelty increases in their minds, and her face turns sinister, its ugliness exaggerated by the pain they feel.

"You need to know the truth," she says slowly, confronting her own weakness. "The truth is that the King and I never had…we never had and could never have children. And we knew you were lost. We wanted you to be close to us. We wanted to help you. We tried..."

"And you never called the police," Rebecca interrupts, "and I mean you didn't. And we still don't even know if our mom and dad are alive!"

"I'm sure that they are. Now listen, I have to go," she tells them, and begins to sit up. "If I stay with you the police will put me in jail too, and I won't be able to help the King."

"And you stink. And we hate you...," Angel bursts out. She fights the urge to cry, but her tears have already welled up.

"And you basically kidnapped us!" Rebecca adds.

"I thought you liked us," Michael says, still not believing.

"Michael," she says slowly, "I'm so sorry. It wasn't that I liked you. It was that I loved you. I really do love you."

Rising from the chair, her back bent over, the Queen moves slowly for the door. As it closes, she moves even more slowly to the elevator.

8:18 a.m.—The Medical office and the Football

Haldeman races across town, revving the engine of his car, releasing the clutch till the smell of burning carbon steel matches his inner rage. There are more indigents on the street than he has ever seen. The rain is coming down in sheets as Hurricane Agnes sweeps into the city, and the Weatherpeople's disregard for lights and crosswalks disrupt traffic. He swings the front of the car past a hooded teenager carrying a sign—"Stop the War!"

The press incursion is the last damn final broken thread, the latest drift toward anarchy. So, now it's time to cut our losses, like Nixon says. The leaking of established power has to stop before it's impossible to run the government, let alone our ambulance business.

Returning to the main office, he sees the Atomic Car and Hinton's green Mustang parked outside. His mind clicks with precision, working its way through the puzzle of how everything is unraveling.

The Weatherpeople—just one manifestation of civil disorder and the undermining of the country. And the greater threats must be coming from higher up, from people with access to both democrats and republicans—who could even know the national defense codes concealed in the Football. The same individuals who would possibly share them with the terrorists or foreign agents. People like Ellsberg, who leaked to the press and may have leaked to the Russians. Kisman has been spying on Nixon, and me but he's not the problem. It's got to be...and...wait...wait... that's it! It has to be! Hinton and Helen! Of course! They've have been connected to Therapy all along. They're deep inside the Medical business, trying to take it over.

Haldeman leaves his car and walks briskly to the dispatching room to relieve me, the nighttime dispatcher. I rub my beard and tell him that as the Hurricane approached the city none of the drivers would answer calls. As a result, all the emergency calls went to Therapy.

"No one answered?" he asks in disbelief. "How can that be?"

"No one!" I respond, as I head for the door. "You know, I could be wrong, but it feels to me like this company is coming apart at the seams. Oh, and by the way, you left this briefcase here in the office. It looks very important."

"I'll take that!" Haldeman says, quickly taking ahold of the Football. Its open wrist chain still dangles free.

While making a quick exit, I turn to be sure that Haldeman connects the stainless-steel chain to his wrist. I know he'll have to take it to Nixon, and that I will have one more chance to see Nixon. As the force of the Hurricane increases steadily, I dread the meeting and the assassination.

Haldeman continues into the dispatch room and turns on his listening device inside the laundry room. His suspicions are confirmed as he hears the voices of Hinton and Helen.

Day 7, 8:20 a.m.—Laundry room

"We have all the information we need now, ."

"Ohhh!"

Soft groans of pain come from the pile of sheets spread out beneath the laundry table. After staying up through most of the night, reviewing the finances of Medical and planning their future, Hinton and Helen remain collapsed on the bottom of the floor trying to get an hour's sleep. The hard floor strains their bones and Helen rises first, pulling a sheet around her.

"Ouch!" Hinton moans again, feeling her move away as his head slips onto the floor. "Jesus! I can't believe we slept in here, Helen. You know what time it is?"

"Damn it! It's eight-twenty!" she answers, looking at her watch, standing awkwardly. "Haldeman gets here at eight-thirty to take over from the night dispatcher. Every morning. He might even be here now!"

She begins sorting papers on the laundry table. "We've got to put all these files back before he arrives. I swear to God, we're in trouble, . Now hurry!"

"Okay, okay, I'm moving. Hey, you think anyone will ever go through our papers? I mean once we get our plan established?"

"With me handling the work?" Helen answers. "Not likely. Now hurry up, before we get...uh, oh shit!"

As she finishes stacking the papers and Hinton pulls the zipper of his jumpsuit, the scowling face of Haldeman appears through an open door.

"Interrupting your plans?" he asks, the edge of his upper lip rising slightly. His right hand holds a stun gun, recently designed and thicker than a 45, pointed in their direction. From his left wrist the Football briefcase hangs by the steel chain.

"My God, man! Put that thing down. Are you going postal?" Hinton asks.

"Well, I may be sending you two off somewhere. This happens to be a very effective gun, and I expect you to follow my orders. Now if you're looking for something," Haldeman continues, "perhaps I can help you. Are those your papers in the folders over there, or do they belong to Medical? And it looks to me that you two we're trying to open this briefcase I have in my left hand. Am I right?"

Helen adjusts her sheet. "We were, uh...checking numbers, Mr. Haldeman," she says. "Trying to see if there's a way to save...make a better distribution...uhh…diversify the Medical plan. Mr. Haldeman, could you...uh...set your gun down so we could talk about this?"

"Right," Hinton adds. "Nothing to hide. We're all in it together."

"Oh, indeed we are!" Haldeman agrees, glowering back. "You know something else, Hinton? It bothers me a little that you as an EMT are doing this paper review without permission. Sort of reminds one of a Break-in, doesn't it? You know, I think I see Therapy written on your foreheads! You people have been working for Therapy all along, haven't you? And now you're trying to get ahold of the Football!"

"Wait a minute," Helen counters. "That's not what this is. We work for you…I mean for Medical. We're making sure the numbers all line up and… Football? What are you referring to? Don't you believe us?"

"Yet another question from you, Helen. I'll be asking all the questions from here on, and let's go!" he interrupts. "Main office. Now! We'll have a special meeting with the police this morning and you're going to do all the talking. Move it, princess!"

The papers are left behind on the table as Helen goes first. Hinton studies their captor, wondering if he has ever used a gun, let alone a stun gun, whatever it actually is.

"Have a seat, won't you, Helen?" Haldeman asks, pointing with the tip of the gun at the barber's chair, to make his intention more obvious.

"You're behaving like a psychopath," Helen protests. "What makes you think you can get away with this, Mr.

Haldeman? You need to put that gun away and quit acting insane."

"And you need to quit trying to take over Medical. I know about your little union strategy. Now sit down!"

He points the gun at her upper body, which she tries to keep covered with the sliding sheet. Sweat forms on Hinton's forehead and he tries to stand in front of Helen.

"Go ahead, Helen," Hinton urges. "Let's do as he says. He'll come to his senses in a few minutes."

Not taking her eyes off the gun, Helen moves backwards and sits in the barber's chair. Haldeman motions for Hinton to sit on the footrest, beneath her.

"You're next, Hinton. If you make any move other than sitting at the bottom of this chair, I'll make your haircut as short as mine with a very big shock!"

Unwilling to risk a struggle, Hinton sits with his back next to Helen's knees. Haldeman pulls a roll of gauze and tape from his pocket and walks behind them. He uses his left hand to tuck the end of the gauze in a corner of the chair, then circles the captives over and over. He stops when their bodies are completely wrapped. Only their faces and feet are still visible, and Hinton's curly hair is pushed back on Helen's body, as he finishes the wrapping with tape.

"There! That will stop your activities long enough for me to get the Football back to the president. We're in the middle of a hurricane and a potential national crisis. So…we'll leave Helen on top. Part of her so called feminine mystique! Hmm…?"

"What's wrong with you? Why are you doing this?" Hinton calls out, as Haldeman heads back for the dispatching room. "We're trying to help this company. We just want to bring health care for everyone."

Haldeman spins around on one foot.

"No, Hinton! You want to destroy health care! Nothing could be further from the truth. You think your motives aren't obvious? Providing free government service to everyone, everywhere! Isn't that romantic, ? And do you know something else? There's nothing more dangerous. Because once you make everything free, society collapses. Our people become like children waiting to be served. Always demanding, never doing—always spending, never earning. They'll cry for an ambulance every time they stub their toe. 'Ouch, it hurts! Oh my God! I have a hemorrhoid! I can't work anymore!'

"Don't you see it, Hinton? All these bands of protestors and Weatherpeople demanding disability, filling up our streets! The endless wave of immigrants asking for dialysis machines. Children out of wedlock, abortions, all the broken families and welfare queens living on the dole. Its just people who won't take care of themselves. And why, Hinton? Because they want it all for free and you want to give it to them. With your so-called union it will be an entire society on life support!"

"You know," Haldeman continues, balancing the gun on his left forearm with the briefcase still cuffed to the wrist, "as we disintegrate, lose our work ethic, our moral fiber unravels. There are other countries out there that would love to see us fail, other governments, like Russia, like China, like Cuba. They'll surpass us, Hinton. Survival depends on discipline and vigilance, but what would you people know about that?"

They hear the sounds of phones ringing inside the dispatching station.

"You're not going to get away with this," Helen intones from the top of the barber's chair.

"No, Helen, you won't. Would you like to contact a lawyer…before the police get here?" he asks, smiling. "Or would you rather represent yourselves? I know damn well you're both attorneys working for Therapy. I've got your numbers, and now, if you don't mind, I have to return the Football to the president, who actually cares about the country."

Chapter 51:

Technology

Day 7. 9:10 a.m.—Returning to the Pyramid

Feeling the pain of his burns as he drives Car 45 through the downtown rain and intensity of the storm, Otieno notes that most of the small businesses have closed in D.C., taken over by larger conglomerates and big boxes modeled after the Hughes Empire. He looks across the street at a gathering of young bloods, staking out their turf and preparing to break windows. Before he enters the financial district, he sees more indigents and Weatherpeople, wandering the flooded streets—the homeless are pushing carts, others drift along and block the downtown traffic. Insects flying through the air and landing on the windshield also surprise him. *Cockroaches*!

Strange, he thinks, *they're common in the poor sections, but these brown walkers have taken flight and found their way into the upper strata of D.C. They're like all the miniature espionage devices that define Nixon's people, invented by Hughes technology, but planted by the CIA, FBI, and military. Kisman, Haldeman, and who else has them? Everyone is spying on everyone! Well, now I'm going to be the greatest spy of all.*

Continuing beneath the downtown buildings, Otieno notes traffic thin as he approaches the Pyramid. Seeing its vertical rise helps to make his pain diminish as he contemplates the magnitude of his goal. With Hughes gone, there's a vacuum at the top. The alternative to Hughes' control of the city is long overdue.

This Pyramid is the country's ultimate needle! If directed into the social body precisely enough, it's possible the government will learn the meaning of universal health care and social equity.. Doesn't matter if it sounds audacious; someone has to try and it might as well be me.

9:11 a.m.—The Oval Office

Kisman hurries down the corridor of the East Wing of the White House, followed by security guards, till he comes to the stairway leading up to the Oval Office. Climbing with urgency he enters the executive sanctuary, where Nixon stands beside one of the windows, mesmerized by the rain and the encroaching crowd of protestors and Weatherpeople encircling the White House grounds.

"Sir, perhaps you should step away from the window," Kisman suggests, his gravel voice signaling the danger. "I thought at first they were pursuing me. But now I think it is you they're after."

"What's that, Harvey?" Nixon turns slowly. Awake through the night while listening to the winds of the hurricane, his face has darkened. The furrows along his cheeks are deep, accentuated by the lack of shaving and rest.

"The window, sir. We know it's bulletproof, but it would be better for you to stay at your desk."

"The people elected me by a landslide, Harvey. I'm not sure what you're talking about. There's nothing here I can't take care of."

"Well, sir, I believe a calamity is already happening. This hurricane is hitting the city and something else is out of balance, or why do we see these crowds, these

Weatherpeople? They want to force you to see them. And, as you know, it may not be that long before a Special Committee comes after you."

"That's...uh, ridiculous! I've begun Operation Candor. There's nothing wrong here we can't take care of, and I don't know of anything we would need to see a Special Committee for. I mean, the Plumbers never really found anything, did they?"

"Stop the war!" voices of the Weatherpeople, barely audible through the thick windows of the White House, cry out. "Nixon's a crook! Stop the war!"

"Well, I don't know either, but I think..." Kisman pauses as he looks out the window in the direction of the protestors. The wind blows more intensely outside, causing the walls to vibrate enough that the photo of the moon falls to the floor. "…that this is starting to look like a real calamity! And we should be prepared for your protection!"

Day 7, 9:12 a.m.—Urning returns to Hughes Hospital

After his nightclub efforts to create rocket verse, as requested by Hughes, Clifton Urning becomes morbidly depressed. Unable to sleep, he wanders the water-filled streets of D.C. Once again, he finds himself standing at the gate to the Hughes Hospital, not certain what has brought him back.

It's futile, humiliating to write a biography about a man whose face I'll never see. I spend a career studying someone who I'll never set eyes on? No one listens to my poetry and certainly Hughes could care less! What have I ever done besides write down a bunch of poems and words about cars?

Rocket verses that he'll never read? Is it just so I can get paid as a biographer?

He glances up at tall columns announcing the hospital, where Hughes's profits are invested, sheltered from taxation, and consolidated in the most profitable human venture since war and petroleum—medicine. The country's medical health budget is four times that of other first-world countries, yet its public health system is minimal, and now he's just another one of the statistics. The wind of Hurricane Agnes builds at the gate as Urning contemplates his position.

Disease! So universal, inevitable, and...susceptible to financial control? The Hughes managers have finessed the empire's liabilities with such perfection, and Howard hid himself away in the apex, until he escaped to the moon! Why is it wealth controls the planet, and will I ever see his face?

The tall columns make Urning feel more diminutive as he walks past the guards and shows them his medical card. He continues past reception desks into the hospital, assuring each person who stops him that he's on the way to a return visit in the Psych department.

Slowly, he realizes a different goal in the back of his mind. Rather than continuing up the elevator to the Psych clinic, he stops on the third floor and walks toward the ICU. He stands outside the private room of the patient he has witnessed before, listening to the "whoosh" of the ventilator, and wondering why David Lovejoy, so desperate to escape his bed, is unable to break free.

If I can never free myself, perhaps I can liberate one other pathetic soul. But how? Maybe this man is the one who really needs help. At least I can see his face!

The life support system of Lovejoy is as foreign to Urning as his literary goals are to Howard Hughes. He knows nothing of ventilator nuances, how a patient is extricated from a machine without causing respiratory failure, or what the solution will be if he fails without the support. But he sees the suffering written on David's face, the bondage to a tube making him squirm in misery. Looking at the entangled body of the insurance executive, Urning evokes the only power he has. He hovers next to the bed and whispers a poem.

Can we know the reason why
In this story of shackled spies?
Ventilated, tied to a bed
Would it not be better to be dead?
Set him free, now hear my plea
From this vehicle let him flee
Before I leave, I bend to ask
Remove at last the plastic mask
You've heard our names, the hidden story
Where we've been, the recent foray
But first I need to see the face
Of just one man and share his space.

As Urning speaks the last word, there's a jolt throughout the hospital. Floors and walls vibrate from the force of the hurricane as the power goes out, and then resumes under a main generator. As quickly as the lights go out, the emergency power system activates and there's a chorus of alarms coming from every bed and monitor in the ICU.

"Power failure!" the supervisor calls out, moving quickly through the rooms to assure that each bed has a nurse available. Alarms are turned off, leads and ventilators are checked, and the ventilator settings are readjusted. Urning, hoping that the hospital building can withstand almost any power outage, thinks that the crisis will pass. He looks around in time to see Dr. James, the first physician available for the emergency.

"Double check!" James orders, walking quickly towards Urning, inspecting each room. He makes his first stop by Lovejoy and tells the nurse, "This man's ready to come off the ventilator. We can extubate him later, after the others are safe. There's a code in bed seven right now and we need to get there, STAT!"

Urning waits till the nurse and Dr. James leave the room, then enters unobserved.

"Whooosh..."

He looks at Lovejoy's desperate face, wrestling against restraints, turning his head from right to left.

"Wait, I'll get you out!" Urning whispers.

Lovejoy kicks and moans, trapped in the network of tubing and wires. The breathing tube, a plastic barb hooked inside his throat, provides both torture and safety. So Urning hesitates.

And if I kill him? If I pull this tube and he doesn't have enough oxygen? Do I really want to yank on it? Am I really that insane?

Fearing the worst, Urning turns slowly away. The whole apparatus and miserable situation makes him realize the futility of his craft. Poetry never frees anyone from life support, let alone Lovejoy. He walks away from the writhing patient, uttering a final verse.

Behind the face a voice
Through which we make a choice.
To live without apology,
In the shadows of technology.

Urning's head sinks. Afraid to face the man he can't help, he listens to the distant sound of alarms coming from room seven.

Pommt!

Ring!

"Lidocaine!"

Pommt!

Whoosh...Whiish...Whiish

Then another sound causes him to look back. And as he does so, he sees David work his arms free. With one smooth motion, Lovejoy pulls the tube from his throat and coughs out a message.

"Whiish...wiishh…you'd get...me...out...!" he coughs, forcing air past his swollen vocal cords. "My children…!"

Day 7, 9:13 a.m.—The Genetic Stairway

Still evading his pursuer in the reactor, after hiding behind a series of deoxyribose structures in the chromosome stairway, Colson continues transcribing downward. Almost immediately he sees Noah's coat again, flowing about him like a sheet in the wind. Colson leaps the last hydrogen bond step, hoping to break loose, heading for a hiding place among the stainless steel Dewar tanks that line the base floor.

"Wait!" Noah cries, just as the reactor building begins to tremble. The stairway shifts perceptively, forcing the doctor to stop and cling to a railing. "Listen, Colson, this doesn't have to be so...damn...difficult!"

Along with the first trembling, Noah looks up at the fluorescent lamps oscillating above them.

I know the seismic capacity of this reactor and all the surrounding structures. Minor wobbling of handrails and stairs doesn't concern me. It will take much more than a hurricane to bring down a complex built on mobile supports. But Colson is requiring more work than I anticipated. Somehow I've got to convince him!

He chases the reluctant volunteer down to the base of the building and then between the columns of tightly packed Dewars.

"Huh...uh huh...." Colson pants more rapidly, oblivious to the shaking as he continues to try for distance. He's spurred on each time he sees the mist-like vapor of nitrogen escaping from the stainless-steel chambers. From their cages the laboratory dogs make an eerie, sustained howl between their stripped vocal cords, producing a high-pitched violin-like sound. Eeeee…eeeee!

"Huh...Colson...you can live, huh, forever...," Noah beckons, as he becomes winded himself. He tosses off his laboratory coat.

"Huh...not...uh, huh...like...this...," Colson answers, pushing on and moving down a small ladder, through another metal webbed corridor, as Noah gains on him.

9:11:09 a.m.—The return of Dr. Cohen

"Wooosh… Wooosh…"

Margaret wakes from another brief nightmare, finding herself still in City Hospital, but moved from the ICU to a private room. She's still connected to a ventilator. With a new recollection of events and days that have passed, she sees both rain and light entering in through a new window not far from her bed. Then she spots Dr. Cohen.

It has to be daytime. And this doctor in my room…wearing a white coat. I remember his curly hair. Does he work here, and is he going to help me? How in God's name did I get here? And how can I ever get out?

"Whoosh."

Cohen knows City Hospital is understaffed, and that with the hurricane there will be a cascade of patient emergencies, so he decides to assist the residents that he is already an instructor for. And he remembers Jane Doe, who he was puzzled by at the Hughes hospital before her transfer. He has a hunch as to her diagnosis, and now, as he finds her in a special delivery bed, still connected to a ventilator, he wonders how he will verify the cause of her seizure activity.

"Hey, Dr. Cohen, we're glad to see you here!"

Margaret watches as a team of residents walks into her room and discovers the attendant physician with her. Cohen notes the young residents making rounds and addresses them calmly.

"Good morning, doctors. Looks like bad weather, and I decided to help out a little. And it just happens I'm already familiar with this patient."

"Well, that's right," says the chief resident. "She came over from Hughes, and she was under your care at the time. We still don't have her identification, but we think she's ready to come off the blower. Blood gases looked good earlier this morning and she's on minimal settings. The respiratory therapist will extubate her soon, except the hurricane is keeping us all a little behind."

"That's encouraging. She's term and may deliver any time now."

Margaret squirms in the bed, pulling against the restraints, trying to cough words past the tube in her throat. They turn to look at her, also assessing her elevated abdomen. She has another strong contraction.

"We need OB to come by and check. We don't have any fetal monitors in this place that work, but she should get checked this morning by our OB resident."

"Maybe we should extubate her now and get her over to the OB ward?" a junior resident asks.

"The trouble is, with this hurricane and a nursing strike going on, we need someone to watch her here right now. Dr. Cohen, are you able to stay with her?"

"I'm happy to watch her, doctors," Cohen assures them. "But I don't do obstetrics."

The chief resident nods. "Yes sir, it's not our area either. But let's get his lady off the vent and see how she does."

After confirming that her settings are on minimal, he sets her up in the bed with the rest of the team. As quickly as the endotracheal tube went in, the resident deflates it with a syringe and pulls it out. An oxygen mask is placed immediately, and the team stands by to see how Margaret tolerates the change. Outside, the storm continues surging, forcing more rain through the open window. And then the electricity goes out.

"Power outage!" the physicians call out.

Within seconds the lights come on again. The residents look at each other in surprise as they hear the emergency generators start up. The monitoring lights come on, but the impact of their problem is apparent.

"Christ! No nurses and a power shutdown! Okay, let's move fast!" the chief announces. "We've got twelve patients on vents, three scab nurses, so everybody needs to split up and cover two patients. Dr. Cohen, can you stay by this lady and let us know if she starts breathing too fast? We'll be back as soon as we can."

"And if she starts to deliver her baby?"

"Well, sir, you remember what you taught us in medical school?"

"Of course. Don't drop the baby!"

Margaret tries futilely to say something, but her voice is hoarse from the trauma of a tube in her throat. Her face turns pink as she breathes in oxygen from the mask. Then the doctors disperse through the ICU while Cohen mechanically lowers the back of her bed, rotating a hand lever counterclockwise. As soon as she lays horizontal, her contractions begin once more.

Chapter 52:

Otieno's Ascent

Day 7, 9:11:10 a.m.—Return to the Pyramid

"Evacuate! Evacuate! This hurricane is not letting up!"

Panic breaks loose on the water-covered sidewalks as employees rush out of downtown buildings, spilling into the street and through the recent incursion of Weatherpeople. Pedestrians continue escaping around Car 45 and the melee of other cars maneuvering through congested, waterlogged avenues, causing automotive collisions and blocking intersections. Otieno's attention remains focused on his goal. As the city is beset with disorder, he prepares to re-ascend the Pyramid.

H

....

PB + M

....

SH's

....

VP's

....

L's

....

M's

....

D's

....

Leaving the ambulance and approaching the building, he sees the first wave of drivers, manual and clerical labor, exiting the ground level of the Pyramid in a tumultuous rush. Dressed in overalls and service uniforms, they flow outward and away from the building. Otieno pushes his way through them to reach a vortex near the corner. It's barely possible to move ahead in the mass exodus, and he's careful to protect his hands, still wrapped in gauze from the previous day's exploding rocket disaster.

A growing din of human voices and the approaching sound of police cars, their sirens blending with the low-pitched municipal disaster signal, join the howling of city dogs. He forges through the stream of panicked employees, made up now of managers who have worked their way down from the second level. As he enters the Pyramid's bottom level, he finds just enough room to squeeze through the mass retreat and reach the outer perimeter. Entering the emergency stairwell, he quickly climbs the first seven floors.

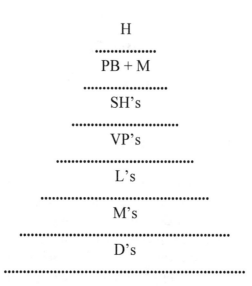

Anxiety permeates the catacomb of offices lining the second level. The majority of managers have escaped to the dubious safety of the streets, but within their offices remain countless rolls of Hughes' fourteen motion pictures and thousands of their copies. The celluloid is threatened by the evacuation's disorder, and a group of diehards remains at the upper corner of the second floor, gathering up canisters.

Other managers help to direct and guide the evacuation and ignore the single intruder ascending past them. Pacing himself, Otieno takes three stairs at a time, encountering fewer and fewer managers as he goes higher. The next wave of employees are the lawyers, toting briefcases and notebooks. One of them carries a two-pound cellular phone, the first of its kind, and is making a call from the eighteenth floor.

Other attorneys make last-minute communications on desktop phones, deciding whether to wait out the commotion or risk traveling through the windblown streets and downtown anarchy. Circuits are overloaded, Security has advised them to stay, and as he interrupts his climb, Otieno watches one group slip into raincoats and grab umbrellas.

"Good luck getting out!" he tells them, loosening the front of his jumpsuit and walking onto the twenty-first floor to catch his breath. "You should go now while you can and those umbrellas won't be much help!" Sweating from exertion, he wipes a layer of moisture from his forehead, wishing the bandages on his hands could be changed. The Security forces next to the stairwell recognize the erstwhile vice president.

"You don't look too good, Mr. Otieno. Is it as bad as it looks out there?" one of the guards asks. "We hear the Potomac's risen up seven feet. The riverbank is overflowing."

"Better to go on foot," he nods.

"Where are you going, sir?"

"Up."

"Well, we hear Mr. Maheu is having a heart attack on floor 42. Hope that's where you're headed."

Otieno begins to feel like he again as endorphins flow through his body and the pain from his burned hands vanishes. He makes his way back into the emergency staircase that now is empty, with the exception of an occasional vice president on the way down from the fourth level. They descend too fast to acknowledge their old associate, and it's not till he reaches the twenty-fourth floor that he pauses and leaves the staircase to greet old partners.

"Gentlemen!"

"Otieno! What are you doing here?"

He grimaces as he takes in the anxious VPs, including a single woman dressed in black trousers. They stand close to the windows looking down on the capital streets, watching the swirling crowds of citizens trudge through water in an effort to get to their homes.

"Playing the paramedic again, Mr. Otieno?" a man in a three-piece suit comments, as he joins the group by the window. The young VP, sporting a wide tie and black vest, brushes back his blond hair and assesses Otieno. "I see you're wearing a jumpsuit, and you're all bandaged up."

"I'm working on a resuscitation," he answers. "And take a look at what's going on out there. It seems the hurricane has made a mess of the city."

"No, it's all the Weatherpeople from the ghetto!" the man vituperates. "This building can handle a hurricane fine, but it'll take months to clean up the situation down there."

"What makes you think they're from the ghetto?" Otieno asks, pointing to the southeast side of the city, where the poor section lies. The young vice president has made his fortune offering real estate to whites only, and in future decades will go on to start his own insurrections. "They're evacuating too, but they're trying to get away from the flood."

"You're wrong. They're a horrible rabble," he counters, "and that's where they're from – the ghetto. They want things they don't own and never earned, like so many elites today. What they need is law and order, and when I get to the top of this Pyramid…it will happen."

He points to a crowd of youths smashing windows and looting downtown stores.

"Pyramid behavior," Otieno counters. "If you didn't work so high over their heads, they wouldn't hate you, and you could live together."

"Nonsense. The Pyramid structure holds the society together, Otieno. Our market system gives people jobs, like yours."

"Is that what the shareholders say? I wonder how they plan to leave?" he asks, changing the subject. Most vice presidents will have evacuation plans that parallel the level above them, allowing departure by helicopter.

"Why should they worry? They know things will settle down pretty soon. These disasters provide us with more incentive to rebuild and grow."

"On top of the people?"

"Clever, Otieno. But not all that accurate. You joke about these things because you get a thrill caring for disasters. Some of us have stayed here to take responsibility for the local economy, and the country too, making decisions that have to be followed up on. Do you have any idea how difficult that is?"

Otieno glances at the surrounding suites of the vice presidents. Their offices look out on the city, furnished with burgundy leather couches and small wet bars. Desktop ticker tapes continue rolling out numbers over polished mahogany desks, documenting the market and facilitating real estate transactions.

"Of course, I remember how excruciating it can be," Otieno responds. "Well, I just wanted to say 'hello.' I'm on my way up." He turns and heads back to the stairwell, leaving the VPs to keep an eye on the pillage.

"Why not take the elevator?" another VP suggests. "We have emergency power here, you know."

"Capital idea!" Otieno agrees, with a sheepish grin. There are generators on the fourth level, and remembering them he walks over to a glass door elevator where a security guard waits.

"Do us a favor," a VP asks, as the door begins to close, "when you get up there, ask the shareholders what the hold-up is. We'd really like to get the hell out of here!"

9:11 a.m.—Hojo's swimming pool and Room 623

Angel and Michael watch from the window as the Trash Queen walks out on the sidewalk where her dog keeps watch, tied by a rope to the side of the shopping cart. Water flows up over the curb, and Revenge is soaked through, but his tail wags when he sees the Queen. They begin forging through the rain but the cart is heavier now, saturated with water. The dog senses his master's sadness as he starts to pull on the rope and it tightens around his neck. Slowly, they slog through the inch deep water, moving a few feet at a time, headed nowhere.

"Is she leaving forever?" Michael asks.

"I hope so," Angel answers, not certain what to say. "I don't know. I think she…" Angel pauses. She bites her lip as she watches the woman and dog seem to dissolve in the heavy rain.

In the same moment, while Rebecca gathers courage to call the police, the windows begin to rattle with the wind outside. The vibrations stop as quickly as they begin, and she takes the phone and dials 911.

"Please stay on the line…your call will be answered by the first available operator. If this is not an emergency, please hang up."

Looking outside the window they continue watching the flooded streets and congested traffic. Cars escaping the hurricane-besieged city splash water into the air, but only a few are able to traverse one open lane on Virginia Avenue and most of the vehicles are backed up for blocks. The workers and residents of the Watergate Complex decide to wait it out, watching the spectacle from their own windows, hoping the river does not reach the bottom floor, but the flood keeps rising.

Rebecca waits. After a minute she calls again.

"Please stay on the line…your call will be answered by the first available operator. If this is not an emergency, please hang up."

The TV goes off, along with the room lights. They watch the streets outside, more with fascination than fear, never having been in a massive storm before. In the distance police cars travel over sidewalks, raising rooster tails of water when their tires go over the curb. Sirens scream, and the escaping traffic of the city is disrupted by the insurgence of homeless people pushing shopping carts and blocking the road. From his elevated vantage point Michael stares with fascination at drivers waving fists outside the car windows.

"God, when are they going to answer?" Rebecca asks. "We're so ready to be rescued! I'm calling the police again. Why don't they just pick up their phones?"

"I bet they never come," Angel says. "Like, they don't even care about us. They're taking care of the storm."

"Yes, they will!" Rebecca counters. "I mean, they're taking care of the hurricane. Like right now. But when they get done, they'll come for us."

"But it's not over," Michael says. "Are we going to drown? Now?"

"Yeah, Michael, I think it's all over," Angel answers. "And we're all going to drown!" She looks small beside the window, wearing her nightgown and barefoot. In the distance the river swells up along the bank, swirling by the submerged edges, sweeping cardboard and trash, tents, and all the detritus of the King and Queen's camp, destined for the Chesapeake Bay. Past the water-drenched clouds a few remaining geese fly off to find shelter. Slanted rain hits against the glass pane. Then Angel has a sudden recollection.

"You guys, you know what? You know what I just thought of? I mean maybe we should just do what Dad said."

"What? What are you talking about, Angel?" Rebecca asks.

"Well, I mean, remember he told us to wait by the pool? Like before he left and everything. What if we just go up there for a little while? Like, we put on our swimming suits. You know? It's hot in here. And we can even swim in the rain! We could go up to the pool right now."

"Are you crazy? You don't swim in a hurricane, Angel! Like what if there's lightning? We have to talk to the police. I called them, and I'm going to call again."

"Well, we can call up there. There's a pay phone and you can dial 911. For free. I used to do that after school, and then run away. You can see a lot better from the top!"

They look at each other, then down on the wild street evacuation below. The employees and guests of the Motor Lodge have either left or sequestered in the restaurant to wait out the storm. The air conditioner has stopped and the humidity is unbearable inside.

"I want to go," Michael says.

"Okay," Rebecca agrees, "There's no thunder right now. We can put on our swimsuits, but I'm gonna keep calling the police. And we have to be ready when they get here. There's no way Mom or Dad is coming now."

In the room across from the children I try to get an hour of sleep. My own mission is almost complete, having acquired the Code from the briefcase when Haldeman left it in the dispatcher's office. I have the Code, but working under Blackbeard I know I still have to take care of Nixon.

Assassinating is not in my blood, but the expectation is clear. And if I fail I will never belong to Cuba. Like children without parents, I'll become a man without a country.

9:47 a.m.—Longevity deferred in the reactor building

Scrambling around the metal observation ring, above portentous columns of cryonic technology, Colson has forgotten the supposed hurricane as he stumbles and falls to his knees, exhausted by the continued efforts to escape from Noah. When he sees Noah approaching once more, he wipes the sweat and grease from his face.

"I can't see... huh...Jesus...Noah...would you just leave me alone...!"

"Quit running around, Chuck. If you would just sign my paper I'll let you rest," Noah urges, pausing to rest and clean moisture from his glasses, which he sets into his pocket. He has narrowed the distance and capture is imminent. "I will only take a second. Once you read this consent, you'll see what we're talking about. Science is the answer."

"I read the damned thing. You're a crazy fucking scientist, Noah! You're Doctor Strangelove! Never! I will never sign up for your craziness!"

Colson is determined to get out of the building. The alternative, like becoming a rat in a time capsule, means being sealed in a steel Dewar beneath the reactor. Reaching cautiously down the side of his jumpsuit, he pulls out a small cylinder of mace and waits for the doctor to approach.

"Don't say no to science," Noah urges. "Say yes! Yes, to a future no one's ever dreamed of, Colson. Today's world shrinks in the horizon of tomorrow! You will travel on a voyage to the future of our race!"

"No, Noah...all we need...is right now!"

"But we have now already, Chuck. You need more. You need forever."

"You...uh huh...can… huh...have it!"

As Noah comes into range, Colson waits for him to remove his glasses and sprays an acrid mist into his unprotected eyes. Noah blinks and screams as the fluid burns his corneas. A new surge of energy allows Colson to pull himself up on the side railing and begin running, bootless, over the metal grid. It works. He sweeps forty-five degrees of freedom into a full half circumference, with the steel center of the reactor's cylindrical building giving him invisibility. Encouraged by his success, he runs faster, widening the gap.

He's dumbfounded, however, by a circular track that brings the two men into a colliding path.

"OOOOF!"

The two drivers spill forward on the metal ring and Colson lands on top of Noah. Struggling to regain breath, with Noah pinned beneath, he lets the sweat drip off his cheek and onto the helpless captor. The two men temporarily embrace, locking arms and legs and rolling on top of a metal grid approaching the edge of the rail.

"Colson! Would you just give up? My eyes are killing me!"

"You give up, you son of a bitch!!"

Over the side railing Colson can read serial numbers and classifications of "volunteers," written above each of the Dewars.

#389752 Chordata—Vertebrata
Mammalia—Carnivora
Rodentia—Muridae
#587298 Chordata—Vertebrata
Mammalia—Carnivora
Canidae—Poodle
#892561 Chordata—Vertebrata
Mammalia—Carnivora
Hominidae—Colson, Charles

"Noahh…nooo…!"

"Come on, Chuck. It's forever! We'll be extending life forever! You and I!" Ignoring the sweat, Noah waits for Colson's exhausted body to gradually slip off, heading ever so gradually in the direction of a human-sized Dewar.

Day 7, 10:14 a.m.—Shareholders, powerbrokers, and Maheu

Otieno rests as he glides in the elevator above the twenty-second floor, observing through glass doors a gymnasium with Nautilus machines, weight racks, and a large Jacuzzi that sends mist over the glass windows of the relaxing room. Masseuses are rubbing down a few diehard vice presidents, indifferent to the recent cataclysm, in orange spandex suits. He continues through the fourth level, past indoor tennis courts, a pool, another spa, putting greens, sports bars, lunch tables, and lounge chairs, while on the streets below, the fleeing pedestrians squeeze past a barricade of shopping carts brought in by transients and Weatherpeople.

On the fifth level, he encounters the shareholders, undistracted by his entrance or the chaos on the streets below. Assembled next to a large screen, they follow digital figures flashing on a dark background. Projected from translucent slides, they analyze stock and bond ratings that trace up and down the screen in graphic regularity—Dow Jones, Nasdaq 100, S&P 500, FTSE 100, the trade deficit, Consumer Price Index, and the growth of franchises. McDonalds and Walmart are looking good. The head of the group, however, argues for value investment and feels coffee can never compete with Coca-Cola. Coffee chains will never work in America. Meanwhile, they fail to notice the EMT till he's looking over their shoulders.

"Everything going okay?" Otieno asks, noting a downward trend of numbers.

"Who are you?" the head shareholder asks in return, startled by the new arrival. His close-cropped sideburns and rimmed glasses define a serious mien as he notes burn blisters on Otieno's face.

"He's an old vice president, Warren," the security guard informs them. "He used to work here, and now he's a paramedic or an EMT. Looks like he got caught in a fire somewhere."

"He looks like *he* needs a paramedic," the leader adds, adjusting his bow tie, then turning back to the screen. "And I could be wrong, but it also looks like his face has turned black. That's a pretty rare color for vice presidents around here!"

"And where the hell are the helicopters?" another man in the group asks nervously. "We should be out of here very soon."

They turn and face a sliding glass window leading to a landing platform on the side of the Pyramid. A group of attendants wait to help direct the escape flight. The attendants are wearing raincoats, braving the wind and rain and searching the storm-darkened sky, hoping for an arrival.

"Right. Exactly. We're ready to go!"

"The copters can't get here till the Weatherpeople are cleared out," a flight coordinator announces. "The pilots are having trouble getting into and out of the airport."

"Unbelievable! And the outlying cities? What about their helicopters?"

"They're on the way. It shouldn't be too long."

"Well, I hope not. Now, what about this man, this uh...vice president? He looks terrible and probably needs a doctor himself. Since when do we start letting vice presidents come up here?"

Otieno grins.

"Something amusing?" the shareholder asks.

"You won't find too many vice presidents leaving their own escape route," Otieno assures him. "They'd also like to know, by the way, when the helicopters will be ready."

"Well, so would we."

The flight coordinator goes through the glass doors and onto a landing shelf. As he does, shouts and noise can be heard, emanating from the streets below.

"It may be a few hours before things settle down on the street," Otieno tells them. "When the transients come out, they don't go under again till they meet with higher levels. My grandmother said this happened decades ago when another rabble insisted on seeing the president."

"Your grandma? What the hell has your grandmother got to do with it?" another shareholder asks, as he looks back out on the landscape. Swarms of people make patterns that flow over the center of the city. The thickest concentration swirls by the White House.

"Well, her time goes back to the days of slavery, so she knew this city from early times. She said the District of Columbia was built on a swamp and, according to her, cities tend to return to their natural state. Entropy or extinction are what we call it. The only way to prevent such a regression is social evolution."

"Well, isn't that's quaint," the shareholder begrudges. "Entropy. And what was your grandmother's answer to entropy and social evolution?"

"Keep a clean house."

"Ha. And when you get anarchy and disruption? From the Weatherpeople? It does look like its time to clean the house, doesn't it?"

They look again in the direction of the White House, obscured by the crowds.

"Homeless people aren't foreign to this city," Otieno answers the shareholder, "any more than the blacks. They've always lived in the street, and they make up the base of the Pyramid, or they live underground. When they come out of seclusion they seek the ones who unearthed them. You must know Cliodynamics? Around every fifty years inequality reaches a point of instability. The Civil War in the 1860s, the Depression beginning in the '20s, and here we are in the '70s. Listen, with your permission, I need to continue on up. I only stopped on behalf of the vice presidents, to ask about the helicopters. "

They look at him warily.

"And just where do you think you're going?"

"The next level. I understand Maheu has had a heart attack. I'm a paramedic."

"Let him go, Warren," another chairman acquiesces. "There's a physician up there taking care of Mr. Maheu, who apparently is really in trouble. Probably his doctor made the request and this so-called paramedic can go with the security guard."

He nods to a guard and turns his attention back to the screen as Otieno heads into the glass elevator again. On auxiliary power it moves slowly, rising for the second time in a week to the sixth level, allowing Otieno to penetrate deeper into the Hughes Empire.

On floor 36 he spots a physician who is carefully writing and examining the contract he's been included in. While Hughes was planning his moon venture, the power brokers changed the name of Hughes Empire to Summa, allowing more control of the Pyramid to himself and the individuals on the five floors above him. Having supplied Hughes with enough codeine and valium to manage his pain and obsessive-compulsive tendencies, the doctor also hopes he'll find himself in the Hughes will.

A second doctor on floor 37 watches Otieno and the elevator rise past his office. He knows he won't be included in the Summa contract or the will, but he merited an office since he saved Hughes' life after the X-11 jet crash, three decades earlier. He remembers Hughes passing in and out of death's door, suffering from massive burns and chest trauma. No will was signed at the time, and Hughes refused morphine, despite the excruciating pain. His addiction to codeine developed in his later years due to the sequelae of the plane crash, but Hughes still depends on the doctor for support.

Dr. Wilbur Thain, who took over the drug supply for Howard by ordering a massive supply from a New York pharmacy, occupies floor 38. Thain tried to reduce the dosage of codeine without success, but he was able to convince Hughes to sign the contract that put him and the Summa leadership in control of the empire. Hughes even offered him a position taking over the Hughes Hospital, and now that Hughes is away, he'll see the empire grow.

Otieno continues the ascent. He recognizes Nadine Henley on floor 39, who moved up from secretary and stenographer to vice president, and now power broker of the Summa Corporation. At her desk, busily filing away the letters that Hughes has written to Maheu, she knows Maheu will never receive them. There's a will on her desk made out by Hughes, but he never signed it.

On floor 40 Chester Davis, Hughes' principal attorney, signs off on paperwork for Toolco, the oil drilling company that Hughes' father founded. The company that once provided Howard a fortune to create his own empire is now Davis's pathway to the billionaire club.

William Gay resides on floor 41. Dressed in a black suit, he sits alone at his desk studying the details of Operation Jennifer, the $350 million covert scheme to recover a sunken Russian submarine. Chosen by the CIA to keep the operation hidden, Gay assists the CIA in obtaining the codebooks and nuclear missiles buried in "K-129." The submarine is three miles deep in the Pacific Ocean, a thousand miles northwest of Hawaii, and the Glomar Explorer will probe the ocean's depth while Howard is exploring the moon. By that time, Maheu will be completely excluded from the empire, if he survives his heart attack.

As Otieno and the guard arrive at floor 42, the final floor of the sixth level, they encounter Hughes' manager, Robert Maheu, lying supine on a thick carpet. Having recently been fired by Hughes, he now is suffering severe angina, aggravated by the onslaught of the hurricane. Dr. James has come from Hughes Hospital on the emergency call and he slips a nitroglycerin tablet beneath Maheu's tongue.

"Great!" he protests, as he looks up and sees the burns on Otieno's face, and gauze wrapped around his hands. "Just what we need—another emergency!"

"I'm here to help," Otieno says, leaning down, removing the gauze to check a pulse. "I'm a paramedic."

"Well, that's just fine," Dr. James answers. "You look terrible and this man needs oxygen. We've got to get him into a helicopter, or an ambulance. And soon! If he doesn't get oxygen it's not going to go well for him!"

"It's too late," Maheu protests. "Hughes let me go me, and it's just as well if I die! Now he's on the moon, the shareholders have taken over, so forget about the oxygen. After all these years I never even got to see his face!"

Maheu clutches at his sternum as coronary vessels constrict in a vise-like spasm within his heart muscle. With no oxygen and a crushing sense of doom, he hopes for a quick end.

"Damn it! Oxygen!" Dr. James curses, sliding a second nitroglycerin tablet beneath Maheu's tongue.

Otieno scans the room, considering the dilemma. It could take an hour to move Maheu down the Pyramid and get him to a hospital. On floor 42 there are no medical support supplies besides what Dr. James carries. So help will have to come from the next level up, the inner sanctum where Hughes has remained hidden from the world. And Otieno knows all the secrets of the Pyramid.

"Oxygen is my specialty," he announces, beginning the last leg of his climb. He searches the ceiling for the single point of access—a screened air conditioning vent. Climbing onto a desk he pulls open a screened vent and a rush of pressurized oxygen pours down from the hyperbaric chamber, where Hughes has immersed himself in the concentrated element.

Chapter 53:
On the Barber's Chair

Tuesday, 10:15 a.m.—The White House

Kisman longs to be back in the barber's chair, where he can rule with authority, rather than preside over a president headed for impeachment and now lost in depression. Instead, he's stuck in the Oval Office, trying to rally the spirit of the free world leader who's in deep trouble. As the city ebbs further into disruption from the hurricane, he spends an hour on the phone making arrangements with Civil Defense. Again, he has to confront the president when he's told of a critical problem concerning the nuclear reactor. Nixon remains by the window of the Oval Office, watching the Weatherpeople as they try to climb over steel fences that surround the White House.

Maybe I should go out and meet with them? Nixon wonders. *These young people, inexperienced in the challenges of our day, the issues of America, and the human race. Maybe I can explain to them what it takes to run a country, the responsibility one carries. But the damn rain and hurricane. It's really not a good time!*

Kisman interrupts Nixon's thoughts.

"There are serious leaks in the water system, Mr. President," he advises, after hanging up the phone. "The streets are overflowing with these people who seem to have been hiding in the drainage tunnels beneath the city. The floodgates at the river somehow were shut off, and as a result homeless people seem to be forced out of the tunnels by the built up sewage. They've joined all the Weatherpeople and terrorists. But more critically, right now there may not be enough cooling supply for Noah's nuclear reactor."

"Really, Harvey?"

"Yes. If a meltdown occurs, we're vulnerable. As you know, the National Defense system should be activated. We have to be prepared for a possible foreign attack. Our intelligence reports that Cuba may still have one missile, and we are in range for it. So, we need to get you to a safer location."

Nixon looks somberly across the room at Kisman, who's now standing next to his desk.

"And, uh...what you're really saying, Harvey, is that...we...well...I should be prepared to evacuate! But that it's not possible, right? In the middle of this hurricane."

"That's correct, sir. Marine One is down, at least until we clear the Weatherpeople out. But we still need to get you to safety."

"Right. And, uh...given the danger of civil unrest, if a terrorist attack or worse, I mean if there were a foreign threat…we have to stay prepared to activate it, don't you think? I mean the Football. Isn't that right? We've never had to do it."

"Yes, sir. I agree. Except that, as I was telling you, we don't seem to have it right now. Security states that it was left behind at the Medical Ambulance office, with Mr. Haldeman. He's still there and currently has possession of it. You're the only one who has access to open the Football, and it should be at your side right now!"

Kisman stands up and fills his chest with a deep breath, while considering the dilemma. Whatever Nixon does, he will have to support it.

"I see. Well then, we need to expedite getting the Football, at whatever cost."

"Yes, sir."

He watches Nixon walk over to the desk and pick up the phone.

"Operator, it's the President. Get me Mr. Haldeman right away."

"I'll try, sir. All the lines have been jammed in the storm."

Day 7, 10:39—Escaping Hughes Hospital

David Lovejoy and Clifton Urning force their way through the crowded streets, going against the exodus of congested traffic and pedestrians, their heads covered with surgical caps to protect against the incessant rain as they head for the Howard Johnson's Motor Lodge. Urning has to prop up his new friend every few blocks, and the two men seem almost inebriated as they work their way back to HoJo's. The white coats they wore while escaping the Hughes Hospital seem to help clear a path through the oncoming evacuees.

Lovejoy's legs are weak, unused to walking, let alone slogging through wet streets and incessant rain. His throat burns as he tries to catch his wind, after six days on a ventilator. But the determination of Clifton Urning and his need to find his children give him new energy.

"You're doing great," Urning encourages him. "A few blocks more and we'll be there. Keep going! We can do this, my friend!"

Day 7, 10:45 a.m.—The Atomic Car

The barber's chair, securely bolted to the floor of the main office, is unshakable, and its occupants remain safe from the storm outside. But as they struggle to break free, Hinton and Helen wrench their bodies together against the gauze wrapping. Then, unexpectedly, Guru Miraj shows up for his shift with the Ambulance company. He takes an uncertain look at the two captives.

"And now it seems you are tied together!" Miraj comments. "Actually, I have always wondered if you wanted to sit there, to have authority, but this is a very odd way. Especially in a hurricane!"

"Miraj, for God's sake, just get us untied," Hinton pleads, still struggling to get a hand loose.

"Yes, of course. But let me talk with the boss. I'm not fully understanding the situation."

Without trying to untie them, he goes to find Haldeman.

"Let's go! Let's go!" Helen urges.

Hinton feels her feet kicking him from behind. It distracts him, interfering with his own work of undoing the layers of gauze.

"Helen, cut it out! We've got to get out of here!"

"I know, I know. Now go!"

He looks around and realizes her hands have unraveled the end of all the tape and gauze.

"I can't believe you got out of this...how did you do it?"

"I'm a lawyer, ," she answers, showing him the bandage scissors. "I know how to get people out of trouble. It's what I do."

Helen leaps off the chair and continues unraveling him while listening to the voices from the dispatching room. Miraj has taken over the calls, trying to handle urgent calls, explaining that all the Medical ambulances are unavailable.

"Actually, right now we don't really have any ambulances free. They are somewhat tied up on missions. May I suggest you call Therapy Ambulance Company?" A pause… "Oh, I understand perfectly, they are also unavailable. Well please call soon, and we shall try to help you."

As Miraj fields the incoming calls, Haldeman continues to establish contact with the president, to learn his whereabouts.

"Okay," Hinton acknowledges, stepping out of the barber's chair and heading for the door leading to the parking lot. "Let's get the hell out of here. Let's get to Therapy before the whole damn city goes to pieces. We need to hurry!"

They slip through the back door, checking to be sure Haldeman hasn't detected their escape. Emerging out onto the parking lot they encounter a mob of indigents and Weatherpeople milling about, pushing shopping carts filled with blankets and stolen goods. They squeeze through the vagabond assemblage, heading for the only ambulance left behind.

"God, what a mess!" Helen protests, as she ducks below a Rastafarian youth. His long hair hangs loosely down, soaked with water, and discolors the white sheet she has wrapped around her. Meanwhile, the rain and wind pelt them as they push forward.

"Why are there so many of these people?" she cries. "Have you ever seen this many homeless?"

"I think I know why," Hinton says, stepping around a man in a wheelchair before finally reaching the Atomic Car. "But we need to get to Therapy. Noah and Colson took Car 22 and all we have is this one. You think you can drive an Atomic Car while I work the radios?"

"Goddamn it, . You keep forgetting that I am a driver! And you know it!"

She pulls herself into the driver's seat, closing the door to escape the parking lot assemblage, feeling a second's relief as they break free of the rain and the masses. Hinton climbs into the passenger's side, but the radio is silent.

"Are you sure, Helen? I know you drive, but this car is kind of different. It's…uhh…well, it's atomic."

She glares back.

"Give me the bloody key, ! I know how to drive and we have to move!"

"There isn't a key."

"Oh shit! Just tell me where it is! It has to have one, for Christ's sake!"

"Honey, you see that set of numbers next to the steering wheel? You have to press out a code. *16 15 23 5 18*. Just do it!"

Helen presses the numbers. Instantly lights come on, as well as the radio, and Hinton dials in Therapy's frequency.

"Okay, you know where to go? This thing runs on batteries, so you won't hear an engine. We need to say goodbye to Medical, Helen, right now!"

Helen acknowledges and is about to step on the accelerator when she looks at the rearview mirror and sees Haldeman running after them, knocking down Weatherpeople as he approaches. The stun gun is in his right hand.

"Or not," she corrects, as Haldeman makes his way in front of the windshield.

Tuesday, 11:00 a.m.—Otieno reaches the Apex

Like a chromosome, the architecture of the Great Pyramid has evolved through time with a decipherable pattern. As Dr. Cohen and the guards attend to Robert Maheu on the sixth level, Otieno contemplates the empty apex on the seventh level. The missing man is now pursuing his future on the moon, and few others besides the Mormon guards and Otieno have ever entered Hughes' inner sanctum. Even fewer understand the arcane circuitry of the Pyramid woven in a way that allows Otieno to continue higher, after pulling open the concealed door from the air conditioning vent. Pressurized oxygen pours down from the hyperbaric chamber, as he ascends into the seventh realm.

"He's found the way!" Maheu whispers, taking deep breaths and feeling the crushing sensation ease in his chest as the nitroglycerin tablets dissolve. Heart muscles re-perfuse with oxygen-rich blood, color returns to his ashen face, and he watches as Otieno takes hold of a ladder and climbs into a narrow corridor, leaving the door of the vent open so the forty-second floor office equilibrates with high-pressure oxygen from above.

Disappearing into a four-foot tunnel of darkness, Otieno hears only muffled shouts and words from the men below, then nothing. Silence, lonely and dark as the sealing up of the Great Pyramid four thousand years ago, envelops him. Driven by the impulse to climb higher, he pushes, a foot at a time, feeling the pain of his blistered hands scraping over rough cement. He continues through the narrow passage. Like the men of early history—Al Mamun, Abd-al-Latif, Greaves, Davison, and Napoleon—he slowly makes his way till he reaches the Ascending Passageway. The arcane design, imprinted to memory from studies of the original Pyramid, forces him to climb a twenty-six-degree incline, 153 feet, till he reaches the higher corbelled ceiling of the Grand Gallery. He pushes forward and the ceiling lifts higher, till he's able to stand in the angled but elevated hallway.

Pulling a flashlight from his belt, Otieno scans polished, red granite walls. His breathing, more labored with elevation, breaks the silence now. He wills away claustrophobia, as the destination becomes perceptible and the walls open wider. Like progressing through a womb, the secret ancestral space of the King's Chamber and its wide, theopneustic proportions allow measured steps to the final entrance of the sanctuary.

Otieno times his breathing with the beating of his heart, waiting till he sees a faint light at the end, then arrives at the monolithic door concealing the inner Chamber. Once again, he finds the numbered locking system on the side panel and presses out the code sequence.

8-21-7-5

16-15-23-5-18

As he enters the interior, he finds the abandoned yellow writing pads, unused BIC pens, and discarded Kleenex that Hughes left behind. The sanctum is still illuminated by a Zenith television and screens for watching old RKO films directed in the past. The large screens surround Hughes' empty reclining chair and, next to it, suspended by steel cables and lowered from the highest level of the hermetically sealed arcanum, is the espionage zenith of the capital.

"The Mummy!"

Hughes' huge, white, clam-shaped enclosure remains open and unattended, left empty by his departure for the moon. No one other than Hughes has ever sat in the cybernetic station, and after catching his breath Otieno slides gently into the ergonomic chair.

As he sits back in the Mummy, it folds together tightly, enclosing him into a digital cockpit of surveillance. Exploring the well-lit interior, he finds a broad instrument panel of buttons and switches that allow control so extensive that the CIA and FBI would marvel, coveting its intricacy. As he toggles the first switch, he's raised by cables robotically to the highest realm of the apex, and realizes the cybernetic locus connected to the District of Colombia's information highway. An electronic core-fiber optically accesses the capital from a single position, providing an audio-video feast with screens that image critical activities inside the metropolis. Hughes, and now Otieno, can see everywhere throughout the sixty-four square acre area of the capital. Slowly, he sets the headphones over his ears and slides a digital control board beneath his resting arms. His fingers dial the circuitry leading to the Medical Ambulance Office.

Day 7, 11:01 a.m.—Handing off the Football

As the Atomic Car's window rolls down, Helen and Hinton look through the wind-driven rain and past the barrel of a stun gun into Haldeman's angry, almost ballistic eyes. Then the dispatcher lowers the stun gun and speaks carefully, in measured sentences. His pupils grow wider and his gaze softens.

"Look, I need...really need you people to help me! Right now! I need you to deliver this briefcase to the White House. We just received a communication that the city's underground water supply is diverted—I'm guessing by the Weatherpeople, and probably under the direction of terrorists. We have to fix it, but it will take time and we don't have any right now. Noah's nuclear reactor is at risk of meltdown. We're vulnerable as a nation at this moment and we're already experiencing mayhem as a result of this hurricane. It's not impossible we could be subjected to a nuclear attack from outside."

"What are you talking about?" Hinton asks. He and Helen suspiciously observe the dispatcher, who has water dripping from his chiseled face.

"What I'm talking about," Haldeman continues, "is that there are fanatics inside the capital, and countries outside that hate us. The Russians to begin with. North Korea. China. Even Cuba. They all would like to undermine us, and they wait for any sign of weakness. If someone accidentally lets go of a nuclear weapon, like the Cubans could have tried in 1962, it will precipitate Armageddon. When the president doesn't have the Atomic Football...this briefcase in my hands…in a time of political instability…we're completely vulnerable. This is protected information, but I'm going to tell you this: Cuba may have a small missile within range of here, and we're worried about it."

"The Football?" Helen asks. "You mean the briefcase you're holding? Whatever's inside it is the Code of the Strategic Defense system, right?"

Haldeman clutches the black leather case in his hand. An unlocked silver wrist chain dangles from the handle.

"You always have a question, don't you, Helen? Listen, you've got to get this briefcase to the president. He's the only one who has access to the Code. And you have the only ambulance available right now. Can you find your way to the White House? Quickly?"

Helen eyes Haldeman suspiciously, but quietly holds out a hand to receive the Football. Haldeman hesitates, and then lifts the heavy briefcase past her to Hinton, who receives it like a package of explosives.

"You're driving," he tells Helen, "so he has to carry it."

"I think we know how to take care of the problem, Mr. Haldeman, and it's not too heavy for me," she responds, ignoring the slight. They all look up at a gathering crowd of Weatherpeople and the traffic-filled street. "But, if we're going to do this, we better get going!"

"Okay," he says. "I can't leave the headquarters until I establish communication with the president, so you need to make this happen fast. The Football holds the Code for our national security, and now you have it in your hands! And if there's a nuclear meltdown, we're even more susceptible. You've got to get it to him!"

"Wait," Hinton says. "Wait a minute, Haldeman. It would seem that now that we have the Football, we need a little support from you."

Haldeman's upper lip rises, anticipating any pushback. Joining the crisis, Guru Miraj approaches from the main office and joins the scene while Hinton finishes making his case.

"If this company is going to survive, we still need a union. The management and drivers are going to have to work together, to minimize losses and...to bring universal health care to the city."

"And you better get that Football to the president, Hinton, or we're all going to be history. Cut the Therapy bullshit and get moving. We're talking about the end of the race!"

"But…perhaps we can activate the Football from here?" Miraj suggests. "In a manner of speaking…I'm quite sure…if anyone can save us, it could be us!"

They stare at the Guru, caught by the sensibility of his suggestion. None of them, including the president, has ever looked in the briefcase. Or witnessed a device that contains a code controlling the release of the nuclear arsenal. The Code could be radioed to the president faster than driving through streets filled with Weatherpeople, clogged traffic, and a hurricane.

"Well, it may be worth a try," Hinton agrees. "We ought to at least take a crack at it!" He steps out of the ambulance and into the rain, trying to pry open the latch, but it's held in place by a five-dial combination lock.

Haldeman hesitates, knowing the president is the final arbiter of any decision to avert nuclear warfare. With conditions of "Mutual Assured Destruction"—the activation of Superior Air Command, ICBMs, ballistic missiles, and a range of smaller nuclear weapons—a small trigger could result in the elimination of not just Russia and Cuba, but China, Pakistan, North Korea, North Vietnam, and most of Southeast Asia. With any activation, the Soviet forces will have time to release their own rockets, and a launch from all sides will end civilization.

"Try five zeros," Haldeman urges. "Nixon doesn't like to clog his memory.

Hinton tries the sequence, dialing in zeros. To everyone's amazement, it works.

"Jesus!" he says, as the briefcase opens. They all peer over his shoulder, at the open briefcase, sitting on top of the ambulance and collecting rain.

"What is it?" Helen asks.

"I don't know. There are two cans of beer, two condoms, and two little black books. Is this some kind of joke? And then there's this transmitter, that requires another code."

They all try to get a closer look. As Hinton unloads each item, they focus on the transmitter, a black metal device containing ten wheels of single-digit numbers. Mystified, they stare silently, till Miraj identifies the device.

"Clever. Actually, very clever," he exclaims. The others turn to him for an explanation.

"It's an electronic abacus. One that converts numbers into alphabet. The abacus was used by spies, long before the pharaohs and pyramids, and whoever knows the initial numerical sequence can release the encoded message, but only one man must know that sequence!"

"So, it's not a computer," Hinton adds. "And the sequence, which only the president has access to, controls our Defense System. That determines whether we launch or not? Unbelievable!"

"That, in a manner of speaking," Miraj continues, "is what I am thinking."

"And that's why the president needs it immediately. We're losing time," Haldeman reminds them, as the wind blows across the surrounding parking lot.

"He's right," Hinton agrees, closing the case and looking over at Helen. "We'll have to take the freeway, Haldeman. Can you get us in contact with the other drivers while we're on the way? We may need them. Get Noah on the radio with me. We're finally going to have to work as a team. And we'll need Noah to help get us there."

The dispatcher looks back at the office. A few Weatherpeople are headed toward the open back door, and he points his stun gun at them, hoping to ward them off.

"Can you do this, Hinton? I'm willing to work with your Therapy people, but it doesn't mean you take over the health care system. That can never happen. I'll connect you with Noah, but we have to deliver this briefcase fast!"

Hinton removes the electronic abacus out of the briefcase and spins some of the wheels.

"Haldeman, I don't know what's inside all this code stuff. But management has to work hand in hand with the drivers and you have to work with Helen and me. It's the union now, or it could be the end of all of us...right?"

Chapter 54:

“Washington, we have a problem”

Day 7, 11:05 a.m.—The moon buggy

“Bo Bop Areep!”

Riding on a cushion of pulverized dust, Hughes feels a childlike release as he maneuvers the Rover around dark boulders, down deep rills, heading for the base of the Sea of Tranquility, and looks back at the Earth, around which his lunar excursion revolves. The planet seems insignificant as he accelerates ahead on his meteorological venture, thinking momentarily about the Pyramid and the capital.

How it’s grown under my supervision! Matured into a thriving metropolis, albeit one that requires more and more coal and oil. And now nuclear energy. Maybe it’s the child I never had. But this damn nuclear waste is a festering sore, threatening to drain into underground waters, or worse, into the hands of Communists and terrorists. Well, burying spent plutonium and strontium deep under lunar bedrock will take care of the nuclear waste, and then we can pursue real technology. Thorium, titanium, elements for solar energy...who knows what else. If there’s water, we’ll prepare for the greatest flights ever—to Mars, asteroids, new solar systems...there’s no end! I’ll be able to pick the next president and my technology will shape it all!

Hughes lets his hand push forward on the Rover’s controls as he considers the advantages of space travel. Zinc and steel tires send up a billowing wake of lunar dust as he travels in sweeping arcs. Seeking out preferred burial sites, he revels in the thought of lunar stations to be built and how they'll be free of the Earth's gravity, disgusting viruses, bacteria—all the parasites of people on Earth! Trade and material salvation in the new millennium begins with a pyramidal extension onto Earth's largest satellite, and its burial ground for the deadliest waste.

"Bo Bop Areep!"

An intoxicating sense of power buoys Hughes along the regolith, between tilted strata of wrinkled ridges, soft hills of a ion-year-old lava flow. A sudden drop-off of a sinuous channel descends into a V-shaped canyon on the opposite side, and he's about to let the Rover slide down into Hadley's Rille, when he feels a spasm of pain in his stomach. Then he remembers he skipped his last shot of codeine.

"Damn it!"

He clutches his lower abdomen. Shifting positions as he drives and descends, he fails to notice a football-sized meteor ahead of the right front wheel. The Rover lifts up unexpectedly, spilling into the cavernous rille. As Hughes topples off and rolls over and over, trapped in his cumbersome spacesuit, the Earth continues rotating 240,000 miles away.

11:11 a.m.—The research reactor

Continuing his efforts to recruit Colson into long-lasting cryonic survival, Dr. Noah squirms underneath the body of the EMT on the metal railing, and then another crisis develops.

"No, no, not now!" Noah explodes, hearing the emergency siren go off. Colson's sweat-soaked body slides away, onto the steel meshed walkway, and at the same moment a group of technicians enters the underground laboratory.

"Dr. Noah! We need you! The cooling system's failing and we have to shut down. We're having trouble getting the core to close!"

Noah struggles to his feet, pulling his leg out from under Colson. He quickly puts on his glasses and adjusts them, hoping to look dignified.

"You're mistaken. Just open up the water system and begin cooling, people. The core shuts off automatically!"

"We have. There's a break in the system and the water pressure's too low! We think it's in critical danger...we're going to have to scram the reactor."

"You can't do that! Not without my permission. Why don't you just activate the alternative system—go ahead and use it."

"We can't without calculations. We need you to direct it, Doctor."

"Okay, okay!" he groans, looking down at Colson, who's still gasping on his back. "I'll need the calculator, which is...damn it...what a nuisance. It's in Car 22. Colson, you have to get me my calculator. Can you do that?"

"Huh...huh...what?"

"The electronic calculator. In my briefcase. It's in your ambulance. I've got to get over to the control room, and I need you to get my calculator. You can forget longevity for the moment."

Colson looks at Noah in disbelief. Some of the technicians head back up the Genetic staircase.

Insane! He's supposed to be a rocket scientist. But he's a fucking madman! And where does all of this lead?

"There's someone named Hinton on the phone," one of the technicians tells Noah, "who claims we're in danger of a nuclear attack. He's calling from the atomic ambulance..."

Tuesday 11:28 a.m.—Lamaze lessons with Dr. Cohen

The atmospheric pressure of Hurricane Agnes and change of position is enough to activate Margaret Lovejoy's metabolism, initiating the final stages of labor. At first concerned, Dr. Cohen is now convinced as he watches her shift her protuberant belly, seeking an impossible position of comfort. She groans, feeling the new life pushing into the world, stretching and dilating her cervix with a rhythm and intensifying force. Cohen realizes she's moved into phase two of delivery as the cervix, stretched from a tubular gate to a wide tenuous ring, effaces into a fluid-distended membrane, which will soon burst…

"There you go," he encourages, helping her to raise her knees. "You can do it. I'm here to help you have this baby."

His encouragement is met with a gush of warm fluid soaking the sheets beneath her. With the water broken, and in the absence of any help, he will have to attend a delivery that he hasn't witnessed in decades.

"Okay, I'm going to help you as much as I can. Let's work on the breathing.

Margaret's eyes form tears and a tiny head presses millimeter by millimeter, squeezing past the ruptured membrane of the birth canal. The uterine contractions are slowly joined by voluntary efforts, and she begins to Valsalva. Ignoring the oxygen mask and holding her breath, then letting her expanded lungs add pressure to her stomach, she forces down on the tightened uterus.

"Push!" Cohen encourages her. "Go ahead and push!"

He tries to lead, but her experience is greater. Having delivered three children and knowing a fourth will come quickly, she instinctively synchronizes with the contractions, bearing down and accepting pain, squeezing until the contractions end, then relaxing.

"Come on! You can do it. Push again."

The previous deliveries have made it easier for the baby's head to force through the pelvis, but it stops at an orifice, just less than the size of the baby's head. Floating effortlessly in the womb, the fetus is caught in a standstill, held back by Margaret's exhaustion, and then rhythmically squeezed ahead by hormonal forces. Cohen tries to assist by humming a Buddhist mantra.

"Ohm.... Ohmm...!"

With her most forceful contraction, she responds by pulling her right arm free, yanking the oxygen mask from her face, and letting out a scream as her hand smacks on top of Cohen's head. Her piercing wail echoes through the ICU.

"Aeeeeeeeee..."

"Beautiful!" he shouts.

She breathes deeply on her own, as he remembers the Lamaze lessons. "Now just pant like a puppy, and when you get ready to push again, just hold your breath. You're doing great!"

"You pant like a puppy," she coughs back, between continued contractions.

Day 7, 11:35 a.m.—The Race

Hinton holds the Football with both arms as the Atomic Car takes a sharp turn and heads onto the Beltway. Traffic is solid in both directions and he watches Helen steer into the emergency lane. They feel the high-voltage acceleration and the experience of a four-ton vehicle maneuvering, with seemingly unlimited speed, toward the White House.

"I like it! , I really like the car!"

"Take it easy, Helen. Look, I'm having trouble getting Otieno on the radio."

"What about Noah? Is he accessible?"

"He's shutting down the nuclear reactor right now. They say if the water pressure doesn't rise soon enough inside the reactor, there could be a spill. This whole city could get contaminated!"

"Great. Just great! Because right now we have one more problem!"

As she speeds down the emergency lane, cars ahead form a backup that extends across all four lanes and into the emergency route. Rain pelts down on the vehicles as water builds up on the asphalt.

"Damn," Hinton acknowledges. "We're trapped."

The emergency lane is filled with stalled vehicles that have tried to skirt the backup, and as far as they can see there are more cars ahead. There's no way forward. Helen brakes to a complete stop while they consider alternatives, measuring in their minds the remaining miles left to travel on foot to the White House through pouring rain. Hinton switches the radio to a connection at the nuclear reactor, where Noah has access.

"Dr. Noah! This is Hinton. Over."

"Now what?" Noah's voice comes distantly from the control room.

"We're in the Atomic Car, doctor. We're caught here on the Beltway. We've got miles to the White House turnoff and there's wall-to-wall traffic. We're going to have to abandon your car and try to run to the White House - to get to the president. I want you to know...I…uh…we…well, we have to make it fast because we have…the Football! It has the Code for the president!"

They continue looking at the jam. Drivers are climbing out of their cars and into the downpour, shouting at each other. Some of them are starting fights. They can jog the remaining mile, but there's the question of time and the thickening infestation of Weatherpeople, and fleeing citizens could make it impossible.

"Well, don't leave the car!" Noah's voice admonishes over the speaker. "There's a toggle switch in the upper right-hand corner...on the dash. It says 'Elevator.' You just flip it. It can get you through any traffic. It was designed by Hughes."

Helen sees the switch covered by a plastic shield. As she pulls the shield and activates the switch, a high-pitched whine comes from the side windows and four robotic arms, two on each side of the ambulance, slowly extend out. The steel arms telescope down perpendicularly and the whining continues as the car rises up seven feet. At the base of the arms are metal wheels that allow the vehicle to roll.

"Hey...!" Hinton shouts.

"Neat trick," Helen agrees, after they're lifted over the road, above all the vehicles ahead of them. "But how do we go anywhere?"

"Okay," Noah says, "once you're high enough, look for the 'Thrust' switch. It's locked up behind the steering wheel, to the right. When you pull it, you've got thirty minutes' worth of propulsion jets to give you forward acceleration.

They burn rocket fuel, so you may have a little trouble steering and braking by way of the small wheels. You'll have to drive over the cars in front of you."

Searching behind the ashtray, she pulls the switch labeled "Thrust." Instantly a roaring sound comes from the back and flaming gases propel them forward. Water behind the car becomes steam.

"Damn, it works!" Hinton exclaims.

Looking out the windshield at the Beltway, ten feet below, they feel the ambulance begin to roll, suspended on the steel arms and wheels. As they maneuver over the top of a long line of abandoned cars in the emergency lane, the fleeing citizens stare back in awe. Red lights flash next to the shooting flames that ignite from the rear of the car.

"Yeah, it works!" Helen cries, as they clear car tops by inches. "Maybe it takes a rocket ambulance, but we've got to save this country. And the union."

Hinton hangs on to the Football as they gain speed and the car becomes more difficult to control.

Chapter 55:

David Returns to HoJo's

Tuesday, June 20, 11:42 a.m.—The last day

Arriving at Howard Johnson's Motor Lodge, sweating profusely in the rain, David looks at Clifton Urning in disbelief.

Six days on a ventilator! I've made it back to the motel, to the same entranceway where my lungs collapsed, and this strange man next to me is the one who delivers me to my family? He's so sad! There's no way to thank him, but if I make it through this, I'll never smoke again. I'm going to change my life and find a way to pay this guy back. I'll start taking care of myself!

"God, I hope my family's inside," Lovejoy tells Urning, "and I want to thank you but I don't know how. I could never have made it without you!"

Urning nods silently, saluting a soft farewell and heading back into the rain. David pauses only for a second before rushing into the motor lodge, struggling up the staircase to the sixth floor, with burning lungs. The pain in his heart is greater when he reaches room 623. Behind the unlocked, open door is an empty room covered with wall-to-wall debris of children's clothes and food wrappers. He looks across the scattered rug at the silent television, sheets and blankets, and Michael's tiny sleeping bag. A notebook with Rebecca's drawings is laying on the couch, and there's a pair of blue swimming goggles on top of the couch. But no children! Tears blur his eyes, and in desperation he kneels onto the floor, grabbing a towel that has been left behind, and presses it to his face. He whispers a prayer, asking for guidance, and in the same moment a thought occurs to him.

"Water! What if?" he gasps, his throat still hoarse. "They love the water! And I last saw them in the pool. What if?"

Still murmuring a prayer, David begins a final climb, step by step, to the rooftop of the motel. The stairway's silent, except for the soft landing of his feet on each step. In the darkness he holds on to a thin rail, his last hope, as he stops to catch his breath. Hanging onto the rail for support, he pulls himself to the end of the staircase. And when he finally gets to the exit door and walks out onto the rooftop the rain comes pouring down, blurring his vision. Then he sees the children, huddled against the side of the building. They look back with wide eyes.

"Daddy!" Michael cries.

"Daddy, we knew you'd come back!" Rebecca calls out.

He heads toward them. They run fast in their bathing suits, leaping onto him, coming together as a tangled mass. Michael and Angel laugh and cry simultaneously.

"I knew it, I just knew you'd come to the pool!" Angel shouts triumphantly.

"Dad, I waited, like you said," Rebecca says, "and then Mom..." She bursts into tears.

From the top of the building, they can hear the noises of streets below. Still holding on to his children, David realizes there are two more family members to be found.

"Where is she? Where's your mom? We've got to make it out of here!"

"The hospital, Dad. At that hospital," Angel says.

"What hospital?"

"City. City Hospital. I know the way, Dad," Rebecca adds. "By heart! The King made me memorize it."

"What King?"

11:44 a.m.—The Mummy chair

Otieno leans over as he sits within the Mummy, the private digital cocoon sequestered at the apogee of the Pyramid. Forty-nine stories below him lines of cars crawl like millipedes along the encircling Beltway, trying to escape the city and the storm. Scattered crowds of Weatherpeople concentrate more and more around the White House, making it impossible for helicopters to approach, and then a voice comes from speakers ensconced within the walls of the Apex—the shrill, rasping voice of Howard Hughes.

"Otieno, what the hell are you doing in my Pyramid? And how did you get there?"

The high-pitched voice is easily recognized.

"Hello, Howard. I'm going to re-establish some control in the capital. How did you know I was up here?"

"I track everything, Otieno, even on the moon. And where's the Mormon guard! And Maheu, who I fired days ago?"

"Maheu had a heart attack, or maybe an acute angina episode. And the Mormon elite are busy making out wills. Seems that you forgot to write one before you left."

"Nonsense. There's no will. And I have no intention of dying! Now listen, I don't know how you found your way up there, but you're trespassing, Otieno. And I..." There's a pause as Hughes struggles to confess a weakness. "...I'm afraid I need some help. I'm having a little problem."

"Well, why are you calling me here?" Otieno asks, slowly. "Where's your Mission Control?"

"Those idiots! They didn't send any direction for constipation, and the doctors hid my extra box of codeine and Blue Bombers. I'm through with Mission Control. I can do telecommunication, damn it, but I need a damned doctor. I'm in a lot of pain and I need my medicines. They hid my spare medicine box somewhere in this lunar module and we can't find it!"

Otieno hears an exhausted note in the voice. The Rover lies in the depths of Hadley's Rille, and Hughes, dragged by Margulis back into the Lunar Module, feels his abdomen has a knife lodged in the center. He's diaphoretic and his hands shake.

"Mr. Hughes, what do you want from me? Acupuncture's not all that good for opiate withdrawal, and you're a little too far away as it is. I doubt hypnosis will do much, so I can't help you."

"I don't want your acupuncture or your damn hypnosis. What you have to do is get a damned doctor on the screen, and find out where my drugs are," Hughes rasps. "You've got the only transmitter with enough power to make it happen quickly, and give images. My attendant can find the meds, but they need some instructions from Dr. Thain on floor 38."

Otieno, controlling the panel of the largest transmitter in the world, has risen to its apex with a plan to manage the capital by changing the vertical structure of the Pyramid to a circular, socially just economy. But now he looks at a screen showing a man agonizing with pain and constipation. Hughes' eyebrows twist like serpents over sunken cheeks, punctuating his misery. Now away from the largest spy edifice in the world, he's lost control of both his empire and his pain meds.

"Ah, Mr. Hughes, maybe you should consider coming back to Earth. Have you talked with Mission about returning?"

"To hell with them! Damn it, man. I may perforate my bowel but I'm not coming back to that bug-ridden planet without finishing my work. Now, call Noah. Get me Noah and Dr. Thain or Crane or any competent doctor on a computer, and hurry up!"

"I'm going to put you on hold, Mr. Hughes."

"On hold? Wait a minute, you imposter! Do you know who...?"

Otieno sees helicopters lifting off the fifth-level platform and swinging away from the Pyramid, finally evacuating the shareholders and vice presidents. And next to the screen showing Hughes, the Pyramid's antenna transmits a scene unfolding in the Control Station of the nuclear reactor. With Hughes on hold, Otieno dials in on his circuit panel and picks up the conversation between Hinton and Noah.

"Noah, it works! We're on our way again. We're headed toward the White House in the Atomic Car."

"Fine," Noah tells Hinton, as he paces inside the Control room of the reactor. "But the water system's still not achieving a cooling state. We've scrammed the reactor but the core is at risk and if no one fixes the water cutoff, wherever it is, I won't be able to stop the meltdown."

"I think I know where the problem is," Hinton says. "It's under the Lincoln Memorial. There's an underground water system and Deed did something down there a few days ago."

"Jim Deed?"

Day 7, 11:45 a.m.—The Floodgate

Locked in a mechanical melee of cars, shopping carts, and angryWeatherpeople, Jim Deed curses as Car 38 inches over the Arlington Bridge and across the river, headed for illusory freedom. He looks down at the river's dark waters, now flooding the banks, and then at Muriel sitting next to him. Calm and beautiful as ever, she's seemingly indifferent to the hurricane and confusion outside.

"There's something I've been meaning to tell you, Muriel," he says.

Deed knows he's tied to the fate of the president as well as her past history, and he knows he'll never escape without having to return to the subterranean backup he caused beneath the Lincoln Memorial. "What I need to say is…I had a plan to help the president and all of us. You know, controlling the leaks and the problem of the Weatherpeople. I thought if we could force all those people underground out of their tunnels, it might get rid of all the riff raff of indigents. I didn't realize how many of them there were, and I never expected Hurricane Agnes. Or that it would flood the city."

Muriel looks outside the car, where the traffic has come to a standstill.

"Or that the Plumbers would get caught," he adds. "It's become a cancer on the presidency, and now I have to do something besides just run away."

"I don't think I understand, Jim. Whatever is going on can only be fixed by the president. I mean, what exactly did you do? You didn't organize the last break-in. Did you?"

"My attempt to control the leaks and expel the Weatherpeople has turned into a catastrophe. It's the floodgate, Muriel. A few days ago, I shut off the water supply from the river that clears the underground drainage system. I wanted to make sure the Weatherpeople had nowhere to hide, and when I closed the gate it made sure the underground went stagnant. But I had no idea there were so many transients down there."

"Is that what you did? When we went to the Lincoln Memorial that night? That's where the floodgate is, and you closed it off? You tried to stop the city's whole drainage system?"

She studies Deed's worried face. Then the radio interrupts.

"Car 38. We have a municipal crisis!" an urgent voice announces. "Where are you? Noah's reactor has lost control!"

"Damn it!" Deed answers. "Who the hell is calling us? We're outside the city."

"Deed! It's me, Hinton. We're on a 10-47. There's a nuclear meltdown alert and we can't get water pressure to the reactor. It may melt down!"

"What are you talking about?" Deed responds, sensing that he may have done more than just unleash the Weatherpeople onto the city streets.

"It's Hinton, Deed! There's a CIVIL ALERT and I'm in the Atomic Car trying to get the Football to the president. Where the hell are you?"

"Well, uh…I'm on my way to the Lincoln Memorial," he says, looking for a way to turn the ambulance around as he talks. "I'm going back to reopen the floodgate."

"Deed, you still there?"

"Yeah."

"What was it you did? Under the Memorial? What floodgate? What were you trying to do?"

"I can't tell you. I just closed the gate temporarily, to get rid of the Weatherpeople. I didn't expect this..."

"Well, can you reopen the gate that runs to the sewage tunnels? You know how to do that?"

"Yeah. That's where I'm headed."

Day 7, 11:46 a.m.—Returning to City Hospital

After reuniting with the children, David returns to room 623 so Rebecca, Angel, and Michael can put clothes over their swimsuits and he can find the car keys. They're buried deep in Margaret's purse and he grips the keys tightly, hoping they will take him to his wife. They rush together to the garage and are about to head off in the station wagon, when instead they find a broken window, a stolen radio, and a dead battery. There's no other choice but to set out on foot for City Hospital.

After no more than a few blocks they reach the Kutz Bridge. Rains falls heavily over the Tidal Basin and David feels the weight of Michael as they trudge forward.

"Kids, I don't know if I can make it," he confesses, sensing his lungs aren't equal to the task. He has to stop and catch his breath, setting Michael down on the almost submerged sidewalk.

A few straggling pedestrians pass by them. Waterlogged shoes make walking more difficult, and Rebecca and Angel remember how long the journey was from the day before. They stop to rest, considering the futility of their quest, just as my Yellow Taxi arrives beside them. From the driver-side window I call out.

"Hey, you kids! I been looking for you!"

"Dad, we know that man," Rebecca tells her father, recognizing my white turban and goatee. "I think it's the man who stole Mon's purse. I left it in the taxi."

"Hey, come here," I call out again. "You left a wallet in my car, and I've been looking for you. You want it back, don't you? Looks like you need a ride?"

Thankful to escape the rain, they cautiously climb into the car. I hand David the wallet and he quickly offers me the remaining cash for a ride to City Hospital, but I refuse his payment. Instead, I find empty side streets and race through the abandoned city center till we arrive at the parking lot, alongside City Hospital. At that moment Rebecca remembers her mother's words and advice.

"Dad, this man is doing us a big favor! It's like the 'great commandment,' like Mom told me to follow. I told him about it, and now he's trying to help us."

David looks at Rebecca, not understanding what she's talking about. I understood her perfectly.

"Rebecca," he tells her, "let's just thank the man and get going. We have to find your mother!"

The desperate family jumps out of the taxi and heads for the hospital entrance. Doctors and volunteer nurses are working outside, attending patients in tents raised on platforms, evacuated from the first floor of the flooded hospital. David scans each bed, thinking he might identify his wife. His throat is still sore from the breathing tube so he searches quietly while Rebecca and Angel hold onto Michael.

"Good luck," I yell to them from the cab window, waving goodbye to them.

"Thank you again!" David tries to tell me, grateful for the rescue, but now starting his own. "Margaret!" he cries hoarsely, as he heads into an assemblage of patients and hospital staff.

"Dad, I think she's on the baby floor, second floor!" Rebecca insists, following close behind with Michael and Angel. "We know where it is!"

The children lead their father in rain-soaked clothes, bathing suits underneath, squeezing past patients in wheelchairs, beds, and gurneys in the white canvas tents. Lovejoy follows through the commotion in his own gown and hospital coat. The mosaic of health care workers and patients, faces and bodies revealing every disorder, tends to impede progress as they head for the main building. The entrance is no longer guarded, and once inside they look for the elevator, but it's without power.

"Here, Dad! Over here! We can take the stairwell," Angel cries, remembering the course of their escape from the lady with long fingernails. "It's right here somewhere."

As they climb the stairs and move down the hall, they search through each room of the OB ward. David fears for the worst, with painful memories of his own hospital stay, just as they find the door to his wife's room.

"Margaret!"

Almost stumbling into the room, he's shocked to see his wife with an oxygen mask, in labor, and a strange man at the foot of her bed. Dressed in a white coat, Dr. Cohen is posed to catch the baby that has already taken too long to deliver. As David approaches, Cohen recognizes David, finally realizing the relationship, and thinks of the cue for the next step.

"Switch on two! It's up to you!"

He hands a sterile towel to David, who looks back at him in shock.

"What am I supposed to do?" David asks, still catching his breath.

"Simple. Just don't drop the baby."
Margaret makes one last push.

Chapter 56:
The End Is Near

Day 7, Tuesday, June 20, 11:47 am

"One...huh.... Two...uh huh.... Three...huh...!"

Colson climbs back up each nitrogenous base of the genetic stairway, a step at a time, pulling onto the side rails for extra strength. Purine to Pyrimidine, Pyrimidine to Purine, he alternates his balance, sweeping the base sequence till he emerges at the garage. Seeing Car 22 brings a sense of relief and he returns to his familiar role of working as an EMT. He grabs Noah's briefcase with the electronic calculator, then heads back to the reactor to find the scientist. Remembering his role in authorizing the Plumbers, he knows he's headed for prison, but at least now he has a straightforward goal.

"Lord...uh huh...have mercy…"

Day 7, 11:48 a.m.—The Freeway

Moving slowly over the car tops of gridlock in the Atomic Car, Helen sees in the distance a ten-car accident blocking the freeway.

"Damn, ! If we can just get ahead of the wreck, I'll have an open road. But with the smallest divergence from our course, we're screwed, trapped behind all the cars still ahead of us! This crazy ambulance. These stupid turbos require constant braking and course correction, and the goddamn robotic arms keep slamming into open doors. All these abandoned cars. Jesus!"

"Helen!"

Hinton takes his attention off the radio as he sees them heading into more wreckage ahead.

"I've got it, . I think I've got it. We're almost there, but this car is not easy to drive."

The open freeway is yards ahead. And then the vehicles ahead of them are frozen into an irregular blockage. Helen makes rapid swings with the steering wheel in order to drive over them and avoid getting trapped.

"Helen, I think I can get Otieno on the air. He's in the Pyramid and we have full communication now! I'll have all the drivers except Colson! We've got Deed, Otieno, and Noah. You know, this is the Union we've been working for all this time! The four of them. All we need is Colson."

"And I think I have clear freeway ahead of us," she adds. "So please just let me drive!"

As they approach the wide-open Beltway, it seems that they will clear the endless wreckage. Then they discover the cause of the wreck and their final obstacle, standing in the rain. A single woman has planted herself in the middle of the freeway.

"Hey, I know that woman," Hinton says, as they near the last of vehicles and approach an open freeway. "It's the Trash Queen!"

Rain drips from her purple felt hat, the sea gull feathers blown horizontally, and her gray hair falls over her wet shoulders. She stands defiantly before the oncoming vehicles and calls out to the drivers, seated high up in the Atomic Ambulance.

"Slow down! Slow down! This freeway is closed. Slow down!"

Just to the side of the lead car, in the four-lane wreckage, the woman has lodged her shopping cart and its wares. Revenge, howls, and barks as the Atomic Car rolls in front of her.

Helen flips off the turbo jets and hits the brake as the ambulance comes to a halt. Only the Trash Queen's shopping cart, filled with aluminum cans, blocks their access to an open road ahead.

"Hello, ma'am!" Helen greets the harridan, leaning out the elevated window of the car, shielding her eyes from the rain with her hand and giving her best smile. "Would you mind moving your cart? We're…uh…trying to save this city. It's an emergency."

"And I said slow down! You never listen, do you, people?"

Half drowned in loose rags, determined not to move, the Queen stares at them defiantly. The purple hat hides her angry face from the approaching ambulance. Her dog lifts his leg to urinate on one of the robotic wheels, and Hinton opens his door, prepared to slide down and move the woman physically. Revenge snarls.

"Wait a minute, . Let me handle this," Helen cautions. The rain has slowed along with the wind, suggesting the strength of the hurricane has abated, and with an empty freeway ahead Helen anticipates a final breakthrough.

"You know, we could all be ashes in about ten minutes if we don't deliver this briefcase," Hinton protests.

"James, if that dog gets ahold of you, we're finished anyway. Let me talk to her."

He looks at the black leather Football and the open freeway, then checks his watch once more.

"Okay. Ten minutes, Helen," he said. "This wraps up in ten minutes. You understand?"

"You're wasting time," she counters. "I think I know how to handle women a little better than you do." She leans out the window again and removes her glasses so that the Trash Queen can see her better.

"Mrs....uh...Ms. Queen. Would you like to go for a little ride with us? We're headed downtown. To the White House. We could drop you off."

"Got my own transportation," she answers, nodding at her cart and Revenge.

"Well, so you do. But it's important for us to get by. We're in a great hurry, and we could take you to the hospital," Helen insists.

"No hurry at all!" the Queen responds, allowing them a toothless smile. "And I don't like hospitals."

"All right, that's enough!" Hinton breaks in. "Listen, lady, you have to move your cart. Now please get out of the way. If you don't...I'm going to have to force you. We're trying to get to the president of the United States!"

"So what?" she responds, looking him in the eye. "This has nothing to do with the president. It's your cars that have done all this. Listen, mister, you ought to wake up. The water's fouled, the Earth's all polluted, the sky's turning brown, and you think you need to see the president? You think all your big cars…you think they'll help you? Look at these cars on the road! You're addicted to them, and now you can't go anywhere. Why don't you just go home? You're too late!"

They look around at the endless backup of traffic. Most of the engines are still running, adding to the soft din of rain falling on the flooded asphalt.

"I read you even put your cars on the moon," she continues, "because there's nowhere left to bury all your damn waste. That Howard Hughes man, trying to hide nuclear waste up there. Tell you what, mister...the only way I move this cart...is if...Howard…Mr. Howard Hughes…kisses my…" She looks behind, then at her dog for a second, and reveals a toothless grin. "…cheek!"

Chapter 57:

Eleven Minutes to Extinction

11:49 a.m.—A lunar conversation

"Speak to me, Otieno. I demand an answer. Do you hear me, man? I need pain medicine and I expect you to answer and make some arrangements!" Hughes' voice comes to the apex of the Pyramid in a cackling tone. "You are trespassing in my Pyramid, and you work for me now. Where are my goddamn medicines?"

Otieno keeps Hughes on hold, looking down from the Pyramid at the Weatherpeople in the street.

Even if there is a meltdown in the reactor, I'll survive up here with Hughes' supply of food and insulation from radioactive fallout. And if I shape the new world, it will be inclusionary, designed with a circular connectivity. Now it's time to forget the autocrats and the Pyramid's vertical dominance. We'll make a world free of domination, reach out for social justice, and...why not? Universal health care. There has to be a place for brothers and sisters besides prisons, jails and mental institutes. Controlling the terrorists, the CIA, KGB, and G2 spies? Hell, I can do all that from up here!

As he begins his negotiation with Hughes, contemplating the future from the cybernetic Mummy, he's unprepared for the next message that comes through a side speaker.

"Otieno, can you hear me? It's Hinton. I have to talk to you right now!"

"I can hear you, Hinton," Otieno answers coolly, recognizing the voice. "Now what's the problem? I'm trying to take care of Howard Hughes."

"Otieno, listen. We've got a 10-47! The reactor's about to melt down and you've got to help us. Helen and I have the Atomic Football. We have to get to the president, but we're stuck on the freeway."

"10-47?"

Spinning the Mummy around, he overlooks a screen monitoring the freeway and identifies the Atomic Car, still trapped on its way to the White House by a woman with a shopping cart.

"Listen, Otieno, for all we know, a nuclear war could be ignited! And I just received word from Haldeman that Cuba is looking for an opportunity to assassinate the president. Even if the hurricane and the Weatherpeople don't destroy the White House first, the president no longer has the Football. We do! Helen and I. And we need to get it to Nixon in case there's any attack from outside. He's the only one who can release the Code for national defense!"

Otieno looks up at the central screen of the viewing room, then activates a switch controlling Hughes' private radar.

"I don't see any rockets out there," he answers.

"Listen! Haldeman has it from the CIA! There are Cuban terrorists out there that hate us, and Cuban spies here inside the capital and our network. We've got to act."

"Just say I believe you," Otieno says, "and someone does come after the president. Exactly what do you expect me to do about it?"

"We need Hughes! I can't get the Football to the president without him!"

"Hughes? He's on the moon, Hinton. It happens to be 1972. We don't do telepathic transport here, even if it is the end of the world. What do you want Hughes for?"

"I can't really explain it," Hinton explains, hoarsely. "We need to get Howard Hughes' image transported somehow, or it really could be the end! The president's the only one who can access the Code, and we need Hughes in order to reach the president. Look, I just don't have time to explain this. I just need Howard Hughes!"

"Hinton, you have a small problem, don't you? You expect me to get Hughes, who's up on the moon, so you can reach the president. Want to explain how that happens?"

"No! No time! Listen, Otieno. Maybe you can use the Pyramid's antennae to bring Hughes here? Take his image from the moon and recreate him with virtual reality. Just, you know, kind of transport his image down through your antennae. Put the image on the video screen in back of the Atomic Car. Noah says there's a way to do it. I know it sounds crazy, but we need this image in a few minutes or it's going to be too late. We need his image now, and, oh…this is important. He's got to pucker his lips. I'll explain it later. Just tell him to pucker his lips!"

"Listen, I think you've lost your mind, and I'm going to put you on hold."

While Hinton and Helen continue trying to persuade the Trash Queen to move her cart, Otieno looks across the row of monitors inside the Mummy. He focuses on Colson, who's rushing into the control room of the reactor with Dr. Noah's calculator. Colson hands it to Noah, who appears to be scanning the device for final calculations to stop the meltdown. It occurs to Otieno that a rocket scientist capable of designing a nuclear reactor might also have the telecomputing capacity to send images of Hughes from the moon to an ambulance.

"Noah?" he says, announcing through a mic to the speaker system in the nuclear reactor.

Noah looks up along with the other technicians, surprised to hear another voice coming through their sound system.

"Who's there? Is that you, Mr. Hughes?"

"No, Noah. It's me. Otieno. I need to tell you something, Noah, we think you're doing a fine job. A fine job indeed!"

"Otieno! What the…? How did you get in the Pyramid? This is no time to play games. I've got a meltdown in the reactor and in the middle of this hurricane we're trying to get the Atomic Car to the president. He seems to have lost the Football, and you need to stop fooling around in the Pyramid!"

"I know. I know everything. I was just checking on you."

Otieno turns back to the lunar screen and sees Howard Hughes clutching his stomach, bent over an instrument panel in the lunar control module. He switches to a screen for the Oval Office of the White House. The image there is sharp and he sees Nixon and Kisman on their knees, making prayers, hoping the hurricane abates, and hoping an impeachment is not on the way as a result of the Watergate break-in.

Running his fingers over the display board, Otieno makes one final check. On the satellite viewing screens he views a foreign launching site in Cuba, with a small ballistic missile in its silo.

Survival of the fittest. Life as it always has been.

"Listen," he tells Hinton. "I can monitor better than anyone right now, but I don't do 'virtual reality.' I'm a paramedic. We don't make rockets go away."

"Otieno, remember when you said you were a 'doctor'? Well, we need your therapy, right now! We need the Code!

Noah can help, if you'll just give him access to the antennae, so we can get Hughes' image in the ambulance."

He looks again at the screen of the nuclear reactor. Noah is now sitting at the control desk, listening nervously to their conversation.

"That true, Noah?" Otieno asks.

"What?"

"Can you do it? Put Howard Hughes's image on a video screen in the back of the Atomic Car?"

"I can put anyone anywhere. But if this reactor melts down it won't make a bit of difference. We need water pressure and we need it fast."

"Okay, I'll give you the antennae, if you tell me what to do. You run your computers, I'll run the power, and we'll see how it works. There's just one other thing."

He switches back onto the screen monitoring the moon, and the man in the lunar module.

"Mr. Hughes?"

The blurred wrinkles on Hughes' face have sunken deeper, with his skin sallow from exhaustion and need for drugs. He doesn't like the conversation taking place on Earth and his voice comes to Otieno from a speaker next to his image, tired and shrill.

"Listen, damn it, you people need to get me some help! I'm in a lot of pain. I need a doctor right now and I need my medicines!"

"We're working on it!" Otieno says. "It's just that we need you to do something for us, while we locate your doctor. Just stay where you are. I'm going to beam your image down here to the Atomic ambulance, and it should help you get your meds. And one other thing. If you could just pucker your lips a little, that would be really helpful!"

Three minutes to the end—On the freeway

Hinton and Helen help hoist the Trash Queen into the back of the Atomic Car as Revenge stays behind protecting the shopping cart. She's dexterous, despite her arthritis, and with help she mounts the short stepladder successfully. Helen sets her down on the gurney next to the computer screen while Hinton holds onto the Football and looks at his watch. He climbs back into the front of the ambulance and puts the headphones back on.

"You're about to see Mr. Hughes on this screen, Mrs. Queen," Helen tells her. "And when you see him, just put your cheek against the screen. I promise you he'll kiss it. We do this kind of thing all the time."

"Oh, sure you do, honey," she answers.

They look in the direction of the White House.

Two minutes to the end

Deed races back over the Arlington Memorial Bridge and emerges onto Lincoln Memorial Circle NW, now empty of cars and fleeing citizens. He stops close to where the Potomac and Anacostia rivers join to form a Y shape, and where the Lincoln Memorial rises up along the bank. The yoke of the two confluent sources passes close beside the memorial as ever watchful, Lincoln looks ahead.

"So, now what are you going to do?" Muriel asks. Her eyes open wider, soft blue reflections of her confusion.

"I have to open the floodgate, underneath. And Muriel, I want you to know something. How much I love you."

Disappearing again into the back entrance of the column-lined memorial, beneath Lincoln's brooding gaze, he steps quickly down to the underground cavern. The valve opening the floodgate to the subterranean tunnel system is unattended, and when he activates it a torrent of water rushes diagonally beneath the city, freeing the deluge of storm water and debris, clearing the underground matrix of drainage pipes.

11:59 a.m.—The Atomic Car

Noah keys in sequences as fast as he can, but it takes a minute to transmit the Hughes image onto the screen in the back of the ambulance. The clarity of Hughes' face, 240,000 miles away, lacks resolution so Helen tries to entertain the Trash Queen with small talk.

"I've always liked baseball…some dogs…and hospitals and nurses. What about you?"

"I told you already, I hate hospitals."

Hinton looks out the windshield at a helicopter rising over the rain drenched White House and spots the president in Marine One.

"It's Nixon!" Hinton shouts, as they hear the noise of the approaching rotor blades. "He's free and he's on the way here!"

"And Hughes is ready," Helen says, simultaneously, as Hughes' image appears more sharply on the screen. Stripped down, his bearded, scraggly face contorted with pain, he looks every bit as forlorn as the Trash Queen. Helen moves the Trash Queen closer to the image on the screen.

"Go ahead, Ms. Queen. Put your cheek by the screen," she urges the woman. "He's going to kiss you now, just like you asked."

Helen watches Nixon's helicopter approach. As it begins to hover over them she grabs the Football containing the transmitter and heads for an extension ladder, giving access to the freeway below. Hinton cries out.

"Hey, wait a minute, Helen. Where do you think you're going? I'm the one with the Football!"

"James, you need to stay here and take care of the Trash Queen. I did my part and anyway, now I have the Football."

Hinton tries to catch her before she disappears, but he's forced back into the ambulance by Clifton Urning, who has suddenly climbed the ladder with hopes of catching sight of Howard Hughes. And then, spellbound, Urning looks at the long hidden face of Hughes on a screen. Simultaneously the Trash Queen holds her cheek next to the computer screen as the richest man in the world kisses the poorest woman on the planet.

"I see it!" Urning shouts. "I see Hughes' face! I've finally seen it!"

"Son of a…why Hughes has kissed her!" Hinton exclaims, shaking his head. Urning dances around the Atomic Car, singing out his verse.

Rich to poor, forever more,
Howard's lips have made a score!
Shall we finally join the moon,
this earthly swoon, it's not too soon.

I sing of rockets, of shopping carts,
Pyramids, hospitals, worlds apart

Arise ye wretched of the earth,
Take hold this moment, a time of birth.

Man meets woman, woman meets man
That's the moment they know they can
Save the planet, our reckless race
A kiss defines the full embrace!

Inside the reactor, Noah is transfixed as he watches water re-enter the cooling chambers and the core begins to cool down. High up in the Pyramid, Otieno looks at an infrared monitor. An underground pattern of waters unfolds into the shape of an X as the Potomac and Anacostia rivers join in a subterranean flow. The opening floodgate releases suspended waters from beneath the Lincoln Monument and when Deed returns to Car 38, Muriel kisses him on the lips.

Chapter 58:

The Code to Survival

12:00, high noon

After climbing down from the ambulance, Helen rushes onto the open Beltway, slipping past Revenge. The president's helicopter lands in front of her and the rotating blades come to a full stop as she carries the fifteen-pound Football in her right arm. Next to Nixon, military officers prepare electronic communications for the defense system while the wind blows around them.

I watch all this from my cab. The Savage M 10 long-range rifle is easy to bead onto a target and a scope zeros on the president's chest, just to the left of the sternum. It has come to this—my chance to protect Castro forever, and maybe allow me to return to my country. My finger slides smoothly over the trigger and I pause.

When Helen moves beneath the helicopter blades of Marine One she carefully hands the attaché case to the president. Nixon looks at her almost dismissively and then opens the Football with his "Biscuit" code of zeros. As he removes the code transmitter, his fingers turn small circular dials with the numbers that release the full Code.—1-19 20-8-25 19-5-12-6. Watching carefully, he sees an ancient message appear on the front of the abacus.

12—15—22—5 20—8—25 14—5—9—7—8—2—15—18

Helen stands motionless as the president quickly returns to the helicopter and raises his arms in salute to all of them.

His chest is wide open. From my vantage point, the rifle barrel rests easily on the opened window of the taxi. In the chaos of the traffic jam, the rain and freeway confusion, the noise of horns and shouting people out on the road, no one notices my taxi or sunken position in the front seat. I have considered this action so many thousands of times in the last week, but in life there is a moment of truth for each of us. I gently pull the trigger back. With the click I remember that I never loaded the rifle, and never will. And when the helicopter lifts off, leaving behind the Atomic Car, a clear freeway lies ahead along with the Great Commandment.

12-15-22-5 20-8-25 14-5-9-7-8-2-15-18 1-19 20-8-25-19-5-12-6

Chapter 59:
Cutting the Cord

June 20, 12:07 p.m.—City Hospital

"I swear to God, Margaret. We're going to fix this system so no one gets stuck like we did, ever," David tells his wife, as he cradles their newborn in his arms. She rests quietly, spent from her final push, having finally delivered a baby boy and at last free of pain. The baby's cry is strong and while the children cling to their mother, David wonders what to do with the umbilical cord.

"Excuse me," Dr. Cohen's voice interrupts from the open door of the hospital room. Margaret looks around and recognizes him. "You are the woman we transferred from the Hughes Hospital, aren't you, Mrs. Lovejoy?"

"And you're the doctor who took care of me at the private hospital, aren't you?" David asks, not sure whether to trust the strange physician, or to ask him about the cord connected to the baby.

Cohen walks over to a table where some instruments are kept and puts on a pair of rubber gloves. He picks up a pair of scissors and metal clamps.

"Yes, I believe I did," he answers, "and you were never discharged so you need to return to the hospital to pay your bill. You'll be in for a bit of a surprise. Oh, and I would appreciate it if you could give back the coat and gown you're wearing. I know now this is your wife. I've also seen her as a patient."

They face each other while the others watch.

"Yes, it is. And just what exactly are you planning to do now?"

"Well, unless you know how to take care of a placenta, I thought I would deliver it for her. After we divide the cord, that is. I also have something I want to share with you about your wife, besides a 'congratulations.'"

Modestly placing a sheet over her legs, Cohen lets David divide the cord with scissors and then he clamps it. After delivering the placenta, he gives Margaret's diagnosis to the family.

"What I'd like to tell you is this...we've identified the cause of your wife's seizures. It took time reviewing Jane Doe's…excuse me, Mrs. Lovejoy's records, going over all the tests, but then it occurred to us that she suffers from a somewhat rare disorder. She has what's known as auditory-induced epilepsy. It's not common, but that's most likely what she has."

"What are you saying?" David's eyes open wide as the doctor takes the purple, fruit-like placenta in a plastic bag and sets it aside.

"Well, a bit unusual, but not unheard of. You see, when you trace back the seizures, you realize each one has been initiated by a sound. Most likely, the siren of an ambulance."

"Are you sure?"

"Of course, I'm sure. I'm a doctor. And I'd suggest that she use earplugs when you're on the freeway, driving through town, or anywhere you might encounter sirens."

David feels weak on his legs. Dr. Cohen reaches over to take the baby from him, then finds a blanket in the incubator. He swaddles the baby and hands it to Rebecca. Michael and Angel watch the events silently, as David collapses into a chair.

Chapter 60:

Leaving the City

Day 7 ½, Tuesday, June 20, 5:00 p.m.

Driving onto the beltway, David notices my cab keeping up with him as our two cars break free of inner-city traffic. I've taken him back to the Howard Johnson's Motor Lodge so he can jump-start the station wagon, gather up the belongings from room 623, carry it all to the underground parking lot, and then drive to the City Hospital. For understandable reasons, the family was eager to leave Washington, D.C., and now he puts his right arm around Margaret. Looking out the passenger side window he can see reverse traffic already headed back into the city center, in the aftermath of the hurricane. It's possible to distinguish the Lincoln Memorial in the distance, and the softer outline of the Watergate buildings. I follow them, making sure they leave the city safely, and I'm able to listen to their conversation through a transmitter in my taxi.

"You know, Margaret, we get cought up in the events of history, and they can change our lives …"

"David, not now. Let's just get home!"

Lovejoy turns to the back of the car where Michael and Angel are waving at me. Rebecca holds the new baby in her lap and watches the Memorial. As David focuses on the road ahead again he sees a strange-shaped ambulance, elevated on robotic arms, with the letters A C written on its side. It's bearing directly at them with flashing red lights. David nods at Margaret, who covers her ears for a moment, and then I catch the conversation from the Atomic Ambulance.

"James, we're almost there!" Helen says, as she steers the ambulance in the direction of the White House.

"Watch out! That cab is headed right at us."

"Look, if you think you can drive better..."

"No, just hit the siren, Helen!"

"James, I swear to God. I hope that cab doesn't run into us! But would you mind just letting me drive right now?"

"Don't worry. He can see us."

"Margaret!"

David looks at his wife, who seems lost in thought, or perhaps a reverie, as the ambulance passes them. She's using earplugs but there's a slight twitching of her left eye.

"What, David? Now what's the matter?"

She looks back at Rebecca, who's smiling at her and her father, still holding the new baby in her arms. Angel and Michael listen to the radio, playing "Don't you worry about a thing!"

"Nothing, dear. Nothing you and I can't take care of."

Afterword

It's been a busy week. After hanging onto the Football while working as temporary dispatcher, on Monday night, I made sure Haldeman received it so he could do a lateral handoff to the president. Nixon, remembering his early days of Bible study as a Quaker, was still puzzled by the Code; and Castro, who underwent Jesuit training as a youth, didn't think much of any of it. Both of them weren't happy, but Castro eventually let the Russians take the missile out of the silo, and Nixon resigned, saying it was not good for us to hate our enemies. He headed off to his San Clemente estate, while all the Plumbers, including Haldeman and Deed, went to prison. Kisman, of course, kept on spying, and the CIA started a few new wars.

No one ever guessed I was the one who switched out the military Code for a biblical one. As for me, I accept that I can never return to Cuba. I'm a man without a country. But truthfully, I'm now a man of all countries. Like Rebecca, still holding onto the new baby as the station wagon leaves the capital, I just smile!

Watergate – Short Bibliography

Secret Agenda, Jim Hougan, 1984

Silent Coup, Len Colodny and Robert Geddlin, 1991

A Piece of Tape – The Watergate Story: Fact and Fiction, James McCord Jr., 1974

Nightmare – The Underside of the Nixon Years, Anthony Lukas, 1973

Will, G.Gordon Liddy, 1980

Mo – A Woman's View of Watergate, Maureen Dean and Hays Gorey, 1975

White House Call Girl, Phil Stanford, 2013

Warrior – Frank Sturgis – the CIA's #1 Assassin-Spy, Who Nearly Killed Castro but was Ambushed by Watergate, Jim Hunt and Bob Risch,

Confessions of a Watergate Burglar – True Magazine, August, 1974, Andrew St. George

Witness to Power – The Nixon Years, John Erlichman, 1982

The Mind of Watergate – An Exploration of the Compromise of Integrity, Leo Rangell, M.D., 1982

The Strong Man, James Rosen, 2008

Dirty Tricks, Shane O'Sullivan, 2018

To Set The Record Straight, John J. Sirica, 1979

The Ends of Power, H.R. Haldeman, 1973

Fidel Castro – A Biography, Volker Skierka, 2004

The Double Life of Fidel Castro, Juan Sanchez, 2017

Secrets: A Memoir of Vietnam and the Pentagon Papers, Daniel Ellsberg, 2002

The Doomsday Machine – Confessions of a Nuclear War Planner, Daniel Ellsberg, 2018

Watergate – The Hidden History – Nixon, the Mafia, and the CIA, Lamar Waldron, 2012

Watergate Exposed, Robert Merritt, 2009

American Spy, My Secret History in the CIA - Watergate and Beyond, E. Howard Hunt, 2007

The Presidential Transcripts, Washington Post Commentary, 1974

In the Arena, Richard Nixon, 1990

Breach of Faith – The Fall of Richard Nixon, Theodore White, 1975

Legacy of Ashes – The History of the CIA, Tim Weiner, 2007

The Wars of Watergate, Stanley L. Kutler, 1990

Watergate, Fred Emery, 1994

Howard Hughes – The Secret Life, Charles Higham, 1993

Howard Hughes – The Untold Story, Peter Brown and Pat Broeske, 1996

Next to Hughes – Robert Maheu and Delta Hack, 1992

Howard, Noah Dietrich, 1972

Kissinger – On the Couch, Phyllis Schlafly, Chester Ward, 1975

All the President's Men, Bob Woodward, Carl Bernstein, 1974

Veil, The Secret Wars of the CIA 1981 – 1987,Bob Woodward, 1987

The Secret Man – The Story of Watergate's Deep Throat, Bob Woodward, 2005

A Woman in Charge, Carl Bernstein, 2007

Living History, Hillary Rodham Hinton, 2003

Spy Stories

A half-century after the events of Watergate very few of the participants remain, yet mysteries and lessons continue to surface. Since the assassination of JFK, the resignation of Richard Nixon, and the impact of Watergate, new discoveries and techniques of espionage now challenge human comprehension, to say nothing of privacy. What happened to the Watergate spies?

G. Gordon Liddy served the longest prison term, four years, before Jimmy Carter released him. He went on to do speaking tours with Timothy Leary, the man he once arrested and hauled away from a hippie paradise in Duchess County. He maintained a radio talk show, never regretting his service or felonies and passed away in March of 2021.

Howard Hunt was paroled after 33 months in prison. He continued writing spy novels and books, adding 20 to the 53 previous publications. The movie production he entertained with Richard Helms never came to be, but his own persona is to be portrayed by Woody Harrelson in an HBO series.

James McCord spent 4 months in prison and after release went back to doing security work in Rockville. He passed away from Pancreatic cancer at age 93. Probably Richard Helms knew the depth of McCord's CIA involvement, but Helms has passed away too.

Frank Sturgis spent fourteen months in a minimum-security prison in Eglin, Florida and was denied a pardon by Jimmy Carter. He went on to teach guerilla warfare in Angola and Honduras and died at age 69, either from lung cancer, stomach cancer, or a mysterious assassination by "blow gun". Was Sturgis one of the three tramps and how was he involved in the JFK assassination? We may never know. Sturgis points out that the last Break-in was a failure, but there were more than a few that were successful. "We Cubans, at the time, knelt down and prayed and hoped the government would keep its promises. That's all we could do then and that's all we can do now," and "I kept thinking, Castro couldn't get to me, and my own country put me behind bars. What an irony!"

Bernard Barker spent a year in prison and then worked as a building inspector. He died of lung cancer at age 92, in 2009. His comments twenty years later – "I sleep good at night. I have no regrets."

Eugenio Martínez spent fourteen months in prison and after release continued his connection with the CIA and even visited Cuba at the request of Castro's government. He was the only Watergate burglar to be pardoned, by Ronald Reagan, in 1983.

Virgilio Gonzalez spent 13 months in prison and when released changed professions from locksmith to mechanic. He did not like giving press interviews but said he was happy."Of course, I am living again.", and of Watergate, "It gave me personality and friends. I'm part of history. My name is in the books in this country." He passed away at age 88 in Miami, 2014.

Alfred Baldwin did not go to prison and was granted immunity after testifying to state. He is still alive and rumored to be writing a book about Watergate.

Photographic Credits

The "Plumbers" – page 69, Getty Images
Heidi – page 325, personal photo, Kathy Dickerson
The Football – page 397, enWikipedia

Acknowledgements – all editorial sympathy, especially Bee Newell and Richard Eastman. Above all my family, Nancy, Juliane, and Steven. The not so new Code – Jesus of Nasareth. The Spy stories – please see bibliography. Book Cover and drawings – Mike Veronin, Kris Weber, and Steven Godfrey.

CPSIA information can be obtained
at www.ICGtesting.com
Printed in the USA
LVHW041134310322
714806LV00005B/938

9 781647 198978